D0278504

The Lemon Tree Hotel

The Lemon Tree Hotel

ROSANNA LEY

Quercus

First published in Great Britain in 2019 by

Quercus Editions Ltd
Carmelite House
50 Victoria Embankment
London EC4Y 0DZ

An Hachette UK company

A CIP catalogue record for this book is available
from the British Library

HB ISBN 978 1 78648 340 9
TPB ISBN 978 1 78648 338 6
EBOOK ISBN 978 1 78648 337 9

10 9 8 7 6 5 4 3 2 1

Typeset by CC Book Production

Printed and bound in Great Britain by Clays Ltd, Elcograf S.p.A.

For Richard Orridge – fellow writer
and much valued and trusted friend
who can always make me laugh . . .
(in a good way)

CHAPTER I

Chiara
Vernazza, Italy – November 1968

After the argument, after Dante had returned home, Chiara went to bed, knowing she would not sleep. How could she sleep after everything that had happened today?

She closed her eyes and tried to steady her breathing. She could see their faces, hear the barely disguised ill-feeling in the words being thrown between them – these two men she loved best in the entire world: her father and Dante Rossi. Dante, she had known for only weeks, but as Mamma always said of her cooking ingredients: *it is a matter of quality rather than quantity, my dear* – and there was that question of destiny . . . Papà, of course, she had known her whole life.

She'd sat at his knee and listened to his stories even before she could understand them. Tales of *L'Attico Convento*, the Old Convent which had been transformed into The Lemon Tree Hotel where they now lived and from which they made their living; tales of the war; tales of how he had first met Mamma: 'I saw her there in the olive grove and suddenly it all made sense.'

'What made sense, Papà?'

'Why, our Resistance, our fight for freedom against those threatening to destroy the country we loved, my whole life. It all made sense, my darling, when I looked into your mamma's eyes.'

Chiara let out a deep sigh. Was it like that for Dante? She thought of the dark, knowing looks he would send her when he imagined no one but Chiara could see them. Did it all make sense for him when he looked into her eyes? She hoped so. She stared up at the high slanted ceiling, illuminated only by slivers of moonlight creeping through the wooden slats of the shutters. She loved this room; liked to think of the nuns who had once slept here – like her aunt Giovanna, who now had her own cottage in the grounds of the hotel. Chiara wanted to think that one day Dante might be saying something just like that to their own daughter. But . . .

It was a very big 'but'. The 'but' included Alonzo Mazzone – her parents' favourite, son of the friends to whom they were indebted (though this was another story, which Chiara refused to dwell on now). A 'but' that reminded her she was only six-teen: 'too young to know your own mind,' Mamma had said only yesterday when she caught her daughter gazing at Dante Rossi as he expertly gathered up the nets of the olive harvest and simultaneously swept Chiara that glance which told her everything she wanted to know and more. And now, it was a 'but' that included the bitter taste of today's harsh words.

A sharp sound at the window snapped into her thoughts and she blinked in surprise. It couldn't be Dante – he had returned to Corniglia and surely wouldn't be coming back in a hurry. Rain? Unlikely – the sky had been clear this evening, and Papà had insisted the weather wasn't due to break for at least two

2

days. A tile falling from the roof? The Lemon Tree Hotel was old and more rundown than they would like. In its previous life as a convent, it had witnessed violence and suffering, but Chiara liked to think that it had retained its sense of peace and spirituality even in adversity. And surely the condition of the roof was not that bad?

Another noise at the window. She sat bolt upright. It sounded like soft hail. Or . . . She felt a whisk of excitement. The sound came again. She jumped out of bed and quickly crossed the old wooden floor, polished by nuns over the years until it shone. Or . . . *olives?* Would he have come back then after all?

She flung open the shutters, peered into the darkness. The haze of the half-moon cast an eerie halo around the olive trees. 'Dante?' she whispered.

A beam of light flashed from the grove – just for a second, then another, then a third. Three flashes of torchlight. It was their agreed signal. She put a hand to her throat. How could he have dared to return here?

Chiara grabbed her own torch from the marble-topped dressing-table. She gave the two-flash signal back. *I'm coming.*

Her body was instantly alert and fired with adrenalin. Dante . . . He had argued with her father about the olive oil, he had stormed off, walking the three and a half kilometres over the mountains and back to Corniglia, his own village, which was next in line to Vernazza in the Cinque Terre, the five lands, five villages built on the cliffs in Liguria, part of the Levante, their section of the Italian Riviera. And now he had returned.

She threw a woollen shawl over her white cotton nightdress and drew it around her shoulders; she pulled on some shoes and opened her bedroom door as silently as she could. She held her body tense and waiting, but there was no sound from the rest of the building. She took a breath and crept down the wide, winding stairs. It was late – almost midnight – and her parents were in bed, of course. There were no guests – it was November and this time was reserved for the olive harvest, although, as Papà often said, the time was gone when a hundred trees would mean security for a family here in Liguria. And it was oil of the finest quality – extra virgin Riviera del Levante. Still, olive oil was needed in *la cucina*, was it not? Olive wood also gave off the most wonderful fragrance and warmth, and both were useful in the hotel . . . Fortunately, her parents' room was on the other side of the building, so Chiara hoped she was safe from discovery.

She made her way swiftly past the reception desk and into the high-ceilinged kitchen, her soft footsteps sinking onto the cool flags, the emptiness of the room that usually had such a bustling and sweet-smelling warmth making her feel quite ghostly. She slipped out through the kitchen door, which led directly to the olive grove that surrounded The Lemon Tree Hotel on three sides. 'Dante?' she whispered again, shivering from the cool air on her skin, and with something else, something powerful that seemed to shimmer inside her and make her almost want to explode.

'Chiara.' He stepped out in front of her and drew her towards him, into the protection of one of their oldest trees, which formed a moonlit-green canopy around them.

'*Dio santo*,' she said. 'My God, I can't believe that you—'

He silenced her with a kiss. The sweet press of his lips on hers was intoxicating. Chiara gave herself up to it with a surge of longing. How could anything in the world be this good?

'My father . . .' she began, when he finally released her. Would kill him if he saw them now.

'I'm so sorry.' Dante hung his dark head. 'He is your father. I should have shown more respect. I should have stayed silent.'

'No.' She stopped him. 'It wasn't your fault. He was wrong. He . . .'

It had been simmering since they came from Corniglia, this grain of resentment between the villages. Usually, only the boys from Vernazza helped with the olive harvest. But recently, some of the local youths had left the area, just as they were leaving many of the rural communities of Italy. There were new opportunities for them in the cities these days, she knew, a chance to earn money working in different industries. Everyone was saying it: life was not all about farming any longer. So, Papà was worried they wouldn't get the olives down, gathered and to the press in time before the weather broke. It was important to pick the olives before they were completely ripe and purple. A green olive gave less oil but was lower in acidity, so the oil was fresher, more delicious and of better quality. Papà had asked in Corniglia if anyone could help, and Dante had come with his friend Matteo. Dante. She had seen him in her life twice before, and those two encounters had made her think about him more than she could say. And now, he was here, at The Lemon Tree Hotel.

Chiara held the face that in the last weeks had quickly become so dear to her between her two hands and examined every detail in the pale moonlight: his gentle dark eyes, the generous curve of his mouth, the slant of his cheekbones, and the dark stubble on his jaw. When Dante had come to the hotel to help with the olive harvest, when she had first seen his frown of concentration as he unwrapped the orange nets

5

from the trunks of the trees and laid them out to catch the fruit . . . She had caught her breath. It was him. Surely it was him? When she had watched him stretch and roll his broad shoulders as he and Matteo beat the tree and branches with the *bastone*, heard his soft deep voice as they lifted the edges of the nets, witnessed the infectious rumble of his laughter as the olives rolled together into heaps to be loaded into bulging oily sacks to take to the press . . .

From that moment, she had been lost. She was standing by the kitchen doorway, he hadn't seen her yet. Then he straightened, called out to Matteo, pushed his black hair from his forehead, shifted slightly, as if he felt the force of her scrutiny . . . And their gazes had locked. He recognised her from before. Had he known perhaps that this was her father's place? She wasn't sure. But she was sure that he felt it too – this strange emotion that she could not name. Was this what Papà had described to her? Was this love at first sight?

Since that moment, Chiara and Dante had grabbed every opportunity to spend snatched minutes together – to chat when she brought out the lunch or the beer, to linger by one another's side while they were working to bring in the olives, the heat building between their bodies even though it was already November, to meet just like this, in the olive grove under the cover of darkness.

'It is you,' he said to her in that first snatched moment alone only minutes after she'd stood there watching him.

'It is me.' She could still hardly believe that it was him. It was the third time. It was as if Fate or some Divine Intervention had stepped in, and . . .

'Can we talk? Later, I mean?' His brown eyes were intent as he watched her collecting the glasses to take back to *la cucina*.

6

'Before you leave. In the grove at the back of the hotel,' she said, quick as lightning, as if she made such assignations every day of her life. In fact she had never done anything like this before – but then again, she had never felt this alive.

The first time she'd seen him had been in Corniglia, as she walked through the village on an errand for her mother last spring. She was still fifteen. A group of boys were eyeing her as she walked down the hill, swinging the basket, oblivious at first to their grins, the way they were nudging one another and looking her way.

'Hey, look what a gift someone has sent us today. How lucky are we, eh?'

Chiara flinched. She was used to the boys of Vernazza – she knew them all well, she had grown up with them – but she hadn't seen these boys before, and she felt a stab of fear. Of course, they were harmless, naturally they were just having a joke with her. But something about the look in the eyes of the one who had spoken – a lascivious look, a greedy look – made her footsteps waver. She tossed her head. She wouldn't let them see that she cared.

'Oh, she is a princess, is this not so?' He sneered. 'Should we teach her a lesson perhaps?'

Chiara stood her ground, glared at him. But she found she could not speak, the banter that usually came so easily to her had left her. The boy took a step closer.

'Hey, Franco! Give it a rest.' Another boy appeared. A boy with dark eyes and an upright bearing. He smiled at her. Don't worry, he seemed to say. He looked back at the other boy. 'Go home to your mamma,' he teased. 'Leave the poor girl alone.'

And it seemed that he possessed an unlikely authority. The boys mumbled and drifted away – all of them.

'Thank you,' she said to him. She felt unbearably shy, ridiculously naïve. He gave a little nod back to her – and was gone.

Chiara hadn't forgotten him though. A few months later she saw him again – this time in Vernazza. An elderly lady who lived down by the waterfront had collapsed – heatstroke perhaps, for it was a hot day in August. Chiara ran to help her, but someone else had got there first. Him. He mopped the old lady's brow with his handkerchief, helped her sit up, fetched her water from the fountain. Chiara had watched him, half mesmerised. Who was he? Some sort of guardian angel?

Now, she knew better. Dante was no guardian angel – he was a hot-blooded, wildly attractive young man who was more than willing to meet her under the cover of darkness and shower kisses on her lips, her neck, her breasts . . . But still – surely he had been brought to her for this reason alone?

But without Chiara noticing – for she had plenty of other matters on her mind – that grain of resentment between the two neighbouring villages had swollen. And when the yield of their olives turned out to be less than previous years, considerably less than Papà had expected despite the fact that the boughs of the trees had been heavy with the little green fruit for months, one of the locals, Salvatore, was heard to mutter that some of the olives might have been kept back for the Corniglia press.

Dante had fiercely protested their innocence. 'It is the climate,' he had said with a frown, the frown that Chiara longed to smooth from his brow. 'It is the same all over Liguria this year. Everyone knows it.'

'Do they indeed?' Papà did not like his tone, Chiara could tell. He was experienced with the olives, and he would not tolerate any of his workers getting above themselves.

Dante held his head high. 'What else?' he demanded. 'What else could it be?'

Papà shrugged. 'You tell me.'

Dante stared at him with undisguised hostility. 'I am surprised you asked us here,' he said, 'if you have such little trust.'

'What choice did I have, eh?' Papà glared at him. 'You come, and you—' He stopped abruptly and Chiara wondered if Mamma had told him what she might have observed these past days. They should have been more careful. Papà was obsessed with Alonzo and his family, and he would not take kindly to another man coming to steal his daughter's heart.

Matteo had gone to stand next to Dante, the two of them facing her father and the others. Suddenly, they had become enemies, it seemed. The tension hung thick in the air.

Papà waved them away. 'Enough,' he blustered. 'You have done your work, you will be paid, and now you can go, both of you. That's it. I don't want to see you again.'

Chiara watched them leave in despair. She longed to run after Dante. When would she see him again? She knew already that his was a proud family, and she was aware how much damage had been done.

'You did not think it?' Dante asked her now. 'What Salvatore said? You did not think it?'

'Of course not.' She knew how good he really was; she knew he would not be capable of such subterfuge and deceit. Chiara settled her head against his chest. It felt as if it was meant to be there. His arms were around her and she was no longer cold in the least. Now, she was warm; warm and loved in a way she hadn't dreamed possible.

Papà had tasted the olive oil straight from the *frantoio*, the press, then he had brought it home and the family had eaten it with freshly-baked bread and bruschetta. It was as light and golden as ever and had the same mild, fruity taste as always – thanks to the Ligurian weather – not too hot in the summer and not too cold in the winter. 'Delicious, my love,' Chiara's mother had declared. But the atmosphere had remained tense.

'I have been thinking, Chiara.' Dante straightened and she adjusted her position against him.

'*Sì?*' She had thought she would not see him for days. But now he was here in her arms once more – and so miracles were possible after all, and she wished she could tell her aunt Giovanna this. But of course, she could not. This was their secret. It had to be.

'If we stay here, we cannot be together.'

'If we stay here? What do you mean?' Where else could they go? She eased slightly away from the warmth of him. What was he saying?

'Your parents will not allow us to meet,' he said solemnly. 'My parents too.'

'Oh, it will die down.' Though Chiara spoke with an assurance she did not feel. Her father's passions did not tend to die down; the opposite was true. 'And until then we can meet in secret. Like we are now.' It was, after all, rather thrilling. She glanced around at the olive trees, threaded with silver in the moonlight, old and wise, standing serene in the grove, endless as time itself. The olive tree was the symbol of peace and well-being. How many loves had they witnessed? Her father and her mother, Chiara and Dante, probably not the nuns though . . . She suppressed a giggle.

'This is serious, Chiara.' Dante put his hands on her shoulders to increase the distance between them. 'At least to me.'

'And to me.' She pushed towards him again, intending to

hold his head to her breast. She didn't want to talk – there was no time. She wanted to feel more of the delicious sensations that spun through her when he kissed her, when he held her, when he—

'But that is not enough, Chiara,' he said. 'I love you. I want to be with you.'

'And I love you, Dante.' The words were like flowers on her tongue. She relished the scent of them, she wanted to taste them over and over. She might be young, but Chiara knew what she wanted. And she wanted this man – with all her heart. 'But what else can we do?'

'Run away.' He whispered the words into her hair.

'Run away?' She stared at him. It sounded impossibly romantic. 'But where to?' She couldn't imagine being any-where save Vernazza. Everything she loved was here – her father, her mother, Aunt Giovanna, The Lemon Tree Hotel . . .

'Milan.'

She blinked at him. Milan was a lifetime away.

'I could get work there,' he said. 'The car companies, they are looking for new mechanics. Alfa Romeo have a factory in the city. I learn quickly—'

'Milan?' she repeated, aghast.

'Why not? I have been thinking for a while that I might leave and make a new life somewhere. There are so many oppor-tunities, you know. Life is not just for farming and fishing. Others have gone—'

'I know.' Of course, others had gone. The new industries in the cities, *il boom* . . . Everyone was talking about it.

'It could be a new start for us. We would be together, at least . . .' His voice trailed as he caught her expression in the moonlight.

'What would I do in Milan?' she whispered. Milan was a city. Milan was very far from Liguria.

'I'll look after you.' He held her closer once more. 'We would work it out. I don't know. But the point is, we could be together, my love.'

'We can be together here.' Suddenly, she wanted to cry. Suddenly, everything that had been so right was going horribly wrong.

'We cannot.'

Chiara saw the stubborn glint in his eye, and she realised. She loved him, and she had even fantasised that he was her destiny, but she didn't know him – not really. What she knew was Vernazza and this place, her home. What she knew were her parents, her life, the fact that she loved The Lemon Tree Hotel with a fierce passion, that she would run it herself one day – her father had always told her so – and that she was sixteen, and so how could she leave?

'It will die down,' she said again. 'They will forget the silly argument. And then we can start meeting openly, and I will tell them how I feel, and slowly, gradually . . .'

'I do not want slowly and gradually.' He held her more tightly. 'I want you now.'

Chiara shuddered with desire. 'I want you too,' she whispered. She felt his hands so warm against her with only her thin white nightgown between them. She took his hand and put it to her breast. How could it be wrong?

'Not like this,' he said, though his voice was husky with longing.

'But, Dante, how can we leave here? What would we live on?' Mamma had always said it was the women in this world who must be practical.

'I have a small inheritance, you know I told you my grand-mother had died?'

'*Sì.*' Her voice sounded ridiculously small and weak to her own ears.

'It is enough to help us start our life together. In a new place. That's what I want.'

She heard his confidence. But she didn't possess that, she realised. Did he have enough for both of them? She wasn't sure.

'If you love me you will come.'

'I do love you, but—' All she could think of was the disap-pointment in Papà's eyes when he found out what she had done.

'Then?'

'How can I leave Vernazza?' She spoke *sotto voce*, but her words seemed to echo around the silent olive grove in the darkness.

'If you love me, you can leave,' he said.

'It is not as simple as that.' But Chiara was no longer sure. Did love and passion sweep you into making decisions that would hurt the ones you loved? Did they pull you away from all that was familiar and dear? Did love have to be that way? She felt that Dante had set her a test, one that she had failed miserably.

'It can be that simple,' he insisted.

'But I cannot leave my parents. I cannot leave the hotel.' There, she had said it. She glanced at him warily. Surely, he would see that his was a reckless, crazy plan?

'Then this is the end for us,' he said.

'No!' She clutched at his sleeve. How could he be so stub-born, so melodramatic? 'Everything will work out, Dante. You will see. I love you. We will be together. I know it.'

13

He shook his dark head. 'Only if we go now. Only if we take this chance. If you trust me.'

'But . . .' It was too much. 'I can't.'

He took a step back. His eyes had a coldness she had not seen there before. 'I am leaving, Chiara,' he said. 'I have made up my mind. I do not want to be in a place where there is no trust, where villagers live close by and yet cannot work together as a team. Where I could be accused of such a thing – and by your father.'

'But, Dante—'

'I am young. I want to see something of the world.'

'But . . .'

'And I will not – I cannot – stand by and see you married to another man.'

Alonzo. Who had told him about Alonzo? 'I will not marry another man.' She raised her head, jutted out her chin. She had no interest in Alonzo. She hated the idea of letting her parents down, but nobody could tell her what she must do – not even Papà. 'I will marry who I please.'

Dante sighed. 'Do you not see? They will not let us be together, my love.'

How could he have so little faith? How could he not believe that they would find a way? 'But in a few years when—'

He put a finger to her lips. 'I will not wait for years. And so . . .'

And so?

'I will leave, my love,' he said. He stroked her hair. 'I will leave, and I am not sure that I will ever come back.'

Chiara's eyes widened. He was headstrong, this man she loved, but this could not be true – he must come back, he

was her destiny. But already he was turning to go, she felt it.
'Dante—'

'*Arrivederci*, Chiara. Goodbye and take care, my love.'

'Dante, wait!'

But he slipped away into the darkness. And Chiara had never felt so alone.

CHAPTER 2

Chiara
Vernazza – October 2011

'How long will you be gone?' Chiara asked her husband. He was away more than he was home, but in some ways, this made life easier at The Lemon Tree Hotel. Mostly, the three women ran the place – Chiara, her daughter Elene, and Chiara's twenty-year-old granddaughter Isabella.

Chiara glanced proudly around the room. Since her parents had bought it in the 1950s, the hotel had gradually grown into the successful business it now was. After their deaths, she had worked to retain as much of the old character of the original convent as possible, keeping many of the original hand-painted and decorative tiles, simple wooden carvings, and niches that paid homage to the hotel's history – and the lemon tree in the courtyard that must have been planted by the nuns and had given the hotel its name. The acid yellow of the fruit was bright as sunshine for much of the year; in years gone by the nuns had made both lemonade and soap from the fruit, and on a summer's day the lemons and the cool green of the waxy leaves presented a picture framed by the Mediterranean blue of the sea and sky that few of their guests could resist. The crumbling, narrow-bricked cloisters had been restored in keeping, and the exposed wooden beams had been repaired, varnished and polished.

What they'd added in recent years was luxury – the best quality Egyptian cotton bedding, deep leather chairs to sink into, marble and stone bathrooms with walk-in showers, and carefully chosen pieces of antique furniture that reflected the history of the building. Chiara nodded to herself in satisfaction. Sometimes a few changes were no bad thing. She thought of Elene. But a few changes could also be enough. One had to know when to stop.

Chiara was the overall manager and owner – she had taken on this role many years ago when her beloved father had died. Her mother, the chef, usually so stalwart, had crumbled then, never recovered from the death of her husband. She'd continued to work in the kitchen, but Chiara soon saw that she could no longer keep things together. Meals did not appear on time, guests began to complain . . . So, they had brought in Marcello, a big cheery bear of a man who took everything in his stride. The kitchen returned to its previous high standards, whilst her mother stayed behind the scenes in *la cucina*, grieving her loss until a year later, she too slipped away as if she couldn't wait to be with her husband once more.

Va bene. Chiara understood about that kind of love, even though she was not fortunate enough to possess it herself. And whose fault was that if not her own?

She watched Alonzo as he examined his face in the mirror, as he peered closer and plucked out an offending hair. Although in his early sixties now and not a tall man, he had not put on too much weight, his hair was a distinguished salt-and-pepper grey, and his eyes were as sharp as ever. He wasn't unattractive, but Chiara felt strangely detached from this man she had married over forty years ago. Perhaps she had always been detached. Perhaps that was why Elene . . .

But, no, it was better not to go down that route. So, she shook the thought of her daughter to one side, and instead busied herself with straightening the cushions on the tan leather sofa that contrasted so beautifully with the clean white walls of the room. After Alonzo had left for wherever it was he must go, she would pop into the kitchen to see Elene and they could discuss the week's menu – for Elene had taken over as head chef when Marcello eventually retired. Perhaps Elene would make coffee and they could carve out some mother-and-daughter time. That was a rare thing these days. She sighed. Truth to tell, it had always been a rare thing.

Taking over the hotel after her parents' death had been the making of Chiara though, and she paused in her tidying as she remembered those far-off days. In the main it had satisfied her. Still grieving for her parents, still suffering from what she now recognised as post-natal depression after the birth of Elene . . . She'd had to knuckle down and get on with it. That or go under.

'Does it make any difference?' Alonzo was watching her curiously in the mirror, perhaps wondering where she was on all these occasions when she was not here with him, although she might seem to be.

In all sorts of places, she thought. *Places I have never gone to. With people I have loved.* 'Hmm?'

'Does it make any difference how long I'm gone?' He didn't bother to hide his irritation at having to repeat the question.

'Yes.' Chiara ignored his tone. She'd been ignoring it for

18

years, but it never got any easier. 'It does, because of course, it would be nice to know when you will be back.'

He shrugged, put his head to one side and straightened his tie. 'I have no idea. Business is business. It has to be attended to. It will take as long as it takes.'

'Not to mention that we are having a dinner party for Giovanna's birthday, and it would be nice if you could attend a family celebration for once.' Chiara was aware of the edge in her voice. This was what they were like these days: leading separate lives, because when they were together, they bickered. And she guessed that neither of them much liked what they had become.

'We've been through all that,' he snapped. 'I have to work. Where do you think the money comes from, eh?'

Chiara stepped away so that she was out of his view. She knew quite well where the money came from. Alonzo liked to pretend that their livelihood came mainly from his property business – he rented out some apartments in Pisa, and no doubt had a finger in a few other pies. But in fact it was the hotel that largely supported their family. Alonzo probably reckoned that the money his parents had put into The Lemon Tree when they married was more than enough of a contribution. But Chiara knew it was passion that had kept the place going through the hard times. Her parents' passion for the hotel that meant so much to them, and then her own. Now, Isabella had taken on that inheritance, young though she was, and maybe even Elene – though Chiara was not so sure about Elene. She never had been. Her daughter was a closed book.

Yet again, Chiara pushed the uncomfortable thoughts of her daughter away. The hotel had started so simply in its early days, still clinging to its old convent life perhaps, but

19

as the world changed and tourism came to Italy, so visitors had discovered the beautiful Cinque Terre, many of them wanting to come back for more. And The Lemon Tree Hotel had opened its doors and embraced them, just as it did to this day.

Chiara drifted towards the window – now draped with elegant curtains where once it had only green wooden shutters – which looked out on to the olive grove. She smiled fondly as she always did. The silver-green leaves shimmered against the backdrop of the cloudless blue sky, the trees were already laden with small but gently swelling fruit, and these olives would be harvested next month just as they had always been. Summer had continued well into September here in Liguria and it continued still, although September had already slipped into the beginning of October. This ancient grove of trees, terraced so that it could be accommodated on the steep slopes of the surrounding hills, still gave her the same sense of tranquillity, even when she thought of what and who she had loved and lost. The whisper of the brittle leaves in the breeze, the rough curves of the gnarled and twisty grey branches, even the abundant olive harvest itself, reminded her that she had done the right thing.

A man was standing almost under their bedroom window staring into the grove, and she gave a start. For a moment, she thought . . . *Certo*, this was not the first time she had stopped short, seen a man of the right age, and imagined him here once more. But of course, it was never him; Dante was long gone, just as he had said he would be; it was a trick of her imagination – nothing more, nothing less. One might expect that over the years she would stop looking for him, stop seeing him here. But she had not.

She remembered all those years ago – how she had waited for him to come back to the hotel, waited in vain for some word. Everything went on as before, and it was almost unbearable: Mamma worked in the kitchen, Papà bottled and stored his thick golden-green olive oil in glass demijohns whilst continuing to sing the praises of Alonzo. And Chiara . . . Chiara went on waiting.

After two weeks, she could stand it no more. She walked the steep path to Corniglia which she had walked since she was a child and which she could negotiate almost as easily as a mountain goat, and she headed straight for the café in the square to find out what she needed to know. Dante's home proved as easy to find as the café owner had told her it would be, as he pointed it out to her, his curiosity evident in his eyes and voice; it was up by the church, amid a cluster of narrow houses that looked down over the bay. She took a deep breath and knocked on the door.

A woman answered. His mother. She had Dante's velvet-brown eyes and his cheekbones too, though she was small and also looked rather severe. '*Sì?*' She glowered at Chiara.

Chiara pulled herself up to her full height; she was at least a little taller than this fierce matriarch, but not by much. 'Is Dante at home?' she asked boldly. 'May I speak with him, *per favore?*'

'Ah, yes.' The woman folded her arms and regarded her through narrowed eyes. 'I know who you are. From Vernazza, eh? The Old Convent?'

'Yes.' Chiara forced herself to stay put. 'Is he here? May I see him, please, *Signora?*'

'You most certainly may not.' The woman smiled, but Chiara couldn't help noticing that her mouth was nothing like

Dante's mouth, and her smile was just a thin unconvincing line across her dour face.

'May I ask why?'

'Because he's not here, that's why.' The woman laughed, but there was no humour in it. 'He's left home, that's what he's done, and you're to blame, as I understand it.'

Chiara's eyes widened. 'But, *Signora*—'

'Oh, I know the story.' The woman nodded. 'No need to tell me. I know what you all thought.'

'Indeed, we did not,' Chiara protested staunchly, knowing she was referring to the incident of the olive harvesting. But something in her belly had turned to liquid panic. Had he done what he said they would do together? Had he gone to Milan – so far from Liguria?

His mother shrugged her thin shoulders. She was dressed in black, Chiara observed, and she remembered Dante telling her that his grandmother had died.

'Where is he?' she whispered.

Dante's mother shook her head. 'Nowhere you can follow him, girl,' she snapped.

'But where?' She could try at least. If she could get an address, somehow, she could try to contact him and tell him that she was sorry, that she loved him, that she needed him . . .

'England,' his mother said.

'England?' Chiara had certainly not been expecting that.

'He's gone to make his fortune.' The woman continued to glare at her. 'He won't come back either. So, I have you to thank for the loss of my son.'

'But . . .' Chiara didn't know what to say. She was still trying to take it in. England. If Milan was far away, England was another planet.

'So, you're not welcome here. Understand?' The woman slammed the door in her face.

Chiara stood on the step, trying to steady her breathing. She couldn't blame his mother for her reaction to her visit. Signora Rossi wasn't to know that Dante might well have left home anyway, even if they had not met. But he could have stayed – at least for a while – and she had to face the truth. Dante had not cared for her enough even to try again. He had gone as far from her as he possibly could. It was over.

The man outside in the olive grove walked down the winding path between the trees and soon was lost in the shroud of the wispy grey branches. Chiara turned away. He was just another guest. The same age as Dante would be – perhaps – and with something similar about his bearing. But that was it. How pathetic she was. What point was there after all this time, in indulging in such wishful thinking? Many of their guests took a stroll around the olive grove. Chiara liked to think that the olives of The Lemon Tree Hotel could refresh their spirits, could bring that sense of peace that could be so elusive in today's busy world where technology dominated everything and people no longer wandered in olive groves and watched time pass by. And fell in love, Chiara reminded herself with a sad smile.

'I shall see you in a few days.' Alonzo picked up his jacket. He glanced over at her and shook his head in disapproval. 'And shouldn't you be doing less daydreaming and a bit more organising, Chiara? After all, this place is so precious to you, is it not? And you are supposed to be in charge of it? Should you not be giving it a bit more of your attention, hmm?'

Chiara bristled as he no doubt intended her to. But of

course, what he meant was that she should be giving him more attention, that she should be attending to his every whim, not standing staring into olive groves. 'We have everything in hand, you can be sure.'

She followed him down the winding stairs that opened out into the black-and-white tiled lobby. They too were the original tiles of the convent, although again many repairs and replacements had been necessary. It pleased Chiara to think that they still walked where the nuns of the convent had walked, on the same worn tiles. Besides – since when had Alonzo cared a dry fig for the hotel? Since when had he even been aware of who did what and how the place was run?

'*Certo*. Of course, you do.' He was placatory now that his barb had made its mark. He bent to kiss her on both cheeks. '*Ciao*, my dear.'

'*Ciao*.' She felt the distant brush of his lips. There was no love in it. But he was still her husband.

Dante had left Italy, and after two years she had married Alonzo just as her parents wished, so she had made them happy at least. It was 1970, and Italy was not alone in experiencing an economic boom after the poverty of the post-war years. The world was changing so fast, just as Dante had known it would. Even here, where things changed so much more slowly, women had more freedom, they were beginning to forge new pathways for themselves; they were working in the cities and becoming more independent in so many ways. They could make their own lifestyle choices, select their own marriage partner. But she still lived in Vernazza, and things had not changed so very much. Her parents were of the old school, and for Chiara, duty and obligation must still win out over love. Or destiny, as she sometimes still allowed herself to think.

As for herself and Alonzo . . . What had she been hoping for when she married and knew it was not for love? Even in the early days, there had been no patience, no tenderness. Chiara had thought that making love would be something thrilling, something wonderful. But she never felt it, and Alonzo seemed to sense this. It wasn't long before he started going away, before he built up his business interests elsewhere. He seemed to resent The Lemon Tree Hotel – as if he thought it was the place that had come between them.

Chiara was not the type of person to sit around doing nothing while her husband was away following his own business interests. She had a hotel to run – alongside her parents. Alonzo had never really talked to her about what he did – he liked to keep things secret; perhaps it was his way of saying: You have your precious hotel, but see here, my work is equally important, and you know nothing about it.

When Elene was born, Chiara had thought this would bring them together, this would make them a family in every sense of the word. But he seemed irritated at the thought of increasing responsibilities, annoyed by the baby's crying, the broken nights. Chiara was soon exhausted trying to juggle the demands of The Lemon Tree Hotel and her new baby, and this seemed to annoy him too. 'You need to make some time for your husband, you know,' he had told her one memorable early morning when, worn out by the interrupted nights and desperate for sleep, Chiara had turned away from him in bed. *And you need to remember you have a family*, she had whispered silently in her head.

He went away, she stayed home; slowly, remorselessly, the distance between them grew. Until she looked at him one day and realised he was – and perhaps had always been – a stranger.

Chiara gave herself a little mental shake. She should not brood. He had given her a daughter, had he not? She should be grateful for that. And that daughter had given Chiara her lovely Isabella. So, she should forget her dark thoughts and remember that despite her disappointments, she had so much to be grateful for.

She wandered past the old picture of the Angel Gabriel in its worn gilt frame, painted by Giovanna's father Luca Bordoni. He had never been a great artist by any stretch of the imagination, and the painting was simple enough. But Giovanna – not an aunt by blood but by affection – was special to their family and to The Lemon Tree Hotel. And so, the painting stayed in its original niche opposite the staircase, lit by a plain white church candle in the evenings, just as it had been lit when the hotel was still a convent.

At the reception desk, Isabella was working on her laptop. She looked up. '*Ciao*, Nonna.' She gave her a beam of smile.

'*Ciao*, Bella.' Chiara thought of the man in the olive grove. Naturally, it was ridiculous, but there was something different about the chord that had been struck this time . . . 'Could I see the register, *per favore*, darling?'

'Of course.' There was a hint of curiosity in Isabella's eyes as she passed it over.

Chiara studied the names. She knew who most people were. Like Isabella, she tried to keep track; they prided themselves on the personal touch. 'A man checked in this morning?'

Isabella raised a dark eyebrow. 'Uh huh. Signor Bianchi.' She pointed to the entry.

'Hmm, yes.' Of course, it was not him. Over the years, a few nuggets of information had come Chiara's way. She had learned that Dante had turned his hand to making *gelato* of all things. She had to laugh at the thought of those strong arms that had held her, those broad shoulders flexing as he pulled in the nets of the olive harvest . . . To think of those same hands making Italian ice cream in an English seaside resort – it amused her, even as it made her feel sad. He had been that kind of a man – who could put his hand to almost anything.

'And another guest will be arriving soon.' Isabella turned back to her laptop. 'Let me find the name. Ah, yes. A Ferdinand Bauer from Germany.'

'Mmm.'

Isabella looked up. 'Is everything all right, Nonna?'

'Yes, perfectly fine. I just wanted to check on the new arrivals.'

'OK.'

Isabella didn't seem to have noticed that she lacked her usual air of calm efficiency. Chiara put a hand to her hair and smoothed it from her face. 'And everything's ready for Aunt Giovanna's dinner party?'

'Mamma's been talking of nothing else all day.' Isabella grinned.

'Excellent.' Chiara took a deep breath. 'Then I'd better go and fetch her.' Because this really would not do. The time was long gone for seeing ghosts from the past, for fantasising about destiny. She had made her decision many years ago – and there was surely no way of ever going back.

CHAPTER 3

Isabella

It had been a warm and sunny day, there were currently no problems or queries with the guests that she should be solving, and she was looking forward to the family birthday celebration with her beloved Aunt Giovanna, but Isabella couldn't help thinking that the atmosphere of The Lemon Tree Hotel was not quite as tranquil as usual. Was there a storm brewing perhaps?

From her position behind the reception desk, which was tucked well into the interior of the cool hotel foyer, she gazed out through the ancient and wooden front doors that had belonged to the original convent building. She didn't think so. The tension could simply be down to the current difference of opinion within the family about how to change – or not to change – the hotel . . . She sighed. This was partly her fault, since she was in charge of the books, and she had informed them all a few weeks ago that there was money available for further investment in The Lemon Tree, if they should wish it.

For a family business, they spent a lot of time not in accord.

Isabella returned her attention to her emails. They were still getting plenty of requests for bookings, thanks to the Cinque Terre's growing popularity and the Indian summer they were experiencing. She couldn't help worrying though. Her grandmother had seemed distracted. Was she working too hard? Should Isabella be shouldering more responsibility? Her grandmother epitomised The Lemon Tree Hotel for Isabella, and what's more, Nonna was the most poised woman she had ever met – nothing seemed to faze her. But something seemed to be bothering her today.

'*Buona sera.*'

The voice took her by surprise. She'd been miles away. Isabella looked up into a pair of cool blue eyes and a lean, pale, but rather attractive male face. She blinked. 'Good evening, *Signore.*'

He smiled, as if well-aware he'd taken her by surprise. Isabella drew herself up to her full height. Why should she feel flustered? She prided herself on her 'front of house' skills. Like her grandmother, she enjoyed meeting people, dealing with any small problems that might arise for their guests, ensuring they enjoyed their stay. Like her grandmother, she hoped that time spent at The Lemon Tree Hotel could be more than a holiday, more than a gateway through which to experience the stunning landscape of her beloved Cinque Terre. Their family-run hotel could be a retreat or a shelter, it could be a spiritual haven, it could provide rest and recuperation for body and soul. They liked to give their guests that little bit extra.

'You have a reservation, *Signore*?' She spoke in English. She didn't need to check the paperwork, however, to know that he was German and that this was Ferdinand Bauer. Until she started daydreaming, Isabella had been prepared to welcome their guest – generally, she was not a girl who liked surprises.

He was fair-skinned and fair-haired. He was tall and dressed in rather crumpled linen shorts, and a short-sleeved shirt and leather sandals. She raised an eyebrow – though admittedly he seemed to pull off the look. She didn't have his full attention now though. Instead, he was gazing with interest around the foyer and out towards the Cloisters Bar.

Then the clear blue-eyed gaze rested on Isabella once again. 'Yes. The name's Bauer.'

She liked his voice. It was low and not too loud – it seemed to acknowledge the serenity of their surroundings.

'Welcome, Signor Bauer,' she said warmly. 'Have you had a good journey?'

He seemed surprised by her question. Many people reacted similarly, but Isabella's grandmother had taught her to use the personal touch. 'A few questions,' she always said. 'Where's the harm in that? Nothing too taxing – they may be tired, they may not want to talk. Take your cue from them. At the very least it will show that you are interested in their lives.'

'Quite good,' he said. 'Thank you. But I was surprised how busy it is here.'

Isabella nodded. 'The Cinque Terre is one of the most popular parts of Italy.' With good reason in her opinion. Where else could you find a landscape that combined rugged mountains, romantic bays and turquoise sea with colourful villages, terraces of vineyards, olive groves, and lemon trees clinging to the hills and shimmering in the sun?

'I can tell. The train from La Spezia was packed full of tourists.'

And you are one of them. She didn't say it though, just gave one of her little shrugs that seemed to agree, sympathise, and deny all knowledge, at the same time. This was a mannerism she had acquired from her grandmother. 'If you could just complete this paperwork, *Signore*?'

'OK.' He gave it a brief glance and scribbled a signature.

Isabella plucked his key from the rack behind her. 'You are in number three,' she told him. 'I am sure you will be comfortable there.' It was a pleasant room, a little smaller than some and so usually sold as a single, but with a narrow balcony and a partial sea view.

'Any rules and regulations?' He seemed to want to linger. And once again he was looking around the lobby with undisguised curiosity. Almost, she thought, as if he were searching for something in particular.

'Only that we try to maintain a peaceful atmosphere.' The ambience of the hotel was perhaps their number one priority.

'Because this place used to be a convent?' He fixed her with an intent stare.

'It has always been the nature of the building, as you say,' she agreed.

'And has the hotel been in the same family for a long time?'

Really, those blue eyes of his were very penetrating. 'It has been in our family since my great-grandfather purchased the old convent in the 1950s,' she said proudly.

'Indeed?' He seemed very interested in this. 'And the nuns?'

'*Scusi*? Pardon me?' Isabella glanced around as if one of the old nuns might suddenly drift out from behind the cloisters.

He leaned on the desk. Isabella wondered if he was there for the duration. Most guests couldn't wait to get into their rooms on arrival. This one, clearly, was different. 'I was wondering

what happened to all the old nuns – from the convent, I mean?'
He didn't even blink.

'Well . . .' There was something almost accusatory in his
tone. Isabella bridled. Who did he think he was, charging in
here and asking all these questions? 'The order was depleted,'
she said stiffly, searching in her English vocabulary for the
correct words. 'Most of the nuns had already left the convent,
shortly after the war, I believe. The building was . . . how do
you say? In danger.' She frowned in concentration. Her English
was fluent, but she wasn't expressing this at all well.

'In danger?'

'In danger of deterioration. Otherwise it would have become
a ruin, sadly the fate of so many of our old and interesting
buildings. My great-grandfather thought it could be saved,
restored, and made into a hotel.' Isabella folded her arms. And,
guest or no guest, that was all she was saying on the matter.

But to her surprise, Ferdinand Bauer lifted his hands in
apology. 'I've offended you,' he said, rather disarmingly. 'I'm
sorry. I always ask too many questions. I'm too curious about
everything. Please forgive me.'

Isabella stared at him. He was certainly a man of many
parts – she wasn't sure she had met anyone quite like him
before. Already, he'd had her on the back foot and on the front
foot, so to speak, and he'd only just arrived.

Isabella was only twenty, but she knew her lifestyle was
very different from that of other girls her age. Most of her
time was taken up with the business, it always had been; she
had lived and breathed The Lemon Tree Hotel since she was
old enough to understand what it was. Her grandmother had
always made her feel that she was fortunate to live here and
she knew that this was true. She had made sacrifices – she had

friends, but not much of a social life down in the village; it was simply too difficult to find much leisure time with all her duties here. Nor did she have much interest in local boys her age – they all seemed immature, more interested in football than anything else.

But any sacrifices were worth it. She had become accustomed to meeting people of all nationalities here in the hotel; there was always interest and variety. Isabella had done a course in business studies so that she could help her grandmother with that side of things, but front of house was where she most liked to be. It was important to feel that they were making a difference; this made her work fulfilling and worthwhile.

'*Va bene*,' she said. 'It's perfectly all right. It's nice that you're so interested in our hotel.'

He beamed at her – and suddenly it *was* nice. Isabella was so used to the place, she'd forgotten how intriguing the story could be to others. But it was their history, and it should be celebrated – her grandmother had always taught her that too.

'Thank you, *Signorina*,' he said. 'And I must congratulate you.'

'Oh?'

'Your English is excellent.' He grinned – and she noticed that he had dimples. When he smiled, his face was transformed.

'Isabella, please,' she said. 'And so is yours.'

He laughed. 'Well, it's useful to have a language in common.'

'It is.' Isabella knew very little German. But she could manage schoolgirl French, and her English was improving daily. 'But do you also speak Italian, *Signore*?'

'A little.' His smile was once again disarming. 'I learned some at college, and I was lucky enough to spend some time here in Italy when I was studying art history a while back.'

'Really?' Isabella wanted to ask more, but there was a limit to the number of questions one should ask a guest on arrival, and surely Nonna would soon be back with Aunt Giovanna and wonder why she was taking so long to sign in their new guest. 'And now would you like to see your room?'

'I would.' He dangled the key between his fingers. 'But I hope I can talk to you some more about the convent, Isabella?'

'Why not?' She smiled back at him. 'But if you are really interested, then the person you should speak to is my Aunt Giovanna.'

'Giovanna?' Again, she felt the intensity of his interest, again the faintest feeling of unease.

Should she involve Aunt Giovanna? But why not? Her aunt would probably enjoy talking to a charming young man about the old days. But she would ask her first, she decided – maybe even tonight. 'Giovanna Bordoni,' she said. 'She used to live here at the convent.'

'She was a nun?' He leaned closer.

'No, she never was.' Isabella surveyed him thoughtfully. 'If you like, I will speak to her. Ask her if she is happy to talk to you.'

'I would be grateful.' He gave her another long look. Plucked a card from his shirt pocket. 'Here's my number. You can contact me on my mobile any time.'

'Oh, yes, thanks.' She had his contact details already of course, but she took the card and glanced at it. It was charcoal grey with white lettering, a simple graphic. *Ferdinand Bauer, Architect*, she read. Hence the art history, she supposed. She placed it carefully on the desk.

'See you later, I hope.' He grabbed his bag and turned to give her another fleeting smile.

'*Ciao.* See you later.' Really, he was a bit of a whirlwind. Someone like that – he could shake things up if he wanted to. The question was – did she want things to be shaken up at The Lemon Tree Hotel? Hardly.

She watched as he made for the stairs. He paused in front of Luca Bordoni's painting for a few moments as if he already knew the connection, though that was surely impossible, since Giovanna's father's signature on the painting was totally illegible. 'First floor,' she called out to him softly, 'turn left at the top.'

'Thanks.' He waved. One last glance at the Archangel Gabriel and then he loped up the stairs, his bag slung over one shoulder and disappeared from view. Isabella let out the breath she'd been holding.

She picked up his business card, glanced at it again, and put in her pocket. Tranquillity was necessary to The Lemon Tree Hotel, this was indisputably true. Even so, she thought. Even so.

CHAPTER 4

Elene

Elene looked around the family group. It had been a simple enough dinner by Italian standards. For *antipasti* she had prepared scallops in a saffron and vanilla sauce and cuttle fish with a black cream – Aunt Giovanna's favourite. The two stuffed pasta dishes – a meaty *ravioli alla Genovese*, and *pansòuti*, filled with fresh herbs, garlic and crushed walnuts – had gone down rather well and nicely prepared the way for the *secondi* – a layered filo tart with ricotta, plus a traditional braised rabbit dish in a sauce of white wine and fresh capers that was another favourite of her aunt's. The dessert was a traditional Ligurian lemon cake with candles, accompanied by Elene's own *limoncino* – what else could it be?

She sipped the citrus liqueur, felt the heat in her throat as she swallowed. There was one person missing, of course – so often, there was one person missing.

And whose fault was that? Their table was tucked away in the far reaches of the Cloisters Restaurant, leaving the courtyard free for their guests, being looked after tonight by

Emanuele and the others. Elene's mother Chiara was sitting next to Aunt Giovanna; opposite her – dark eyes shining – was Isabella. Silvio and Elene sat opposite one another, Elene as always nearest to the kitchen, so she could nip in and out as necessary to attend to the food. Not that she minded. Cooking was, perhaps, the most important thing in her life – after her family, she supposed. Of course, she loved her daughter Isabella – Elene smiled as she tuned in to Bella's latest story about a demanding hotel guest who had categorically stated that their high quality Egyptian cotton sheets were not sufficiently soft on the skin, and that the view from their window was slightly obscured by an open parasol on the terrace below.

'So, what did you tell them?' she asked Isabella.

Her daughter gave a theatrical roll of the eyes. 'I showed them the label on the sheets – no one was going to argue with that level of luxury. And I pointed out – diplomatically – that the yellow of the parasol perfectly matched the lemons on our tree.'

They all laughed. 'Perfect!' Elene's mother clapped her hands, then looked for a moment towards the olive grove as if something was distracting her, or as if she was looking for someone perhaps. It wouldn't be Papà though. When had her mother ever looked for Papà? She was far too independent, too self-sufficient. So no wonder he went off to Pisa to attend to his business there. No wonder that he missed family celebrations, birthdays like this one. When had he ever been made to feel wanted?

Not that Aunt Giovanna was a blood relation, so not truly family. But she had been so close to Elene's grandparents to make her as good as. She had lost her own parents when still very young, soon after the war apparently, and so had gone to live at the convent with the few remaining nuns. When they left, when Elene's grandparents bought *L'Attico Convento* and vowed to do it up, to make it into a very special sort of hotel, it was only natural that Giovanna would be part of the arrangement. Since that day she had lived in her own cottage in the grounds – independent, but part of their family for sure.

'And did you also point out the significance of that lemon tree, my dear?' Giovanna's faded brown eyes twinkled. She still had a hearty appetite and had managed to have a taste of everything on the table. Elene was satisfied – the birthday dinner had been a success. And as for her family – of course, she loved every one of them. It was just that sometimes she felt excluded, undervalued, that was all.

'I did. I explained that it is iconic. Its fruit enables Mamma to make her *limoncino* and her Ligurian lemon cake after all.'

'Indeed.' Silvio rubbed his stomach appreciatively. 'And very good they were too.'

'Exactly, Papà.' Isabella leaned over to pour him another small glass. 'We *are* The Lemon Tree.'

'Perhaps we are booked up too far in advance to even worry about such awkward guests?' Elene suggested. She pushed her plate away. Who really cared if they didn't come back? Not that she had anything to do with the guests, the bookings, or the way the hotel was run . . . She bit back the sense of grievance that never seemed far away. But she listened to conversations her mother and her daughter seemed to have at every opportunity – consulting constantly about the hotel, the rooms, the staff, the advertising, everything else under the sun. Elene knew they ran a successful business. Which was why, after what Isabella had told them . . . She sneaked a glance at Silvio, her husband, her supporter, perhaps also her best friend. It was time for them to think about making some big changes around here.

'We always have to worry about awkward guests,' her mother was saying now. Come to think of it, she had not eaten as much as usual. Elene frowned. 'If it's not the bed linen or the view it will be the windows being too stiff to open or a speck of dust discovered on a bedside table.'

They all laughed again.

'But not the food, Mamma,' Isabella added diplomatically.

'Oh, no.' Chiara's smile was breezy. 'Of course, never the food.'

'But how things have changed, my dears.' Aunt Giovanna's smile was wistful.

'For the good, Aunt?' Elene knew that life had never been easy for the inhabitants of the Cinque Terre – not even before the war, when steep slopes had been terraced to make the vineyards and olive groves – back-breaking work in near-impossible conditions, some might say. When men had fished for anchovies and other seafood, but had relied on the olives for their living. Their people had been focused on survival back then – not on tourism and the continual stream of visitors whom they now had to keep happy. It was enough that they grew and caught enough to live on. But who could blame them when they saw the glimmer of light provided by people who found the area so beautiful they wanted to spend their vacations here? The Ligurians knew already that Vernazza and the other villages were tiny and precious jewels in the crown of the Levante. Couldn't they then use their land in a new way? Couldn't they celebrate their good fortune at having been born in such a glorious landscape rather than struggle to make that landscape provide them with a meagre living? Anyone could see how it must have been.

'Mostly for the good,' Giovanna conceded. She took a small sip of her *limoncino*. 'But may I say that I am relieved I am so very old . . .'

There were groans and shouts around the table at this remark. No one knew Giovanna's exact age – though she must be eighty-three or eighty-four years old today, Elene guessed.

'Not to have to witness what might happen next.'

What might happen next. For a moment there was silence around the table.

Elene glanced across at Silvio, who gave her a little nod. It's all right, he seemed to say, she cannot know what we are thinking of.

And he was right. They might not have the strongest marriage in the world – Elene would readily admit that she had married Silvio because he was reliable and hard-working, and because he clearly adored her. But they were on the same wavelength, as it were, they wanted the same things – for themselves, for their daughter Isabella, for future generations who hopefully would continue to run The Lemon Tree Hotel.

'But we will do all we can to keep things as they are now,' Chiara was saying staunchly, as if to reassure Giovanna – and perhaps herself. She was such a traditionalist, so stuck in her ways.

'Hear, hear!' Isabella was raising her glass of lemon liqueur.

Elene tutted. It came out louder than she had anticipated. She saw her mother frown.

'What, Mamma?' Isabella was waiting, still smiling.

Again, Elene glanced at Silvio. 'Nothing,' she said. 'To The Lemon Tree Hotel.' She raised her own glass.

'And the peace and tranquillity it provides for our guests,' Isabella added.

Elene met Silvio's eyes yet again. And to our plans, he seemed to say. When the time is right – at last – for things to change.

CHAPTER 5

Chiara

In the end, Chiara didn't get around to talking to Elene about the week's menus until the following day. She had been faintly relieved when the family dinner was over, and when Silvio offered to take a tired Giovanna back to her cottage so that she could retire for the night. Chiara wanted to rest too, but more than that, she wanted to be alone. She was still distracted, still not sure what – or who – she had seen. Although she had checked the hotel register yesterday, there was something still bothering her.

She headed for the swing doors that led to the kitchen with her customary slight trepidation – for it was a place that was very much her daughter Elene's domain.

'Mamma.' Her daughter greeted her with a cool nod. 'The menu is on the table.'

'Good morning, Elene.' Chiara sat down, picked up the menu and ran her eye over the list of dishes written in her daughter's neat and precise hand. Many guests liked to have dinner at the hotel, so they ensured there was a good choice, while keeping the small bill of fare both fresh and manageable for Elene and her team.

'It all looks wonderful as usual, my dear.' Chiara was aware that she sounded appeasing. It was an integral part of the relationship pattern she played out with her daughter. She was always apologising – but for what? The wrongs of the past? At any rate, determined not to cause further upset, she avoided treading on conversational eggshells – which was, quite frankly, exhausting. Whilst Elene . . . *Allora*. Who knew what went on inside that head of hers?

'You don't want to change anything?' Elene shot her a look of disbelief.

'Let me think.' Chiara frowned, shifted her weight and looked more closely. She was still preoccupied; she was finding it harder than usual to focus. 'Perhaps the *antipasto* on Tuesday . . .' She ran a fingertip down Elene's list.

'Yes?' Her daughter let out the smallest of sighs.

'Wednesday might be better for the *mozzarella caprese* – because—'

'Of the market, yes, I know, I have thought of that, naturally. I have plenty, and *certo*, it will stay fresh, but—'

'*Allora*, well then, fine.' She glanced at her daughter's face, which was inscrutable as ever. Sometimes Chiara wondered if she was testing her. Elene knew as well as she did what they could get hold of and when. There weren't many roads that led into the villages of the Cinque Terre; residents and restaurants alike must organise their culinary needs accordingly. There was a poor excuse of a track up to the hotel, which was easily negotiable in an Ape – the practical three-wheeled truck that was really just a Vespa with a cart on the back – still used in these parts. But to make things simple they collected most of

43

their fresh food from the village, particularly on market day, although they still grew much of their own vegetables and fruit, and Giovanna still looked after the chickens in the coop next to her cottage in the grounds. Living on a mountainside had both its advantages and its problems – both undisputed. But Elene was a creative cook, and a good one. Chiara quite liked it when her daughter forgot to be practical.

Elene swapped the *antipasti* around with a double-edged arrow and refrained from further comment.

'The rest is perfect,' Chiara said quickly. She wondered as she often did where she had gone wrong with Elene – how things between them had become so strained. Where was the easiness that characterised her relationship with her grand-daughter, for example: the love and laughter? Had it started with that painful birth, that feeling of being so literally ripped apart by this small being that she couldn't face another preg-nancy? Or had it begun even earlier perhaps? Had it started when she married Alonzo?

The wrong man. Chiara watched her daughter as she plucked her white chef's apron from the peg and wrapped it around her slim waist. Elene wore that apron like armour. In the kitchen, she was in charge, and they all respected that. But Chiara knew that she wanted to make changes to The Lemon Tree too, and that was where Chiara drew the line.

Elene had been left to her own devices as a child – was that the reason why? – and she'd taken to running to the kitchen almost as soon as she could run anywhere. Chiara thought of her mother; it must be in the genes. She remembered how grateful she'd been at first. How hard she had worked to get things right after the death of her parents – and with very little help from Alonzo, it must be said.

'It is your hotel,' he had remarked when she questioned his frequent trips away, his obvious lack of interest. 'It will always be your hotel.' And since Chiara knew this to be true, she hadn't pursued the subject. Let Alonzo disappear off to Pisa, to his apartments and his wheeling and dealing. She could run The Lemon Tree alone – why not?

But now, Chiara wondered about the repercussions. Could she have given Elene more attention? Perhaps. But she was always so busy in those days. The hotel – much as she loved it – often seemed like a greedy child itself, dragging her attention back to it whenever she showed any sign of taking time out. And if she were truly honest, she had relished the challenge of it, she had almost resented those times when she'd had to look after her daughter and been unable to focus fully on the problems and practicalities of running an increasingly busy enterprise. She'd loved Elene – naturally, she had loved her. She had done her best for her. But Chiara was a woman who needed more than child-rearing to satisfy her – that was something she could not deny. While Alonzo . . . She truly believed that he too loved his daughter; he was always ready with an affectionate hug when he came home, he always took Elene's side when there were disagreements – the matter of Elene's marriage to Silvio came to mind – he was not a bad father, no indeed. It was just that he had often been an absent one.

As for Elene . . . Chiara's heart softened as she watched her daughter catch up her nut-brown hair, swirling it into an efficient chignon. Elene was an attractive woman, but in an understated way; she wore a bare minimum of make-up – a flick of eye-liner, a sweep of pale lipstick. Her bone structure, skin, and posture allowed her to get away with it, though. The women of their family were fortunate in that regard.

45

'Is there anything else, Mamma?' Clearly, Elene wanted her out of the kitchen. Behind them various members of Elene's team were washing, peeling and preparing, ready for the lunch service.

Chiara put a hand to her own hair. 'I need to talk to Silvio,' she murmured, half to herself. She still felt slightly spaced out, as if a dream from last night had not quite left her, was still misting around her mind, determined not to let it clear.

'What about?' Elene's eyes were sharp as her father's, and she was defensive of Silvio, always had been since the day she first brought him back here. Even back then, Chiara had known that there was nothing wrong with Silvio Lombardi – a boy from the village – he could be trusted, and he seemed to adore Elene. But . . .

'I have some jobs for him, that's all,' she said mildly.

Elene straightened her chef's apron as if she meant business. Her eyes were steely. 'He's busy, Mamma.'

'Doing?' Chiara arched an eyebrow. It was an instinctive reaction and so she could not take it back. Silvio was supposed to be answerable to her – which she knew was tricky, given that she was his mother-in-law – but this never seemed to happen. Instead, she had to chase after him constantly to find out what he was doing, drag him away to see to what actually needed doing, and then watch him return to his original task the second her back was turned. Of course, he was busy. Why wouldn't he be busy? He too worked full-time here at the hotel.

'I imagine he's working in the kitchen garden.' Elene glanced outside. The window looked out on to the olive grove, but they had created a small area for herbs just outside the back door.

The trees stood, soft and serene, reminding Chiara of the

46

man she'd seen yesterday. Maybe she too would take a walk outside later, she thought; the trees always seemed to soothe her, maybe they would chase that dream away.

'Such a lovely day.' Elene sounded almost wistful. 'A shame to be cooped up inside.'

'As we all are.' Too late, Chiara bit her tongue.

Silvio meant well. And he worked hard enough. But right from the first, Chiara had questioned her daughter's judgement – perhaps wrongly, she realised now.

'Do you love him?' she had asked her when Elene first broke the news of their engagement. The words came out more harshly than she'd intended – so many words did. He seemed a decent boy – but where was the edge, the spark? Would he be enough for her daughter, for any woman of their family?

'Mamma . . .' Elene's eyes told her nothing.

'Do you?' This mattered so much to Chiara – she, who hadn't been allowed the luxury of love.

'There are other things.' Elene's chin jutted in that way Chiara recognised. It told her there was no point in pursuing this line of conversation, and yet still she did.

'What things?'

'More important things.'

'Elene.' Chiara gripped her daughter's arms. 'Nothing is more important than love.' She heard the tremor of passion in her own voice.

But Elene shrugged her away as she had shrugged her away so often. 'Silvio is reliable,' she said. 'I can trust him. He gives me what I need.'

And what do you need? But Chiara did not ask this question. Perhaps she was afraid of what she might hear, that what Silvio provided was precisely what she and Alonzo had failed to give their daughter: solidity, attention, the kind of security she craved.

Elene was stubborn as always. 'Papà likes him. He has already given his blessing.'

'You have spoken to him already?' Chiara was surprised.

'He's my father.' Elene stood straighter. 'He said it was my decision. He said that I was old enough to know my own mind.'

There was no denying the sub-text behind her words. 'And so it is.' Chiara sighed. 'And so you are. But . . .'

'But?'

How could she put this to get through to her? 'I just want you to know, *cara*, that you do not have to make this choice,' she told her. 'You can wait. You can reconsider. You can marry anyone. Anyone you choose. And perhaps one day—'

'I do not want to wait. No one is going to appear like magic with a glass slipper in his hand. Life is not a fairy story.' Elene had glared at her. 'I have chosen Silvio. You put him down. But what do you know about him, really?'

Chiara shook her head. 'I'm not putting him down.' Though she supposed that she was. 'And I know better than anyone that life is not a fairy story.' She swallowed. Better not dwell on that. Elene looked up to her father – even seemed to idolise him, which seemed hardly fair given his lack of parental contribution over the years. Oh, of course, it was good and right for her to love her own father. But did she love a version of Alonzo that didn't really exist? Sometimes, Chiara couldn't help but wonder. 'It's only that if you don't love him—'

'Oh, you pretend to be so gracious.' Elene was angry now. Her eyes were bright, as if she might cry.

Chiara had handled this badly. What was meant to be a

loving mother and daughter chat had turned into something quite different – again.

'But you always criticise me. There is always something wrong. I can't do anything well enough for you, Mamma . . .'

'Elene . . .' She tried to soothe her. 'It's not that, Elene. I'm only thinking of—' *You*. But her daughter had turned on her heel and left the room. Leaving Chiara to reflect once more: was it true? Were her expectations too high?

No. It was just that she wanted her daughter to have what she could not, that was all. She wanted Elene to be happy.

And so, Elene had married Silvio, and he had come to live and work at the hotel. It was a good plan. Silvio was practical – he could turn his hand to plumbing, gardening, and all kinds of building maintenance. Chiara had to admit that he'd added to the smooth running of The Lemon Tree, and that she had grown to appreciate him too. And then of course there was their daughter Isabella, *ah, Bella* . . . the granddaughter she adored. But was Elene truly happy? That, she would love to know.

'And the jobs on your list, they are important, *sì*?' Elene was bustling around the kitchen now, fetching a large pan and a glass bottle of rich green olive oil, grabbing two fat bulbs of purple-white garlic from the terracotta jar.

'Yes.' Chiara turned around to leave the kitchen. They hadn't shared a coffee or a cosy chat after all – why had she thought this might happen when it so rarely did? Instead they had ended on the usual note of tension. 'I'll go and find him.' Too bad if Silvio would rather be weeding the kitchen garden. This was an old building and it required tending – inside as well as out. There was broken plaster work in one of the rooms – the maid had reported it – and this was not good enough; it needed to be repaired before the next guest arrived.

As she left, she heard the unmistakeable sound of Elene slamming the pan on to the marble counter. But Chiara was still in charge – however difficult Elene and Silvio might find that. Nevertheless, she exhaled with relief as the swing doors of the kitchen closed behind her. As someone once said: *if you don't like the heat* . . .

She fanned herself with her clipboard, glanced towards the reception desk where Isabella was smiling and chatting to a guest – and froze. She stared at the man who had his back to her. There was something so familiar about the way he stood, the set of his shoulders, the angle of his head. Surely? She remembered the man she'd seen in the olive grove yesterday. Of course. He bore even more resemblance to Dante at close quarters. But it couldn't be him. *Oh, mio dio* . . . How could it be him?

Chiara found she couldn't move. And by the time she'd half recovered, taken a step forwards, stepped back again, the man had nodded to Isabella and walked away past the desk. Now, he was almost out of sight.

'Nonna?' Isabella had seen her. 'Are you all right?'

'Yes, yes.' Chiara approached the reception desk, struggling to remain calm.

'You're very pale.'

'Nonsense.' Chiara leaned heavily on the desk. Truth be told, she was feeling a little dizzy, she almost thought she might fall. 'I'm perfectly fine.' She was hardly in her dotage. Fifty-nine and fit as a fiddle.

'If you say so, Nonna.'

'I do.' And she forced a smile. The man had disappeared from view. He'd probably gone into the courtyard. 'That man,' she asked Isabella, 'was he the one who checked in yesterday?'

'Yes, that's him, Signor Bianchi.' She tucked a strand of raven-black hair behind her ear. To Chiara's secret delight she had inherited the colouring passed down to them both by Chiara's mother. 'Is there a problem?'

'No, no, it is nothing.' Of course, it was not him, just a coincidence. A man who happened to be around Dante's age and height, his arrival coinciding with that half-forgotten dream. And after all, how could she even guess what he looked like now? How white his hair might be, how bent his back, how weathered his skin? Once she had thought that he was her destiny – but that was a very long time ago.

Isabella was frowning. 'Could you look after the desk for five minutes, Nonna? I need to check something in the office.'

'Of course.' Chiara pulled the hotel's register towards her and stared at the name. *Bianchi*. There was something . . . But. For a moment she was lost, once again, in thought.

'It was a feeble disguise.' The voice was a soft growl. It was one so familiar and yet one she had not heard for over forty years.

For a moment, she was motionless. Then she spun around. 'Dante,' she breathed.

'The very same.'

He was smiling. His face was broader and his skin more lined. His dark hair was now flecked with silver. His eyes were the same though – velvet-brown and deep as a well. He had put on a little weight around the middle – but not too much. Chiara couldn't take her eyes off him.

'But – why?'

'Why the subterfuge?' He was still smiling. 'It has been a long time.'

'Yes.' Such a long time.

'I didn't want to charge in and create any kind of problem for you.'

'Then what did you want?' She was still staring at him. She was surprised she could even speak.

'I just wanted to . . .' He paused. 'Observe.'

'Observe?'

'Exactly.' His eyes were searching her face.

Madonna santa . . . After forty years apart – what did he want to observe?

'But then I saw that you might have recognised me, and so . . .' He shrugged. 'I came clean.'

Chiara nodded, though her thoughts and emotions were so tangled she could barely make sense of what he was saying. Bianchi and Rossi . . . Honestly. White and red, she got it now, of course. 'But, why are you here at all?' Wasn't he supposed to be in England? Making his *gelato* miles away from The Lemon Tree Hotel, from Vernazza?

'You could say that I am paying a visit to an old friend.' He leaned towards her, kissed her on both cheeks.

The touch stung. Chiara felt as though she were on fire. It was the shock. Or perhaps another hot flush? Or something altogether more dangerous? Whichever, she couldn't use her clipboard to fan herself again. It would be too obvious. 'Or?'

'Or you could say that sometimes, even after forty years, it can still prove impossible to get a woman out of one's mind.'

CHAPTER 6

Isabella

Isabella hadn't had a chance to speak to her Aunt Giovanna last night, so she nipped down to the cottage the following morning to ask her about Ferdinand Bauer.

She found her on the back terrace feeding her hens, murmuring to them gently as if they shared a language all of their own. And for the first time, she wondered, was her Aunt Giovanna lonely living here in the cottage in the grounds of The Lemon Tree Hotel? Had she wanted to live here when the idea was first presented to her? Or was there a different kind of life that she might ever have desired for herself?

'Bella. What a lovely surprise.' Her aunt fetched a jug of lemonade and they settled themselves on the worn wooden bench on the back terrace opposite the olive grove.

'There's a guest at the hotel who would very much like to talk to you, Aunt,' Isabella began.

'Oh? Why on earth would anyone want to talk to an old lady like me, my dear?'

Isabella laughed. 'Who wouldn't want to talk to you?' Her

aunt had so many visitors; Isabella knew that over the years she had become a bit of an unofficial counsellor for the inhabitants of Vernazza and the other four villages.

'Ah, well, people think because I am old that I must be wise,' she said, 'when you and I are sensible enough to know that this is not necessarily the case.'

But in her case, it definitely was. Isabella regarded her thoughtfully. 'This young man wants to talk to you about the old convent, I believe.'

'Is that so?'

Isabella felt her scrutiny. 'I have no idea why,' she added. 'Though he seems to be very interested in the history of the building.'

'Hmm.' Giovanna sipped her lemonade. 'And is that all he is interested in, do you suppose?'

'Who knows?' Isabella pretended not to understand her aunt's meaning. Yes, he was young, yes, he was attractive, and Isabella was certainly not blind. But that was absolutely all there was to it – and all there would ever be. Guests were off-limits – she had learned that to her cost.

'And what is he like, this young man?'

'Oh, late twenties, tall, fair, inquisitive . . .' Isabella's voice trailed.

'Then, yes.' And Giovanna's milky brown eyes positively gleamed. 'I would be most happy to talk to him, my dear.'

Back at the hotel, things were not running as smoothly as usual. One of the guests was asking about gluten-free bread, so Isabella went into the kitchen to quiz her mother about it.

Elene was not in a good mood. 'They want this, they want that, they want the other. Since when can people not eat good, honest bread baked in the same way it has been baked for centuries?' She was clattering pots and pans around and slamming cupboard doors and the rest of the kitchen staff seemed to have retreated to the other end of the room.

If they weren't careful, they wouldn't have any staff left. Emanuele had already got into a complete grump about having to look after things last night, and he'd been late for his shift twice this week already. Isabella didn't want to bother her grandmother with the matter. When Isabella had come back from the office to reception this morning, Nonna had been white as a sheet. She'd insisted she was fine, but Isabella was far from convinced. That made twice in two days that Nonna had looked near to passing out.

'Mamma – what's wrong?' Isabella wondered if she should fetch her father. He was always calm in a crisis, and they needed her mother to supervise lunch, otherwise they would have a lot of very unhappy guests to contend with.

'Wrong? Why should anything be wrong?' Another pan clattered on to the stove.

Isabella winced. 'I don't know. You seem unhappy.'

'Unhappy – *pah*! Wouldn't anyone be unhappy working in a hot kitchen all day?'

Well, yes, but her mother usually welcomed it. 'Did Nonna come in earlier to look at the menus?' This was a fair guess. Life would be a lot easier if her mother and her grandmother could get along better, but they both knew which buttons to press and sometimes they pressed them with wild abandon and total disregard for each other's sensitivities.

'Don't talk to me about the menus, Bella,' Elene snapped. 'God knows they take long enough to prepare in themselves – and that's without any cooking.'

'I know, Mamma.'

'As if I can't decide what dish should be eaten when. As if I don't know what ingredients are available and when it's market day and—'

'Perhaps we should talk about it with Nonna,' Isabella soothed. 'Perhaps you should always make the final decision and be done with it.'

'As if I could be trusted to make any final decision.' Elene took hold of her kitchen knife and sliced it neatly through an innocent and glistening onion.

Once again, Isabella winced. 'We could bring it up at the next meeting?' she suggested.

'No point.'

'Mamma, there's always a point.' Isabella put an arm around her mother's shoulders – they were thin and tense. 'Come on now, don't get so upset. Nonna would hate to think she'd upset you. She's not quite herself today, you know, maybe she's coming down with something and—'

'Oh, that's it. Defend her – you always do.'

'Mamma!' Sometimes Isabella wondered who was the daughter and who was the mother around here.

Elene shrugged her away. '*Basta*. Enough. I have work to do, Bella.'

'Shall I fetch Papà?'

'Why? Can he cook lunch all of a sudden?'

No, but he could talk to you. Isabella didn't say this out loud. She peered out of the window. Very likely he'd be out in the grounds somewhere. There was no time to lose. Her mother was pressing bulbs of garlic as if she meant them actual bodily harm. 'I'll just . . .'

'Better not dare,' she advised. 'Your grandmother – she is

on the warpath. Your father must do this and then he must do that. He must not stop for a second – oh, no – because if he does, the entire hotel will collapse, just like a house of sand. Whoosh!' She made a wild gesture with her hands.

Isabella worried about the knife. Her mother could be as cool as a cucumber most of the time. But when she got angry, she got very angry, and only Isabella's father could calm her. 'I'll find him.' She slipped out through the back door.

Outside, Ferdinand Bauer was – rather bizarrely – standing staring up at the back of the hotel.

'What on earth are you doing?' The words were out of her mouth before she could catch them.

'Oh, hello.' He seemed nonplussed. 'Just, er, looking up at the building.'

'Looking at the building?' Honestly?

He shrugged. 'Wondering about the old convent – what it was like back then, you know.'

Ah. He was an architect, of course. Perhaps they often went around looking up at old buildings – wondering.

'This part of the grounds is meant to be private, *Signore*,' She put on her best reproving voice. Although it was hard to be stern when he was grinning at her like that. And those eyes . . .

'I do apologise.' He held up both hands. 'I had no idea.'

'It's OK.'

Her mother's angry voice rang through the kitchen and leapt through the open window beside them.

Ferdinand blinked. Isabella remembered that there was a crisis in the making.

'Please excuse me.' She took a step away.

'Is everything all right? Is there anything I can—?'

'Yes. No. Everything is fine.' Though the near hysteria

evident in her mother's tone seemed to render this statement ridiculous. 'I have to find my father.' She took another step away.

'But can I just ask you . . .'

'Yes?' She hesitated.

'Your friend? The nun who is not a nun? Giovanna, wasn't it? Have you spoken to her yet?'

He didn't seem to appreciate the urgency of the situation. 'She isn't a nun, I told you.' Isabella tried not to let her frustration show in her voice. No point in him thinking the entire family were crazy-mad-Italian. 'And yes, but . . .' She spotted her father in the distance. 'I'll tell you later, *Signore*.' She waved. 'Papà!'

'Ferdinand,' he said softly.

She looked back at him for a moment. His eyes were the exact same shade as the sky. 'Ferdinand,' she repeated.

CHAPTER 7

Chiara

Chiara eased herself on to the bar stool beside Dante. Her body felt not quite hers, it was rather too aware of him; and she could smell his aftershave, oddly reminiscent of cypress trees and the ocean; that was new. The old Dante Rossi had never bothered; he had smelt only of honest sweat and toil and bitter-green olives.

She had promised to meet him for an *aperitivo*, that was all. 'To catch up on the last forty years,' he had said with a wry smile.

How could she refuse when she wanted to know so badly? And where was the harm? Dante had in fact invited Alonzo too, though she could tell he was relieved when she told him Alonzo was away on business. 'Just you and me then, Chiara,' he'd said.

'Just you and me,' she'd agreed. And she'd pretended to herself that the slow thrill of excitement that rippled down her spine at the prospect wasn't really there at all.

She'd taken her time in deciding what to wear tonight –

because what could possibly suit the occasion? Her red lacy dress was surely too frivolous. But the white linen might be too casual? High heels? Espadrilles? Jewellery? There was simply too much choice. Why did it seem so ridiculously important to get it right?

'Good evening, Chiara.' Dante had got to his feet and greeted her with a kiss on both cheeks and a look of appreciation that made her glad she had made the effort.

The white linen hit the right note, she'd decided, but with a splash of bling to make it special. She always took care with her make-up. At fifty-nine she still prided herself on her maternal family's cheekbones and the fact that she hadn't put on too much weight – despite Marcello's and now Elene's excellent pasta – but these days, less had generally become more and a touch of blusher and mascara went a long way. Tonight though, she had added a rich slash of lipstick in a shade of vermilion she hadn't used for almost a decade.

'*Bella* . . . You look beautiful,' he told her. 'What can I get you to drink?'

'A glass of prosecco would be lovely.' She smiled at Emanuele, who looked after the bar most evenings and sometimes doubled up as a waiter when they were pushed. 'Very cold, with some ice and perhaps a dash of Aperol, no soda.' Aperol spritzes were becoming all the rage, and here at The Lemon Tree they were getting through more bottles of Aperol and prosecco than ever before.

Dante ordered a beer, and when the drinks were served, they raised their glasses in a toast. 'So where do we start?' he asked.

'From when you left the olive grove here at The Lemon Tree Hotel and headed for England without a word?' Chiara suggested dryly. He looked pretty good himself, she had to say. It didn't always follow that attractive young men became good-looking and distinguished in late middle-age, but Dante had. There was a different sort of confidence about him now – the confidence that came, she suspected, from having created a successful business and perhaps from having learned a lot along the way. The silver in his grey hair contrasted with dark brown eyes that looked so much wiser than before. And the lines on his face were full of character and suggested that he had lived a lot – and laughed a lot too.

'*Va bene*. OK.' He took a long draught of his beer. 'So, I travelled around England for a while . . .'

'Why England?' She wanted to know everything.

Those eyes twinkled. 'Why not? My grandmother – she always had a bit of thing for the place. Nonna adored the Queen.'

Chiara giggled. 'Did she ever go there?'

'Good God, of course not. She never left the village. But that woman could dream.'

Chiara saw the light still in his eyes that she'd been drawn to when they first met. It had barely dimmed. Nothing wrong with dreaming, she thought, as long as you didn't make the mistake of mixing it up with reality. As for Chiara, she was as untravelled as Dante's old grandmother had been, though it didn't seem that way, with all the international guests who stayed in the hotel. 'We have more English tourists here than before,' she told Dante, 'but many more Americans, Australians . . .'

'And rich Italians,' he guessed.

'*Sì*. Certainly, many rich Italians.' Dante would be able to see for himself how The Lemon Tree Hotel had changed. But she hoped that they had kept its heart intact. Chiara sipped her prosecco. It was deliciously icy with a good fizz, and Emanuele had added a slice of orange and a sprig of mint for good measure. She gave him a nod and smile of approval.

'I wasn't long in London,' Dante continued. 'It was great to see, but too busy for me. After that I went to West Sussex. It's in the south of England.'

'I know.' She eyed him over the rim of her glass. She didn't add that she had made it her business to find out much more about England since that visit to his mother in Corniglia. Their love affair might have been short, but it had been oh-so-sweet, and Dante had stayed in her heart for so long that sometimes she wondered if it had really been destiny after all.

'I made for the coast, just looking around, you know?'

'*Sì.*' She could imagine. He would be feeling a little lost, alone in a strange country. It would be exciting – but he might also be wondering what he was doing there at all.

'I found building work in a place called Worthing. There were other Italians there.' He took a swig of his beer. 'It was cold and it was rainy, but . . .'

Chiara watched him as he was drawn back into the past, into his memories. This was what she had wanted from tonight – to hear how it had been. And this was what she had given up, she realised. The chance for adventure. The chance to be with this man as part of his life. 'Building work?' She wondered how he had gone from that to *gelato*.

He nodded. 'To start with. I was always a labourer, was I not?'

He certainly was. Chiara remembered the tautness of his muscled brown body, the glow of sweat as he worked on the olive harvest. She took another sip of her prosecco and tried to banish the image from her mind.

'One of the Italians had started up his own ice-cream parlour on the seafront. That first summer, he offered me a job there. He reckoned there was good money to be made from Italian *gelato*.'

'I'm sure.' Naturally, Italian *gelato* would be an improvement on English ice cream, just as Italian coffee must have shown them what coffee should be all about.

'So, Mario, he taught me the craft. He was happy to; he took me under his wing.'

Chiara was pleased to hear that. She hated the thought of Dante being sad and friendless. Italians were good at sticking together. There was no one like an Italian for welcoming someone into their family with open arms. 'Tell me how you make the *gelato*,' she suggested. She just wanted to hear his voice – it was as comforting as a lullaby.

'It is a delicate mix.' Dante began to gesticulate as he explained the procedure. 'We use more milk than cream, you know, so it is much healthier and the ice cream is churned at a slower rate incorporating less air, which leaves it denser, richer to the taste.' He smacked his lips.

She smiled at his enthusiasm. 'So, you stayed in Worthing?'

'For a while.' He shrugged. 'But there was only enough work for me in the summer. And I was still restless, you know?' His dark eyes searched hers.

'I know,' she murmured. But don't go there . . .

'Mario's sister told me about Dorset. They had more relatives over there. She said I could go and stay with them, take a look around, think about what I wanted to do next.'

Chiara sipped her drink. The ice had melted, and although she had not intended to, she was drinking faster than usual. 'And that's what you did?'

'Yes.' He had finished his beer, so he gestured to Emanuele and ordered more drinks for them both.

'With some olives *per favore*,' Chiara said to their barman. 'And some nuts perhaps.' She should be careful; drinking on an empty stomach might not be such a good idea.

Emanuele served them with fresh drinks and a platter of nuts, olives, and *antipasti*.

'And what did you find in Dorset?' Chiara asked Dante.

'Somewhere I could live,' he said simply. 'It's rather beautiful, Chiara, though it's not the Cinque Terre, admittedly.'

She bowed her head in acknowledgement. Most of their guests told her that this part of Italy was one of the most stunning landscapes in the world, so, as untravelled as she was, she guessed it to be true.

'I got a job in a coffee kiosk in a little seaside town,' he told her. 'The guy who owned the place sold ice cream.' He pulled a face. 'But not good ice cream.'

'So you showed him how it is done?' Chiara laughed. So far, they were avoiding difficult subjects, so far there were no tricky emotions to shy away from. And it was easy, this talk between them, there was none of the awkwardness she'd feared. Already she could almost feel herself slipping into the old banter they'd shared.

He chuckled. 'I did.'

'And it was a success?' she guessed.

He looked a little pleased with himself now. And why not? 'Two years later I bought the kiosk,' he told her. 'Now, I run my own *gelateria* and supply my *gelato* to other cafés and restaurants in the area.'

'That's very impressive.' He'd always had ambition. She remembered what he had said about going to work in a car factory in Milan; he would probably have been equally successful there.

'Thank you. It's hard work, but worth it.'

'But why didn't you go to Milan?' Chiara took a sip of her prosecco. She had to ask this.

'It wasn't far enough away.' His dark eyes were brooding.

Chiara thought she knew what he was thinking. She must change the subject and fast. 'But, however is your *gelateria* managing without you?' she teased. When what she really wanted to ask was: *If I was really that important to you then why did you never come back before?*

He laughed out loud now in that sudden and infectious way she remembered. 'I didn't trust anyone to do my job for years,' he admitted. 'When you've built up something from nothing . . .'

'*Sì*.' She knew that better than anyone. And there was even more pressure when it was your parents who had built it up from nothing.

'Is that how it has been for you, Chiara?' His eyes were serious again now.

'Every day,' she admitted.

'But you have achieved so much. Just look at this place.'

They both looked around the cloisters at the vaulted ceiling that was pretty much the original from its convent days, at the ornate brickwork behind the bar that echoed it, the delicate sheen of the marble surfaces and the carefully chosen décor in shades of amber and earth-green. As always, Chiara felt a quiet sense of satisfaction. Outside, in the central courtyard, the lamps were lit and glowed soft and golden in the growing dusk.

'*Grazie mille*, Dante,' she murmured. 'Thank you so much. I am proud of it, yes.'

'And the charming *signorina* at the reception desk?' He arched an enquiring eyebrow.

'My granddaughter Isabella.'

'I saw the resemblance.' He nodded.

'And yes, she is a treasure.' A thought occurred to her. She couldn't believe she hadn't thought it before. 'Do you have children, Dante?' For he was here now, but he couldn't be alone.

'Sadly, no.' He seemed about to say more, but stopped himself.

'But are you married?' Her voice shook a little as she asked this question. Given her own marital position, it was ridiculous to mind, but the very thought of Dante . . .

'No.' He put a palm over her hand, which was resting on the rail of the bar. 'I should perhaps not say this, but . . .'

'But?' His hand on hers was both warm and comforting. And Chiara wanted to know more than anything what it was that he should not say.

'Only that I never met a woman I wanted to marry,' he said in a low voice. 'It is entirely inappropriate to say this to you now, but I never met a woman who could hold a candle to you.'

Mamma mia! Chiara was suddenly finding it hard to breathe. Italian men were renowned for their charm, their unashamed skill in the art of flirtation, but Dante was not like that, he never had been. Dante was sincere. She struggled for composure, looked up to see Elene coming into the bar to speak to Emanuele. She spotted Chiara immediately and shot a look of curiosity Dante's way.

Chiara saw the exact moment that her daughter noticed Dante's hand on hers. She took it away, *pronto*, but it had all happened so fast, and it was too late.

Dante followed the direction of her gaze. 'Your daughter?'

'Elene, yes.' She tried to sound unconcerned, but a knot of anxiety had already formed in her chest. She should have met him in a bar in Vernazza – but surely that would have suggested some sort of clandestine element to this innocent meeting. And it wasn't like that. It really wasn't like that.

'I apologise.'

'There's nothing to apologise for.'

He raised a hand in disagreement. 'I forgot for a moment – that you have a family here, a life, a past, a present.' He hesitated. 'And a future too.'

'It's fine, really.' She would tell Elene about Dante later. At least she would tell her that he had turned up here, an old friend, an affectionate old friend, and that this was all.

Her daughter had not been in the best of moods earlier – and Chiara realised that this was partly her fault. She shouldn't have criticised the menu, she shouldn't have told Elene she was looking for Silvio. But, really . . . Elene blew so hot and cold, it was sometimes hard to keep up.

Chiara tried to grasp back the initiative of the conversation, but the mood had changed and she couldn't quite let the subject go. 'You must have had girlfriends,' she said. 'Lovers.' Dante was not a man who would not have had women.

'Yes, more than one over the years.' He picked up his beer. 'But that, *cara*, is a different story.'

And one that she didn't much want to hear, thought Chiara, though the endearment gave her a little glow. 'Perhaps we should take our drinks outside?' The Cloisters Bar was beginning to feel a little claustrophobic somehow.

'Good idea.' He got to his feet and took her arm. 'It will be more private there.'

67

Chiara almost turned right back again. That wasn't what she had meant. But, no. He was right – she didn't want their conversation to be heard by the staff; she did require privacy for this strange encounter with the past.

In the courtyard, tables and chairs were set out in random groupings over the grey stone flags. Chiara led the way over to the bench under the lemon tree beside the old well. As Isabella had pointed out at Giovanna's birthday dinner, not only had the lemon tree given their hotel its name, but it produced gloriously scented fruit almost all year round, which Elene used to make her lemon cake, her lemon chicken, and that delicious *limoncino*, the Ligurian version of *limoncello* – and it was definitely no coincidence that the parasols in the courtyard were the exact same colour; Chiara had sourced the fabric herself.

They settled themselves on the bench, and Chiara breathed in the sharp citrus fragrance that always seemed stronger at night-time as the lemons glowed in the golden light from the lamps in the courtyard.

'So you married Alonzo,' Dante continued.

They now had a good view of the pinkish-grey stone of the old convent building, still crumbling in places despite its restoration, the blood-red bougainvillea planted in huge clay pots so that they clambered up the narrow brick arches, and the clumps of agapanthus surrounding the benches and the little stone fountain. It was a warm night, and the breeze was like silk on her skin. Chiara had always loved this courtyard, but it was most special at night when the lamps were lit and the stars glinted in an indigo sky. Tonight, the waxing moon was only a narrow crescent, but Chiara could see as clearly as she ever could.

'Yes, I married Alonzo.' She placed her glass carefully on the table. What else could she have done? Her one and only love, the man she had thought to be her destiny, had travelled many miles away to another country – she'd had to try to forget him.

'Just as your parents wished you to.'

Chiara gave a little shrug. He was making it sound as if she'd taken an easy option – but that showed how little he knew. 'It meant so much to Papà,' she said. 'Alonzo's father was very special to him. He was bullied at school you know, and Papà stuck up for him. Their friendship lasted their whole lives.' Her hand trembled as she reached for her drink. Too much wine on a near-empty stomach perhaps? Or the effect of this warm night combined with the unexpected presence of the man by her side? She realised that it was important for her to make him understand. 'Alonzo's family had money. They helped out with the hotel in the early days. Papà could not have done it without them. And so . . .' And so, it was felt the debt must be repaid. All four parents were keen for Alonzo and Chiara to marry, to cement the bond of friendship, to reinforce the security of the hotel and the livelihood it could provide for generations to come.

'It also left a burden of repayment,' Dante remarked. 'Your father must have felt bound to offer his daughter to his friend's son.'

Chiara frowned. 'What do you mean?' He made it sound as if she was just part of a bargain.

'I mean, what sort of friendship is that?'

'He didn't feel bound exactly.' She struggled to find the right words. 'It was something they wanted, that's all.'

But it was as if she hadn't spoken. 'What age are we living in, Chiara? The 1940s, the 50s maybe? For God's sake, this is the twenty-first century.'

For a moment Chiara was taken aback. But of course, Dante had always had this spikiness in his character. 'It *was* a long time ago, Dante,' she reminded him rather tartly. 'It was the twentieth century if you recall.' She couldn't decide if she were more annoyed or flattered by his outburst. 'We are talking about 1968, remember?' Which was dangerous territory indeed.

Dante shot her a probing look. It reminded her of that last night in the olive grove, and she shivered – although she was not cold, not in the least. 'You married him in 1968?'

All of a sudden, the years seemed to have dissolved and the past was as raw as if it were yesterday. 'Of course not.' Chiara took another sip of her drink and once again fought for composure. She was determined to bring a pause to this conversation. It was getting out of hand. 'I married Alonzo in 1970.'

'*Pah!*' There was so much feeling in this one exclamation that Chiara almost laughed. Except that it wasn't funny. And she understood his frustration, even after all these years.

And so, this time it was Chiara's turn to put a hand on his. 'I waited for you, Dante,' she said. 'I waited two years.' And two years was a long time when you were sixteen and your parents were so eager for you to marry another man.

His expression softened. 'I apologise once more,' he said. 'When I met with you tonight, I intended to be so cool, so collected . . .'

She smiled. 'Me too.'

He leaned closer. 'And you should know that I understand your decision, my dear Chiara,' he said, 'much more than I understood it back then. I was headstrong, crazily in love with you—'

Inside, she let out a low, deep sigh. *Crazily in love with her . . .*

70

She closed her eyes – just for a moment – to let this reckless thought sink in.

'All I could think was that you didn't love me as I loved you.' He took her hand in his, and all of a sudden she was oblivious to the few other guests around them in the courtyard, to the fact that Elene or Isabella or even Alonzo could walk out here at any moment. 'But now I see how it was – your sense of duty and obligation to your parents, to this place . . .' He flung a hand towards the hotel that she loved in a gesture that was far from affectionate.

Chiara nodded. She didn't trust herself to speak.

'And did you love him?' His voice was soft as butter. It seemed to slide into her, this question that was really the only question about the past that mattered. 'Do you love him still?'

When she had been getting ready earlier, Chiara had guessed this moment might come. It had been part of the thrill, the excitement, the pure blind terror. Maybe it was even part of why she'd chosen the red lipstick, as if she were going to war. She couldn't guess though, how she might respond to the question.

She turned to him and realised that his face, although older, had remained just as dear. Somewhere, somehow, a piece of this man had stayed in her heart. Then she thought of Elene and Isabella and her beautiful hotel, and she knew what she must say. 'Alonzo and me, we get along fine.' Her voice had a breezy lilt to it that she hated.

And Dante obviously hated it too because he let go of her hand as fast as if it had burned him. 'I am pleased to hear it,' he said. 'It is a relief to know that everything has turned out for the best after all.'

Chiara said nothing more. But she heard the politeness in

his voice, and her spirits sank. She got to her feet. She couldn't stay here with him any longer. This was a magical night, but it wasn't their magical night – there was far too much at stake.

'You are leaving?' There was a note of acceptance in Dante's voice.

She nodded. 'I have things I must see to, I'm afraid,' she said. 'But it has been . . .' she hesitated '. . . lovely to talk to you.'

Dante rose from the bench. 'It has, Chiara.' He bent towards her, and his lips barely brushed her cheek. Once, twice, three times.

Chiara stepped away. Dante was her past. Her family and her hotel – these were her future.

CHAPTER 8

Chiara

'So, Mamma,' Elene asked her at breakfast, 'who was that you were with last night?'

Chiara had been expecting this. 'Just an old friend,' she said with a studied casualness she was far from feeling. Last night, she had stayed awake for hours replaying their conversation, the touch of his hand, his kiss on her cheek – rather like the teenager she had once been. 'He used to live in Corniglia. He left forty years ago and went to England.' Chiara decided not to mention the ice cream. She plucked a *cornetto* from the plateful on the table and helped herself to coffee.

'You seemed very . . .' Elene was clearly choosing her words carefully '. . . close.'

Close. But despite what she'd witnessed, at least Elene seemed in a better mood this morning. Chiara bit into the soft, sweet *crema*, giving herself time to answer. French croissants with their buttery, flaky layers of pastry were also delicious, but personally she preferred the denser, richer Italian version. The dough was sweeter and more perfumed. And the *crema* was the final touch of sweetness on the tongue.

'We were good friends.' But this was a conversation she didn't want to prolong. She pulled her phone from her bag and checked for messages. Nothing from Alonzo. Nothing from anyone. Her entire life suddenly seemed awfully empty.

'He was practically holding your hand.' Better mood or not, Elene clearly was not going to let it rest.

'We were talking about our parents. It got a bit emotional, you know how it is.'

'Poor Nonna.' Isabella touched Chiara's shoulder as she went by.

The back door opened. 'Any coffee for the workers?' Silvio pulled off his boots and came inside.

Grateful for the diversion, Chiara rose to her feet. 'I'll get it.' She refilled the scoop and slotted it into the espresso machine. 'I'll be out between three and five by the way.' She directed this at Isabella – it would be a pragmatic change of subject. '*Va bene*, my dear?' She needed to get away from the hotel – for a couple of hours at least, and the rota pinned to the office door had informed her that she had no particular duties to attend to this afternoon.

But her granddaughter blinked as if she were lost in thought and not here with them at all.

'Bella?'

'Oh. Oh, yes, of course, Nonna.'

Chiara shot her a curious look. She put Silvio's coffee in front of him on the table. 'I'll be going into the village if anyone wants anything? And I'll look in on Aunt Giovanna on the way.'

She was glad that they had thrown Giovanna a birthday

celebration. Although all the family – bar Alonzo – worked here in the hotel, there were few occasions that they all – bar Alonzo again – managed to be in the same place at the same time for a family celebration. Giovanna was special. She had been Chiara's mother's closest friend; it was only fitting that when the order of Vernazza nuns dissolved, Giovanna had stayed – in her small cottage beyond the olive grove – close enough for the family to keep an eye on her. Or, as Chiara often thought, close enough for her to keep an eye on them.

Later, armed with an offering for Giovanna and her swimsuit and a towel, Chiara followed the winding path through the grove, trying not to think about Dante Rossi standing here amongst the silvery olive trees. He had come back – to observe, he had said. He had stood in the olive grove and remembered. He had told her that he had not been able to forget her . . .

Giovanna would be able to heat up Elene's *trofie de pesto* for her supper. Her aunt was fiercely independent; she used to make all her own pasta as well as tend the chickens and her *orto*, a small allotment, which had originally supplied all the fruit and vegetables for the hotel. These days, Giovanna was too old to do much gardening, and Silvio had taken over the *orto*, and even expanded it, though Chiara's aunt still cultivated tomatoes that Chiara considered the reddest and most flavoursome in all Liguria – Elene bottled them when there was a glut in late summer to use for pasta sauce in winter. And Giovanna still cared for the chickens – her 'girls', as she called them.

'Chiara, my dear.' Giovanna was still waving away her last visitor, Siena Gianelli, a retired nurse who lived in Monterosso and who was a frequent visitor and good friend. She kissed Chiara and accepted the bowl of pasta with a wrinkled smile.

'How kind of you. Please thank Elene. Come through. Shall we have some fresh lemonade?'

'Thank you, Aunt.' Chiara knew that many of her aunt's visitors brought small gifts of fruit or a dish they had baked the night before, making an extra portion for the woman of the Cinque Terre who had spent her life trying to help others.

It was a warm and sunny afternoon, and so they settled themselves on the terrace on Giovanna's wooden bench, surrounded by terracotta pots of scarlet geraniums. As usual, the hens were wandering around the cobbles, clucking and pecking at grain, out of the coop that kept them safe at night. They were on the outskirts of the olive grove here, but through the twisty branches, Chiara could see snatches of blue and for a moment she longed to be down there already, ducking her head underwater, swimming in the ocean, feeling free.

'What is wrong, *cara*?' Giovanna had poured the lemonade and was regarding her fondly.

'Does something have to be wrong?' Chiara smiled. Perhaps she should visit her aunt more often. But Giovanna understood more than most how busy they were at the hotel. She had always been around, she had watched the place grow.

'It does not have to be, no.' Giovanna wrinkled her nose. 'But you are frowning, my dear.' She reached out to smooth Chiara's brow with bent and arthritic fingers. 'And there is in your eyes, a distraction. I saw it the other night too, although of course I would not mention it in front of the others.'

A distraction. 'Thank you, Aunt.' She was grateful for that. Dante was indeed a distraction. Amazing though it seemed, Chiara had never entirely stopped thinking about him – though sometimes she wondered if it was some idealised version of the man that she kept in her head as a reaction to a marriage that had never become what she had hoped. And yet forty years was a long time and, after the first rush of grief when she'd heard that he had left her and gone to England, after the hollowness of regret that had lasted for days, months, longer perhaps . . . life had gone on. It had had to.

Except that when he'd stood beside her in the foyer yesterday afternoon, when she'd sat with him in the courtyard at dusk, when he'd put his hand on hers . . . she had felt something dormant in her come alive again. Ridiculous to say it, ridiculous to think it – but it was true.

'It's nothing,' she told her aunt. 'I'm just not feeling quite myself.' Which was accurate enough. She was someone else. She was that sixteen-year-old girl kissing Dante Rossi in the olive grove – kissing him as if her very life depended on it.

'Very well.' Giovanna bent her head to sip her drink. Her hair was fine and white as cotton thread. She looked entirely unconvinced.

Chiara remembered what her aunt had said at the family dinner about how things had changed and how she was glad she wouldn't live long enough to see things change still further. 'Does it make you feel sad, Aunt Giovanna?' she asked. 'Seeing The Lemon Tree Hotel as it is now and remembering what the place once was?'

Her aunt's milky eyes clouded. 'Things move on, do they not, my dear?' she murmured. 'Vernazza is a very different place these days. And you and I – we live in a very different world.'

Chiara nodded. True enough. 'But what was it like?' she asked. 'Before?' She had asked this question many times – both of her aunt and her parents too. Her father had fought for the anti-Fascist Resistance when Mussolini was still in power, although he rarely spoke of those difficult times.

'It was not even our war.' He would gesticulate angrily when he said this. 'We were only drawn in because of Hitler's admiration for Mussolini. That's what led to them forming an alliance.'

'So what happened?' Chiara had asked. She wanted to know more about something that had affected her beloved papà so deeply.

'It was an uneasy alliance at best,' he told her. 'Many Italians were resentful. Let me tell you – we didn't want to be in that war.'

Who would want to fight in a war? Chiara was only young – but she could imagine the fear and the horror. 'Is that why Italy had to surrender?' she asked.

'Something like that, *cara*. The ill-feeling grew, and eventually *Il Duce* was forced to resign. We didn't surrender though until September 1943. I remember that day well.'

'Was it a good day, Papà?' Chiara couldn't imagine her father surrendering over anything. But then again, he hadn't surrendered himself to fight.

'Ah, *sì*.' He sighed. 'We thought that after that day our part in the war would be over.'

'But it wasn't?'

'No, *cara*. Still, our country was ripped apart.' He looked so sad that Chiara ran to him, wanting to hold him close, to help him forget. 'We were all ripped apart, even as Germany retreated and the Allies forced the Liberation. Poverty, looting, the cutting of our electricity lines, the bombing of our bridges. Some liberation, my dearest . . .'

And Chiara knew, as surely as she could feel his heart beating through his linen shirt and see the dazed look in his eyes, that he would never forget. She already knew the story – from her mother, from school, from people in the village. She knew of the terrors and the deprivation, she even knew that it was Allied bombs that had destroyed Castello Doria, Vernazza's castle, even if it was the Nazis who had been in occupation and the British had only been trying to get them out. It was still destruction. It had taken a long time for the German army to be forced back through Italy.

'*L'Attico Convento* was always a spiritual place.' Her aunt's voice was soft and low. She gave it the name it had been given when all the nuns had left, when the building stood isolated, rundown and empty, before Chiara's parents had got the money together to buy it. 'A place that saw more than its share of suffering, as you are aware, my dear. But it also saw love.'

Chiara nodded. 'And the nuns?' She liked to think of them drifting around the convent in their black-and-white robes, kneeling to pray, tending their kitchen garden and their precious olives, making their soap and lemonade from the lemons on the tree that still stood in the courtyard by the ancient well. She liked to think that there was something left of the nuns in The Lemon Tree Hotel, some tranquil vibration from their prayers and their chanting perhaps that had been absorbed into the very walls.

'Even before the war there were not many nuns left at the convent.' Giovanna gave a sad smile. 'Life was simple. I was only a girl, don't forget. I first came to *L'Attico Convento* with Mamma's bread to exchange for olive oil.' Her eyes grew misty with the memory. 'During the war, it was even harder to get food than usual, you see. I still remember the taste of that chicory coffee.' She pulled a face of disgust. 'Mamma and I

79

used to walk to Pignone to buy potatoes, flour and corn – it was too dangerous on the train.'

'*Mamma mia* . . .' That was ten kilometres or more.

'We stretched out the flour with ground chestnuts to make it last that bit longer.'

'That was enterprising of you, darling Aunt.'

'We had to be. You learn quickly when you're hungry.'

'I can imagine.' Chiara could only be grateful that she had not had to live through such hardship herself.

'And the planes . . .' Giovanna stared up at the blue sky as if they might suddenly appear once more. 'We were terrified. They were so loud, so dark and forbidding.' She shuddered.

'Bombers?' Chiara whispered.

'Ah, *sì*. Some of us sheltered in the convent, but many of the villagers ran all the way to the sanctuary.' She closed her eyes. 'We could hear them screaming. "Our Lady of Reggio, help us",' she whispered. 'That was the worst year.'

'And the young men who resisted, the Partisans?' Chiara leaned forwards. She wanted to hear this story again, because it was Papà's story.

'Oh, yes, my dear. Joining a partisan group was almost the only way to escape the fighting. But they were fighting too – for Liberation.' Giovanna nodded. Her old neck was wrinkled as a turtle's. 'They mostly stayed up in the mountains, and when they came to the town, they hid in the convent. They were runaways. Where else could they go?'

'And when someone came looking for them?' Nazis, Republican Fascists. No doubt, the more men who joined the Partisan groups, the worse the reprisals would be.

'They climbed up the old bell tower.' She gestured towards it, just visible beyond the olive grove.

Chiara tried to imagine the fear, the shootings, the torture. She shivered and leaned back against the stone wall, warm from the afternoon sun. A few metres away, the last of Giovanna's tomatoes were still ripening on the vines. What must it have been like to live in an occupied town? She remembered her mother telling her that there had been a curfew at eight o'clock. 'We Italians hate sticking to the rules, as you know, *cara*,' she had said. 'But if anyone was caught outside after that time, they'd be arrested and spend the night in a cell in the castle tower, you can be sure.'

'It was brave of the nuns to help the Partisans,' Chiara said. She sipped the lemonade, wondered if Giovanna still used the nuns' old recipe.

'Many people were brave, my dear,' said Giovanna. 'On all sides.' Her eyes grew dreamy as if she had slipped back to that time.

'But on that day when Papà was injured . . .' Chiara's voice broke.

Giovanna's expression grew more serious still. She seemed to understand that Chiara needed to hear the story again today. 'On that day, we had no warning, my dear. No one saw it coming. The soldiers forced the gates, they charged in. There was no time to climb the bell tower. Your papà and the others, they ran off through the olive grove – it was all they could do.' Giovanna let out a deep sigh and her thin shoulders sagged. 'There were shots.'

'You were there?' Chiara stared out into the grove. These trees had witnessed so much. But surely her aunt had not lived at the convent until after her mother died?

'I was there.' Giovanna clasped her gnarled hands together. 'I often came to the convent as a girl. Not just with the bread,

81

you know.' She paused, and Chiara had the distinct feeling of something left unsaid. She stared into her aunt's eyes, waited for her to go on. What was it? Some other sadness about that time? Her mother had always said that Giovanna had experienced a most traumatic war, and of course there was the death of her family. 'And then . . .'

'Then?'

'Your father was injured, but at least he escaped.' Giovanna's voice changed. 'For that, I am grateful. Your poor mother – I always knew how close they were.'

Others though had not escaped. Chiara knew that her father had seen two of his brothers at arms shot dead as they raced desperately through the olives, up the terraces, out on to the mountains thick with chestnut trees. The olive grove had not been able to protect them all. He had spoken of this part of the story to Chiara only once, his entire frame shuddering with the memory, the pain. No wonder the old convent had meant so much to Papà. No wonder he had wanted to save it after the war when the nuns had all left.

Chiara held her face up to the sun. 'But why did the nuns all leave?'

Her aunt gave a little shrug. 'There was so little money. The community was gone. The village was bombed. We had been so violated, my dear. Valuable artefacts were stolen from the convent, just as they'd been stolen from the church and the castle.' She shook her head. 'Many of them were never recovered.'

Chiara knew that Vernazza was not alone in this. The rape of Italy, it had been called.

'But didn't you want the convent to remain a religious building?' Chiara persisted. 'When the war was over, I mean?'

Giovanna looked out into the olive grove. 'Why would I?'

'Well, the nuns had taken you in . . .' Though Chiara didn't want to upset her aunt by talking too much about that time.

'Yes, they did. They helped many people in times of trouble – whatever their faith.'

'But you were never tempted to join the order?'

'I was not.' She chuckled. 'A woman can serve God and her village in many ways, my dear.'

And she certainly had done that. Chiara sometimes thought the entire Cinque Terre came to Giovanna with their spiritual and emotional problems. There was no chance for her aunt to be lonely.

Chiara reached for her hand. 'You're a marvel.' She honestly was. And if Chiara were going to confide in anyone, her aunt would be the person she'd choose. But . . .

'Nonsense.' Giovanna's voice was brisk. 'I simply did not want to see *L'Attico Convento* become a ruin. Your parents wanted to save the building. I respected them for it. They only wanted to bring people to the Levante again. There is nothing at all wrong with that.'

Chiara smiled. She was always so loyal. Though even her parents might be shocked at what had happened since. These days, so many visitors came to the Cinque Terre that sometimes she thought the five villages had truly reached saturation point and that something had to give.

'People have always wanted to stay in Vernazza.' Giovanna clicked her tongue at one of the hens pecking in the yard and the bird looked up at her, cocked her head. 'Even before there were hotels, before *il boom* and all that shiny *macchine*, televisions and such, you know?'

Chiara knew.

'The local boys knew which people were willing to rent out a room and for a coin or two, they'd take them there.' She chuckled. 'There might not be a bathroom mind, but there was always hospitality. Then and now.'

Chiara thought of the understated luxury of The Lemon Tree Hotel, how they had transformed the simple building that had been the old convent into the elegant and historical place it was today. 'You're right. How things have changed.'

'Exactly, my dear, that is life, as I say.' Giovanna shrugged. 'But you mustn't worry about me. I have always been happy here in my cottage. Your parents were good to me.'

And where else could she have gone? Her father had died fighting, and her mother had died giving birth – to a baby who was stillborn. Chiara's mother had told her this many years ago, and Chiara knew that this was when their friendship had begun to deepen. Gently, she patted her aunt's hand. She was sorry. For these deaths, all the suffering, perhaps even for coming here this afternoon and bringing up the past.

'It was a long time ago.' Giovanna blinked her rheumy eyes.

'It was.' And yet Chiara knew that for Giovanna too, that long ago past could sometimes seem as close and real as yesterday.

CHAPTER 9

Isabella

Isabella saw Ferdinand Bauer sitting out in the courtyard.
This was unusual. Since he'd arrived a few days ago, he always
seemed to be on the go, wandering around the hotel and
grounds as she'd discovered yesterday, checking things out,
disappearing behind cloistered walls, down stairs and corridors.
She'd meant to come back to him yesterday about the proposed
visit to Aunt Giovanna, but she hadn't had a chance. So now,
she went out through the cloisters to speak with him. He was
sitting by the small stone fountain, studying a map of the area,
and he jumped to his feet when he saw her.

'I was just looking at some hiking trails,' he said. 'Maybe
you could advise me where to go to get off the beaten track?'
And he fixed her with a certain look from his cool blue
eyes.

'Hiking trails?' Isabella couldn't help feeling that there was
something quite different he wanted to say. 'Yes, there are a
few.' She glanced at the map – it was one of the good ones.
'But I really came along to apologise for yesterday.'

'No need.' He grinned – almost as if he was enjoying her discomfort.

'And to tell you that I spoke to my Aunt Giovanna.'

'And?' His voice was eager.

'And she's happy to talk to you.'

'That's great. When? Did you fix up a time?' Already he was folding his map away and stuffing it in a canvas bag.

Isabella couldn't help laughing. 'We could go now, I suppose,' she said. 'I've just finished my shift on reception, and Giovanna's usually around.' People came to Giovanna, not the other way about these days.

'Fantastic.' He glanced at his watch. 'How far away does she live?'

'Her cottage is in the grounds.'

Isabella led the way through the olive grove towards Giovanna's place. As always, the trees seemed to give off an air of gentle protection. When she was a young girl she had spent many happy hours playing in the grove, sometimes lost in her imagination, sometimes playing hide and seek among the gnarled trees and crooked branches and making her poor parents frantic when they couldn't find her. Her mother had always scolded her, but her father had only laughed. Isabella suspected that he too would like to take time off from the hotel now and again – *magari*! Chance would be a fine thing.

She felt a little awkward being alone with Ferdinand Bauer like this; the olive grove was such a peaceful and private place. But she was looking forward to the meeting between him and her aunt Giovanna. She sneaked a sideways glance at him. He was tall and lean, not muscular, but sinewy and probably quite strong. Already, his fair skin was lightly tanned from the sun, and his hair seemed even more streaked with blond than before. He had told her that he planned to stay for at least a week – which was longer than their average visitor – and she was pleased about this. Not that she had any feelings about him one way or the other, and he was only a guest after all, but . . . The sun was very warm and she noticed a faint bead of sweat forming above his upper lip. Quickly, she looked away.

Ferdinand turned towards her as they walked along the gravelly path. 'Don't take this the wrong way, Isabella, but I was wondering – does Giovanna still recall past events clearly?' He held an olive branch up out of their way.

'Very clearly, I'd say.' Her aunt's mind was still razor sharp. Isabella glanced at him once more. He seemed lost in thought. 'But remember, *Signore*—'

'Ferdinand please,' he reminded her once again.

'Ferdinand.' Again, she tasted the name on her tongue. '. . . That some of those past events might have been traumatic for her.' Isabella wanted him to be warned. 'It is the history of the building you wanted to talk to her about, you said?' After all, Vernazza had been occupied by the compatriots of this man walking beside her in the grove. Some of the older people in the village still talked of it. Of course, it was a long time ago, and naturally Isabella was of a generation that had no feelings of bitterness whatsoever, but . . .

'I understand that.' He stopped walking for a moment and put a hand gently on her arm. 'Don't worry. The last thing I want to do is upset her.'

'Thank you. Then I'm sure you won't.' She looked at him, conscious of a jolt of connection between them, a mere blink of awareness – of him, his height, his fair skin and striking blue eyes. She shook it off and they walked on. It was nothing, she thought. Probably just the heat of the sun.

They arrived at the cottage and she knocked on the door. Not waiting for a reply, she opened it wide and called out. 'Aunt Giovanna? It's me – Isabella.'

'I am out the back, Bella,' came a faint but welcoming voice.

Isabella exchanged a small smile with Ferdinand. 'Let's go around the side.' She led the way.

Giovanna was seated in her usual place on the worn wooden bench surrounded by orange and red geraniums, several hens of similar colours scratching the cobbles around and beyond. 'Hello, my darling.' Spritely, for a woman of over eighty, she got to her feet. 'Goodness me, I have been so lucky today – so many people have come to see me.'

Isabella remembered that her grandmother had also called in. 'Should we come back another time?' She hesitated. 'If you're too tired . . .'

'Nonsense. I'm never too tired to see people.' Giovanna was peering behind her, curious to see the young man she'd mentioned, Isabella supposed.

'Good. So, Aunt, this is the guest I was telling you about who is interested in the old convent.' Isabella had been standing in front of him, but now she stood to one side and Ferdinand stepped forwards.

The afternoon sun must have been in Giovanna's eyes for she stared, blinked, seemed mesmerised. For a moment, Isabella thought that she would keel right over, and she and Ferdinand both dashed forwards to help her back on to the bench.

'Aunt, Aunt, are you all right? What is it? Are you ill?'

Giovanna grabbed Isabella's hand tightly. 'I am fine, Bella,' she whispered. But her eyes were locked on to Ferdinand's.

'What's wrong?' Isabella asked her. Perhaps after all she

shouldn't have brought him here – her aunt was clearly upset already.

'Nothing. Just . . .' Giovanna let go of her hand. 'Memories. You didn't tell me he was . . .' She faltered.

'German?' Ferdinand took a step closer.

Isabella was horrified. Hadn't she? 'I'm sorry, Aunt, I didn't think—'

'No, no, my dear.' Giovanna silenced her with a raised hand. 'Please don't misunderstand me.' She was still staring at Ferdinand. 'It is not a problem, not at all, why should it be? It's just that for a moment, I thought . . .'

'What did you think?' Isabella frowned.

'A face from the past,' she murmured. 'That is all.'

'Thank you for agreeing to talk to me, *Signora*.' Ferdinand spoke more softly than he had before. And he spoke in half-decent Italian – Isabella recalled that he had told her he had learned the language when in Italy studying art history. He dropped down and sat easily on the ground at Giovanna's feet. 'And I'm so sorry for giving you such a shock.'

Giovanna's eyes were watering from the sun. Or was she crying? Isabella was about to step forwards once more. But now Giovanna was positively beaming at her visitor. It was most confusing. 'Not at all,' she said. 'You know how it is. I am old. I see things – and people . . .' She gave him an intent look '. . . that aren't really there.'

'I'm so pleased to meet you, *Signora*.' Ferdinand cocked his head to one side. 'I came here to find out a bit more about the convent, as Isabella mentioned.'

Giovanna nodded as if this were the most natural thing in the world. 'Of course, you did,' she said. 'And what is your name, young man?'

89

'Ferdinand Bauer.'

Giovanna didn't seem able to take her eyes off him. 'Ah, sì, sì.'

They both looked at Isabella. It was odd, but it was almost as if they wanted to be alone. She must be imagining things surely? But they both remained silent as if they were waiting for her to go. 'Shall I make some coffee?' she suggested.

'Ah, yes, please, my dear, if you would.' Giovanna folded her wrinkled hands in her lap. She now appeared the picture of serenity.

Isabella went into her aunt's tiny kitchen to put on the percolator. She could see the two of them through the windowpane, talking intently, gazes locked; an unlikely twosome it had to be said, this tall fair-haired young man from Germany, and the diminutive, elderly Giovanna. But charming nevertheless, she thought. And there was a real emotional intensity in their body language – she could tell that even from this distance.

By the time she took the coffee out on a tray, the conversation was of the old convent building and how it had changed since becoming The Lemon Tree Hotel, and they continued to chat about this as Isabella passed milk and sugar and settled back on the bench to listen. They clearly had no need of an interpreter.

'Vernazza has always been a hub of the arts,' Giovanna was saying. 'It has always attracted artists, musicians, actors, dancers, ah, sì . . . Very colourful, yes, indeed.' She sipped her coffee. 'There were many avant-garde gatherings down in the piazza.'

'Really, Aunt?'

'Ah, yes, people were shocked, scandalised even.' She beamed. Isabella had rarely seen her so animated.

'There were impromptu parties – so loud that the people who lived nearby took to throwing tomatoes at them to try to get them to go home to sleep. And someone – probably Gianni, Aldo and Giorgio – even bought the old olive mill and turned it into a club.'

'Did you go there, *Signora?*' Ferdinand asked her. He was teasing, but Isabella liked the respect in his voice when he spoke to her aunt, she loved the fact that he was so interested in her memories of Vernazza.

'Oh, my goodness, bless you, no.' She put a hand to her mouth. 'And no parent in Vernazza would let their daughter go there either.'

'A real den of iniquity then?'

'Probably not. It didn't even have a license to sell alcohol as far as I know, but that wouldn't have stopped anyone.'

They all laughed.

'Did I ever tell you, Bella, about the Rotunda delle Rose?' Giovanna was on a roll. 'The open-air dance hall where an orchestra would play and everyone would come in summertime to dance?'

Isabella smiled and nodded. 'You did, Aunt, yes.' Her grandmother had talked of it too.

'An entire orchestra?' Ferdinand marvelled.

'Oh, well, a drummer, a trumpet player, and someone playing the accordion.' Giovanna chuckled. 'People joining in humming and tapping a spoon.'

'It sounds wonderful.'

'Ah, yes, it was.'

But fascinating though her aunt's memories were, Isabella couldn't escape the feeling that this conversation was for her benefit, and that the other conversation, the one she'd witnessed through the window but unfortunately not heard, was the one that really mattered.

After coffee they said their goodbyes and returned to the hotel. Ferdinand was unusually quiet. 'Did you find out what you wanted to know?' she asked him.

He gave her a sharp glance. 'You could say that.'

She raised an eyebrow. 'Good.' But it was all rather intriguing.

Back inside The Lemon Tree Hotel, she watched him lope up the stairs to his room, pausing as usual to stare at the painting of the Archangel Gabriel in the niche. What was the fascination? Had Giovanna mentioned that her father had painted it? But why would she? Isabella was confused. She couldn't help but feel that something was going on – and that much to her annoyance, she wasn't party to it.

CHAPTER 10

Chiara

After leaving Giovanna's, Chiara took the steep path through the prickly pears and the chestnut trees down towards the clutter of rooftops that made up the village. At every twist and turn of the steps, she caught a tantalising snatch of the clear blue ocean. She loved The Lemon Tree Hotel with all her heart, but sometimes it was good to take some time off, to get away from the place, to taste a different air. Seeing Dante again, talking to him . . . It had made her think again how untravelled she was, how little experience she had of the world. And now – was it too late?

She stepped from the *caruggi*, the honeycomb of narrow, stepped interior passages that climbed up and around and eventually led to the castle, down into the warmth, noise and bustle of Via Roma – the main street – which was divided in two by a row of blowsy oleanders in pots. She felt the full warmth of the afternoon sun on her head and sniffed appreciatively as she passed the *panificio* . . . rosemary focaccia, you couldn't beat it, though of course, Elene's was the best. The little shops were all busy – the *gelateria*, the boutiques, the art gallery; Chiara knew all the owners and exchanged a cheery greeting with them as she passed by. A delivery man wheeling polystyrene trays of anchovies in ice boxes down the street called *buon giorno* and promised her that he was on his way to The Lemon Tree straight after this delivery. Chiara sniffed the freshness of the fish, smiled, and told him that she hoped so.

She went on through the narrow alleyway between tall and shadowy pink buildings whose paint was peeling to reveal the original underbelly of stone beneath. These houses were ravaged by wind, rain and storms in autumn and winter. Spray from the biggest waves sometimes reached the top of the castle tower and, *Madonna santa*, that was something to see. It meant there was always much re-building to do. But then, the Cinque Terre had always been about building – in what seemed like impossible conditions. Look at how her ancestors and the other inhabitants of the town had once terraced all the high slopes to create their vineyards and olive groves. Those dry-stone walls, the *muretti*, were an early masterpiece of engineering; it was said that if you laid them end to end they'd be longer than the Great Wall of China.

'Hey, Roberto!' She waved to their old family friend who was squatting in a corner of Piazza Marconi, busy re-varnishing his boat. 'How are things?'

'Good, good. And you?'

'Yes, yes, very good. And your mother? How is she?'

'Well enough to shout at me this morning for waking her up, God bless her.' He mopped his brow and grinned ruefully. 'Going for a swim?'

'I certainly am.' The square was lined with boats, the rainbow parasols of bars and restaurants, shiny-leafed magnolia trees, and a row of tamarisks at the waterfront casting their feathery shadows. It drew the tourists, but the piazza was also a meeting-place for the locals – it always had been. She stood on the stone steps facing the sea. Some local kids were playing football on the harbour beach of gritty brown sand – they were usually here: swimming, running, kicking a ball; it was their playground all year round, just as it had been when Chiara was a child.

She looked out towards the end of the pier where the local young men dived into the waves to impress the tourists. There were steps into the water too, but she could see that the rocks were crowded with onlookers today so although she was a strong swimmer, she decided to keep a low profile and stay where she was. She took a route around the children on the *spiaggia*, stepped along the narrow harbour wall, slipped off her sundress, and picked her way over the dark rocks towards the inky blue sea.

She was also here, she silently admitted to herself, to avoid Dante. It was all very well talking with him and telling him that her life was fine and dandy, *grazie mille*. But of course, it was not, and the longer he stayed, the harder she might find it to hide that fact. So here she was again . . . She negotiated a slippery rock. Running away by staying exactly where she was – among her friends and family, safe within her comfort zone. Perhaps it was the story of her life – hey?

She stepped into the water. It was cool and inviting on her sun-warmed skin; another few steps and it had crept up to her thighs. Heaven. She swept forward into the surge of a wave, in a smooth breaststroke. Beside her, the multi-coloured boats bobbed and rocked with the tide. She kept near the buoys and swam her usual route out towards the harbour mouth and the open sea beyond – which glittered in the sunlight as if it had been scattered with gold dust. *Ah*. They had built the swimming pool at the hotel more than twenty years ago – it had meant creating a terrace near the entrance, below the olive grove – and it was wonderful to have it. Even so, she preferred to leave the pool for the use of their guests, and besides, there was nothing quite like swimming in the sea.

She turned and floated for a few moments on her back, her body too now rocking gently with the waves, as she filtered out the voices and laughter from the shore and breathed in the fresh salty air. Squinting into the sun, she could see some labourers high up on the steep hillside terraces carrying red and green baskets of grapes on their shoulders to stack on to the little monorail train that swept up the mountainside for this purpose alone. *Vino d'uva*. Once, it had been important to differentiate their own pure local wine from what was available in the bigger supermarkets springing up in Liguria – who knew what might be in *that*? Now, the wine of Cinque Terre tasting so fresh and clean on the palate was justifiably celebrated. At The Lemon Tree Hotel they prided themselves that even their house wine came from this region.

She swam towards the shore and the terrace of houses above the church – dusty pink and bright tangerine, green shutters flung open to the day. The afternoon sun slanted across the decorated portal, the old stone walls and pale peach and grey bell tower of Santa Margherita di Antiochia, situated on the waterfront and forever iconic of Vernazza. This was the view that drew people to their village and, although it was familiar, every time she saw it, Chiara seemed to fall in love with it once more.

At last, she swam in and picked her way back through the

rocks – she could probably do this blindfolded, she sometimes thought – to her bag in which she had packed a thin beach towel that doubled as a sarong.

'*Ciao*, Chiara.'

'Dante.' She stood there in her swimsuit, dripping and at a loss.

He realised immediately. 'Is this your bag?' It was on the rock beside him.

She nodded.

'Here.' He handed it to her, saw the towel. 'Let me.' He wrapped it around her shoulders.

'*Grazie.*' Chiara shivered. She wasn't cold, only embarrassed, she realised. Here she was – fifty-nine years of age, and yet vain enough to take a lot of trouble to look her best for their meeting last night. And now she was almost fully exposed – her not-so-young body on show to her childhood sweetheart. How absurd it all was. She shivered again and laughed at the same time.

'I am so sorry.' Dante seemed to understand her mixed emotions, though his eyes gleamed with mischief. 'I did not mean to . . .' He gestured with his hands. 'You know.'

'I know.' And why shouldn't he be down here in the harbour? He had once, after all, been almost a local. More to the point, why should *she* be here? He would have expected her to be at the hotel working, which was where she should go, right now.

Instead, she sat down on the rock. Perhaps *he* was trying to avoid *her?* It was not a comfortable feeling.

'May I?' He gestured to the rock beside her.

'Yes.' It struck her that this older version of Dante Rossi was much politer than the boy she'd known.

97

He sat down beside her, thankfully not too close, but close enough. 'I was walking along the beach when I spotted you in the sea.' He spread his hands. 'Swimming.'

'*Sì* . . .' Again, Chiara laughed, and this time he laughed with her.

'I was going to sneak away before you came out of the water,' he confided. 'I didn't want to spoil your . . .' He hesitated. 'Me-time.'

'But you didn't.'

'Sneak away, or spoil your me-time?'

'Both.' She sat with her knees bunched up to her chin, the towel wrapped around her to preserve her dignity.

'Remember when they used to play waterpolo here?' he asked her.

'I do.' Once, the waterpolo team of Vernazza had been among the best. And Chiara remembered everything.

'Hmm. Good times, eh, Chiara?' How could he sound so casual?

'How long are you staying in Vernazza, Dante?' She hadn't meant to ask this so abruptly, though it had been on her mind ever since his arrival. She had even checked the hotel register, but it was an open booking. Isabella wouldn't do this at the height of the season, but now that things were slowing down, it was possible . . . She frowned. Though Dante must have used his charm on her granddaughter, she guessed.

'Two or three days,' he said. 'There are a few people I want to visit. Friends and family.'

'Yes, of course, you must miss them.'

'I miss Italy.'

She couldn't mistake the regret in his voice, the passion. 'And yet you have made a life in England,' she reminded him.

'You are successful with your *pistachio gelato*, your melon and your prickly pear, is that not so?'

'No prickly pear in England.' He glanced up at the steep mountainside next to them where the plant was growing in abundance. 'I do not know how that flavour would go down in Dorset.'

Chiara chuckled.

'And it is good to have some sun.' He held his face up to the cloudless sky, his eyes crinkling in the light.

He looked vulnerable like that. She glanced quickly away. Two or three days, she thought. That wasn't so long. She wasn't sure whether to feel disappointed or relieved. 'It is grey in England, yes?'

'Very grey.' He spoke solemnly. 'Though England, she has her charms.'

'Such as?' With a corner of the towel, she rubbed at the damp tendrils of hair on her shoulders.

'The landscape,' he said. 'Cornwall is very beautiful, with granite rocks and sea as blue as the Mediterranean on a good day.'

'Is that so?' She gazed out to sea. The colour shifted from navy to turquoise to pale green where it was shallow by the rocks at the end of the harbour.

He ran his fingers through his hair. 'Almost as blue anyway,' he amended.

'And Dorset?'

'There's real history there,' he said. 'Green fields and hedges, villages with thatched cottages and little streams running through by the roadside. Sloping hills and farmland with dry-stone walls. Beaches that seem to go on for ever. And stunning sandstone cliffs. It's a Jurassic coast – very, very old.'

'It sounds wonderful.' She'd love to go there. And London. How she'd adore to see Buckingham Palace and the changing of the guard. 'And the food?'

'It could be a lot worse.' He gave a small shrug. 'There are Italian restaurants everywhere now – some more authentic than others as you might guess. Indian too, Chinese, you name it.'

Chiara nodded. 'Though Italian is the best,' she said.

He shot her a glance. 'Oh, naturally.'

She wondered if he was teasing – it wasn't always easy to tell. 'Did you eat at the hotel last night?' After their drink, she'd got something from the kitchen and taken it to their rooms so as not to run into him if he was still around.

'Yes, and it was very good. There are very few restaurants in England up to the standard of your hotel's.'

Chiara was not surprised at this. 'You know that my daughter Elene is our chef?' She looked out to sea once again. A little motor boat was just chugging through the harbour mouth. The thought of Elene made her realise that she must get back.

'You must be very proud of her.' He stretched out his legs. He was wearing jeans and summer sandals on bare feet. The olive skin of his bare arms was certainly paler than it had been when warmed by the Mediterranean sun in the old days. He still looked strong though, she decided. At sixty-one, he remained a fine figure of a man; his shoulders not quite so broad perhaps, but he held himself very upright. He looked – distinguished, she realised. The boy she'd known had been lovely, but never distinguished. She smiled. 'Oh, yes, I am very proud of her.'

'What are you thinking, Chiara?' He smiled back at her, and once again the atmosphere was easier between them.

She improvised. 'Have you never been back here before, Dante?'

'I have.'

'But you didn't come—'

'No, I didn't.'

They stared at one another while she struggled to understand. Did she have the right to question him? She was still curious, still smarting perhaps even after all this time from the manner in which he had left. It was not as if she had sent him away.

'In the early years when I could afford it, I paid for my mother to come and visit me in England,' he told her gently. 'As you know, I was the only child. I felt guilty. I thought perhaps she might want to come and live in Dorset too.'

'And did she?' From her one and only interaction with Signora Rossi, Chiara would be surprised.

'No, she most certainly did not.' They both laughed. 'I couldn't blame her. Her life was the Cinque Terre, Corniglia, her friends. She couldn't speak the language. Who would she have talked to all day?'

Chiara smiled. 'You speak English fluently, I am sure?'

He laughed, for she had said this in English, to tease.

'After all these years, I do, yes.'

And I am also sure that the Englishwomen love your Italian accent. But she did not say this out loud.

'I came back to Corniglia only once,' he said. 'For Mamma's funeral.'

'Oh, Dante.' Chiara put her hand on his arm. After her swim his skin felt almost hot under hers. 'I'm sorry.'

He turned towards her. 'Your parents too?'

'*Sì.* Many years ago now.'

He took her hand in his. It seemed natural. How could there be any wrong in it? 'At our age, we must accept losses,' he said.

Dangerous territory, she reminded herself. 'I should get back.' She rose to her feet.

'Dressed like that?' Again, she saw the mischief in his eyes.

'*Allora* . . .' Normally she would shower in the small cave that had been cut out of the rock face and fitted with a cold-water shower and change using the sarong. But once again, she felt at a disadvantage.

He took pity on her and held up both hands. 'Go ahead. I will look away.'

'Very well.' She hurried to the shower and changed behind a rock just to be sure. But Dante's gaze remained fixed on the distant horizon.

'May I walk you back to the hotel?' he asked when she returned.

Chiara hesitated.

'No funny stuff, I promise.' Those velvet brown eyes twinkled.

It made her realise how silly she was being. He was an old friend, nothing more. He was part of a different world, a different life now. And the feelings she was experiencing . . . she could put them down to a general dissatisfaction with her marriage, the rose-coloured memory of past love. 'Why not?'

So, they walked back through the village; past the restaurants in the piazza where cutlery and glasses gleamed expectantly on empty tables, and past the Bar Capitano where the local men played *scopa*, shuffling their cards while stray cats lounged by the water fountain soaking up the late afternoon sun. They passed her favourite *gelateria* on the upper pier alley before weaving a pathway through the blue and yellow boats parked on the main street, just as they always had been, Chiara thought with some satisfaction. It was good to know that some things had not changed. She and Dante passed comment on which shops had appeared, which had changed hands, which restaurants were good, and which catered for the more dubious tastes and deep pockets of tourists. And with the idle chat, Chiara began to relax more than ever.

They took the steps to the right past the jewellery shop and the trattoria, and then tackled the steeper steps towards La Torre, winding their way through the houses built on the higher terraces, gradually leaving the splashes of blue sea that continued to come into their line of vision behind. A few more twists and turns and they reached the acid-yellow tablecloths and grey parasols of La Torre bar. 'Is this place any good?' he asked as they paused for breath.

'It certainly is. They do a very decent *spaghetti della pesto* with green beans,' she said. 'Not to mention one of the best views in the whole of the Cinque Terre.'

They looked out past the succulents and grasses clinging to the hillside and towards the smooth royal-blue of the sea. In the distance, the colourful houses of Monterosso al Mare perched by the shore. Closer to home, the village of Vernazza jutted from the mainland like a fat, crooked finger filled with a jumble of misshapen buildings, rooftops, alleyways, and palm trees. Beyond the knuckle was the L-shaped jetty, the rows of boats in the harbour where she had swum and above this the rugged and serrated cliff rose high towards the skyline. The castle's tower stood at the fingertip and the tall skinny buildings in burnt terracotta, earth-green and misty blue, with lines of washing on skeletal balconies bordered both sides of Via Roma right up to the station.

'You're right about the view,' he said. 'I have missed that too. And I will certainly bear the spaghetti in mind.'

Chiara had the urge to giggle. Had he always had that serious manner? In a way, yes. She only had to recall that last night in the olive grove (though she should not think of that now). He had certainly been serious when he proposed that they run away together. What would have happened if . . .

More dangerous territory. She held on to the handrail as the dusty path wove higher past the lemon trees, pines and figs. There were pine needles on the stone steps now and she could smell the scent – both sweet and bitter drifting on the breeze. Although the path was steep, Chiara was relieved that Dante didn't take her arm. She'd been climbing this path since she was a girl and too much bodily contact would bring that 'what if' far too close to the forefront of her mind.

'I do not blame you for choosing to stay in such a beautiful place,' Dante said as they approached the side entrance to the hotel via the wrought-iron gate and the gravel pathway that snaked through the olive grove.

'It wasn't that. At least it wasn't only that.' Chiara had not meant to say this – somehow it had just come out of her mouth. They had entered the olive grove now and the place was dense with memories.

'Chiara.' He breathed her name and she felt her knees almost buckle. They both stopped walking. For the love of God . . .

'What is it?' She forced the words out with some difficulty.

'I should explain.'

'There's really no need.' She tried to carry on walking, but he caught her arm. She paused.

'When I came back to Corniglia for my mother's funeral,

104

I wanted to see you, of course.' He took her hands. 'I need you to know that.'

'But I was married,' she said.

'Yes, and I could not disrupt that – even if I had had the power to.'

And what about now? She stared at him, taking in the shape of his face, his mouth, the lines of laughter and worry perhaps that had never been there before. He had always been attractive, but he had been a boy. Now, as a mature man he was having exactly the same effect on her. Did he not think he could disrupt her life now? Was he not trying to do just that?

'It was too painful for me to come to Vernazza,' he admitted, and she could see the old grief still written there on his face. She took her hand from his and traced a pathway along his cheek with her fingertips. This man . . .

'I was already grieving for my mother, there were already so many regrets . . .'

'You could not take any more.' Chiara understood.

'Exactly.'

'And now?' She hesitated to ask this. But here they were in the olive grove, the late afternoon sun glinting through the silvery green trees and gnarled twisty branches. The ancient olives surrounded them with their aura of peace and wisdom. It was their place, had always been their place.

'Now, so many years have passed that I thought we were safe.' Their eyes met.

Were they safe? Chiara knew that this spark between them could so quickly be fanned into a flame – yes, even at their age, even after all this time. For it had never gone away and it seemed to be a part of them. He was already holding her hand. All she had to do was move a little closer.

But she could not do it. How could she do it? What about Alonzo, Elene, Isabella? There was still the hotel, always the hotel. There was simply too much to lose. Dante had made his life in England, and it was a successful life. Chiara could not leave Italy. And she was married, for God's sake, she was still married, albeit to a man she did not love.

'Dante . . .' Almost, she could not speak his name, when once she had whispered it over and over before going to sleep at night. She couldn't look at him, not at this moment. But she could feel him here, close as ever.

'You tell me you are fine.' He turned and put his hands on her shoulders just as he had before, reminding her of his touch, his kiss. 'And I want that.'

She waited.

'But can you truly tell me that you are happy?'

At his words, she felt a sudden and overwhelming sadness flood over her. And yet she had so many things to be thankful for.

'I saw your face, Chiara,' he said. 'When you were swimming in the ocean. And you looked so sad. I would hate for you to be sad.'

'I have so many things to be thankful for,' she repeated aloud. 'I have almost everything I ever wanted.'

'Almost?' he echoed.

She bowed her head. Sometimes there was simply too much to say.

CHAPTER 11

Elene

Elene was getting ready for bed. She had a fixed routine – as she did for most things. She brushed her hair and clipped it back. She cleansed and moisturised her face, and then she flossed and cleaned her teeth. She could hear Silvio in the bedroom, whistling, which she was finding profoundly irritating. Whistling suggested that all was well with the world, and this was simply not the case. Something was very wrong.

Because of the whistling, Elene found herself glaring at her husband as she returned to their bedroom to undress. What did he have to be so cheerful about? Had he even seen them? Elene certainly had. Her mother and this man – a guest of their hotel apparently – had been practically holding hands that night she spotted them in the bar. Then when she happened to look out of the window yesterday afternoon, she'd seen them in the olive grove, talking and looking very serious. What was going on? What was her mother up to? Who *was* he? It was both odd and unsettling.

'What's wrong, my love?'

107

Elene shot him a surprised glance. Like most men he tended to take a rather simplistic view of things and so she was always surprised at these rare moments of perception. Perhaps she should tell him – get a man's point of view on the matter? 'It's Mamma.'

He frowned. 'Is she ill?'

The opposite, thought Elene. She looked almost unreasonably well. 'No.' In one fluid movement, she pulled off the sleeveless shift dress she liked to wear under her chef's apron while she was working. 'It's nothing like that.'

'What then?'

Elene knew he was looking at her body. She was never quite sure whether she liked this or not. 'There's someone staying here at the hotel, a man called Dante Rossi, though Isabella said he checked in as Signor Bianchi, which is a bit suspicious for a start.'

'Hmm.' Silvio was lounging on the bed still fully dressed. He folded his arms behind his head. 'Why would he give a false name?'

Precisely. 'Mamma knows him. She says he's an old friend.' Though Elene had not been impressed by that casual performance in the kitchen. It had been far too glib.

Silvio nodded encouragingly. 'That's nice,' he said.

Elene shot him a despairing glance. He seemed to have entirely missed the point. 'I've seen them together a few times,' she said. 'Laughing over some joke, talking together in an . . .' she hesitated '. . . intimate way.'

He shrugged. 'What's wrong with that if he is an old friend?'

Elene sighed. As she'd thought – simplistic to the core. 'It's the *way* they are doing it,' she said. Shouldn't that be obvious? 'It's the *look* she gives him.'

'The look?'

She shot him a flirtatious smile. It was called spelling it out.

'Ah.' He reached out to grab her waist and she slapped his hands away. To the core, she thought again.

'And it's more than that.' It was the unexpected light in Chiara's eyes. Her mother looked younger suddenly, less harassed. Elene didn't like it, not at all. What would her father say?

'More, eh?' Silvio got up, took off his shirt and threw it across the back of a chair. 'Lucky guy. Maybe she does fancy him then.' He flexed his muscles.

'Silvio!' Really, he was not taking this remotely seriously.

'*Allora*, why not? Maybe she finds him attractive. What's wrong with finding a man attractive?' He sidled up closer to her again.

Elene snorted. 'You're my husband,' she reminded him sternly.

'I'm glad you realise that, my love.' He slipped one of the narrow silk straps down over her shoulder.

'The point being that he is *not* my mother's husband.' She pulled the strap back into place. And if Silvio couldn't see the difference, then he was more stupid than she had thought. Although he wasn't, of course. He was practical, reliable and intelligent. He supported her, they were friends and their relationship was contented enough. He was everything she wanted. Wasn't he?

When Silvio Lombardi had first started paying attention to Elene, back in the day, she had been flattered – few of the other boys from the village had bothered; she was too quiet, she found the banter wearing and frankly a waste of time. She put her nose in the air and ignored them and she wouldn't care if they called her stuck-up and superior (which they did). Silvio didn't though. Silvio came up to the hotel and asked her to go to La Spezia or to Monterosso al Mare with him at the weekend. Silvio brought her gifts – once, a bottle of olive oil from his uncle's land, once a special balsamic that his mother swore by. Right from the start, he knew what kind of presents Elene would appreciate. He picked wild flowers and gave her little posies and bracelets plaited from wild grasses; he pursued her with a single-minded loyalty that both touched and moved her. It was the kind of love she'd never had.

'Something is definitely up.' Elene climbed into bed and pulled the covers up to her chin. 'I don't like it,' she said again. 'Especially with Papà away.'

Silvio raised his dark eyebrows. 'My love, your papà is nearly always away.'

Elene turned from him, burrowing her head further into the soft comfort of the pillow. She knew that this was true enough. But who could blame him? Elene's mother had always made it perfectly clear that The Lemon Tree Hotel belonged to her and to the women of the family. She loved this place probably more than she loved any of them – except perhaps Isabella. With this thought came the unavoidable twinge of jealousy. Elene loved her daughter too – of course, she did. But when she saw her mother and Isabella together, when she saw the easy affection between them, she sensed that it was something she would never share. Those two were just on the same wavelength somehow.

'You mustn't worry, Elene.' She felt Silvio climb into bed next to her. 'Your mother can look after herself.'

She knew that all right. 'Yes, yes.' But what about her father? He certainly wouldn't like it. Elene rolled on to her back and stared at the ceiling. 'And you don't think there is any funny business going on?'

'No way. Your mother, she is not like that. I am sure of it, my love.' He kissed her shoulder.

She glanced across at him. 'I don't know why you defend her.' After all, her mother had never exactly been Silvio's greatest fan. She bossed him around as if he were of little importance in the grand scheme of things. When Elene had first announced they were going to marry, Mamma had been so patronising, so negative. He wasn't enough for her, that was why. Her mother didn't value his qualities of honesty and integrity; she didn't realise how important it was for Elene to be loved. Papà though – he had realised, he had given his support. Because although he wasn't around much – had never been around much – Elene knew that her father loved her. And she loved him too. Her love for him was uncomplicated, never fraught with sensitivities, jealousies and criticisms – imagined or not.

And Silvio? Elene bit her lip. She was fond of Silvio and she could not imagine her life without him, no indeed. But had she ever loved him as he loved her? No – not even in the early days. So? Was that so wrong? No, it was not wrong, it was sensible, that was all. That was how to avoid getting hurt. Things were safer that way.

'I defend her because she is your mother,' Silvio said mildly. 'She is not so bad as employers go.' He was propped up on his elbow looking at her. 'And I also defend her because some-times, my love, you attack her with no reason.'

'Attack?' Elene stared at him. It was a strong word to use. 'And with no reason?'

'*Allora* . . .' Silvio looked doubtful at this point.

111

That was it. 'I will phone Papà.' Elene began to scramble out of bed. 'He really should know what is going on around here.'

'Now?'

'Now.'

'No, Elene.' He caught her arm in his powerful grip. It was so rare for him to say this to her that Elene blinked at him and for a moment, she was still.

But not for long. 'Why shouldn't I phone my own father?' She was angry now – with Silvio and with her mother too.

'Because it is your mother's business and you shouldn't interfere.' His voice was soft but unusually authoritative.

'What is it to you, Silvio?' she snapped, pulling away from him again. 'What right do you have to tell me what to do? This is my family. Mine. And what have they ever done for you?' Too late she saw the sadness in his dark eyes, that sadness that never entirely vanished, no matter how much he might enjoy their life together, no matter how often he might whistle.

He sat up in bed, but let her go. And now she didn't want to go anywhere. She felt awful.

'They have given me my living,' he said. 'They have given me my wife. But you are right.' His voice changed. 'It is nothing to do with me. I am only your husband. I just hate to see you eaten up like this.'

'I'm not eaten up.' She stayed sitting on the side of the bed. Suddenly she felt like crying.

He put a hand on her shoulder and gently turned her around to face him. 'We have each other, Elene,' he said.

She nodded, not trusting herself to speak.

'I love you, you know that.'

'Sì.' She did know that. It was the one thing she was always sure of, little though she did to deserve it.

112

'I only wish that was enough for you.'

She lifted her face and stared at him. *Oh, Silvio* . . .

'Don't phone your father – that's my advice.' He opened his arms and she crept inside his embrace. Together they lay back on the bed, her head nestled into the crook of his shoulder, her favourite place, the place she would always feel safe. And as for her mother and this Dante Rossi . . . She would decide what to do tomorrow.

CHAPTER 12

Elene

Elene was still brooding about the conversation she'd had with Silvio the previous evening as she moved in her accustomed manner around the kitchen, checking that the necessary preparation had been done, that every dish needed only twenty minutes or so to be ready to go. She had three helpers in the kitchen tonight: Ghita, Febe and Raphael, all practised and capable and used to her methods. Elene knew that she was exacting. Perhaps she cared too much. But it was a matter of pride. Since she was a girl, she had been pulled into this kitchen by its warmth, its comfort, her love of the food produced within: the fragrant tomato sauces cooked with fresh herbs until they possessed a depth that made the palate sing; the *trofie* with pesto she insisted on still making herself from the freshest ingredients and rich with olive oil, pine nuts and the best *Parmigiano*; the walnut sauce that her old friend Marcello had made with such love and gusto. The scent of *la cucina* still intoxicated her – it always had.

Tonight, they were preparing various regional specialities.

There were the usual *antipasti* including anchovies cured in lemon and olive oil and thin slices of squid terrine served with a warm potato salad, while the first courses included her *trofie al pesto* prepared this morning with fresh basil from the kitchen garden. Pesto might be popular throughout the world, but in her opinion their own small-leafed Ligurian basil, buffeted by sea breezes as it invariably was, was by far the best and most flavoursome. Among the *secondi*, were *muscoli ripieni* – stuffed mussels, and *cappon magro*, an elaborate layered dish made of lobster, sea bass, prawns and anchovies with vegetables – a sort of Ligurian caponata. The food had been prepped and the fish lightly poached. Everything, she decided, was under control.

Silvio was a good man and she should be kinder, she knew. But he would never understand the complex emotions that surrounded Elene's relationship with her mother. She wasn't sure that she understood them herself. Elene checked the mussels that Ghita had prepared earlier, ensuring they were well-cleaned and that all the shell valves were still attached to one another.

As a girl, she had never been badly treated; on the contrary, both her parents had worked hard to ensure she had the best start in life, and when she was younger she knew that her mother expected her to take over the running of the hotel at some point in the future, so that Chiara could step down. The Lemon Tree Hotel was Elene's legacy, after all, or so she had been given to understand. She discarded a mussel with a broken shell. That one would certainly not do.

Running the hotel was what her mother had done for most of her life, so why not Elene when her turn came? She inspected the filling for the mussels, of which Ghita had also been in charge. As well as mussels, it consisted of garlic, chopped thyme, parsley and marjoram from the kitchen garden. To this, Ghita had added breadcrumbs that had been drenched in milk and then squeezed, *Parmigiano*, eggs and *mortadella*. Elene tasted the mixture and added a few more grinds of black pepper. '*Bene*,' she said. It was good.

And this, it suddenly struck her, was the crux of the problem between them. Her mother had always thought that Elene should do everything just as Chiara had wanted to do it. So, Elene should have looked for the kind of man her mother would have looked for (given the chance; Mamma had always made it clear that she had not been permitted to marry for love – which was pretty tough on poor Papà), Elene should have preferred hotel management and administration to cooking, just as her mother did, Elene should want the hotel to remain unchanged, just as her mother did – an echo of its former self that refused to step into the twenty-first century.

'You can fill the mussels now,' Elene told Ghita. 'And then make the sauce, OK?' The point being – where was Elene in all this? Where were her wishes, her thoughts, her desires? Nowhere. She might as well not have a mind of her own. Her father on the other hand, whilst being largely absent from her life – more so, as the years went by – encouraged her to follow her own star.

'If you ever feel you don't want to stay at the hotel,' he had told her once when she admitted to feeling particularly disgruntled, 'come to me first, OK?'

'Mamma would kill me,' Elene had told him.

And his face had darkened. 'Mamma will have to understand.'

She never had though – the truth was that Elene loved The Lemon Tree as much as her mother did – but it was nice to know that she had a choice.

She nodded her approval as Ghita assembled the ingredients for the sauce – more garlic, parsley, white wine, and tomatoes. The stuffed mussels would simmer in this for about thirty minutes before service.

Elene wiped her hands on her apron. The irony being that her mother had got what she wanted in Isabella. Isabella had never wanted to run to the kitchen as Elene had done when she was a girl with busy parents and left very much to her own devices. Isabella liked to deal with the guests; she wanted to talk to people, she was good at managing things, and her business and technology skills ensured that she could keep the hotel running smoothly. She was only twenty, but she already possessed a natural authority similar to her grandmother's. She was cut from the same cloth as Chiara; they understood each other without even trying.

And so. Elene sighed. She tasted the sauce, which was bubbling nicely, and added just a touch more salt. Elene made her contribution to the running of the hotel, of course. She was appreciated – to some extent. But she was made to feel somehow not quite as indispensable to the continuing success of The Lemon Tree Hotel as her mother and her daughter were. And whenever she or Silvio dared to suggest any changes . . . her mother and Isabella closed ranks. Elene simply didn't understand their stubbornness. Just because the hotel had once been a convent – why should that mean it must always make a nod to its past life? Why not restructure the building, build an extension or two? Why not add a few touches of luxury that would bring in the guests who had money? They could afford it, and it would be a good investment for the future.

'I want the hotel to retain its tranquillity,' her mother had said when they had last talked of the matter. 'That's vital.

The shape, the structure of the building, the history of the convent . . .'

'Is part of its integrity,' Isabella had added. 'Whatever we do, we shouldn't compromise on that.'

'I agree.' And they had shared a conspiratorial look.

'But you're both businesswomen.' Elene was exasperated. 'Surely you can see that we can bring in more money if we update things a little?'

'It's not all about money, Mamma,' Isabella had said, making Elene feel like an avaricious skinflint.

'I know.'

'It's about the hotel being accessible for people who need it.' Her mother had always pushed this idea as if The Lemon Tree Hotel was some sort of spiritual retreat.

'But in the meantime, we get left behind.' This was Silvio, putting in his contribution. 'Five-star hotels need to have five-star facilities.' He was always loyal to Elene, but sometimes she wondered if that was all it was. Her mother clearly thought so.

'We don't need to be a five-star hotel in order to attract visitors.' She seemed to be looking down on the very idea of such a notion. 'And we won't get left behind.' *Allora*. Once again, the matter was closed.

'Do what you like then. I'll just get on with the cooking.' Elene knew she was being childish, but, what the hell, she *felt* childish. She had no part in the decision-making around here, and this just proved it.

Elene had already made her *trofie* pasta and prepared the pesto. As all Italians knew, it was necessary for pasta and sauce to marry; the pasta must be perfect for the sauce. In this case, the ribbed twisty spirals of Ligurian *trofie* were able to pick up the delicacy and fine consistency of the fragrant pesto to

118

perfection, so that the full experience was in every bite. Elene liked to prepare her dish with blanched green beans and basil that was young and fresh, but she didn't add potatoes and she had her own way of using the pestle and mortar with the salt and basil to coax the flavour from the young leaves – this was why it was a dish she felt unable to delegate to any of her assistants.

It wasn't only the comfort of food that had pulled Elene into the kitchen when she was a girl; it was also Marcello the chef. Whilst her parents often seemed tense and anxious, whilst the atmosphere in their rooms was too often rather like the one you get before a storm . . . Marcello had been free and easy. He was a great bear of a man; a burst of loud laughter or a hug was never far away.

'There you are, little one,' he would roar as if her seven-year-old presence was somehow necessary to his delicately flavoured Ligurian prawns or his famous *salsa di noci*, walnut sauce. 'I was wondering where you'd got to. And so . . . *allora*.' He would put his head to one side and watch her. 'What shall we prepare today, hmm?'

She never considered at the time that he was teaching her. He made her feel wanted, that was all, and the kitchen soon became her favourite place to be. But as months and then years went by, Elene realised that she could prepare a *ragù* with the necessary layers of flavour, that her sauces were as glossy as required, and that her *panna cotta* had what Marcello referred to as the 'perfect wobble'.

It made her feel good. It was a release. People's reactions to her food warmed her belly and her heart. This was something she could do. This was something in which she could excel and be proud of. Even her mother – who had never been free with her praise – raised a perfectly plucked eyebrow and remarked on Elene's skills. 'You are an excellent chef, Elene, so maybe . . .' Elene knew the way her mother's mind was working. The hotel, she was always thinking of the hotel. Maybe it didn't matter that Elene had no interest in the business side of things. Maybe she could do what her grandmother had done and make her contribution that way? Her words made Elene feel both happy and resentful. It made her want to cook both less and more. When she was young, her thoughts about her mother always seemed to have this ambivalence.

They still did. Was Chiara a bad mother? No. Was Elene a bad daughter? Perhaps. Living in the same building, working towards the same ends should have brought them closer. But it had only served to make the distance between them grow.

Even so. Silvio was probably right about this thing that was bothering her – she was letting her imagination run right away. Her parents had never been love's young dream, and they had never pretended to be, but that didn't mean they weren't solidly attached. They were a unit. They were her parents. They belonged together. Spending so much time apart might even make them closer in the end. They always spoke nicely to one another, they seemed concerned about one another's welfare and she'd never even heard them argue. Perhaps it was all a bit too polite to be true. But Elene had no real reason to doubt them. They had been together for ever – very few couples went around holding hands all the time after almost forty years, and if their closeness wasn't always apparent, well . . . No, she was glad now that Silvio had persuaded her not to make that call to Papà – why bother him unnecessarily? And this unsettled feeling – no doubt it was down to something else entirely.

She glanced at her watch. It was time for a short break before things got a bit hotter around here and she decided to pop back to her room for a quick freshen-up. They could manage without her for now. 'I'll be back in five minutes,' she called.

She pushed open the swing doors of *la cucina* just in time to see her mother turn to speak to this old friend of hers. They were standing just beyond reception in the arched doorway that led to the bar. But Chiara didn't just speak, she laughed in a soft and intimate way that set Elene's teeth on edge, her nerves jangling. And the man – this Dante Bianchi or Rossi or whatever he was called – put a hand on her mother's arm and bent closer to whisper something in her ear. Elene stood by the swing doors, waiting for her mother to step away in that gracious way she had when a guest got too close but she didn't want to cause offence – Elene had seen her do it hundreds of times.

Only, she didn't. She reached up to the lapel of his jacket and she brushed away a speck of dust.

And that was it. That told Elene everything she needed to know. People could pretend all they liked, but there was no mistaking the intimacy of that simple gesture. Mother of God, it was worse even than she had thought. What might it lead to? Indeed – what had it led to already? What could she do? There was only person who could stop this.

Elene slipped back into the kitchen and she reached for her phone.

Chiara

Dante had somehow persuaded Chiara to have dinner with him.

It was against her better judgement. She had spent the last few days shifting between trying to avoid him and wanting to catch sight of him more than anything. 'I'm on the desk until seven,' was her first excuse. Even she found it weak.

'I can wait.'

'And my family . . .'

He raised a questioning eyebrow. Who is the boss around here, he seemed to be saying. And he was right. But: 'We could go somewhere else?' So clearly, he understood her reservations.

'*Allora* . . .' She weighed up the options.

'It's only dinner I am proposing, *cara*. And it is my last night.'

'Oh.' She tried not to feel upset about this, at least not to allow her emotions to show on her face – Dante was all too good at reading them. And *certo*, he was leaving. Why wouldn't he be leaving? His life was not here in Italy – it hadn't been for years. She swallowed hard. She wanted to experience every last minute with him that she could, she realised. 'In that case, it seems churlish to refuse.'

'And where would you like to go?' There was just a hint of a smile playing around his mouth. 'Here, or . . .'

Chiara looked away. 'Here is fine.' At least she would be showing that she had nothing to hide. At least there would be no temptation – to get too close. She repressed a small shiver. How was it that he had this effect on her still?

Once again, she dressed with care – this time in a forest-green dress that she knew complemented her hair and eyes, high-heeled sandals that she hadn't worn for years, and with her favourite gold necklace, given to her by her parents, at her throat. Elene might see them dining together, but what did it matter now? He was leaving tomorrow.

What would have happened if Alonzo had been here these past few days, she wondered, as she clipped the necklace into place. Would he have accepted Dante's initial invitation for them both to have a drink with him? Hardly. He had always been jealous of Dante. He knew of his existence – Chiara had been foolish enough to mention their brief liaison and how she'd once felt about him, when Alonzo had made his first declaration.

'You still think of him now?' His brow had furrowed.

Chiara had reacted quickly enough. 'No, not now,' she had lied. 'It was almost two years ago.'

But . . . Somehow, Alonzo had seemed to know that he was second best, that he was not Chiara's true choice, that this was more a marriage of duty and obligation than of love. 'I will make you love me,' he had vowed, fists clenched.

Back then, Chiara had prayed that he could. Now, she knew that he could not.

Stilling her nerves, Chiara checked her appearance in the mirror, gave a little sigh – oh well, she would never be young again – and went down the stairs to meet Dante.

Halfway down, she almost bumped right into their young German guest the Signor Bauer. '*Signore.*'

'Excuse me. *Signora.*' He had a charming smile. She watched him go on up the stairs, lean and bursting with energy. She hoped she was wrong about his reasons for being here, but after what Isabella had told her . . . she had her doubts. She had noticed the way Isabella's eyes lit up when she saw him – it was almost impossible not to – and then when her granddaughter had told Chiara about the encounter with Giovanna . . . She'd had to say something. She had a protective role to play where both Giovanna and Isabella were concerned. No one was ever going to hurt them – not if Chiara had anything to do with it.

She paused on the bottom step, hand on the curved oak banister, opposite Luca Bordoni's painting of the Archangel Gabriel in the niche, the white candle already lit. She could see Dante from this vantage point, about to go through the archway into the Cloisters Bar, cutting a rather fine figure in his navy suit and a dusky pink shirt, the silver in his greying hair illuminated by the glass lamp above. As she watched him, he turned and saw her, held her gaze. Oh, Dante, she thought. She had given herself away.

She crossed the black-and-white tiles of the foyer and he came to meet her. He kissed her hand.

'*Ciao*, Dante.' She forced a lightness into her voice.

He leaned closer and whispered into her hair. '*Ciao*, Chiara. You are looking especially beautiful tonight.'

Chiara gave a little laugh. She wondered if some men continued to pay their wives extravagant compliments long after they were married, or if she was just unlucky in this respect. It was meaningless, of course, she reminded herself sternly, quelling the blush that she knew would be staining her cheeks. He was merely being polite, just doing what Italian men would always do best.

To distract them both, she brushed a speck of dust from the lapel of his jacket and then was immediately embarrassed at the intimacy of the act. It was the kind of thing a woman might do if the man were her husband or her lover, not simply an old friend.

But Dante just smiled and thanked her. *Mamma mia* . . . Nothing was simple. How could it be when she still felt so open to him, with every look, every smile? The past: it seemed to crouch behind her shoulder, leaping out to confront her at every opportunity.

The tables in the Cloisters Restaurant were laid with white damask cloths, gleaming cutlery, and elegant glasses. In the centre of each was a tiny vase of flowers cut from the flower patch by the herb garden at the back of the hotel. Chiara nodded her approval. Everything was exactly as it should be.

Some of the other tables were already occupied, but Chiara had reserved her favourite, slightly tucked away but with a good view of the courtyard. She nodded a greeting to the other diners, most of whom she recognised. There was an American family with two young children who were chatting animatedly – Chiara noticed that Emanuele had put them at the far end of the Cloisters Restaurant, where they would disturb the fewest number of people. A young Australian couple she'd taken rather a shine to, who were hiking the entire *Sentiero Azzurro* Cinque Terre trail, were drinking Aperol spritzes and gazing into one another's eyes, and the

Signoras Veroni who came here every year from Milan were both studying the menu intently. Chiara wasn't fooled though, they didn't a miss a thing. One gave her a smile and the other *signora* – the one who was apparently looking for a husband when she came here every year – actually winked. Oh, dear.

Over the *antipasto*, she and Dante chatted about The Lemon Tree and the future of the hotel, and Chiara found herself telling him about Elene and Silvio's wish to make it more exclusive.

'*More* exclusive?' he teased.

'This is the Cinque Terre,' she reminded him. Though as she glanced out at the darkening courtyard, the grey stone flags lit by the golden lamps, the wrought-iron furniture casting its knotty shadows, the lemon tree shimmering gently in the moonlight, she couldn't help but agree.

'And?'

She cut a piece of the squid terrine and popped it into her mouth. Elene's *antipasti* were always delicious. 'You can see for yourself how the area has changed.' Like Chiara, he had grown up in this region where people still made their living from fishing or from their olive groves and vineyards built into the terraced hillsides. Time was when you could go down to the harbour and catch a netful of anchovies in minutes and the rest of the fishing was done by *lampare* – night trawling with lamps – along the sea beds near the five villages. They weren't rich in the material sense of the word, but it was a good and simple life – at least, until the price of olive oil plummeted, until factories grew up in nearby towns, until their rural lives threatened to change.

With more and more people visiting the area, and tourism promising to give financial security back to the region, what the family possessed in The Lemon Tree Hotel up on the hillside was a valuable slice of history; a place of peace, protected from the crazy bustle of the five villages. Authenticity. Ah, yes. A lot of tourists expected lobster, but in Vernazza most restaurants had stuck to their traditions, and The Lemon Tree was the same. What was traditional and what could be found on their own doorstep was not only authentic to the region but delicious too. And Chiara hoped that would never change.

She paused as Rosalie, their waitress, appeared to clear away their *antipasti*.

When she had done this, Dante leaned towards Chiara, chin cupped in his hands. 'And exactly how would they like to change things?'

'*Allora* . . .' She began to speak, but the pasta course appeared before she had the chance to go on. The perfumed fragrance of the pesto was heady. Chiara speared one of the delicate *trofie* and took a taste. It was delicious. Once again, Elene had excelled.

Where to begin? 'They'd renovate all the rooms. Add more contemporary furniture.' Elene had even mentioned giving each room a theme. Chiara shuddered. Who knew where *that* might lead? 'They would make everything about the hotel more luxurious and less traditional. She – they – would like it to be less reminiscent of . . .'

'A convent?'

'Exactly.' She told him about Elene and Silvio's other suggestions: the infinity pool and hot tub (both of which she found unspeakably pretentious), the spa centre in a new extension (was that really necessary?), the rooftop terrace, which admittedly would have a glorious view, the pool bar (which sounded too tacky for words) . . . Chiara had already agreed to a piano in the cloisters; she could imagine a laid-back jazz evening creating a relaxing atmosphere for their guests, or gentle piano music serenading their diners, but as for the rest of it . . .

Dante had been tucking into his *trenette* pasta served with *salsa di noci*, Elene's delicate walnut sauce, but now he sat back in his chair. 'It seems disrespectful of its history to me.'

Chiara glanced at him in some surprise. He seemed very sure. 'Exactly,' she murmured.

'I know the history too, don't forget.' He toyed with his fork. 'Your parents – they would not want it.'

'No, they would not.' As for Giovanna – she had no shares in the hotel, it was true – but she would hate it too. After all she'd been through . . . Chiara could not allow it to happen – and it would not, while she had the strength to stop it. She took another forkful of pesto.

'And what does your granddaughter think?'

'She agrees with me.' Though that never went down well with Elene. Their latest discussion on the matter had taken place in the kitchen where Elene had been making focaccia – pounding the dough as if her life depended on it.

'And Alonzo?'

The atmosphere seemed to change as her husband's name was brought into the conversation. Chiara shrugged. 'He is a businessman. He would favour whichever would be most successful.' Dante would know that by success she was referring to money, and she felt a small stab of guilt at this small betrayal. But it was the truth. Alonzo didn't care for the hotel – not like the rest of them did, not even as his parents had when they were alive, when they had been generous with their money as well as their support. Sadly, Alonzo was not like his parents, whom Chiara had got on with rather well – he lacked their integrity, for a start, though it had taken her years to fully realise this. She felt another stab of betrayal. She should stop thinking this way – he was her husband, for better, for worse; she must remember that. He went away often, but he had given her no reason to think that he was disloyal to her.

Rosalie came to their table to take their plates back to the kitchen. Chiara wondered if she had told Elene that Chiara was in the restaurant tonight with a male guest. Would Elene care? Chiara had to remind herself again that she – they – were doing nothing illicit. Even so, she had drunk a little too much white wine and was on her way through at least three courses – not counting dessert – which was very unusual for her these days. This was probably why she felt intoxicated. Because, *certo*, it could surely be nothing to do with the man sitting opposite her and the little dances of electricity that seemed to exist between them.

Their main courses were brought to the table, and Chiara let a small sigh escape her lips. She tried to draw it back, but it was too late.

'What is it, Chiara?' He took her hand.

She flinched at his touch. The warmth of his skin was a sweet and guilty pleasure. 'Only that I will miss our chats.' She forced a smile. 'It has been good to see you again, Dante.'

He bowed his head. 'Then I am glad I came.'

Even though, she reminded herself, she had not yet answered his question.

'And tomorrow, you will return to England.' Chiara withdrew her hand while she was still able and before anyone should see. She took a mouthful of delicious seafood. She must compliment Elene on tonight's dishes, she decided. She must be more attentive, more thoughtful. She valued her daughter in so many ways – but how often did she let her know?

'*Sì*. I must.' Dante had chosen the gleaming, garlicky mussels as his main course, and he seemed to be enjoying them. 'I cannot expect my assistant to look after the place for too long, you understand. And of course, I must make more *gelato*.'

She smiled. 'Why ever did you decide on making ice cream for a career?'

Dante demolished another mussel and dropped the shell in the bowl provided. He gave a little shrug. 'I spotted the need,' he said. 'Why do you think so many Italian coffee shops have sprung up in England?'

Chiara acknowledged this. 'But you could have opened a coffee shop.'

'I could, yes.' He seemed to consider this, head on one side. 'But the big chains dominate most of the towns and cities, you know, and besides, with *gelato* . . .' He paused to eat another mussel. 'I could be more creative.'

'I suppose that you could.' Chiara pushed her plate away. Dante demolishing a bowlful of mussels was quite a sight – and it was making her harbour thoughts that were entirely inappropriate.

'Besides,' he added, 'making *gelato* is more complex than it might seem to the uninitiated.' The quirk of his mouth suggested he was not being entirely serious.

'What do you think of when you're making it? What's your aim?' It was perhaps rather an odd question. But she could picture him testing the flavours, churning the milk, and she wanted to know more. She wanted to know what made Dante and the man he had become, tick.

130

'I suppose I think of the children,' he said. He finished the last of his mussels and wiped his hands with the lemon-scented tissues provided.

'The children?' She hadn't been expecting that.

'The children who are going to be eating it.'

'Ah.' Now, she got it. And they could have had children of their own . . . Shocked at this thought, she turned her attention back to the courtyard. Night was deepening now. She could no longer make out the colours of the plants and flowers, though she fancied she could catch the citrus tang of the lemon tree drifting in the night breeze.

Rosalie returned to clear their plates and give them the dessert menu. Chiara took it, though she wasn't sure she could manage any more food.

'I think about those who come next in life. The future.' He glanced at the menu and smiled at Rosalie. 'Definitely the *gelato* for me,' he said.

Chiara laughed and handed back the menu. 'I couldn't eat another thing.'

'Really?' He feigned surprise.

'One would think,' she teased, 'that you would have had enough of ice cream in England.'

He shrugged. 'Can one ever have enough of a good thing?'

Once again, Chiara held his gaze. His eyes still seemed to draw her, just like they had drawn her all those years ago, bringing her in closer and closer, until . . . 'I hope that ours lives up to your expectations,' she murmured.

A few minutes later, the dessert arrived, along with two glasses of their delicious dessert wine, the Sciacchetrà – which Chiara never could resist. It was made from partially dried Cinque Terre grapes, and the large quantity of grapes required to make just one bottle of Sciacchetrà helped explain the high pricetag.

Dante surveyed the *pistachio gelato* with a critical eye. He tasted it. 'Not bad,' he conceded.

'We get it from the best *gelateria* in Vernazza, you know.' She leaned forwards. 'But tell me, Dante, how exactly do you put the future into ice cream?'

His eyes gleamed. 'I use the best ingredients – no preservatives, no colouring. I keep it fresh, pure and organic, just as the future should be.'

'*Bene!*' Chiara grinned back at him, and this time it was she who placed her hand on Dante's. 'I love that.'

'Of course,' he said. 'This is how you operate too here at The Lemon Tree Hotel. It is all about authenticity, no?'

They shared another long and conspiratorial glance. Authenticity . . . He was right, and yet she'd hardly kept to this ethos where her marriage was concerned, had she? Chiara felt ashamed. There was so much she could say, so much she could allow herself to feel. But, how could she? Just the look of him seemed to throw her into a spin, take her back to a time in her life when everything was still possible. But now it was not. Now, whatever the authenticity of the matter, whatever she felt in her heart . . . there were other things – other people – to consider. It was no good. She had to accept that all there could be between them was this one last supper, this gentle conversation, this spark that could never become the fire that she longed for.

Rosalie brought coffee and liqueurs. It was already late. Chiara was aware that they were both trying to prolong the evening, knowing that very likely they would never see one another again. And yet. And yet the thought was almost too difficult to swallow.

'It was brave of you to come here, Dante.'

He seemed to hesitate, his dark eyes clouded with sadness, and the desire to reach over the table to kiss him was so sudden and so intense that Chiara had to use all her strength to fight it.

'It is incredible, and I can hardly believe it myself. But the fact is that my feelings are still the same,' he said. 'Even after all these years.'

Even after all these years . . .

'Dante . . .' She hesitated.

'*Allora.*'

Chiara jumped at the sound of her husband's voice. In the next second, she realised it was a guilty jump, but by then it was too late.

He was scowling. 'This is all very cosy, I must say.'

'Alonzo.' Feeling at a disadvantage, Chiara rose to her feet, slightly unstable on the unfamiliar heels, slightly dizzy from the wine. 'This is—'

'Dante Rossi,' he finished for her. 'I know perfectly well who he is. Because we all know about Dante Rossi – is that not so, my dear?'

CHAPTER 14

Chiara

'I am pleased to meet you, *Signore*.' Dante rose to his feet. He seemed remarkably unperturbed by the interruption even though Alonzo was glaring at him as if he were the devil incarnate.

'I regret that I am unable to say the same.' Alonzo ignored Dante's proffered hand. 'As I said, I know exactly who you are and I can guess what it is that you want.'

Chiara was grateful that there was only one other table still occupied in the restaurant although unfortunately it was the one where the Signoras Veroni were both gazing open-mouthed, clearly enjoying the drama that was unfolding. She had to find a way to diffuse this situation, and fast. Alonzo seemed determined to make a scene.

'Indeed?' Dante's dark eyes grazed over him. He did not look at Chiara, and she was grateful for this. She was already hanging on to the edge of the table to stop her knees from buckling completely.

'And so, I must ask you to leave The Lemon Tree Hotel immediately.'

For goodness' sake . . . 'He can't leave immediately,' Chiara burst out. What was Alonzo thinking of? 'It's past midnight. And he is a guest.' Added to which, this was *her* hotel. Alonzo had no right to dictate who should leave and when. She was about to say this, when she caught Dante's swift glance of caution. She swallowed back the words. He was right. Why antagonise Alonzo still further?

'I leave in the morning.' Dante remained calm. 'But if I may say, I think you misunderstand the situation, *Signore*.'

'It seems clear enough to me,' Alonzo muttered. 'You sneak in here as soon as my back is turned . . .'

'Not at all. I came here not aware that you were away. Your wife and I are merely having dinner for old times' sake,' Dante continued smoothly. 'If you had been around, I should certainly have asked you to join us.'

Alonzo snorted. 'And I should certainly have refused.'

But, thankfully, his initial hot temper seemed to have cooled. And after all, what could he accuse them of? He had not discovered them doing anything wrong. However, he had a point. How would Chiara have reacted if she came across her husband enjoying an intimate dinner with another woman – some old lover perhaps? She wasn't sure. She assumed he was loyal, yes, but perhaps that was rather naïve. In fact, she knew almost nothing of her husband's life; he could have intimate dinners with other women three times a week for all she knew.

'Alonzo, please.' Chiara put a gentle hand on his arm. How little things had changed between the sexes after all this time. He would always be in charge. She ran this hotel, but to all intents and purposes, she stayed here – effectively 'at home' – while Alonzo went out into the world, doing whatever business he did, without sharing any part of it with Chiara.

135

And she had accepted that – perhaps because she was aware of how much of herself she also kept from him.

'In the morning then,' he snapped. 'I want you gone first thing.'

Dante raised his dark eyebrows but said nothing.

Chiara took a deep breath. This was awful, but she was relieved that Alonzo had calmed down and that a terrible scene in the hotel dining room had been averted. Damage limitation, she thought, although no doubt the *signoras* would be disappointed. 'That is enough, I think. Perhaps we should all now say goodnight and go upstairs.'

All the pleasure of the evening had evaporated. Alonzo had brought reality back into the room. And perhaps that was a good thing in some ways, because would Chiara have otherwise been strong enough to say goodnight to Dante without a touch of the hand, without even a kiss perhaps? A tremor ran through her body at the thought, and she pushed it from her mind. Either way, she couldn't be sure.

'*Andiamo*, let's go.' Alonzo turned away from them.

Dante nodded. 'Goodnight,' he said stiffly, shooting Chiara an apologetic glance that said an awful lot more.

Alonzo strode away without a further word. Chiara knew she must follow him immediately if she wanted to avoid any more argument. But she also knew there would be more words between them whatever she chose to do now. '*Buona notte*. Goodnight, my friend,' she said softly.

'Chiara – wait.'

She watched Alonzo's retreating back as he left the cloisters through the archway by the bar. She breathed a sigh of relief. But: 'I must go.'

'Will you be all right?' Dante grabbed her hands.

'Of course.' Alonzo had a temper, but he'd never been a violent man. And besides, she had betrayed her husband in her thoughts alone. How could he tell what she'd been thinking? How could anyone?

'Are you sure, *cara*?' Dante let go of her hands, but his voice seemed to caress her.

'Absolutely sure.'

'I am so sorry to have put you in this position. I should not have come here. I should certainly not have persuaded you to have dinner with me. It was wrong of me . . .' He tore his fingers through his hair.

'No.' Chiara met his gaze once more. 'It was my decision to have dinner with you. It was not your fault at all. And you know that I am glad you came here.' Chiara was once more aware of the two elderly women from Milan trying to catch every word. She forced herself to break away. 'I must go,' she said again. She would have to fly up to their rooms or Alonzo would certainly have a lot more to say.

'It has been . . .' For a dangerous and delicious second, he drew her closer, '. . . everything to me,' he whispered.

Everything to me. Chiara shivered. One last look at him, one last touch of his hand, and she walked swiftly away.

Upstairs, Alonzo was pacing the room. 'You make me look like an idiot.'

'You're mistaken.' She took off her earrings. If she acted as if she were innocent, then wouldn't she be innocent – at least as far as Alonzo was concerned? *Nothing has happened*, she whispered to herself. *And tomorrow, he returns to England.*

'And a fool.'

'No.' She took a step closer.

He grabbed her arm. 'Do you still have feelings for him?'

'Of course not.' She pulled away. 'It was forty years ago, Alonzo. And I haven't seen him in all that time.'

His eyes narrowed. He was not convinced. 'So why did he come here?'

'I suppose, just to say "hello".' This sounded unlikely, even to Chiara. 'He was in the area. You know, he lives in England now.' How chatty she sounded, how unconcerned. When in reality her belly was churning – with anxiety, with regret.

'But he has been here for several days.' He followed her into the white marble bathroom.

'Only two or three,' she corrected him. Three days that had disappeared much too fast. She had wasted the opportunities. But how could she have done otherwise? However she felt about Alonzo, however empty their marriage, however little they shared, he was still her husband.

'But in those three days you have been meeting with him, *sì?*'

Chiara realised with a lurch of apprehension why Alonzo had returned so suddenly and with no warning. Elene must have phoned him. She had seen them in the Cloisters Bar. Perhaps she had even seen them tonight? It wouldn't have taken long for Alonzo to return from Pisa. Elene must have called her father and told him that something was going on. Alonzo had come here in order to catch them out. Chiara felt an ache of disappointment, of sadness. She couldn't blame her – he was her father after all. But, oh, Elene.

'Well?'

'A few conversations.' She shrugged. 'Dante had many people he wanted to see. I was just one of them.' And that was all it was, she reminded herself. Just talking. That was what had spun her back into the past. That, and the way he touched her hand . . .

'A few conversations . . .' he mimicked. 'That dinner tonight looked like much more than conversation.'

'Not at all.' The bathroom was making her feel claustrophobic. Alonzo was making her feel claustrophobic. She began to take off her make-up with a cotton-wool pad and cleanser. Her face looked garish in the light of the bathroom, shiny and unreal.

'And look at you.'

'What?' He was standing behind her, staring into the mirror. She didn't like the expression on his face.

'You have gone to some effort, I think. A nice dress, high heels, a little more eye make-up than usual, hmm?'

'Not really.' She must keep calm. Chiara finished washing her face and went back into the bedroom.

He followed her. 'In fact, you look like a whore.'

'Alonzo!' She was shocked.

'Did he touch you?'

'No!'

'Did you—'

'No.'

He was glaring at her now, and there was a cold light in his eyes. She turned away so that she didn't have to see the hatred there. It was worse than she had let herself believe, she thought now. Their marriage was a sham.

'And how much did you have to drink, eh?'

Chiara sat down on the bed. She must take off these shoes. She must regain some balance. She glanced up at him. He seemed to tower over her. He was scaring her. But what right did he have to cross-question her like this? 'You want to limit my alcohol intake now, is that it?' she snapped.

'When you are drinking with an old lover, sì.' His words were measured.

139

'He's not . . .' She should tell him that Dante was not an old lover. She should tell him that although they had been in love, they had never *made* love. They had been so young, they had been together for such a short time. But, she would have. Chiara remembered how she had felt when Dante had come to her in the olive grove at night. How he had kissed her breasts and she had held him so close that he had felt a part of her. It wouldn't have taken much. One word from him, one of his deep kisses and, regardless of her parents, her age, the morals that had been pounded into her since she could remember – she would have.

'You don't have to tell me the details,' he sneered. 'I don't want to know.'

'There is nothing to say.' Chiara sat up straighter. 'Nothing happened between us. Besides, we were only children back then. We—'

'It is written on your face, my love,' he spat.

Chiara sighed. It was hopeless, she realised. But, 'Why should you care, Alonzo?' The wine finally seemed to give her more fire in her belly. 'It was long before you and I were married.' She got to her feet and approached him. 'And now? You are hardly ever here. You don't tell me anything that is happening in your life. We have a daughter together, and yet we may as well be strangers. You stay in Pisa and who knows what goes on there—'

He slapped her face. Chiara was so shocked that for a moment she felt nothing. Then the sharp sting penetrated her senses. She put her hand to her cheek, stared at him. He had never hit her before, never so much as raised his hand. But then again, she had never defied him like this before, she had never given him reason.

He stared back at her. 'I apologise.' But he still looked defiant. 'It is him – Dante Rossi – I've always known you loved him.' He raised his hand again and she flinched. He sighed. 'Don't deny it, Chiara, *per favore*. I always knew you married me only to please your parents. And so . . .'

'And so?' She held her back stiff and upright, her face still smarting from his slap. She could hardly believe that he had done it, and yet her cheek felt swollen and sore under her fingertips.

'And so, I've always hated the bastard.' He turned again to face her. 'For God's sake, tell me, Chiara. What was it he gave you that I could not?'

She lowered her eyes but remained silent. This was her chance to be honest, to be authentic, to be true to herself. But how could she possibly answer that question? 'Nothing,' she whispered.

'I've always wondered what would happen if he came back . . .' And she thought she could hear the fear in his voice.

'Still – after forty years?' And yet he was right to be afraid. He had sensed it in her. And perhaps Elene had sensed it too.

'Even now,' he confirmed. 'Seeing you with him, smiling at him, your eyes just glowing . . .' His voice trailed. 'Have you ever smiled at me that way?'

In truth, Chiara could not recall. She was deeply ashamed. She should have worked harder at her marriage, she should have ensured that Alonzo never felt second best. But he had always seemed so cold, so distant, even in those early days. She had tried to love him, but there had never seemed to be enough to hold on to. And when he started to go away so much . . . It had become easier to play the part, to pretend that all was well. 'Then I am sorry too.' But he shouldn't have slapped her. He should never have slapped her.

She thought of Dante. How sour the evening had become. How much bitterness could be produced by something that had belonged so firmly in the past? And now?

'Tomorrow morning, I have a meeting in the city.' Alonzo spoke almost as if nothing had occurred between them. 'I would not have returned tonight had it not been for this.'

She nodded. 'And so you must leave early.'

'Yes.' He paused. 'I will trust that you will not try to see him. That you will stay out of the way until he has left.'

'Of course,' she muttered. For God's sake – she would have a bruise on her face. She wouldn't want to see anyone tomorrow.

'The following day I will be back here. I hope we will never have to speak of this again.'

Never speak of it again? Chiara was stunned. She watched him go into the bathroom, heard the tap running as he washed his face, cleaned his teeth, and she continued to watch him as, seemingly oblivious to her, he stripped off his clothes and got ready for bed. At last, feeling weary, she followed suit.

But she lay awake for hours, thinking about what had happened. Alonzo's property interests in Pisa couldn't take up so much of his time. So what did he do there? Why did he spend so much time away? She had always assumed he didn't want to be with her. He was not a demanding man in the bedroom. So perhaps he did have lovers? It wasn't just a case of being naïve – Chiara had never wanted to know. Their marriage had been unsatisfactory in so many ways. This was just one of them. And now? It seemed that Alonzo's moment of honesty was over, that he was prepared to continue as if nothing out of the ordinary had occurred, to go on just as before. Chiara glanced across to the other side of the bed. He was sleeping peacefully, snoring lightly.

Clearly, Alonzo could put it all behind him. She touched her face once more. But the question was – could she?

CHAPTER 15

Isabella

The following morning, Isabella was at the front door of The Lemon Tree Hotel chatting to the Signoras Veroni; the two women of seventy-something almost didn't seem like guests, they had returned so often.

'And how is your dear grandmother this morning?' the taller sister, Antonia, was asking. 'We were quite concerned . . .' She fanned herself rather theatrically with the map of Monterosso that she happened to be holding.

'Concerned?' Isabella spotted Ferdinand Bauer loitering at the edge of the olive grove. She'd been meaning to catch him. There was something she wanted to ask . . . But she forced her attention back to the two sisters. 'Why would you be concerned, ladies? I'm sure that Nonna is fine.' Though, hadn't she been thinking the exact same thing these past few days? Isabella frowned. Had something happened last night?

'I'm sure she is, my dear.' The younger sister, Caprice, caught Antonia's arm. 'And we are not the kind of people who gossip, as you know.'

Isabella folded her arms. Ferdinand must be coming from the olive grove towards the hotel otherwise she would have seen him leave the lobby. Where had he been? Down to the village perhaps for an early morning stroll? Or . . . She glanced at her watch. It wasn't even ten o'clock. 'Gossip?' she echoed. 'What about?'

Antonia's old eyes were bright with mischief. 'We saw her having dinner last night with such a nice man,' she said. 'And we couldn't avoid hearing little snatches of the conversation, you know how it is.'

They were so naughty – like a couple of mischievous school-girls. 'My grandmother has many friends here in the Levante,' she told them. Though she couldn't think who it could be. Their family were wedded to The Lemon Tree, and running a busy hotel tended to make social events hard to organise. They all had friends, yes, but mostly they socialised in the winter months when things were a lot quieter.

'It was a man who is staying at the hotel,' Caprice supplied. 'A guest. We have spoken to him. Very well turned out. Italian, of course. From around these parts.' She made a gesture that encompassed the landscape around them.

So that was it. 'Signor Bianchi,' Isabella supplied. Or was it Rossi? She had to admit to being slightly confused herself. 'He's a friend of Nonna's. A very old friend, I believe.'

'Ah, sì, sì, an old friend, that would be it,' said Antonia. 'Though not a friend of your grandfather's I'm guessing.'

What on earth were this pair suggesting? Isabella giggled – she could hardly take it seriously. 'Now, that I couldn't say. My grandfather is away at the moment – he has a business in Pisa, and—'

'Oh, but we saw him.' Antonia's eyes widened. 'Last night and again this morning, rather early.'

'Oh really? He must be back then.'

'Antonia is merely jealous, my dear.' Once again Caprice caught at her sister's arm. 'She has been coming here for thirty years to find a husband. And still she has no success. How much longer do you think she will hold out hope for, eh?'

This was a longstanding joke, and so Isabella laughed politely. 'It's never too late,' she said.

'Hmm, and then your grandmother has two men fighting over her. *Magari*! Chance is a fine thing, eh? She is a lucky woman.'

Two men? Fighting over her? These two must have both lost their marbles. Isabella shook her head as Antonia eventually gave in and they headed off down the drive towards the front gate. '*Ciao*, my dear,' they called.

'Have a good day.' Isabella waved them off. What a strange couple they were. Nevertheless, she decided to have a little chat with Nonna this morning – just in case something was amiss. She had been quite disconcerted when Nonna put her head around the office door yesterday and asked about Ferdinand.

'He seems a nice man.' She had come in and sat down on the edge of the desk. 'I hope you don't mind me asking, Bella, but I saw you talking to him earlier and I just wondered . . .'

As usual, Isabella had jumped at the chance of confiding in her grandmother. 'Nonna, the strangest thing happened . . .' And she told her about the encounter between Ferdinand and their Aunt Giovanna.

But her grandmother frowned. 'Do you know anything about his background, darling?' she asked.

'No.' Apart from the fact that he was apparently a freelance architect based in Germany, Isabella knew nothing about him at all.

'It's possible . . .' She hesitated.

'What, Nonna?' Isabella leaned closer.

'I was thinking that perhaps he has a relative who has been to Vernazza in the past.' She seemed to speak reluctantly. 'If you get my drift, Bella.'

'You mean . . .' She could only mean one thing. That Ferdinand Bauer was so interested in the old convent and in Vernazza because one of his relatives had lived here, been part of the Occupation of their town during the war. 'But that's—'

'Unlikely, yes.' She shrugged. 'And perhaps I am wrong.'

'And of course, the war has been over for a very long time, Nonna,' Isabella reminded her. 'We welcome all international visitors here, do we not? We are all Europeans now.'

'You're right, of course.' She nodded. 'But perhaps you should ask him why he is so interested in the old convent, Bella.'

'Oh, it is nothing to me.' What did she care one way or another? It was only her aunt Giovanna that she was concerned about.

'Is that so?' Her grandmother arched an eyebrow.

'Of course.' Isabella got to her feet. She tossed back her hair and ignored her grandmother's unsubtle implication. She should be getting on. She must take over reception duties from Marco and get some emails sent.

'Even so, you should take care, my darling.' Her grandmother's voice became very serious all of a sudden, and Isabella had stopped in her tracks.

'Why, Nonna?'

'Because there is always a reason for everything – and your Ferdinand Bauer may not be exactly what he seems.'

Meanwhile, that same Ferdinand Bauer was now walking out of the olive grove, and so she went over to meet him. At the edge of the grove, the sunlight dappled the gravel path and veined the leaves of the olive trees with gold.

'Isabella!' He seemed surprised to see her – though why this should be so, she couldn't imagine; she lived here after all.

'Good morning, Ferdinand. You're up and about early this morning.' The path was a cut-through to the *Sentiero Azzurro* – which led either up to Corniglia or down to Vernazza – but of course it also led to Giovanna's cottage. Isabella considered this. He wouldn't have gone back to see Giovanna again – would he?

'Oh, yes . . .' He shrugged. 'You have such picturesque grounds here. How can your guests resist exploring a little?' Was it her imagination or was there a glint of guilt in the expression of those blue eyes?

'Exploring?' Isabella put her hands on her hips and faced him. 'So, you have not been back to visit my Aunt Giovanna?'

'Isn't that allowed?' he parried. 'Didn't you say no rules or regulations?'

'Of course, it is allowed . . . If she wishes it.' Isabella knew he was teasing her. Why shouldn't he visit her aunt again? It was surprising – he'd only just seen her, and surely he'd had plenty of opportunity to find out everything he might want to know. Besides, why should a young man like Ferdinand be drawn to an old lady like Giovanna in the first place? But . . .

'It bothers you though?' He put his head to one side.

'No . . .' Why should it? She'd introduced them after all. But that was before her grandmother had pointed out a possible connection between a member of Ferdinand's family and the occupation of Vernazza during the war. 'But I don't want you to upset her.' She tried to look stern. 'She's old. We are responsible for her welfare. She doesn't really know you, and—' Neither did Isabella. She remembered her grandmother's words. *He may not be what he seems.*

'Isabella . . .' He took a step closer. 'I wouldn't dream of upsetting her. I like Giovanna, and I respect her too. She's a lovely lady.'

'Yes.' She looked up at him. In the light of the sun shimmering through the grey-green leaves of the olive trees, his eyes were almost translucent. 'She is.'

'I'm sorry.' He raised his hands. 'Perhaps I should have said something to you first.'

'You should.' Because he was right. She didn't like the fact that he'd sneaked off to see Giovanna again behind her back. After what her grandmother had said, she almost wished she hadn't introduced them at all.

'But she did tell me to call on her any time.'

'She did?' Isabella frowned. Why would Giovanna have said that – especially if it turned out he was related to her old enemy?

'You find it strange?' He touched her arm, the lightest of touches.

'No. Well, yes, a bit.' Isabella was certainly confused.

'Trust me.' He leaned a few centimetres closer still. 'It's nothing to worry about. We were talking – that's all.'

Through the trees she saw a couple arrive at the front door. New guests. She must go and greet them. 'Sorry,' she said. 'I have to go.'

He nodded. 'But do you ever get a day off?'

Isabella turned back to him. 'Day off?' she echoed.

'Or doesn't that happen with a family-run hotel?'

She noticed how the sunlight filtering through the leaves was glancing off the blond of his hair, turning it almost green-gold. 'Yes, it does.' She smiled. 'My grandmother insists on it. Plenty of time off and a flexible rota. There's no point otherwise, she says.'

'Very wise.' He was leaning against the trunk of a large and wizened olive tree, watching her lazily. He looked like some other-worldly woodland creature. 'So, when's yours?'

'Tomorrow,' she said, without thinking.

'Excellent.' He stood up straighter. 'Then would you come out with me?'

Isabella looked over to the hotel entrance. She just hoped that her grandmother or someone was around to take care of the new arrivals. 'I really must—'

'Would you?'

'But you're a guest.'

He laughed and revealed those dimples again. 'Is that another rule?'

'No.' She didn't laugh with him. He was teasing her – again.

He caught hold of her arm. 'Please, Isabella? Would you show me one of your favourite places?'

Why was he asking her this? After all, he would be gone in a week or so, and she would never see him again. What was the point? 'I've got things to do,' she hedged.

'Better things than go out for the day with a troublesome guest?' He pulled a face. 'Can't say I blame you.' His eyes gleamed. 'But it could be fun.'

She hesitated. It would at least give her a chance to ask him why he had come to Vernazza; she might even be able find out if Nonna was right. And she had to admit, she enjoyed talking with him. Yes, it could be fun. 'We could go to Sestri Levante,' she said. 'It's a real town. Some say that the *Baia del Silenzio*, the Bay of Silence east of the old town is the most beautiful beach on the Riviera Ligure di Levante.'

He beamed. 'It sounds perfect.'

'And now . . .'

'You have to go, I know. See you later, Isabella.'

She gave him a small smile. 'See you later.' She hurried back inside.

Fortunately, Marco had come through to look after the guests and was handing them their room key.

Isabella took her place behind the reception desk and smiled at the new arrivals. 'We hope you will enjoy your stay,' she told them.

Was she mad? Her grandmother had told her to take care where Ferdinand Bauer was concerned, and now she had agreed to go out with him for the day. So yes, she thought, she probably was.

CHAPTER 16

Chiara

Alonzo had left first thing that morning and Chiara stayed tucked away in the office for most of the day, pleading a headache and arranging that Marco would cover her reception duties. Although she had disguised the livid mark on her cheek with a careful blend of foundation, Chiara wanted to see as few people as possible. She felt bruised and raw – and not just from that slap. The shock of it seemed to have penetrated to her inner core. Of course, things were not right between her and Alonzo; *Madonna santa*, they had never been right, but she had never thought that he would strike her.

As for Elene – Chiara guessed that her daughter was equally keen to avoid her. She would know that her father had returned, she might have heard that there had been words between them, but she would not know of his violence – not if Chiara had anything to do with it. Elene had called him back here – but she didn't need to know what had taken place.

Most of all, she didn't want to see Dante – she was deeply

ashamed. She would stay well away from the public areas of the hotel, she decided, and by the time she emerged, he would be long gone. *And she would never see him again . . .* She pushed this thought away. It was a necessary sacrifice. She had no choice. And she must not torture herself with thoughts of what might have been.

Isabella popped in to bring her a cool drink of lemonade. 'Do you still have that headache, Nonna?'

Chiara kept her head down. 'I'm afraid so, my dear.' She was keeping the light dim and the blinds half drawn.

'Would you like me to get you something for it?'

'No, no, thank you, but this is lovely.' Chiara gestured towards the glass of lemonade. She glanced at Isabella, who seemed temporarily lost in another of those daydreams of hers. It was fortunate that her granddaughter had other things on her mind today, though Chiara suspected that unfortunately, those things were connected with their guest, the Signor Ferdinand Bauer.

'Nonna.' Isabella suddenly seemed to wake up.

'Yes, Bella?' Chiara put her hand up to shield her face. Had she noticed the mark on her cheek?

'Did my grandfather come back here last night?'

Oh, dear. What had she heard? Of course, people would always talk, and although they had averted a scene, it had still been dramatic enough. 'Yes, he did.' She tried to remain calm. 'Just briefly, to collect a few things for a business meeting. He's gone back to Pisa, but he'll return tomorrow.'

'Right.' Isabella clearly wanted to say more. 'And did anything happen?'

'Happen?' If only she knew. Chiara's entire body seemed to ache from what had happened – and not happened.

153

'Oh, nothing, really, just ignore me.' Isabella slumped on to her chair looking suddenly dejected.

'Bella? Is anything wrong?' For a moment Chiara forgot about her own troubles.

'Oh, it's just . . .' Isabella bit her lip. 'It's nothing.'

Chiara shook her head. Really there was an awful lot of nothing going on in the hotel today. 'Have you seen Giovanna since the other day?' She tried to keep her voice casual. She would go to see her herself if she weren't so concerned that in the daylight the old lady's sharp eyes might notice the bruise she'd tried to conceal on her cheek.

Isabella gave a little start. 'No, I haven't. Do you think I should?'

'Perhaps it is an idea . . .' Had it been wise to take the young man there in the first place? Chiara didn't think so – and if she'd known of Isabella's plans, she would have questioned it. 'Just in case . . .' she added.

'In case?' Isabella blushed.

'I worry about her, Bella,' she admitted. Giovanna's closeness to her parents made Chiara feel responsible for her aunt. How had she dealt with the encounter with this young man? How had it affected her? Isabella had insisted they'd got along well, but what if Giovanna was simply being polite?

'I'll call around there later.' Isabella gave another start when her mobile beeped in a message and as she pulled it out of her pocket, a slightly crumpled business card fell out too. She blushed even more as she bent to pick it up, smoothed it between her fingertips, and replaced it in her pocket.

Chiara raised her eyebrows. 'Thank you, darling.' Was it really possible, as she'd already mentioned to Isabella, that the Signor Bauer was related to someone who had been part of

154

the terrible Occupation of their town? Even someone who had committed atrocities here during the war? Chiara shuddered. She hoped not. It would explain his interest though. Isabella was right and, naturally, they were all European now. But some people had long memories, and it was hard to shake off the thought of what her father and the other Partisans had suffered at the hands of those men.

Not that it would be Signor Bauer's fault – no, not at all. But what about that look in Isabella's eyes when she talked of him? That message was probably from him too, judging by the secret little smile on her granddaughter's lovely face. And she was very jumpy. It wasn't good to develop a crush on a guest – not good at all. Guests came and went; they were on holiday, they could not be relied on. But then again – who could?

Chiara did not emerge from the office until past six o'clock. She glanced through to the Cloisters Bar, and there he was. Dante. Her eyes widened in surprise.

'Chiara!' He had seen her, and was on his feet already.

'Dante! I thought you were leaving this morning . . .' She broke off. She'd felt such a dull ache of disappointment all day. Dante had left, and under such a dark cloud, that she'd been convinced she'd never see him again. It would be just like before. He would go back to England and take all her dreams with him. But now . . . It was ridiculous, but at this moment, despite everything, she felt like a young girl again.

'I was told by your husband to leave this morning,' he corrected her with a wry grimace. 'But I thought I'd take my chances and stay another night.'

'Why?' Mindful of the mark on her face, Chiara stepped back a little so that they were standing in the shadows. There

155

was nothing to be gained by seeing Dante just one more time, but she couldn't help being glad.

'Because I was worried about you. Because I wanted to see you before I left.' He frowned, took a step closer. 'But you have been hiding away all day, and I didn't want to draw attention—'

'I am fine.' She glanced down at the floor. It was too hard to look at him and lie. And she didn't want him to see . . . But she could hardly help her heart leaping. This man cared for her, really cared. It was too late now, of course. But how foolish she had been all those years ago, to throw something like that away.

'But, surely . . .' He was very close now. He bent his head, examining her face.

Chiara looked up.

He ran his fingertips so gently across her cheek.

She winced.

Dante looked very serious now. 'Did he . . . Did he *hit* you?' She heard the disbelief in his voice.

'Ssh.' Chiara glanced around. They were not alone. There were a few guests in the Cloisters Bar on the other side of the arch, including the young Australian couple, and Isabella was still working on reception, chatting to some new arrivals and handing them their room key.

He swore under his breath. 'We must talk.'

'Not here.'

'Can we go somewhere private? Is he around?' He sounded controlled. But she could see it in his face and she could feel it – a white-hot anger. She'd seen him this angry once before. The night he'd walked away from her in the olive grove forty years before.

'Alonzo? No.' She shook her head, put a restraining hand

on his arm. 'He will be back tomorrow. But you must not . . .' Her voice trailed at the expression in those dark eyes. '. . . Do anything foolish,' she murmured.

'Will you come to my room?'

The words were spoken so softly, but they seemed to spin in her head, making her dizzy. She fought for composure. '*Certo*, I cannot.'

'Where then?'

She caught the urgency in his voice. She thought quickly. They couldn't talk in her rooms – what if Alonzo should return unexpectedly? Where else was there? This was a hotel – there were guests everywhere. The olive grove? That was far too risky. And what if Elene should see them again in any of the more obvious public places? She sighed. And yet she wanted to talk to him. Just for a few minutes. Just to say goodbye. '*Va bene* – your room then.'

'Fourteen. Come as soon as you can.'

A few minutes later, Chiara slipped along the upper corridor before she could doubt her own wisdom or question why she was doing this. She tapped softly on the door and went straight in.

'Chiara.'

All she wanted at that precise moment was for him to hold her, all she wanted was to be in his arms. But he kept his distance. He gestured to the two chairs at the window and she sat down on the nearest one. Thank goodness that one of them had some sense of propriety.

'A glass of wine?'

'Please.' She needed something to fortify her.

Dante poured a glass of white from the bottle in the ice bucket on the table. His movements were measured as he handed her the glass, but she could tell that he was finding it hard to hold back.

He sat down and raised his glass up to hers as if in a silent toast.

Chiara did the same. They did not speak, but his gaze held hers for a long moment, before she broke away and took a sip. The wine slid down her throat – chilled and heady.

Dante put down his glass. He took a deep breath. 'So, he hit you.' He clenched a fist in his palm, and now she could really see the anger flaming in his eyes.

'He has never done it before.' Listen to her, still defending him. Chiara felt the cold dampness of the wine glass seeping into her palms and she put it back on the table.

Instantly, Dante reached forwards and grabbed her hands. 'But don't you see, Chiara? Now that he has done it once, he will do it again.'

'Not necessarily. I provoked him, you know that.' But inside herself, she felt a shadow of foreboding. Was Dante right? Would striking her unleash some further aggression – allow Alonzo to lose whatever inhibitions had held him back this far? She didn't think so. Alonzo was usually so calm, so composed. 'It was seeing you. Knowing . . .' Her voice failed.

'Knowing what?'

'Knowing how much I loved you,' she said simply. 'Knowing that when I married Alonzo, my heart was still yours.' It seemed pointless to lie any more. For he must already be aware of this, and what was there to lose?

Dante's gaze did not leave her face. He kept hold of her hands too. 'And since then?' he asked. 'You have had a good marriage, *si*? You told me that you get along fine.'

She shook her head. 'It wasn't true,' she confessed. She felt that she had to be honest now. 'We've struggled. We don't share our lives. Alonzo is away most of the time. Though it's probably my fault.'

'Your fault?' He let go of her hands and sat back in the chair. 'How could it be your fault?'

There were so many reasons. 'I did not love him enough. I am always busy with the hotel. He always seemed so distant.' And cold, she thought, he always seemed so uncaring and cold. She drank more wine. It was one of her favourites from their cellar and had a boldness in its flavour – a characteristic that apparently came from the high mineral content of their soil and the fresh, salty sea air. Under different circumstances, she would have complimented him on his good taste.

'You have done a wonderful job here, Chiara.' Dante looked around the room.

It was true that everything was tastefully done – she hoped – and it was true that everything ran smoothly at The Lemon Tree and that the hotel was doing well. But . . . Once upon a time it was her sense of responsibility towards the place that had stopped her from running away with him. And now . . . She doubted he appreciated the irony.

'Alonzo says I care more for this hotel than for my own family.'

He clicked his tongue. 'We all have to make sacrifices. This hotel was your legacy.'

'And still is,' she reminded him gently. Just in case he had another agenda on his mind. Alonzo had hit her, yes, Dante still had the same effect on her, certainly, but despite these things, she would survive what had happened and she would put it behind her. She had to. She was not a woman who needed saving.

'Of course.' He sipped his wine and regarded her over the rim of the glass. 'But are you really going to stay with him after this?'

She too picked up her wine glass to give herself time to think. This was what she was ashamed of. 'I am, yes.' She had considered all the options during her sleepless night. And she had come to the conclusion that much of the blame must be laid at her door. 'I am sure it was a one-off incident.'

'Incident? My God, Chiara . . .' He shook his head in disbelief. 'He *hit* you.'

'And there is Elene to consider.' Elene, who was so often angry with her, so often resentful. How could she do something that could only make their relationship worse? Alonzo might not be around for his daughter most of the time, but he was still her father, and they could still at least pretend to offer a united front for her.

Dante sighed. 'How many times, *cara*, must you choose duty and obligation over love?'

Love. She found herself staring at his mouth. 'I should go.' She could imagine the scene if Alonzo were to return early. She could see him frantically searching the hotel for her, becoming more furious by the minute, checking the register, storming into this very room . . .

'I can't let you go until you have answered my question,' he said.

'What question?' Though she knew.

'Are you happy, Chiara?' He gestured towards her bruised face. 'You are such a strong woman – at least I have always thought so. Is this really how you want your life to be?'

She got to her feet. She'd been wrong to come here. She had told herself she simply wanted to say goodbye, but that was not the honest truth. She had been hurt, and she'd wanted comfort. But she was not in a position to accept comfort from this man. 'I don't know the answer,' she confessed. 'You ask me if I am happy – right now, you can see that the answer is "no".' She looked out of the window where the olive trees were shimmering acid-green in the evening light. 'Something bad happened, I can't deny that.' Her voice was low. 'But I have so much to be thankful for – I have told you this and it's true. There are so many things – my daughter, my granddaughter, my work here . . .'

He nodded. 'I understand. But you could leave him and not lose all that, is this not so?'

'My daughter . . .' She shrugged. She simply did not have the energy right now to explain. And besides, with Dante gone, she could manage her half-life with Alonzo. She had given up on love a long time ago.

'You cannot bear for her to suffer?'

'Exactly.'

'So, you will stay with him, even though it might happen again?' He drained his glass.

'It may not be true happiness,' she went on, 'but it's the life I have chosen.' She shot him a final look of regret, turned around, and walked to the door.

'Wait.' He got to his feet and took a step towards her.

Chiara turned back. How close would he have to come before her resolve failed?

'I thought when I saw you again that you would have become some stately matriarch,' he said, 'with children and grandchildren running around your feet.'

She laughed, grateful that the atmosphere between them had lightened. 'I am a grandmother.'

'Yes, you are a grandmother.' He took another step closer. 'But not that sort of a grandmother.' He was within reach of her now and still she did not move away. He ran a fingertip along her cheek, just as he had done downstairs, touching the very place where Alonzo had slapped her. 'You are still a beautiful woman.'

'Dante . . .' Beyond the soreness of her face, she felt the tenderness of his touch. And it was a tenderness she craved.

'I have never forgotten you, Chiara.' He took her so gently into his arms, as if she were some precious thing.

How could she walk away from something so healing, so good? She rested her face – just for a moment – on the curve of his shoulder, and it felt familiar, a perfect fit, almost as if it were a place reserved just for her.

'You are always so brave, so selfless,' he whispered into her hair. 'When will you do something for yourself, hmm?'

'Such as?' She lifted her head and looked into his eyes. They had seen so many different things and yet they were still the same eyes. She and Dante were standing so close to one another that she could smell the faint tang of that citrussy, resinous aftershave that he must have put on this morning; so close that she could feel the heat of him.

'Anything,' he said. 'Anything that you want to do.'

Anything. There was of course, only one thing. But could it ever be just that between them – only one night of love? 'What good would it do, Dante?' she said.

His eyes gleamed in that way they had always gleamed before. 'Why don't we try it out, Chiara, and see?'

And then his lips were on hers and the shudder of longing swept over her and into her, that same shudder she had not felt

162

for forty years. And she kissed him back because she wanted to. She kissed him back with all the love and pain she had felt in her heart for so long.

Why don't we try it out, and see . . .

CHAPTER 17

Chiara

The first thing Chiara was aware of when she awoke, was a feeling of warmth running right through her to the core of her being. She was being held. She took a moment to adjust. This was a new sensation. Alonzo never held her like this through the night. And then it all came back to her. She was with Dante. She was in The Lemon Tree Hotel, but she was in Dante's bed. *Madonna santa . . .*

She couldn't move. For one thing, she was so close to him physically, breathing in the heat and sheen of his skin, that if she moved, she would . . . what? Break the spell? Because it had been magical. Something so longed for, so often imagined and desired. And in the end, even better than she had imagined, because every second had been real. And so, she didn't want to move. She didn't want to wake him, she didn't want this present moment – when everything was still possible – to end.

But it did. Dante shifted sleepily under the duvet and she felt the second when he awoke, when he realised she was there lying next to him, when he went through the same thought process that she had.

'So, you are still here, my love,' he whispered, holding her closer.

'I am still here.' She snuggled in. Though she probably shouldn't be.

'You have not run away.' Gently, he nibbled her earlobe.

She wriggled. 'Not yet.' But she must. There was a faint shaft of light coming through the shutters, falling at an angle on the polished wooden floorboards. It was still early. But it was morning.

'Before you do . . .' He moved closer, she could feel his breath and the roughness of the morning-after stubble of his jaw on her neck, and the desire swept over her again.

His fingers were circling her belly, her hips. His mouth was on her breast. She wanted to arch towards him. 'Dante, I must go.' There were a million reasons why she should get up now. She must get back to her rooms before anyone was up and about, she had to prepare for the day – for heaven's sake, she was supposed to be opening up reception at eight o'clock this morning. She had to think about what she had done and what exactly she should do now. Alonzo. She had betrayed Alonzo with hardly a second thought. She closed her eyes. What was happening to her?

But there was one good reason to stay just a little longer. And as he caressed her, as he kissed her, as he held her and they made love – even more tenderly than they had done last night, when each motion and each caress had been filled with the urgency and passion of forty years of waiting . . . that became the only reason that mattered.

Afterwards, he held her close and stroked her hair. 'You know that I love you, Chiara?'

'Yes.' She had no doubts. 'And I love you too, Dante.' If only she had known forty years ago what it would be like to lose him. If only she had known that theirs was a love that would not fade away . . . She couldn't blame her parents. Chiara had been so young; they weren't to know it was so much more than a childish infatuation – no one was to know that. Chiara suspected that back then, Dante was the only one who had known for sure.

'But . . .?' He raised a dark eyebrow as she slipped out of bed.

Embarrassed at her nakedness, she grabbed the soft white towelling bathrobe the hotel provided for their guests and wrapped herself up in it. She glanced at the clock radio on the bedside table. 'No time for "buts" now,' she told him. 'I'm on duty in less than an hour.' She began searching for her clothes, which had somehow ended up all over the room. Her dress was flung across the chair, her bra was hanging on the doorknob, her knickers half-hidden by the coverlet, were on the floor under the bed. It was too late for blushes. She was fifty-nine years old. Up until now she had only ever slept with one man – Alonzo. Only ever loved one man – Dante. And now this.

'Ah, duty . . .' He rolled his eyes and continued to survey her from his recumbent position, arms folded behind his head. A thought seemed to occur to him. 'Do you regret it, *cara*?'

She turned from her clothes retrieval to see the concern in his dark eyes. 'No, my love.' She scurried into the bathroom to get dressed. 'How could I?' she called out as she pulled the door half closed behind her. It hadn't felt wrong. It hadn't felt a sin. She had always felt he was her destiny, had she not? She was a married woman, and she had never dreamed that she would be capable of such a thing. But, in fact, nothing in her life had ever felt quite so right.

'Then you can't just leave my bed as if it meant nothing.' But she caught his tone – he was half-joking, half not.

She poked her head back around the door. 'It meant everything.'

'*Bene*. That's good. I'm glad to hear it.' He grinned.

She pushed it from her mind – that 'but', and retreated once more. She pulled on her underwear, and when she was half decent, she opened the door wider again. He was at least sitting up in bed now. And he looked so inviting, his body still in such good shape, she found herself thinking, that she almost leapt back in there again. She remembered what he had said after their dinner the other night. *This means everything . . .* And now she had said it too. She opened her mouth to speak.

'I know, I know,' he spoke before she had the chance. 'I can't ask anything of you.' He swung his body out of bed and stood up.

Chiara suddenly felt short of breath. She returned to the bathroom, looking around the marble wash-stand for mouthwash, toothpaste, something to freshen her mouth until she could get downstairs, have a shower and clean her teeth. The morning after – she had never experienced this kind of thing before; suddenly in the harsh light of day there were so many more unanswered questions, so many doubts, pragmatism seemed to overtake romance and was determined to have its say.

Stark naked, Dante followed her into the bathroom and stood behind her at the basin. It was most unsettling.

'I know you have told me how you feel – about your hotel, about your family – as if I don't already know all these things.' She saw him catch sight of his own reflection in the mirror and smiled as he automatically ran his fingers through his thick, silvery hair. 'Even so . . .'

167

'Even so.' She turned and gave him a minty kiss. She couldn't think about it now. One thing at a time.

'After this, I feel as if I can't lose you.' He tucked her hair behind one ear. Kissed her nose. 'Not again. That's all.'

This was what they would be like, she realised, if they were together. And it hurt to think of it, because it was just so nice. 'I know.' She felt the same. How could it be only one night? Neither of them would be interested in any sort of illicit affair, and anyway, they lived in different countries, for heaven's sake. It was all or nothing. Chiara had always known that.

'We can do it, Chiara.' His voice became urgent. His hands were on her shoulders. His brown eyes were pulling her into the world of their possible future together. 'This could be our second chance.'

'How?' she whispered. She wanted to believe it, so much she wanted to believe it.

'I can deal with Alonzo,' he said.

'Oh, no doubt.' She laughed as she slipped from his hold. It was incredible that she was laughing about it. But she felt joyous. This man had made her feel joyous. She turned around and waggled a finger at him. 'But there won't be any of that macho stuff – whatever happens.'

'And what will happen?' He was suddenly serious again. Serious, and still, disconcertingly, naked.

'I don't know.' She slipped her dress over her head and grabbed her bag.

'Chiara . . .'

Her hand was on the doorknob. 'I must go,' she said again.

He grabbed hold of her again, kissed her, long and slow. 'Come back later to talk,' he said.

'I'll try.' She nuzzled briefly into his warm shoulder. Shocked herself by putting a hand on his bottom.

'You must.' He didn't need to say what she already knew – that he was supposed to be leaving today, that Alonzo was returning, that decisions must be made.

Dante had played his trump card though. How could she leave him now?

She was walking on air as she crept out of Dante's room and along the corridor towards her own suite. Not a sound could be heard. It was still early enough. No one was around.

Could it work out? Was it possible that against all the odds she could make a future with this man? That he could be that future as well as her past? She couldn't help smiling at the thought. It had to be possible. She felt as if a burden had been thrown from her shoulders. She had to make it happen somehow. She had to be with him. He had made her come alive.

'Mamma?'

Chiara hadn't even seen Elene standing in the shadows by the top of the stairs. She jumped. What was she doing up so early? And more to the point – why would she think her mother was creeping along the corridor from the guest rooms at this time in the morning, in the dress she was wearing yesterday, and with not a scrap of make-up on? The walk of shame. She understood it for the first time.

Chiara straightened her back. This was it then. It had happened sooner than she had expected. It was time to return to reality.

CHAPTER 18

Chiara

What would be, would be. Chiara was her own person. She would deal with this with dignity, if it killed her. 'Good morning, Elene.' She tried a smile.

Elene did not smile back. 'I came to see you last night after dinner, Mamma.' Her voice was measured, accusing. 'But you weren't in your rooms.'

Not like this, thought Chiara, not like this. She hadn't even had time to think. 'Come along there now,' she said. 'I need to—' *Shower and change and stop looking as if I have just got out of another man's bed . . .*

'I waited, Mamma. I waited a long time.' Elene's eyes were cool and distant.

Chiara remained silent. What could she say in her defence? There was no defence. If Elene knew, then she knew. *Allora –* perhaps Chiara's decision was going to be made for her after all. Because if Elene told Alonzo what she had clearly worked out for herself, then Chiara wouldn't have to end her marriage – Alonzo would do it for her.

'And then . . .' Elene paused. 'I came back this morning and you still weren't there.' Her gaze shifted.

She stared back along the corridor to the guest rooms where even now Dante was probably in the shower, maybe humming or whistling to himself as he replayed the events of last night and this morning in his head.

'Come with me, Elene.' Whatever she had done, Chiara was not prepared to stand here in the corridor any longer. Guests would be waking up, getting up, going out for a morning stroll perhaps. She needed to get washed and changed. And one thing she was sure of – this conversation was not going to take place in front of an audience. She moved purposefully towards her own suite. Thankfully, Elene followed her, though at a distance.

When they got to the door that led to her rooms, Chiara turned to her daughter once more. 'Why did you want to see me?' Though she wasn't sure it even mattered now.

'I wanted to apologise.' Elene stood straight, tall, and rather intimidating, it had to be said. No one ever warned you that your small child, dependent on you for all things, could end up looking at you this way.

'What for?' Chiara groped in her bag for her key. She found it and let them in.

'I wanted to tell you that it was me who called Papà.' She flashed Chiara a look of pure defiance as the door swung shut behind them.

'Oh, Elene. I guessed.' And in truth, it felt like such a long time ago now. Since then, Chiara's world had spun on its axis and deposited her in what felt like another lifetime.

'So, what happened?' Elene remained by the doorway as if she might need to make her escape. 'Where is Papà now?' For a second, a flicker of vulnerability showed in her eyes, but then it disappeared even more quickly than it had come.

'He had a business meeting back in Pisa.' She wouldn't go into details. 'Elene—' She stepped towards her. Elene flinched and Chiara hesitated, just as she always did when her daughter put up the barriers.

'And so you went to *him*?' Elene's icy gaze was unforgiving.

Chiara surveyed her daughter. How would she respond if she knew the truth, the whole truth? Would she blame her mother for seeking love? Probably. 'Yes,' she said. 'I went to him.'

'For God's sake . . .' Elene's voice dripped scorn. If anything, she held herself even more erect, her back ramrod stiff. 'You know, when I phoned Papà I felt guilty. I didn't want to get you into trouble. I wasn't sure what was going on, or even if anything was going on, I just wanted it to stop . . .'

'Elene . . .' Another step closer.

'But I can see now that I was right to call him.'

Chiara took in her daughter's expression. There was no doubt what she was thinking, what she was feeling – that her mother was little more than a common whore.

She had to summon up every gram of self-assurance she possessed. 'Elene, I know how hurt you are. I know you're upset.' Deep breath. 'But I'm your mother,' she said. 'You think that you can talk to me exactly as you please. But I'm also a grown woman. You might want to judge me – that's your prerogative. But you don't know the full situation. And if you would just let me explain . . .'

'What is there to explain?' Elene's lip curled as she looked her mother up and down. 'Isn't it embarrassingly obvious, Mamma?'

Chiara supposed that it was. And perhaps Elene was right – there was nothing to explain. She had slept with another man, she had betrayed her husband and her daughter too. Dante might be the man she loved, but she was not free to love him back. She had got carried away, and Elene was quite right – it was unforgiveable.

'And what about Papà? How could you deceive him like this?'

Chiara took a deep breath. 'Your father and I . . .' But how could she even begin to tell Elene about their marriage? How her father had become a stranger? 'We have grown apart.' It was all she could say, but it wasn't nearly enough.

'Maybe you should inform Papà of that fact before you go to bed with some old flame.'

'Elene . . .' Had she honestly believed that her parents had a happy marriage? Hadn't she ever sensed the distance between them that had always seemed so obvious to Chiara? She guessed that sons and daughters saw what they wanted to see – they could hide their heads in the sand if necessary, anything to preserve the illusion that their parents were what they needed and wanted them to be.

Elene took a step closer. She folded her arms and narrowed her eyes. 'And he likes it rough, does he – this Dante Rossi?'

'What?' Chiara realised Elene was staring at her face. She put a hand to her cheek. 'No, he does not.'

'Then what did you do, Mamma? Walk into a door?'

Oh, my God, she had almost forgotten about that. 'Yes.' She stared her out. 'I walked into a door.' Because how could she tell her the truth?

Elene's eyes filled, and she burst into tears.

For a moment, Chiara simply gazed at her, horrified. Elene

never cried – she was the poised, cool, practical one – until she flew into a rage, that was.

Then she opened her arms and, after a moment's hesitation, Elene walked into them. 'I'm sorry, darling,' Chiara whispered. And she stroked her hair and held her close until slowly the shaking subsided and her tears became a sniff, a gulp, a sigh. Oh, Elene.

'What will you do?' her daughter asked at last.

'I don't know.' But this was the fall-out, Chiara realised. She had spent the night with Dante, not considering the consequences, allowing herself to be swept away by the moment, by her own longing, her own dreams. She had failed to consider the feelings of those she was responsible for. But there were always consequences. Always a price to pay.

'Please don't leave us.' It was little more than a whisper and, for a moment, Chiara thought that she must have misunderstood. She'd never heard her daughter sound so sad, so vulnerable, so childlike.

'There.' She stroked her hair some more. 'There, my darling.'

Elene drew away. Her eyes were red and her face streaked with tears. Chiara felt her emotions twist inside her. This was Chiara's chance to change her life, her last chance of true happiness perhaps. And already she could see it dissolving in front of her.

Elene took a hiccupy breath. 'I know that you and I have different ideas about how the hotel should be run, Mamma, and how things should change. I know that we have our differences. I know that Papà goes away a lot, but—'

'I won't leave.' Chiara could bear it no longer. She would not put her daughter though this. And besides, how could she leave? Her parents had built The Lemon Tree Hotel up from nothing. Dante was right. It was her legacy and her responsibility.

'And Papà? Will you leave Papà?'

There was very little Elene had ever asked for. As a young girl she had been so independent, so sure of what she wanted. Chiara had often wanted her to ask for more, but she never had.

But now there was Dante, and she had asked for the most important thing of all.

'People grow apart, Elene,' she said gently. 'You know that. People who think they will stay together for ever, suddenly realise that they have nothing in common any longer. It's life. It happens.'

'But you have things in common.' Elene lifted her tear-stained face. She looked like a young child again. 'You have the hotel and you have me – and Isabella. We are the life that you share.'

'Yes, you are and we do.' Chiara pulled her daughter back in to her arms and stroked her hair some more. She could remember her own mother doing this to her, she knew how soothing it could be.

'Please don't leave Papà. He loves you. I know he does. He needs you even though he sometimes pretends not to care. Please don't leave him.' Elene's voice was small, but desperate too.

Chiara could have coped with anger, with coldness, with anything really, but this. Once again, she was torn between love and duty. Once again, she knew that whatever she decided, a part of her would be gone. She had waited for so long for her daughter to come to her with affection, and now at last she had. She thought of how Elene adored her father, how little she had ever asked for. 'Ssh now,' she told her daughter. How could she deny her this? 'I won't leave Papà. And I won't leave the hotel – of course I won't.'

The decision was made. What else could she do? Her first loyalty was to Elene. Otherwise, what sort of a mother would she be?

But she felt the bitter disappointment rise in her throat like bile. She would have to tell Dante straightaway – he must leave before Alonzo returned. And once again, the decision was made and she must learn to live without him.

CHAPTER 19

Isabella

'It is rather unusual,' Isabella said to Ferdinand Bauer, sneaking a look at him from under her lashes, 'for any tourist to come and stay in Vernazza for more than a week.' This was her opening gambit. She had more lined up to follow. Because Isabella was determined to find out why he had come to the Cinque Terre – and what he was up to while he was here.

She'd had such a lovely day that she was in danger of forgetting that Ferdinand Bauer was just a guest at the hotel – one who would be leaving very soon. It had slipped her mind – almost – that he might be related to someone who had been part of the Occupation of Vernazza during the Second World War. And she had quite forgotten her grandmother's warning. Isabella was too busy having fun.

They had begun their day out by walking along the wide promenade of Baia delle Favole, known as the Bay of Fables in tribute to Hans Christian Andersen, who once lived here in Sestri Levante. And yes, Isabella had always thought it a fairy-tale setting. Sestri Levante had once been an island, but was now connected to the promontory of the shore by a thin sliver of land.

Next, she and Ferdinand followed the path leading from the old town to Punta Manara – she wanted to show him the magnificent view of the Ligurian coastline from Levanto to Portofino, the crystal light on the sea reflecting the surrounding mountains.

'Wow!' He was as impressed as she had expected him to be.

'From here, you can understand why this town was known as "the city of the two seas".' She pointed. On the one side was the Bay of Fables, on the other, the Baia di Silenzio, the romantic Bay of Silence. Sestri Levante sat on the rocky point, the Isola, which divided the two.

'I can, yes.' He followed her gaze. From up high, the bands of blue on either side of the narrow town with green mountains and another band of blue in the sky above was an incredible sight, almost an optical illusion. Like their own view of Vernazza, Isabella never tired of it.

They descended the path towards Baia di Silenzio, where people were gathered on the water's edge, some of them paddling in to scoop up jellyfish in their children's buckets so that the lifeguard could dispose of them. 'Jellyfish?' Ferdinand pulled a face.

'Not everything can be perfect – even in paradise,' she laughed.

There were several cafés and bars perched right on the beach and the scent of the cooking was too much for either of them to bear. 'Lunch?' Isabella suggested, and they went in search of antipasti and beer in the old town.

After lunch they bought *gelato* from Gelateria Ice Cream Angels, Isabella's favourite. And now they were strolling through the narrow streets and piazzas, past old and decorative buildings, cafés, bars and shops, soaking up the atmosphere of the old town. She had already shown him the basilica and the old palazzo – now Sestri Levante's town hall. The shops here were elegant but not over-priced; Sestri Levante was a working Italian town, and Isabella liked that.

So far, Ferdinand had proved himself to be an entertaining companion, and she was pleased that he too seemed to like this town. But this wasn't all about pleasure and having fun. Isabella was enjoying his company and she couldn't deny that she was attracted to him, but she must remember that she also wanted some answers. Why had Ferdinand come to Vernazza in the first place? Was he just another tourist – or did he have a different agenda?

'You do not think there is enough to see in the area of the Cinque Terre?' he asked innocently, glancing across at her. He was wearing knee-length cotton shorts and a T-shirt, both in muddy shades of beige and khaki that suited his fair colouring. She also liked his well-worn leather sandals and the fact that he wasn't wearing socks – the same could not be said of all male tourists from certain countries.

'Yes, there is a lot to see,' she conceded, as they wandered down another narrow road. The old town was a honeycomb of alleyways and winding streets, and Isabella knew that any minute they'd come upon the beach again. The Riviera Ligure di Levante certainly had more than its fair share of attractions, from Genoa to Lerici. There were the hiking trails, and each of the five villages of the Cinque Terre all had an individual charm. One could travel by boat to Portovenere – another of Isabella's favourite places – or venture into Tuscany by train, to Lucca, Florence, or Pisa. Most people used one of those towns as their base – not little Vernazza with its rather pricey hotels and restaurants – or they stayed a night or two and then moved on. 'But . . .'

'But?' As she'd predicted they had arrived back on the sandy *spiaggia* of the Bay of Silence. Despite its obvious appeal, it was never too crowded here; there was a grey boardwalk leading out to sea and a crescent moon of pastel-painted houses, hotels, and villas lining the bay.

'Shall we sit down for a while?' Isabella reached in her bag for the cotton sarong she'd brought with her. She sat primly on it. The afternoon sun was still hot, and she'd like to strip down to her bikini, but she felt unusually shy. She hardly knew him, she reminded herself. She shouldn't have brought him to a beach destination at all. She should have taken him to a city, like Florence, where they would be surrounded by people.

'Why not?' He followed suit, pulling a striped beach towel from his bag and laying it out next to her sarong. He didn't seem to share her body-revealing qualms though – he gave her his *gelato* to hold and promptly pulled off his T-shirt to reveal an almost hairless chest which was still pale, only slightly tinged with a golden tan. He was lean but wiry, the muscles of his arms tensing as he leaned on one elbow, seemingly perfectly at ease.

Which was annoying in itself. Isabella gave him back his *gelato* and turned her attention back to her own. 'There is a lot to see, yes . . . But a week . . .'

'Or longer,' he added. 'Given the attractions of the place.' He licked his ice cream.

Isabella was conscious of a little internal shudder. 'Is it possible, Ferdinand, that you have an ulterior motive?' There, it was said.

He finished his *gelato* and wiped his mouth with the white napkin that had been wrapped around it. 'Such as?' He looked from the smooth blue sea of the bay where the glassy water held barely a ripple, and back to Isabella. 'Aren't you going to take off your dress?'

She frowned. 'You have ice cream on your chin.'

Lazily, he wiped it off.

'Maybe. In a minute.' She watched a little girl paddling by the boardwalk and wondered how to re-word her question.

'You're German,' she said.

'Very observant, *Signorina*.'

'Funny.' She pulled a face. 'And more to the point, you've been very interested in talking to Giovanna. On two occasions.' Maybe even more that she didn't know about.

'I told you – she's a nice lady. Why not?' He stretched out his legs and lay back on his beach towel. 'Tell me – do you give the Italian Inquisition to all your guests?'

'Oh . . .' Isabella finished her *gelato*. It was hopeless. He was exasperating. He knew quite well what she was getting at. She shook her head at him, though he couldn't see, as even behind his sunglasses she could tell he had his eyes closed. She took the opportunity of wriggling out of her sundress while unobserved. 'I'm going for a swim,' she announced.

His eyes blinked open. 'Good idea.'

But she didn't wait for him. It was only a few steps to the water and she took them almost at a run. She strode into the sea.

'Be careful of the—'

She was already in. She swam out towards the boats moored in the harbour, keeping her head above water, wanting to put as much distance as possible between them. He was infuriating.

181

He didn't answer direct questions, he liked to tease, he didn't take anything seriously, and he was evasive in every aspect of his behaviour. Nonna had told her to be careful of him, and she was right. Her grandmother certainly wouldn't approve if she knew Isabella had come here with him today.

She gasped as he appeared from nowhere, grabbed hold of her bodily and threw her to one side. 'What—' she spluttered. 'What the hell do you think you're doing?' She was out of her depth, she realised. Water was stinging her eyes and her hair was drenched. She kept going under.

'Jellyfish.' Treading water, he held her until she'd found her balance. He pointed to the purply-blue fronds of the transparent blob trailing in the water where she had been swimming.

'Oh.' Isabella blinked the water out of her eyes. 'Thanks,' she added grudgingly. In her hurry to get into the ocean she'd forgotten about the jellyfish.

He had water on his eyelashes and his hair was flattened and wet. 'We're a bit far out. Let's go in.'

'All right.' Though he did have a tendency to keep taking charge – and although Isabella quite liked this, she also wanted to remind him that this was her territory and she could take very good care of herself – jellyfish notwithstanding.

'And does it matter?' He threw this into the air between them. But he didn't wait for an answer; he set off at a fast crawl towards the beach.

'Does what matter?' She followed him in a sedate breaststroke that wouldn't get her hair any wetter, towards the shoreline of pink and terracotta houses with yellow shutters that lined the bay. The salt water was still in her nose and throat, and she kept having to cough.

He pulled himself out of the water, reached out a slippery

hand to help her as she almost lost her balance again. Isabella took it — briefly. He might have saved her from a jellyfish, but she'd been stung often enough to know that was no big deal. She still didn't trust him. Why should she? And she still shouldn't have brought him here.

'Does what matter?' she repeated as they reached their spot on the *spiaggia*. Her sarong was a bit thin to act as a towel, but the sun would soon dry her.

'Why I've chosen to stay in Vernazza.' He grabbed his towel and threw it around her shoulders. 'Do my reasons for staying around here really matter?'

'Thanks.' Isabella considered. It wasn't any of her business, she supposed, but . . . 'Yes, they do.' She bunched her knees up to her chin. Thought of her great-grandfather and how he had hidden in the convent, in fear for his life, no doubt. She knew that awful things had happened, she knew that people had been ill-treated, shot and tortured in Vernazza during the war. 'Giovanna was there,' she reminded him. 'My great-grandfather was there. So, I need to know if . . .' Her voice trailed as she recalled Nonna's theory. But what other reason could there be — for all Ferdinand's questions, his desire to meet with Giovanna, the obvious curiosity in The Lemon Tree Hotel that he'd shown ever since his arrival? 'If a member of your family was there too.'

'Oh, you need to know, do you?' His glance was both searching and teasing.

She shrugged. 'Yes.' At least for her own peace of mind.

'In that case, I will tell you, Isabella.'

She waited.

'You're right, of course.' He sighed. 'It's true. My father Karl was stationed in Vernazza during the Second World War.'

183

'Your father?' Isabella blinked with surprise. She'd imagined any connection would be a generation further removed.

'He was fifty-five when I was born,' he explained. 'And he was only a boy of eighteen when he was living here.'

Eighteen . . . Isabella shuddered to think of what that boy had seen and done at such a tender age. 'Is he still alive?' she whispered. Poor Giovanna – that must have been why she was so startled when she first saw Ferdinand. He must look like his father, and Giovanna must have thought the days of the war had suddenly come around again to haunt her.

'He's coming to the end of his life.' Ferdinand stared out to sea. It was getting late. The light was turning gold, coating the sea with the metallic sheen of early evening.

For the first time since she'd known him, he seemed over-whelmingly sad. So, she had got through to him at last. Punctured that air he had of never taking anything seriously. Tentatively, Isabella placed a hand on his arm. 'I'm sorry.' Because it was a terrible thing to lose a father – whatever that father might have done.

He looked back at her, forced a smile. 'Thank you. But he's had a good life. He's eighty-five.'

A good life . . . Isabella was conscious of the irony. Ferdinand's father had fought in a world war. He had fought in an occupied town – her town. Had it really been a good life – in any sense of the word?

'And since he hasn't got long to live,' he went on, '. . . the time has come for my father to reflect on his life, as you can imagine.'

Isabella could.

'And so, he asked me to come here on his behalf. On a sort of pilgrimage, you could say.'

184

Isabella digested this. A pilgrimage? She scooped up some of the soft grey-brown sand in her palm and let the rough grains trickle back through her fingertips to the ground. 'To make amends do you mean?'

'Something like that.' He continued to stare out to sea.

'And does Aunt Giovanna remember him?'

He closed his eyes for a moment as if he couldn't bear to think about this. 'You'll have to ask her that question,' he said at last.

Isabella let out an audible groan. 'Why?'

'Because it's her business, not mine.'

Isabella sighed. Didn't he know? He must do – he'd visited her twice already, and they'd hardly been discussing the unseasonably good weather. He was indeed infuriating. He gave her one snippet of information only to withhold the rest. 'What did he do here – your father?' she demanded. She wanted to know what it had been like, what her great-grandfather had gone through, what Giovanna might have seen.

'Exactly? I don't know.'

'What?' She wanted to stamp her foot. He had talked to his father about it. He was here on his behalf – on this pilgrimage he'd mentioned. How could he not know?

'At least . . .' He turned to her. 'I know some of it, but look, Isabella, I don't really want to talk about this. Do you mind?'

Isabella shrugged. She wouldn't show that she cared. But actually, yes, she did mind – she minded very much. What right did he have to come back here to Vernazza and then refuse to say why he was here or what had gone on? What right did he have not to tell her any details? Didn't he think it concerned her? Was that it? Didn't he think that it mattered?

She could feel an unaccustomed anger building inside her and she had to let it out.

'So, where do you stand on the sins of the fathers, Ferdinand?' She got to her feet, still holding the towel around her neck and struggled to pull off her wet swimming things from under it.

'Are you getting ready to go already?' He watched her. His mouth twitched with amusement as she almost lost her balance pulling off her bikini bottoms, and she glared at him. It was not funny.

'Yes, I am.' She turned her back on him. 'But no doubt you will not bother to answer the question.'

'What question?'

She turned towards him again. 'Should sons be responsible for the sins of their fathers?'

'No.' He regarded her more seriously now. Which was good, because as far as Isabella was concerned, this was no laughing matter. 'Do you?'

She flung the towel towards him. 'No.'

He dodged it and laughed, damn him. 'Well then . . .'

Isabella waited, arms folded, though she was tempted to walk back to the train station alone. It was true that sons shouldn't be responsible for the sins of the fathers. Neither should fathers – nor mothers come to that – be responsible for the sins of their sons and daughters. And she had no right to cross-question him about why he was here. She knew that. He was a guest. The purpose of The Lemon Tree Hotel was to nurture, to replenish, to provide tranquillity. As she had told her grandmother, the war was long gone, and they were all part of the European Union now. But it was insensitive and crass, she felt, to assume that people could so easily forgive and

186

forget. And that wasn't the only thing. She knew for a fact that there was a lot more to the story than he was telling her.

'It's too nice a day to argue, don't you think?' Lazily he grabbed his clothes and pulled them on.

She picked up her sarong, gave it a shake to get rid of the sand. 'As you like,' she muttered. All right, she would let the matter drop – for now. But she would go and see Giovanna at the first opportunity, she decided, and see if she could find out anything more. She had promised to drop in on her anyway. And surely her aunt would tell her what she needed to know?

'Don't be angry, Isabella.' He had got to his feet and was looking at her with those cool blue eyes, and they were drawing her in again, she felt it. The sun was warm on the top of her head, her hair hanging in damp rat-tails to her shoulders. He bent down, she looked up, and his lips brushed hers. It was the lightest of touches, hardly a kiss at all. She stared at him. And yet she hadn't stopped him – hopeless, hopeless girl. Her heart gave a little leap, but it was against her better judgement. Because a man like Ferdinand Bauer certainly couldn't be trusted for so many different reasons, and as usual her grand-mother had been right.

CHAPTER 20

Chiara

Alonzo returned that evening, still behaving as though nothing was amiss. All the drama, all the emotion . . . And yet here they were eating dinner together in their apartment, and making bland conversation. But this was not how it was going to be. Something had changed and they must acknowledge it. Chiara pushed her plate to one side and straightened her posture. Enough, she thought. She had promised to stay with him, but her heart was not in it and she could not pretend that it was.

Alonzo refilled his wine glass. He was drinking more these days, perhaps they all were. Running a hotel, they should be careful of such things – with a cellarful of wine, there was always another bottle easily available . . . He picked up his glass and leaned back in his seat, surveying her. 'You're very quiet tonight.'

'Yes.' They had both behaved badly, though in very different ways. Chiara got to her feet and began clearing the plates. She remembered the slap – the sound of it, the shock of it, and the sting of it too. She remembered the rawness, the way the bile had risen in her throat. The shame she'd felt the following day was still lingering with her. And so was Dante . . . Would she have slept with him if Alonzo had not hit her? Truthfully, she couldn't say for sure.

'Did you see him before he left?'

Fortunately, Chiara had her back to Alonzo as he asked this question. *Yes, I saw him.* Though she didn't say this. Instead, she plunged the plates into a bowlful of hot water she'd just run. She had seen him, and she had slept with him – all night. He had comforted her and he had loved her. Oh, how he had loved her. And she had loved him back – and meant it.

After her conversation with Elene early this morning, after she had showered and got dressed and carefully made up her face to hide the lingering bruise on her cheek, Chiara had made her way to Dante's room with a heavy heart. She knocked lightly and he came to the door.

'That was quick.' He drew her inside. 'I must have under-estimated my powers.' Then he saw her face. 'What is it, *cara*? Is he back already? What's happened?'

'No. It's not Alonzo.'

'So?' But she could see that already, he had guessed.

'You must leave The Lemon Tree Hotel, my love,' she said.

'And you?' He lifted her chin.

'I must stay.'

He let out a deep sigh and swore softly. 'What has changed?'

Nothing, she thought, and everything. She told him how Elene had been standing in the shadows of the corridor when Chiara had left his room that morning. She told him of their conversation.

Already, he was shaking his head. Already he was moving

189

away from her, standing by the window looking out on to the olive grove, a bitter reminder of that other time.

'You don't know how hard this is for me.' Chiara spoke softly. She couldn't see his face, but his back was stiff and unyielding. She was heartbroken. But what else could she do?

'She is your daughter, yes,' Dante said, 'but she is also an adult woman with a husband of her own. Give her time and she will understand her mother's choices.'

'And what would we do?' For they had not even discussed this. She came up to where he was standing at the window. His eyes flickered to her and then away. 'Would I leave the hotel and my family and come to England with you? Would you leave your business in England and come to live in Vernazza with me?'

He spread his hands. She knew that he had no answers. 'We could at least talk about it, *cara*.'

Outside, the morning sunlight gleamed on the narrow grey-green leaves of the olive trees. The fruit was ripening. Soon there would be another harvest. 'I can't do it, Dante,' she said. It wasn't even Alonzo. 'My family still needs me.' Elene still needed her – she had made that plain. And The Lemon Tree Hotel still needed her too. Dante had managed perfectly well without her all these years, but her family could not. Alonzo would always go his own way, and she knew now more than ever that any love between them had died. But they still shared a daughter. Elene was more vulnerable than she had ever realised. Chiara must focus now on repairing the damage she had already done – this was her chance, her duty.

'Very well.' And to her horror his face seemed to close up to her, just as it had done forty years before.

She caught at his arm, wanting him to understand. 'Sometimes, Dante, it is impossible to choose love.'

'So, it seems.' He pulled away from her. She didn't think that she could bear it.

'Do you understand, Dante?' she begged him. 'Can you forgive me?'

He turned back, his dark eyes at once both wistful and calm. 'I understand that your hotel and your family are tying you down, Chiara,' he said. 'I understand that you will never be free to live your own life.'

She looked down. She knew that he was right.

'And there is nothing to forgive you for.'

'I'm so sorry, Dante—'

'You need not worry.' And his voice grew hard. 'For I tell you this – I will not come back for you again.'

Chiara turned around to face her husband. His eyes narrowed as he waited for her reply. 'Well?'

She thought of Elene and what she had promised. The truth would help no one. 'How could I see him?' she demanded – regally, she hoped. 'After what you said? After what you did?' Instinctively, she put a hand to her face, to the mark of his slap. 'Believe me, Alonzo, I did not want to see a soul.'

She had not been able to watch Dante leave. She had asked Marco to take over on reception, and she had waited in her room upstairs. And then she had run to the window and seen him at the moment he walked away. He had not looked around, and she had not expected him to. She had longed to run after him. She wanted to catch his arm and tell him it was a mistake, and she wanted to see his eyes light up as she told him that they could be together, that she agreed – somehow, they would find a way. It was like the night in the olive grove all over again. The same old love, the same old heartbreak.

Then she thought of Elene – poor Elene, who wore the armour of her kitchen whites to hide her vulnerability and her fears. Would Elene tell her father what she had seen? Would she tell him that her mother had spent the night with Dante Rossi? She didn't think so. Why would she, when she was so desperate for her parents to stay together?

'*Bene*.' Alonzo nodded with satisfaction – the satisfaction of a bully who has been obeyed, she found herself thinking. 'The mark on your face – it has faded.'

Chiara remained silent, chin held high. She almost didn't want it to fade. She almost wanted to show the world what he was. And what about what she was – a woman who had betrayed her husband? A woman who had made love with another man? She would have to carry the guilt of that for ever.

Alonzo got to his feet and approached her. She tried not to wince. He lifted her chin still higher with his forefingers so that her face was in the light. '*Sì*, it is almost gone.' He didn't take his hand away.

Chiara met his scrutiny without flinching. She thought of Dante's words to her last night. He will do it again, he had said. Was he right? Possibly. And there was no way she was going to play victim in a marriage of domination – whatever she might have done to deserve it. 'You know it is over between us, Alonzo?' She kept her gaze strong, she refused to let her voice shake. He must know that she was in control of this situation. Otherwise . . .

'Over?' He frowned, stared at her some more, narrowed his eyes again. 'What are you talking about? Our marriage?' And for the first time she heard his voice falter.

'Not our marriage, no.' She couldn't do that to Elene. She had promised.

'What then?'

'Our intimacy.'

He laughed as he let go of her face at last. 'Not that there was much of that,' he said.

Chiara bowed her head and looked up again. 'Not that there was much of that,' she agreed, still watching him.

She could see him trying to work it out. What did she mean exactly, and how would it affect him? What could he do to regain the upper hand? Should he hit her again – maybe he also considered that. She would just have to hope that he decided against it. 'Or – what?' he said.

Chiara had her answer ready. 'Or we separate,' she said clearly. He didn't need to know what was holding her to him – that promise to Elene. It was a bluff, but she could carry it off; she'd done it before.

Alonzo frowned. 'You'd leave the hotel?'

What was he thinking? 'You would leave the hotel,' she corrected. 'Obviously I would stay. I work here. I own the hotel.' She didn't think she'd gone too far. She had to show strength – that was imperative.

'Separate beds, my love?' he sneered. 'Is that what you're proposing?'

'We have a spare room.' She hardly need point out how frequently he was not here.

'People will know,' he muttered.

Maids, he meant. The housekeeper. The employees who came in and cleaned. She shrugged. 'I can make the bed in the spare room when you have stayed here, if that's the only thing bothering you.' She didn't trouble to hide her disdain.

193

This wasn't about whether or not Alonzo lost face in front of the employees of the hotel, for God's sake. This was about somehow managing to be true to herself, to Dante, and yet also keep her promise. She didn't think she could bear to touch this man, or worse, for him to touch her. Not now. Alonzo had assumed it was because he had hit her. He didn't need to know the rest of the reason why.

He returned to the table to pour more wine. 'And the rest of our marriage?'

What else was there, she wondered. For most of her life she had been in a loveless marriage. She didn't yet know if this new state of affairs would be better – or worse.

'Will be as before,' she said. 'For the sake of appearances.' And for the sake of Elene. Dante's return had changed her life. But she would not admit that to anyone.

CHAPTER 21

Elene

Elene was in the kitchen doing the prep for her *salsa di noci*. She would serve it with *trenette*, a narrow, flat pasta similar to linguine but made from wholewheat flour; in Liguria they valued the variety of their pasta and they preferred to be precise. She was just reaching for her pestle and mortar when Silvio appeared at the back door.

'*Ciao*,' he said.

'*Ciao*.' Elene glanced across at her husband and caught his worried look a microsecond before he changed it to a smile. She sighed. 'Hungry?'

Silvio had worn this worried look ever since the morning when Elene had virtually caught her mother emerging from Dante Rossi's bedroom. Would he always be sad or worried? Was that the best she could do for this man? She closed her eyes for a moment, remembered how she had felt as she waited in the shadows of that corridor. Her mother was not in her apartment, had not been there all night. Elene had hardly slept

195

for thinking about it. It was almost impossible to imagine – but there was only one place she could be . . .

Elene watched her husband as he pulled off his boots. She had been so frightened at that moment, though she couldn't say exactly why – pulled into some old childhood fear she couldn't even name. Was it a fear of her parents' impending separation? It was true that they had always spent more time apart than together, true that – now she came to think of it – they were rarely openly affectionate with one another. But they were her parents nonetheless, and parents came as one unit as far as she was concerned. Elene snipped a bulb of garlic from the strand hanging from a hook. It had been wrong perhaps to give in to it. Was it a fear of how any separation might affect her and the hotel? Was it a fear of the unknown? Or was it something deeper – was it a feeling that everything, her whole world, was somehow falling apart?

Elene determinedly pushed these thoughts away. She pressed hard on the garlic with the bridge of her hand and the cloves cracked and separated. Silvio winced. Elene didn't want to analyse how she felt – she couldn't. But she had let down the barriers. She had – unusually for her, apart from when she was in her kitchen – acted on instinct. She only knew that when she saw that ugly mark of violence on her mother's face . . . she had felt the strangest surge of love and protection mixed with that fear of the unknown. She had been determined to save her – and Papà too.

'Am I not always half-starved?' Silvio grinned and grabbed a *cornetto* from the tray on the counter.

Expertly, Elene peeled the sticky garlic cloves with a minimum of neat movements and without a knife – it was something that every chef learned at the start of his or her career. 'Help yourself,' she murmured, but not unkindly.

196

She didn't even want to know the full story of what had happened between her mother and Rossi – indeed, something inside her had blocked off that need to know and replaced it with a desire simply to sweep it out of sight. She only knew that before Dante Rossi had come to The Lemon Tree Hotel, things had been fine (though perhaps 'fine' wasn't quite the word; she was aware that her mother wasn't truly happy, and obviously the relationship between Elene and her mother was strained, had always been strained, but . . .) and that after Dante Rossi arrived, everything had gone terribly wrong.

Elene removed the chunks of bread that had been soaking in milk, ready to combine with the walnuts, parmesan cheese, marjoram, and seasonings. Perhaps she shouldn't have called her father when she saw her mother reach up to him with that intimate gesture – she knew that Silvio thought she shouldn't have – but now it was done. Dante Rossi had left the hotel, and now hopefully they could all go back to normal.

The trouble was though, that they had not. She still remembered the feel of her mother stroking her hair – it had been so long since Mamma had held her that way . . . Elene sniffed. She wanted her to do it again – and at the same time she thought that she would do anything to stop her. She grated the parmesan into a wide bowl, sniffing the strong flavour as she did so. But now her mother looked unbearably sad, her father looked grim and angry, and the atmosphere between her parents was one of a chilly politeness that made Elene shiver inside. What had she done? *Allora*, things could only get better – she hoped.

'And how are you, my love?' Silvio asked.

'Busy.' Elene began to add her garlic. It was a delicate job. It had to be worked towards a paste, but it was necessary to stop just short – for it must not be too smooth. Food processors and electric blenders were all very fine and dandy, but for this job, a pestle and mortar was better. It allowed things to be more gradual, for the chef to blend at a slow rate and to catch the perfect point.

After the confrontation with her mother, all Elene had wanted to do was run to the kitchen – that was always her first instinct when things went wrong in her world. But she could hardly take charge of *la cucina* in the tearful, red-eyed and blotchy state she was in, and so she swiftly returned to their rooms and of course it was early, and Silvio was there, getting washed and ready for his day and probably wondering where on earth his wife was.

'What is it?' he had demanded, fists clenched as if he were ready to go out and punch whatever had caused her distress.

Despite everything, Elene had to smile. She'd told him what had happened with her mother, and then she'd cried some more. When she was done, she'd washed her face, re-applied her make-up, brushed her hair, and coiled it neatly into the chignon she wore in the kitchen. That efficient chignon symbolised her no-nonsense working mantra – with that, she put the emotion behind her and became a focused and capable chef once more.

'Shouldn't you be getting to work?' she'd asked Silvio, who was still hovering, looking both sad and worried at the same time.

'But what are you going to do?'

'Do?' Elene checked her face in the mirror. No one would know she had been weeping for Italy.

'Are you going to tell your father?' Silvio's eyes were wide. It almost looked as if he was frightened too.

'No.' Elene had known that from the moment she'd walked into her mother's arms, even before Mamma had promised that she would not leave The Lemon Tree Hotel. This time, she would not betray her. Her father was a proud man, and Elene wanted to keep them together, not prise them apart.

'Then—'

Elene put a finger to her husband's lips. 'I don't want to talk about this again. *Per favore.*'

Silvio frowned. 'But—'

'I mean that, Silvio.' She had opened the door of their room, ready now to face anything. She didn't need reminders, she didn't want this kind of emotion that threatened her working practice. It had been dealt with. And that was enough.

'What you did . . .' He wasn't taking 'no' for an answer.

'You think it was selfish?' She turned to face him.

'Yes.'

Of course, he was right. Elene was an adult woman and old enough to allow her mother to lead her own life, to deal with her mother's decisions. Only at that moment in her parents' rooms she hadn't felt it.

'I know what you wanted though.' And there was a certain wisdom in Silvio's eyes that Elene wasn't sure she had seen there before.

'Oh?' She put her hands on her hips. 'And what did I want?'

'You wanted to make your mother choose.'

'I won't disturb you if you're busy,' Silvio said now. Even so, while Elene had been adding the garlic, he had helped himself to coffee, eaten another three *cornetti*, passed the time of day with Raphael, who was on the other side of the kitchen preparing vegetables, and he was now peering into Elene's mortar as if her *salsa di noci* could somehow tell him the meaning of life. It was good. It was an underestimated sauce that was only fully appreciated in the tasting. But it wasn't that good.

So – she had made her mother choose. Why then, didn't she have more sense of satisfaction, since her mother had – against the odds – chosen Elene?

She began to mix in some of their best and purest olive oil from last year's harvest, a teaspoon at a time, grinding and smoothing as she went. The oil was so special to their cuisine. Homer had called it liquid gold – that was true enough. The rhythmic nature of these tasks she found soothing – especially when everything else at The Lemon Tree seemed so fraught. Marcello himself had taught her how to make this sauce – Elene had hardly changed a thing, though she had departed slightly from Marcello's purist Ligurian method by adding a little cream; in her opinion the walnut sauce was even more delicious that way.

'What are you up to this morning anyway?' she asked Silvio. She was conscious that he was lingering.

'Laying down some gravel outside the front door.' He went to take another *cornetto* from the tray and she slapped his hand.

'*Basta*, Silvio! Too many pastries are no good for your waistline. I will do you some lunch soon.'

He shrugged and grinned. Sometimes, Silvio looked just like a little boy. Sometimes, he made Elene wish that they had been blessed with another child, a boy, a miniature version of her Silvio, a dear son who would give all his love to his mamma. She smiled grimly. As if . . .

'And I have been chatting to one of our guests,' Silvio added.

'Oh, yes?' Elene added the ricotta cheese to her sauce – but only after Silvio had filched a small cube.

'We have an architect staying here at the moment.' He gave her a knowing look. 'A young guy. Very friendly.'

'Is that so? Where is he from?' And now for the cream, she thought. She began to add it carefully, along with the remainder of the oil.

'*Benissimo*! It smells great.' Silvio sniffed appreciatively. 'Somewhere in Germany.'

'Ah, yes.' She thought she could recall her mother mentioning someone – and there was something else she thought she should remember, but for the moment it escaped her mind. The *salsa* did indeed smell delicious; fresh and herby, the nuts providing the grounding, the cream adding the richness. She took a teaspoon and tasted the sauce. A little more pepper perhaps?

'Is it good?' Silvio looked so forlorn that Elene took pity on him.

'Here.' She offered him the teaspoon. 'What was his name?'

'Ah, that is wonderful, my love.' He smacked his lips and blew her a kiss. 'Signor Bauer, I think he said.'

'*Va bene*.' She added the pepper and tasted again. Perfect. Not that his name mattered a jot. Elene and Silvio rarely had much to do with the hotel guests. She supposed it was inevitable, given that her time was taken up in the kitchen and Silvio was usually working in one of the unoccupied rooms or away in the grounds somewhere, but she resented it all the same. It was just another of the ways in which she and Silvio felt less important at The Lemon Tree Hotel, less valued. Their work comprised of slaving away behind the scenes, and so people were hardly aware of them, while Chiara and Isabella dealt with their guests; taking their money, allocating them their rooms, and receiving their grateful thanks and praise, no doubt.

Silvio came a step closer. 'He was saying how much he liked the old convent building,' he told her. 'How much he appreciated the . . .' He waved his arms around in dramatic fashion '. . . peaceful atmosphere of the place.'

Elene snorted. It hadn't been very peaceful here lately. She had missed the scene in the restaurant when her father had returned to find her mother enjoying an intimate dinner with Rossi (missed it on purpose in fact, feeling bad that she was the one to have caused it) but no doubt some of the guests had enjoyed the spectacle – even Isabella had mentioned something about it and asked Elene if she knew what was going on. Yes, there had certainly been an emotional whirlwind in full flow. She covered the saucepan. The sauce was thick, but when she added the pasta it would come right. Some people made the mistake of allowing the *salsa di noci* to cook in the pan, but it must not – this would make it lose its vibrancy.

'Maybe we should ask him what he thinks of our ideas for the hotel, eh?'

Silvio was at the door already, putting his boots on again. He turned back to Elene and lowered his voice. 'There's no point,' he told her. 'Your mother would never agree to it. You know what she's like about protecting everyone's privacy while they're staying here. And anyway, no one wants to talk about work when they are on holiday.'

Elene shrugged. 'He told you he was an architect though, *sì*?'

'Yes . . .' Silvio had his worried look on again. He'd obviously been trying to distract her with his mention of architects and it had turned into something he now wanted to avoid.

'So, he doesn't mind people knowing what he does for a living.'

'Maybe.' Silvio now clearly couldn't wait to get out of the door.

'He could even be looking for more work. Who isn't?'

Silvio pulled a face. 'Quite a few people, now you come to mention it, and—'

'So why not take the opportunity?' Elene had the bit between her teeth now. The more she thought about it, the better an idea it sounded. Synchronicity, it was called, was it not, when such a thing fell your way at the right time? 'Just a little conversation. He can only say no. What harm could it do?'

'Just a little conversation?' he repeated as if he didn't think she was capable of such a thing.

'Exactly.'

'And your mother?' He looked towards Raphael. But he was over the other side of *la cucina* slicing peppers as if his life depended on it. 'Is this another test?'

'My mother?' Elene moved closer to him, reached up and kissed him briefly on the lips. He looked surprised – as well he might, for this was a rare occurrence. She thought of her mother and the uneasy truce they'd shared since the other morning. She thought of Dante Rossi and the look on her mother's face when she came out of his room. She didn't think of whether it was or was not a test. '*Allora*. Why does she even need to know?'

CHAPTER 22

Isabella

Once again, Isabella was conscious that the atmosphere in The Lemon Tree seemed to lack its usual tranquillity. Everyone seemed on edge. Emanuele had been late for his shift again this morning, and Ghita had not turned up at all, much to her mother's irritation.

She volunteered to collect the eggs from Giovanna. After what Ferdinand had said – and not said – in Sestri Levante, she hadn't forgotten that she wanted to have a word with her aunt and check up on her too.

She walked through the olive grove to Giovanna's cottage, half-expecting Ferdinand to be there. But of course, he would not be; she was imagining things, getting it all out of proportion. Instead, there was Giovanna in her black dress, wrinkled stockings, and flat black shoes, sweeping the step with her old-fashioned broom, her sweet face wreathed in smiles the moment she caught sight of her. Thank goodness – all was well.

'Ah, Bella, how lovely,' she said. 'Come through, sit down, let me look at you.'

Isabella accepted a glass of fresh lemonade, and they sat on the little terrace at the back of the cottage discussing the welfare of the chickens.

'Lia is laying well at the moment,' Giovanna told her. 'Just look at her.'

Isabella smiled at the note of pride in her aunt's voice. *Her girls* . . . But it was true that Lia's feathers were bright, and she had a perky look to her as she strutted around the cobbled terrace where Isabella and Giovanna sat on the old bench watching the hens peck at the feed she had scattered for them.

'And this one?' Isabella indicated a rather more dull-eyed hen on the edge of the clucking crowd. 'She doesn't look very full of the joys of spring?' Or late summer, in this case.

'Mara.' Giovanna shook her head. 'She's rather sullen today, my dear.' Her old aunt clicked her tongue, sounding rather like one of the hens herself. 'She's laying – but not as well as usual.'

'What do you think's wrong with her?' Isabella watched the sad-faced hen and found herself wondering what range of emotions a hen might experience in her life. Might she, for example, be resentful if the cockerel overlooked her in favour of another bird? Might she be happier when the sun was shining or when she had laid a perfectly formed egg? At any rate, at least these chickens were well cared for and allowed to roam free. They would also escape the pot, if Giovanna had anything to do with it.

'Who knows?' Giovanna frowned, got to her feet, and threw Mara a handful of feed from the tin.

'And the eggs?' Isabella knew that her mother wanted at least two dozen. If there were fewer, they'd have to go elsewhere – and perhaps invest in some more hens for the future.

'It's not only Mara who's quieter than usual.' Giovanna

shook her white head. 'Even so . . .' She disappeared and came back with a few cartons from her cool larder. She opened the boxes to show them to Isabella.

They were brown and smelt sweet and fresh, one or two fluffy feathers still stuck to the shells. Isabella breathed in deeply. 'Wonderful.' She knew that her mother loved to cook with eggs freshly laid in the grounds of The Lemon Tree Hotel. And Giovanna took great pride that her large family of hens provided them.

They sat on the bench and drank their lemonade. The sharp citrus was both dry and sweet on her tongue. 'I spent the day with Ferdinand Bauer yesterday,' Isabella told her aunt. Giovanna's reaction would probably tell her all she needed to know.

Giovanna took in a sharp breath and then let it go. 'Ah, *sì, sì*.' Which frankly told her nothing.

'Can I ask you, Aunt . . .' She hesitated. She didn't want to bring up the painful past again, but . . .

Giovanna's eyes clouded. 'Bella, my dear,' she said. 'You can ask me anything you wish.' Despite her words though, Isabella sensed a reticence, a closing down of emotions. Her aunt placed her glass on the worn and pitted table and folded her hands in her lap. She was waiting.

Isabella watched her closely. 'Do you remember him?' she asked.

'Him?' Giovanna's old eyes flickered.

'Ferdinand's father.'

She gave a little start of surprise at this, though she must have been expecting it, surely? 'Yes, Bella,' she said. 'I do. I remember all the men who were stationed here – what they looked like at least.'

Which was exactly as Isabella had suspected. But why had Ferdinand made such a thing about it? 'Ferdinand – he looks like his father, doesn't he?'

'Why, yes.' She gave her gentle smile. 'I suppose that he does.'

'It must have been awful.' Isabella could hardly imagine. They had tried to make the hotel an oasis of peace. What had it been like when the town was occupied, when the Partisans hid in the convent, given refuge by the nuns, when the fascists and the occupying German forces came to search them out? 'The nuns must have been terrified every time someone came to the gates.'

'I'm sure that they were.' Giovanna's milky brown eyes glazed over as if she were remembering those far-off days of brutality, poverty, and fear. 'But they always believed that God would keep them safe in the convent.' She crossed herself swiftly. 'They were probably far more frightened for the men taking refuge there – men like your great-grandfather, whose lives were at risk.'

'Of course.' They had been selfless those nuns – and very brave. 'But how you must have hated the men who were taking over your town.' Men like Ferdinand's father, Karl Bauer.

An expression of disapproval flickered across Giovanna's lined face. 'Hate is a strong word, my dear.'

'I suppose it is.' But justified surely? Perhaps the nuns' faith and religious beliefs prevented them from hating even the perpetrators who filled them with such terror. But Giovanna hadn't been a nun – just a young teenage girl at the time. 'So are you saying that you didn't hate them? Even though they were occupying Vernazza? Even though—' But here, Isabella could not go on. She didn't know all the details of the atrocities that had taken place, but she knew enough not to offer any reminders to this dear woman who must have witnessed at least some of them as a girl.

Giovanna bowed her head. 'It's true, Bella. I did not hate them.'

Isabella stared at her. How truly good she was.

'Some were worse than others, of course. Most were just ordinary men following orders you know, my dear. The war, the occupation, the way we were living – these men were not to blame for all this.'

'But surely—' Isabella had heard that there were men who had taken advantage of their new-found sense of power – that always happened, did it not, in times of war? There would always be men from all sides who enjoyed the suffering of others, who were born to bully. Wasn't her aunt simply blinded by her need to see the good in everyone?

'The men who gave the orders to shoot, to maim, to torture . . .' Giovanna's voice broke. 'They were the ones to blame. As for the others – they had to follow those orders,' she whispered, 'or pay the price for disobedience.'

'Yes, I see.' It was a fair point. And Isabella could guess what that price would be. Perhaps she was seeing things in black-and-white, when in fact there were many shades of grey. She let her gaze drift past the hens and the terracotta pots of scarlet geraniums and through to the olive grove. It was such a paradise – now. And yet, these old trees had witnessed everything – all the atrocities, all the pain. Some of those responsible for war crimes had paid the price, at least. But how many more were there – who had colluded, who had taken advantage, who had committed cruel acts out of greed, or even for the sheer buzz of it? Human nature could be a frightening thing to witness, now just as much as back then.

Giovanna put a wrinkled hand on her arm. 'Life is so much more complicated than it sometimes appears, Bella,' she said. 'Is that not so?'

Isabella thought of Ferdinand Bauer. His hair shining gold in the sun, his eyes of a blue as untroubled as the water in their swimming pool, his pale tan body when he had taken off his shirt on the beach at Sestri Levante. That faint brush of his lips. 'Yes, I suppose it is.' Her feelings towards him were so mixed, so confusing. Soon he would be gone. Soon, she wouldn't have to concern herself with it at all. But until then . . .

'And yet sometimes, life is so simple.' Giovanna chuckled softly. 'Ah, *sì*.' She bent to snip off a dead geranium head between her thumb and forefinger.

'What are you saying, Aunt?' Isabella frowned. Once again, she couldn't escape the feeling that she was being left out of some mysterious scenario. There were secrets, she was sure of that. And perhaps those secrets were shared by Giovanna and Ferdinand Bauer. Only . . . she couldn't imagine what those secrets could be.

'Oh, don't listen to the ramblings of an old woman.' Giovanna got to her feet. She put the empty glasses on the tin tray to take back to the kitchen.

'Let me.' Isabella took it from her.

'Do you like him, Bella?' Giovanna was watching her intently.

'Ferdinand?'

'*Certo*, Ferdinand.' She refastened a strand of fine, white hair that had come un-pinned.

'I don't know.' Isabella rinsed out the glasses at the old porcelain sink and put them on the drainer to dry. 'Yes. No. I'm really not sure.'

Giovanna patted her arm. She reached for a drying-up cloth. 'My advice is to give him a chance,' she said. 'He's his own man. It doesn't matter who his father was or what happened here in Vernazza. You've met him and you like him. That's all that matters.'

'Really?' Isabella stared at her. 'You are very forgiving, Giovanna.' After everything that had happened . . . And was it all that mattered? What really mattered, surely, was to be able to trust someone?

Giovanna shrugged. 'The past is past, Bella.'

'Yes, but—'

Giovanna was giving her that look – as if she understood everything and more.

'Why do you think he came here, Aunt?' How could he possibly make amends for anything his father might have done all those years ago? It didn't make sense. 'To seek the forgiveness of the villagers?'

'Ah, yes, perhaps.' Giovanna nodded wisely. 'Sometimes there are things that still need to be resolved, wouldn't you say, Bella?'

Isabella had no idea. 'What things, Aunt?'

But Giovanna was just staring out of the window, her expression many years away.

'He'll be leaving soon,' Isabella said. And so, was there any point? She dried her hands on the square of white towel that Giovanna kept near the sink.

'Maybe.' Giovanna looked out of the kitchen window towards the olive grove. 'But these things – they do not take so long to happen, you know.'

What things didn't take so long to happen? And how much the wiser was she now? Isabella carried the basket of eggs carefully back through the olive grove. The trees provided a welcome shade from the morning sun, sharp rays glinting on gnarled and twisted tree trunks, forming arrows of light on the gravel path. Although she had always known the history; now, for the first time, it had become real for her. As she walked, she seemed to hear some long-ago echo from the past in the whisper of the leaves in the breeze. A shout went up, a flurry of gunfire, footsteps thundered past her along the path and then disappeared among the ancient trees. She gave a little shiver and hurried on.

Inside the hotel, Ferdinand Bauer was loitering by reception. 'I was just heading off to Lucca,' he said when he saw her.

Isabella put the eggs on the desk. 'Have a good day.'

'I suppose there's no chance . . .' He shook his head even as he asked the question. 'You're working?'

'All day,' she confirmed. Much as she might love to spend it with Ferdinand Bauer in Lucca, there was a hotel to run.

He leaned on the desk. He smelt cool and freshly shaven. 'How about tomorrow?' His eyes were so blue, so clear. He seemed uncomplicated – but with that family history, how could he be?

'I'm afraid not.' He was keen, she'd give him that.

'I was thinking of walking up to the Santuario di Reggio.'

She looked up at him, remembered the short discussion they'd had about hiking trails that were off the beaten track. The path to the sanctuary was certainly not as popular as those to Corniglia or Monterosso – which was one of the reasons she liked it so much. There were magnificent views of the coast-line, and the sanctuary was one of those much-loved pockets of peace in the area, a traditional place of refuge, cherished by all who lived in Vernazza. Refuge, she thought, was becoming

211

rather a theme. 'I'm sorry – I'm on the desk from ten-thirty in the morning.'

'An early morning hike then?' He grinned.

Isabella was tempted. She tried not to stare at his dimples. She thought of what Giovanna had said about giving him a chance. About the past being past. About how it didn't take long . . . 'All right,' she said. 'Yes, that would be . . . very nice.'

Those cool blue eyes gleamed. 'Good. I'll see you later to discuss the arrangements, shall I?'

She nodded. 'I'm helping out in the bar this evening.'

'*Ciao* then, Isabella. I'll catch you later in the bar.'

'*Ciao*.' Isabella watched him walk away, tall, rather gangly, and somehow very appealing.

'Your Signor Bauer is still with us, I see.' Her grandmother was standing just behind her – Isabella hadn't even noticed her come out of the office.

'Yes.' Isabella opened her laptop. 'Though he isn't *my* Signor Bauer, Nonna.'

'Hmm.' Her grandmother sighed. 'And have you found out anything more about him, Bella?'

Isabella glanced up. Her grandmother looked concerned and she still had a sadness in her dark eyes. She put an arm around her shoulders. Nonna hadn't been herself for some days. Isabella remembered what the Signoras Veroni had said the other day about two men fighting over her. If it was true, Nonna didn't seem to be thriving on it.

'Don't worry, Nonna,' she soothed. 'I can look after myself you know.' She decided not to tell her what she had found out. Giovanna might have forgiven Ferdinand's father for his part in what had happened to Partisans like her great-grandfather – but

212

Isabella suspected that her grandmother would not feel quite the same.

'Of course you can.' Her grandmother patted her hand. 'But please take care, Bella. I don't have a good feeling about that young man — he looks as if he's hiding something. Whatever you do, my darling, take care.'

CHAPTER 23

Elene

Elene had an hour to herself before she needed to do any further preparation for dinner, so she undertook a little detective work, which mainly consisted of getting Silvio to point out Signor Bauer as soon as he spotted him again.

At 4 p.m. he called her. 'He's just entering the lobby,' he said, in a suitably low and melodramatic tone. 'Grey T-shirt and green shorts, tall, fair hair, slim build.'

Very succinct. Elene made her way to the lower curve of the sweeping stairs, preparing to linger by the painting of the Archangel Gabriel that her mother and Isabella insisted on keeping in the niche, even though it was old-fashioned and not even very well painted, in her opinion. Elene had as much affection for Giovanna as any of them, but that didn't mean they had to display her father's painting in their foyer for evermore.

Signor Bauer was having what seemed to be rather an intimate conversation with Isabella. Elene saw her daughter laugh and lean forward to look at his phone – perhaps he was showing her a photograph. And that was exactly it, Elene thought; her mother and her daughter both possessed this easy charm, this way with people. Elene wasn't sure how they did it; it seemed to come naturally. As a girl, Elene used to watch her mother in action, she even tried to mimic her welcoming smile in front of the mirror in her own bedroom. But it lacked sincerity somehow. Her mother and Isabella would smile and nod, and somehow know when to ask another question or when to hold back. They always said the right thing. They seemed so interested in all their guests, they had warmth. It was beyond Elene. She was glad she only had to work with pasta, tomatoes, and *melanzane* and the like in the kitchen. Food was far less demanding.

At last, the young *signore* made his way out to the courtyard, and Elene followed, with a casual hello to her daughter as she passed by.

'*Ciao*, Mamma.' Isabella shot her a sharp look.

But there was nothing strange about Elene walking into the courtyard at this time of day, nothing at all. Why should she not enjoy the sunshine like anyone else?

Signor Bauer took a seat under the lemon tree by the well and Elene wandered over. He unfolded a map on to the table top and began to study it intently.

Elene knew that this wouldn't be easy. It wasn't in her nature simply to go up and start talking to people. She would have to give the performance of her life. She went over to the lemon tree and made a pretence of examining the fruit. For a moment she was distracted by the sharp green of the leaves, the zesty citrus scent. Lemons were fundamental to the very history and identity of this land. Mmm. Perhaps she would make another lemon cake later? She hadn't planned to, it hadn't been so long ago that they'd enjoyed Aunt Giovanna's lemon birthday cake – although so much had happened since then that it felt like a lot longer – but a few of these beauties were ripe for the picking. She neatly plucked one from its stem and drew it in closer to inhale the fragrance.

The *signore* looked up at her and smiled. Nice eyes, she thought. No wonder her daughter found it easy to be friendly and pleasant with this one.

'Good afternoon,' she said.

'And to you.' He gave a little nod.

'I see you are investigating our hiking trails,' she said warmly, looking closer at the map. If her mother or daughter were to see her, they might be surprised. But why shouldn't she fraternise with their guests? Had anyone ever suggested that she should not? Just because she worked in the kitchen, didn't mean that she couldn't also mingle in the courtyard, pass a word or two with anyone she chose – just as she was sure her mother and Isabella did if they so desired.

'Yes.' He looked up, vaguely curious, she could tell.

'Elene Lombardi.' She held out a hand. 'I'm the chef here at The Lemon Tree Hotel. Chiara Mazzone, the general manager, is my mother.'

'Oh.' He rose to his feet. 'You are Isabella's mother, I can see the resemblance.'

She acknowledged this with a nod. So, he was on first-name terms with her daughter. Did that mean anything? Probably not, she decided. It was the way of the younger generation.

'I'm very pleased to meet you.' He shook her hand. 'I've already experienced your delicious food, *Signora*. Thank you. The sea bass at dinner last night was out of this world.' He rubbed his stomach appreciatively.

'Thank you, *Signore*. The *branzino* was indeed very fresh.'

216

Elene beamed at him. He looked as if he could do with fattening up. He was one of those young men – a little like Silvio had once been – who were so lean and yet ate such a lot that you couldn't help wondering where they put it.

'Bauer. Ferdinand Bauer.' He smiled. 'I'm just looking at the trail up to the sanctuary.' He showed her on the map. 'They say it's a lovely walk.'

'Oh, it is.' So far, so good, she thought. He was very charming. Perhaps it was easier to be friendly with the guests of their hotel than she had realised. 'May I join you for a moment?' She indicated the chair next to his. It was very pleasant out here in the courtyard garden, the blue agapanthus waving slightly in the breeze, the faintest hint of ozone in the air mingling with the sharp sweetness of the lemons, and the sun warm and golden as honey.

'Of course.' He was very polite – especially for someone so young – but also a little surprised, she could see. Perhaps he wanted to be left alone to study his map. But she would only take up a few minutes of his time.

'You are enjoying your stay with us, I hope?' She made a nod towards the pinkish-grey of the convent walls, visible beyond the cloisters. 'It is atmospheric here, *no*?'

'Oh, yes.' He nodded. 'It is a restored convent, I understand.'

'Yes, it is.'

He put his head to one side. 'The restoration has been carried out very sympathetically. And so many of the original features have been retained. I congratulate you.'

'And yet . . .' Elene let her voice trail. 'There is so much more we could do.'

'Perhaps.' His smile gave nothing away. 'There is always more that can be done with these old buildings.'

She tapped his arm playfully. 'You sound as if you know what you are talking about, *Signore*.'

He gave a modest little shrug. 'It's what I do for a living, as a matter of fact.'

'Really?' Even Elene wasn't convinced at her own performance, but the young man seemed to notice nothing amiss.

'I'm an architect, yes.' He sat back in his seat. 'And I have to admit that I'm very interested in your old convent, *Signora*.'

'Ah, I suspected as much.' Elene smiled to herself. So, he was already interested in the building – this might be easier than she had thought. Of course, the creatives of this world – such as painters, architects, chefs . . . they never really let go of what they felt passionately about. A painter would always be thinking about the landscape or the light, a chef would never completely forget about food, and an architect would always look at buildings with an architect's eye.

But although this Ferdinand Bauer was young, and although he was an architect, he was also – no doubt – like all men, susceptible to flattery. Like all men, he seemed to be ruled by his stomach. She wondered how to progress. 'And so, I imagine that you are working on some exciting project right now?'

'Right now?' His brow furrowed. Had she touched a nerve perhaps? 'I'm not here in a professional capacity,' he began. 'It's more of a . . .' He hesitated. 'A family affair.'

'How intriguing.' She resisted the impulse to ask more. That was not her purpose here. 'But no doubt people are always trying to pick your brains for ideas? I suppose it is a bit like being a doctor? Suddenly, everyone you talk to has some ailment they need to discuss.'

He laughed at this. 'Sometimes, yes.' He gestured towards the old convent building. 'But here, it's all been done already,

I can see. The staircase is elegant, the lobby cool and welcoming and yet retaining its original simplicity, the cloisters so romantic.' He let out a small sigh and gazed towards the fine narrow brickwork, the decorative tiles set into the various niches in the walls, the ruby-red bougainvillea clambering up the crumbling arches of pale stone.

Elene wondered what or who he was thinking of. Some young girl back at home in Germany no doubt. She wondered if she'd been mistaken about this young man. She would have expected the young to be interested in new ideas, to favour the contemporary, to be innovative, explorative . . . But this one sounded a bit too much like her own daughter. One last try, she thought. 'But as you yourself said, there is always more that can be done with an old building, is that not so, *Signore?*'

'Ferdinand, please.' But she saw a new light in his eyes, a new interest. 'It is a historic building, *Signora*, and very individual, very special. But . . .'

Elene made sure she kept a smile on her face. 'I need hardly tell you that we are catering for the luxury market here.'

'Yes, of course.' He frowned. 'But I'm still not sure . . .' He looked back towards the cloisters. It almost seemed as if he was waiting for someone to come out and save him.

'And as such, there are certain facilities that we are expected to provide.'

'Such as?' He raised a sandy eyebrow.

Elene took a deep breath. It was now or never. 'Spa facilities. An infinity pool. A rooftop bar . . .'

The other eyebrow went up. He whistled. 'You don't do things by halves around here, do you?'

'And generally, a more contemporary feel.' She plunged on.

'Contemporary?' he echoed.

She nodded. '*Sì.*' Just because the convent was old, didn't mean they couldn't provide a more up-to-date vibe in the place. It could still be restful and tranquil and all the other things that her mother and Isabella wanted, but it would belong in the twenty-first century – for the first time.

'Are you quite sure?' he asked her. 'It's hard to see how the place could be improved and yet still keep its original charm. It's already quite minimal. It's such beautiful stone, such exquisite carving . . .' He was frowning again, and Elene's heart sank. But just because this young architect didn't think they should do it, didn't mean that her ideas were bad ideas. It just meant that he was the wrong man to be talking to. What they needed, she thought, was not necessarily someone young, but someone more willing to embrace change.

'Yes, I am sure.' She didn't add that she and Silvio were the only ones that felt this way. To be honest she wasn't even convinced that Silvio did feel the same – or if he just supported her because she was his wife. She wanted to put her stamp on the place, that was all. She wanted to be valued. She wanted to be recognised as a co-owner.

'And the others?' There was a smile twitching at his lips now, and she got the definite feeling that he was teasing her.

'The others?'

'The owner – Chiara Mazzone, isn't it? Your mother, I think you said? And . . .' His voice trailed.

'We're co-owners.' Though what business it was of his she had no idea. She hadn't even asked him to do anything yet. 'We don't agree about everything, naturally. Not all the time. Whoever agrees about everything?' She gave a light laugh.

'So where were you thinking of housing the . . . spa?' He

looked around the charming courtyard with its stone flags and bright planting.

It had once been a simpler and more contemplative place. Elene guessed that when it was a convent, the flags had been bare, the stone well uncovered, the fountain the only decoration. The lemon tree had been here for almost a century, she believed, and was still going strong – there were many lemon trees in Liguria; in Monterosso they even had a festival of lemons every May, *Sagra del Limoni*, with lemon-themed decorations and menus in every restaurant. Lemon statues, market stalls selling lemon pie, lemon cake, lemon custard and *limoncino* – though not necessarily up to the quality of that produced in Elene's kitchen.

Her mind began to wander. It was the lemon that made the difference; so it was all about choosing the right lemons for this delicate recipe, which was made by steeping lemon zest in spirit and then diluting the mix in a sugar and water syrup. The intense aroma of essential oils in any lemon skin came naturally from its environment – and was therefore dependent on the microclimate, the proximity of the sea and protection from the cold winds in winter. Then it also depended on when the lemons were picked. Marcello had taught Elene that the first blossoming lemons, picked at dawn, had the most concentrated flavours – this was undeniably true. The syrup to alcohol ratio mattered too; Elene used grappa of prosecco, just as Marcello had done.

But she knew that her mother had planted the bougainvillea, and that she and Isabella had put their heads together and come up with the plan for the drifts of agapanthus and other flowers. Elene had to admit that as a whole, the colourful splashes of planting contrasted, complemented, and worked.

221

The terracotta urns and the original stone well and fountain completed a pretty much perfect picture.

'Not here,' she said hurriedly. God forbid. 'In a separate building perhaps?'

'The lines,' he murmured.

'Lines?'

He shook his head. 'An annexe of some kind?' The words almost seemed to pain him.

Elene held her breath. Was he taking this seriously after all? 'Yes,' she said. 'Would you be interested in taking a look around, perhaps giving us some ideas?' She gave him her best smile.

He hesitated. 'I don't think . . .'

Elene thought of the way he had been talking, heads together with Isabella earlier on. 'We would all appreciate it so much,' she said.

He seemed to at least be considering the idea now. 'Informally, do you mean?'

'For now, yes.' She beamed.

'And you're all on board?'

'We will be.' Elene had not realised what a good actress she could be. 'But at this stage, I would appreciate it if this little chat could be kept between the two of us.'

His expression grew wary at this.

She spread her hands. 'Who knows where it might lead?' Actually, she was rather good at all this chatting to the guests sort of stuff. Perhaps she had more of her mother's genes than she had realised.

'You haven't asked anything about me or my work,' he pointed out. 'What makes you think I can help you? I haven't had much experience of this sort of project.'

'But you are here.' Elene lifted her face to the sun. 'And I can tell that you understand the place.'

'I don't—'

'Just a few initial ideas,' she said. 'Just your impressions.'

'But—'

'Maybe a few sketches?'

'Well . . .'

She shrugged. 'Whatever you think is appropriate,' she whispered. 'We'd pay you for your time, of course.'

'Oh, no, I couldn't dream of—' He seemed very flustered all of a sudden.

Elene decided to leave it there. '*Grazie mille*,' she said. And she kissed him enthusiastically on both cheeks. He looked rather shell-shocked, but that was no bad thing. 'This is my email.' She pulled a notepad from her bag and scribbled the address down. 'Please send any communications to me here. And here's my mobile number.' She wrote this down too. She wanted everything to be professional and clear.

'Right.' He gave her a dazed look.

'Do you have a card, Ferdinand?' she asked him.

'A card? Oh, yes.' Somewhat reluctantly, he pulled a business card from his back pocket and handed it to her. It was crumpled around the edges and slightly squashed from having been sat on, but it looked like the real thing.

'Thank you.' She tucked it carefully into the zipped pocket of her bag. 'And now, please excuse me, but I must return to *la cucina*.'

'Of course, yes.' His eyes lit up. 'I'll be eating in tonight, *Signora*.'

As she had thought . . . A man and his stomach. 'And

remember . . .' She put a finger to her lips. 'It will be a wonderful surprise for the rest of my family.'

Elene practically skipped back inside with the lemon she had plucked from the tree. She felt a surge of excitement, of joy. She could do this, she realised. With this young man's help, she could make things visual, she could show her mother and her daughter how it could be done, how amazing it could be. She imagined her mother's smiling face, the warm tone of her voice. *Well done, Elene*, she'd say. *These are fabulous ideas. I didn't know you had it in you, but I can see now how much we could improve The Lemon Tree Hotel. You're so clever. You've really helped me to see.* Something like that anyway.

'Oh, there you are.' Silvio was lurking in the Cloisters Bar. 'You were talking to him for ages.' He was eying her suspiciously. 'What did you say? You didn't commit us to anything, did you?'

'I was setting things up, that is all.'

'And?' He caught hold of her before she could slip away.

'And I'll tell you later.' She looked meaningfully at the arm restraining her. Because no one was going to stop her carrying this through. She had enough money in their joint account to pay the young man – at least for his initial sketches. And after that – *allora*, who knew . . .

CHAPTER 24

Chiara

Chiara looked up as her granddaughter burst into the office.

'Sorry to disturb you, Nonna . . .' She seemed flustered.

'What is it, Bella?' She thought immediately of their guest, this Ferdinand Bauer who seemed to be having such an effect on Isabella. Had he upset her? Perhaps Chiara should have done more, said more to warn her, but . . .

Isabella looked behind her and pulled the door to. 'There's a woman in reception.' She shook her head as if she was unable to convey more in words.

'A woman?' Chiara's thoughts did a rapid turnaround.

'She is asking for Nonno.'

'Do we know her?'

'*Madonna* – no.'

Chiara put down her pen. 'What sort of a woman?' she asked. It might be a strange question, but from the way Isabella was acting, she was already getting a bad feeling about this.

Isabella shrugged. 'She is wearing very bright orange lipstick,' she said.

Chiara raised an eyebrow. That was hardly unusual.

'Tatty clothes, greasy hair, down-at-heel. Let's say she doesn't look like any of our guests, Nonna.'

'I see.' She was getting the gist. And yet this woman knew Alonzo? She hoped to God it wasn't some woman of his from Pisa or who knows where. Their marriage might have lost its intimacy, and God knows she had forfeited any right for him to be loyal to her, but that didn't mean she wanted the evidence thrust in her face.

Isabella hesitated. 'Shall I bring her in here?' She seemed worried. 'I could stay around in case you need me.' She bent closer towards Chiara. 'She's very loud, Nonna,' she warned.

'Don't worry, Bella. I'll deal with this.' Chiara got to her feet. She had expected to feel so different after Dante's departure from her life, after that talk with Alonzo about how their marriage would be from now on, after her decision to separate herself from her husband even though it would not be apparent to the world outside that anything had changed. But she didn't feel very different at all. Things with Alonzo were much as before – a cold body in bed was not so different to no body in bed – Elene had kept Chiara's secret, but seemed almost as distant as ever, and Dante . . . *Allora*. At least *she* knew that there was a little more truth in her life.

Chiara opened the door, took a deep breath to muster all the dignity she possessed, and swept out into the lobby.

The woman standing by the desk did indeed not look like any of their usual guests. She couldn't have been more out of place if she'd tried. She was dressed in a short black skirt and a pink blouse slightly stained under the armpits, and was wearing high-heeled gold sandals that unfortunately emphasised the skinny muscularity of her legs. Her dark hair was drawn back from her thin face, and she wore not only the orange lipstick Isabella had mentioned, but also thick and poorly-applied black eyeliner and an awful lot of bright coral blusher. She was gazing around her at the wide looping staircase, the pale walls and shadowy niches as if The Lemon Tree Hotel was another world.

Chiara didn't waste any time. '*Buon giorno, Signora.* You are looking for my husband Alonzo, I understand?' She kept her voice brisk and efficient, but polite. Over the years there had been many problems to deal with – both personal and concerning the hotel. Chiara had found that it was best to remain as cool and unemotional as possible. Practical issues could always be solved with thought, money, and time; everything else she had little energy for. 'He's not here at the moment. Perhaps I can help, *Signora* . . .?' She made it into a question – it was always better to know who you were dealing with.

'Conti.' The woman looked Chiara up and down.

What was she thinking? And could her husband really be involved with a woman like this? Chiara realised that she simply had no idea. She didn't know her husband at all.

'And you are?' She might look out of place here, but the woman didn't seem fazed in the least. Chiara felt a grudging respect for her.

'Chiara Mazzone – co-owner and general manager of this hotel.' Chiara stood straight and tall. This woman was a few years younger than her perhaps – in her mid-fifties, Chiara would guess, but she was too old for the clothes and make-up she was wearing. It was not just a question of money, surely, it was a question of style.

'His wife, eh?' The woman laughed – it was not a pleasant sound.

227

'Yes.' The bad feeling was getting stronger. Chiara was unwilling to stand in reception with this woman any longer. There were guests around, and she might make a scene. *Allora*. It was time to deal with whatever she had come for. 'Perhaps we could go into the office to discuss this matter?' she suggested. 'Or the bar?' Why was she here? Did she want money, or revenge – or both perhaps?

The woman smoothed the fabric of her skirt. 'Am I creating a bad impression for your charming hotel?' she said loudly.

So, she was aware of this? Interesting. Chiara shrugged as if it was of no importance. 'We can be more private in the bar, *Signora*, that's all.'

'*Va bene.*' The woman looked around her. 'Very nice, very nice. The bar then.'

Chiara shot a swift and despairing look at her granddaughter and proceeded to lead the way.

She headed for the far end of the cloisters. She didn't want to take the woman outside; it was far too tranquil out in the courtyard, and several guests were lounging with drinks and a book – she wouldn't want to disturb them. The young Australian couple were out there too – it was their last day and they were finally relaxing.

Chiara paused at the bar to order espressos for them both on the way. God knows she could do with one.

'You know my husband then, *Signora*?' she asked, as they sat facing one another. She may as well cut straight to the chase.

'I certainly do.' The woman was taking her time now. She sat back, taking stock of her surroundings, nodding occasionally as if everything was exactly as she'd pictured it: the graceful crumbling arches of pale stone, the narrow brickwork, the hand-painted decorative tiles set into a nearby niche. 'It's all so perfect,' she said. 'So peaceful.'

'We like to think so.' And for the first time, Chiara felt herself warm to the woman slightly. She wasn't so bad. She appreciated beauty and tranquillity at least. Chiara just hoped she wasn't out to try to destroy it in some way.

The coffee arrived and Chiara took a grateful sip. 'And so, what can we do for you, *Signora?*' she asked.

The woman drank her coffee in one gulp. When she replaced her cup on the table, the white porcelain was stained with the orange imprint of her lips. 'Do you know what things are like in Pisa, *Signora?*' she asked.

Chiara was taken aback. That wasn't quite what she had been expecting. 'Pisa?'

'In the apartment block your husband owns. Do you know how different it is from this place?' She gestured angrily towards the peaceful courtyard with its grey stone flags, gently dribbling fountain, and old stone well.

The apartment block. Of course. Chiara was beginning to understand what had brought the woman here. That was why she was so interested in this building, its appearance and atmosphere. She was comparing it to where she herself lived. She wasn't involved with Alonzo at all – *certo*, he would not look at a woman like this; he was much too fastidious. This woman lived in Pisa. She was here to complain about her landlord. 'You live in one of Alonzo's apartments?' She let out a breath she hadn't known she was holding.

'I don't.' The woman frowned. 'God forbid.'

Chiara raised an eyebrow. *God forbid?* 'Then . . .'

'But my mother does – and that's why I am here today.'

'I see.' Though she didn't. At least not yet. 'But I don't

understand how I can help you. I'm sorry.' She wasn't sorry either, mind – just angry with Alonzo for allowing this to happen, for the serene atmosphere of The Lemon Tree Hotel to be shattered in this way. 'You see, I have nothing to do with my husband's business, and so I'm unable to discuss it with you. You'll have to phone him direct. Or make an appointment to go and see him at his apartment in the city—'

'Oh, I've been there, don't you worry.' She leaned forwards, and Chiara winced from the smell of the woman – a mixture of cheap perfume and stale body odour. It wasn't her fault perhaps, but anyone could achieve personal hygiene – it cost almost nothing.

'And he wasn't there?' Chiara took another sip of her coffee. If he wasn't in Pisa, then she had absolutely no idea where he might be. She could phone him perhaps, but not at this precise moment, not with this woman sitting here in her hotel, expecting her to do something about a situation she knew nothing about.

'Sometimes he's there and sometimes he's not – but when he is there he won't see me.'

'Really? Is this true?' Chiara was surprised. Alonzo had always seemed so on top of things; it didn't sound like him at all.

'As true as I'm sitting here right now in your delightful hotel, *Signora*.'

Chiara didn't know what to say to this. What did the woman expect her to say? 'So, you came here.' Alonzo could be avoiding the woman for a very good reason. Perhaps she was unstable, crazy even. Perhaps she had created problems for him in the past, he might even have called in the police to deal with her. She could be a stalker or an arsonist or anything.

What did Chiara know? Alonzo told her nothing (which was ridiculous, of course). She could be dangerous, and Chiara would have no idea.

'I found out his other address, didn't I?' The woman looked pleased with herself, but Chiara had to admit that she didn't appear dangerous – at least not yet.

'That was enterprising of you, *Signora*.' She hoped this didn't sound sarcastic. But the woman's words were fuelling her fears. How did she find out exactly? 'But if you have a problem with your mother's accommodation . . .' She spread her hands. Subtext: what was Chiara supposed to do about it?

The woman stared at her. 'Have you ever seen it?' Her eyeshadow had creased and the eyeliner smudged in the heat. But the clownish look seemed sad somehow.

'Seen it?'

'The apartment block.' She rolled her eyes.

'Actually, no.' Chiara finished her coffee and pushed the cup to one side. She had never had any interest in the place. Why should she? It was Alonzo's business, and Pisa was his domain. She had visited her husband's apartment – the one he lived in whilst in the city – but not the places he rented out. She didn't even know the address.

'Then perhaps you should.'

Chiara blinked at her. 'May I ask why, *Signora*?'

The woman rolled up her sleeve and scratched her arm. 'Because it's a dump, Signora Mazzone. Because it's unhealthy.' Her voice rose. 'Because your husband doesn't give a fuck about any of his tenants—'

'*Basta*! That's enough now.' Chiara made to get up. She had tried to be polite. She had given this woman a chance to voice her grievance. But she certainly wasn't willing to sit and listen to her making these claims against her husband, using *that* sort of language in the Cloisters Bar.

'Go there.' The woman reached into her bag and grabbed a notebook and pen. 'This is the address.' She scribbled it down. 'Here.'

Chiara sank back into her seat.

'Just go and look. Please?' The woman looked so earnest, so forlorn.

Chiara began to feel sorry for her. It must have taken some nerve to come here to the hotel, to walk into the lobby, to take control of the situation in the way she had. But she didn't seem to understand that none of this was Chiara's concern. It was Alonzo's. 'I'll talk to my husband,' she said. 'I promise.'

The woman shook her head. 'Talk to some of the tenants instead, I would. They'll tell you what kind of a place it is.' She handed her the piece of paper.

Chiara took it. What else could she do?

'Though you might find out a lot more than you ever wanted to know.'

Perhaps that was what she was afraid of. 'And your mother?' Chiara asked.

'She's elderly and frail.' Signora Conti picked up her bag, which Chiara could see was made of a cheap imitation leather. Clearly, she was finished here. She'd said her piece and now she was expecting Chiara to sort the problem out.

'And what is the problem exactly? Does her apartment need redecorating or some maintenance done – is that it?' Because perhaps she could get Silvio to go there and help. He was so practical, and he'd always got on well enough with Alonzo. Perhaps Alonzo couldn't find anyone to do the necessary work in Pisa and simply hadn't mentioned it?

Signora Conti eyed her with pity. 'Yes, but that's not the issue. She's a long-term tenant. Your husband's given her notice so that he can get a higher rent. And she's got nowhere to go. Nowhere. She can't stay with me – we're already overcrowded.' The woman got to her feet and put her hands on her skinny hips. 'That's why I'm here,' she said. 'To ask him to reconsider.'

'I had no idea.' Chiara was still trying to take it all in. Some scummy apartment block? An elderly woman being evicted? Things that she wouldn't want to know? Was this the kind of place Alonzo ran in Pisa? She felt a flush of shame creep over her.

'Thank you for listening,' her visitor said. '*Grazie mille.* I'm grateful for that. Grateful for being allowed in here really.' She laughed her harsh laugh once more, but this time Chiara heard it differently. She heard the brashness, but also the vulnerability it was trying to hide. 'Even if nothing comes of it – at least I've tried.'

'I'll speak to him,' Chiara said again. She steeled herself. 'And I'll go there.'

'You will?' She looked pathetically grateful and, once again, Chiara felt ashamed. Just as she had told Dante – she had so much. And lifestyles could be decided on the toss of a dice.

'I certainly will.'

'*Arrivederci* then, *Signora.*' She held out her hand, and Chiara took it. 'And thank you.'

'Goodbye, *Signora.* All I can tell you is that I will do my best.' She hesitated. 'Can you add your number here?' She held out the paper. 'I could let you know how I've got on.'

'*Grazie.*' She was clearly surprised at this, and her eyes filled with tears. She bent to write her phone number. 'My mother is Beatrice Gavino. Apartment 5.'

Chiara nodded. 'Thank you.' She couldn't promise anything. But at least she could find out for herself how bad things really were.

'All this . . .' As Signora Conti went to walk away, she paused. She looked through the cloisters, into the courtyard where the vivid blue agapanthus flowers and the shiny lemon tree were gently glimmering in the sunlight. She shook her head. 'I don't know how your husband can live with himself, that's all.'

CHAPTER 25

Isabella

Isabella was doing some last-minute checks in the Cloisters Bar before they shut down for the night. Emanuele was pretty efficient – he'd wiped down all the tables and washed all the glasses, even given the hand-rail a quick polish before going home. The marble counter gleamed in the soft amber light, and the bottles lined on the shelves under the ornate narrow brick-work shone out their warm promises for tomorrow. Isabella moved a couple of chairs back into position. She didn't want to hang around. She could do with an early night – she was due to meet Ferdinand Bauer at 7 a.m. in reception for their walk up to the sanctuary, she reminded herself. As if she could forget – it had been playing on her mind all evening.

Because it was against her better judgement? Isabella paused in the doorway. She switched off the lights. Everything was in order in the Cloisters Bar. They kept a few lamps burning in the courtyard all night long; there was no one out there now, but the lamps still cast their blanket of golden light over the high walls, the stone flags, the ancient lemon tree, and the

235

spiky agapanthus flowers. She took a few steps forward, leaned on a pillar, and breathed in the night air. It tasted softer than daytime air. Could darkness make it less abrasive? Or was it something to do with synaesthesia – that confusion between the senses, that blurring of certain signals to the brain?

Which was rather like the blurring of signals when it came to Ferdinand Bauer. Isabella yawned. It had been another eventful day, and now the prospect of tomorrow's hike was giving her a not unpleasant fluttering in the stomach. Would she sleep tonight? Could she sleep? Ferdinand's invitation had been unexpected, but she had been pleased nonetheless. It was, as her grandmother might say, an unresolved situation – half-kisses often were, she supposed. Giovanna had said she should give him a chance, Nonna had told her to be careful. What was the answer then? She supposed she would have to decide that herself.

Thinking of her grandmother made Isabella's mind jump to what had happened earlier today when that woman had walked into the hotel lobby and demanded to see her grandfather. She shook her head and retraced her steps to the door. What was that all about? Her grandmother had dealt with the matter with her customary efficiency and calm – but she had been very quiet afterwards when Isabella had taken her some cold sparkling water at the end of her stint on reception. And then earlier this evening she'd taken Isabella aside and told her she was going to Pisa.

'Is something wrong, Nonna?' Her grandmother looked very serious. 'Is it something to do with my grandfather?'

She had sighed – and oh, she had looked so weary at that moment, that Isabella had wanted to gather her up in a protective hug and tell her to go and lie down for the rest of the evening. She probably would have done it as well if there hadn't been so many guests around – poor Nonna would not have appreciated such a public gesture drawing attention to her tiredness.

'It's nothing to worry about, *cara*,' she said – rather unconvincingly in Isabella's opinion. 'But I need to check up on something to do with the apartments – and see your grandfather too, I suppose.' Though she didn't sound enamoured at the prospect.

It crossed Isabella's mind – as it often did – that her grandparents lived very separate lives. Had it always been that way? When her grandmother used to sit her on her knee and tell her fairy stories about princes and princesses, woods and wolves, Isabella had assumed that her grandfather must be Nonna's prince; as she told those stories she always had such a wistful expression. But some time during the past fifteen years Isabella had realised – this wasn't the sort of love her grandmother had spoken of with such passion in her voice, such love in her heart. How could it be? She remembered that comment the Signora Veroni had made about two men fighting over her grandmother. She remembered their guest, Dante Rossi, who had turned out to be an old friend of Nonna's. And she wondered about this new sadness in her grandmother's eyes . . .

'Let me take care of the rota,' Isabella had told her. 'What time do you want to go?'

'Mid-morning will be fine.' And her smile was a little warmer and relaxed. 'Thanks, Bella.'

'*Prego*.' She was welcome. But what was the problem? Isabella shrugged. No doubt she would find out soon enough. But it was odd. Was it her imagination? She couldn't say for certain. But nothing had been quite the same since that day

237

both Dante Rossi and Ferdinand Bauer had arrived at The Lemon Tree Hotel. Of that, she was quite sure.

Isabella left the bar and headed for the lobby. She had even seen her mother talking to Ferdinand in the courtyard this afternoon, and that was practically unprecedented. Her mother rarely ventured out of the kitchen, and when she did, she tended to avoid the guests as if they had the plague. So, what? Was her mother charmed by him too?

She jumped, startled. The lights were low – she'd turned them down herself an hour ago – but there was a figure in the niche opposite the staircase, standing right up close to the painting of the Archangel Gabriel, up so close that he was touching the worn, gilt frame. In the base of the niche, the white candle flickered. 'Hey!'

His head jerked around.

'Ferdinand?' Her voice was sharp. What in God's name was he up to?

'Oh.' He took a rapid step backwards and almost tripped over the step. 'Isabella. Hello.'

'What on earth are you doing?' She came closer. And hadn't she asked him that once before not too long ago?

He stuck his hands in his pockets. A bit late for that, she thought.

'This painting.' He nodded at it as if she might not have noticed it before, living here as she did. 'It's quite beautiful.'

'You think so?' Isabella put her hands on her hips and regarded him sternly. Inside, she felt a deep disappointment. She had been fooling herself. Nonna was right, and she should have listened to her. She had allowed herself to be fooled by eyes as blue as a summer sky.

'Of course.'

Beautiful wasn't the first word that came to her mind. In fact, the painting was rather an amateurish affair – which made it all the stranger that Ferdinand was interested in it. 'It's not valuable, you know.'

'Oh, my goodness.' And he actually blushed. 'You didn't think I was going to steal it, did you?'

Isabella merely raised her eyebrows. What else was she supposed to think? Everyone to his own taste. She had never thought much about the painting herself – it had simply always been there. This was an old convent. The artist's daughter – Aunt Giovanna – was the last person who had lived here – taken in by the nuns when she was only about seventeen. Hence, the painting would always remain. It belonged here in The Lemon Tree Hotel.

'I was wondering what techniques the artist used to catch the light like that.' Ferdinand frowned up at Gabriel as if the archangel might share the secret of his conception. 'And the framing – I wondered whether it was gilt or painted wood. You know, it's very interesting.'

He had been doing a lot of wondering – rather like all the wondering he had been doing when she'd caught him in the kitchen garden that time when her mother had been so angry. And he certainly didn't give up easily. Isabella narrowed her eyes. 'Are you an artist as well as an architect, Ferdinand?' She'd be surprised at that too. He was clearly rambling because he was embarrassed to be caught in the act, not because he was some kind of undercover art expert.

'No.' He took another step away. 'Sorry.'

Isabella wasn't sure what to do. Should she tell her grandmother that Ferdinand Bauer was showing more than a passing interest in the painting? Was there any reason that she should?

Nonna wouldn't like it —even without knowing who his father was or why he had come here. Or was Isabella overreacting again? She didn't think so. He hadn't simply been admiring the picture; he'd been examining it, at least as far as she could tell, though for what reason, she had no clue.

'As I said,' she repeated, 'the painting isn't worth much. But it's valuable to us.' She stressed the last word. Surely, he had some integrity? Surely, she wouldn't be attracted to him if he didn't have even a few measly grains of the stuff?

'You did think I was up to no good, didn't you?' Those eyes were so clear and honest. Challenging too.

'No.' Although . . . 'Yes.' If it had been anyone else, she'd have thought that, for certain. 'Perhaps,' she compromised. Because something was going on – but she had to have some faith in her instincts too. And her instinct was to like him.

His gaze never left her face, though his mouth twitched in amusement – at her indecision, no doubt. It was a manifestation of how she felt about the man. 'Who painted it?'

'Luca Bordoni.' A flicker of something – understanding? – danced into her mind and then flitted away. 'Giovanna's father.' Did he know that already? Surely, he knew that already? She pointed. 'That's his signature in the corner.' She recalled Ferdinand's initial interest in the painting when he had first checked in. And his interest in Giovanna. It couldn't be one massive coincidence. There had to be a connection.

'Ah.' Ferdinand nodded. 'So, is this the only painting of his at The Lemon Tree Hotel?' he asked conversationally, as if they were two art critics taking morning coffee.

'*Basta*. Enough. I'm going to bed.'

As she brushed past him, he caught her arm. 'But we're still on for tomorrow?'

Isabella hesitated. How had he managed to charm Giovanna in the way he had? And what exactly was he up to? Even now, she wanted to trust him, but how could she if he wasn't honest with her? She wanted to like him too – but how could she when he seemed to be everything her family should feel embittered towards? It was one thing not wanting to talk about this unlikely pilgrimage he was doing on his father's behalf, because that wasn't Isabella's business, not really. But this . . . this was more closely connected to The Lemon Tree Hotel itself, she felt. This concerned her directly. She looked back at Luca Bordoni's painting, illuminated by the white candle. She bent down and blew it out.

'Please, Isabella?'

'Very well.' But she would be asking him for a further explanation, she decided. And this time it had better be a lot more convincing.

CHAPTER 26

Isabella

The following morning, Ferdinand was waiting for her in the lobby – standing, not by Luca Bordoni's Archangel Gabriel, but by the front door, dressed for the hike in sturdy walking boots, green shorts, and a T-shirt, with a straw hat on his head, a small rucksack on his back, and a camera slung around his neck. The typical tourist. Despite her worries about the wisdom of this expedition, Isabella suppressed a smile. She was wearing a cotton dress and sandals because the warm weather was showing no signs of disappearing any time soon. But they were strong sandals – she knew what was required on these trails. All she had in her shoulder bag was a bottle of water, some sunscreen, and her mobile. Not that she was planning to use it – and she could hardly zip back down the mountainside should she be required at the hotel – but she liked to be contactable at least.

'Good morning.' She kept her voice cool. She hadn't forgotten the events of the previous night – in fact, thinking about them had kept her awake for more than an hour before she eventually fell asleep. The next thing she knew, her alarm was playing its waterfall melody and it was time to get up again.

'Morning, Isabella.' Ferdinand seemed cheerful enough. He opened the front door. 'It's a lovely day. Perfect for our early morning walk, don't you think?'

'Yes, it is.' Outside, it was just getting light, though the hotel faced south-west and they'd have to wait until they were out on the cliff to see much of the sunrise. The sky was a silvery pink and blue with woolly ribbons of grey on the far horizon. He was right. It was a beautiful morning and she couldn't wait to get out there. She inclined her head. 'Shall we go?'

They walked through the olive grove, the trees still dewy from an early morning mist, until they reached the *Sentiero Azzurro*. They took the path down towards the village. In the pastel light of dawn, the colours of Vernazza shimmered softly like unpolished jewels against the silvery-grey sky and sea. There was a feeling of peace about the landscape that had not yet fully woken up – even the train station was deserted. They paused to take it all in.

'That's Vernazza's other convent,' Isabella told Ferdinand. She pointed to the old building perched on the hillside beyond. Its roof was bright terracotta and its façade a dark salmon-pink, but as with all the buildings in Vernazza, the paint had peeled to reveal the grey render beneath.

Ferdinand looked over to where she was pointing. 'Any nuns still around?'

She shook her head. 'They all left a long time ago. It's used for community events these days.' The church beside the convent was of a simple design – white with a central rose window and a grey bell tower. Next to it, snaking through the vines, terraces and trees, were the steps leading up the mountain.

'And that's where we're going. It's where the path to the Sanctuary of Nostra Signora di Reggio begins,' she told him. It was ironic, she found herself thinking, that she should be visiting a safe house with a man who might be dangerous – in more ways than one. Not that he looked dangerous this morning in his tourist get-up. She smirked.

Ferdinand glanced over towards the sinuous mountainside path and did a double take. 'Shit. It's pretty steep.' He turned back to Isabella. 'Will you be OK?' He looked pointedly at her open sandals.

'Yes.' She laughed. 'Will *you* be OK, Ferdinand?'

He held up both hands and gave a rueful grin. 'You're right. This is your territory.' And the ice of the morning was broken – or at least cracked – for now.

They continued along the path lined with dry-stone walling that protected the *ortos*, the little allotments where villagers grew their artichokes and their beans, their *melanzane* and their onions. 'See the *trenino*?' She pointed again, this time to the steep hillside above.

He stopped walking and peered towards the little red-wheeled train already twisting up through the terraces. They started work early in Liguria, to make the most of the cooler hours. 'Hey, that's ingenious.'

'It's the monorail wine train. It takes the workers high above the village to the small family vineyards, and then brings the baskets of grapes back down again.'

'Wow.' He seemed impressed. 'Does every family have its own small vineyard then?'

She smiled. 'Historically, yes. In reality, not every family, not any more – they're too labour-intensive, I suppose.' She looked up at the men already working on the mountainside.

244

'There are still small co-operatives though. They grow various grapes – the Bosco, Albarola, and Vermentino.'

'You're very knowledgeable.' There was a note of respect in his voice.

'I like to keep an eye on our wine list.' Not to mention that her grandmother had given her tiny glasses of wine to taste since she was about ten years old. 'And lots of people want to keep the old methods going.' Which was a good thing in Isabella's opinion. 'It's an important part of our heritage,' she added proudly.

They continued along the old mule track where the white grapevines were hanging over the path. 'Imagine what it was like in the old days though,' he remarked. 'It's amazing what they've managed to do on the side of a mountain.'

'You're right.' She was glad that he got it – not all tourists appreciated how hard life must have been. 'These hillsides have been terraced for centuries.' How they had achieved it though, she'd never truly understand. 'We've certainly had more than our share of great stonemasons.' She let her hand trail along the stone wall as they walked. Higgledy-piggledy yes, but that was for practical reasons. Those builders had used every stone available – from big to small, flat to curved.

'Like jigsaw puzzles.' He bent closer to examine the stone-work. Odd pieces of marble and brick had been added to the wall over the years in order to keep it solid. 'Built to last.'

'Yes,' she agreed. 'But the weather around here has different ideas in the winter. If these walls aren't well maintained and can't hold back the soil . . .' She looked up at the terraces. With fewer people working to cultivate the land and tend the vineyards and olive groves, the walls and the terraces were bound to be neglected. They couldn't be expected to survive.

'Landslides,' he murmured.

'Exactly. The Cinque Terre has been made a conservation area, and people are certainly trying to protect the environment here, but . . .'

'It was a different life,' he said, 'when your people worked the land.'

It was. Things had changed – and surely there would be some consequence.

They continued along the path and called in at the old convent. The arches were crumbling, the paint was peeling, and the bricks of the old well were broken – nevertheless, in the cloisters the faint lines of an ancient fresco were still visible and a delicate painting had been tucked into a small niche in the wall. Niche. Painting. The events of last night flashed back into her mind once again. She showed Ferdinand the mural and the tiny work of art. 'Since you're so interested in paintings,' she teased. She just wanted to get a reaction, she supposed.

He shot her a look she couldn't interpret, but didn't rise to the bait. 'Very nice,' he said. 'That's one of the things I love about Italy.'

'The frescoes?'

'The sense of history.'

She nodded. 'Me too.' It was hard to imagine not being surrounded by these historic buildings, this legacy of her ancestors, this sense of the past. 'And what do you think of this other convent, Ferdinand?' she asked. 'Is it as fascinating as ours?' Because his interest in The Lemon Tree Hotel was evident.

'Nowhere near as fascinating.' His gaze shifted from the convent building to Isabella herself. It was another of his appraising looks. She felt a blush rise to her cheeks and willed it to go away. 'It's definitely not as classy as The Lemon Tree,' he added.

She gave a light laugh. 'I should hope not.' Though if her family hadn't saved it, who knew what the future of their own *L'Attico Convento* might have been?

They retraced their steps past the church of Santa Margherita di Antiochia. 'It's fourteenth century, maybe earlier,' she tossed the information to him over her shoulder. 'And we'll have to miss out the cemetery . . .' Even though it had staggeringly beautiful views over the harbour. 'Otherwise we'll never get there.'

Ferdinand was right – the stone steps lined with passion flowers and jasmine were charming but very steep. Isabella was used to them of course, but to her secret delight, after a few minutes he was out of breath from the climb. She turned and surveyed him, enjoying the all too brief sense of superiority. '*Allora*, we call this the Via Dolorosa.'

He frowned. 'Way of Suffering?'

'Exactly.' She gestured to the first station of the cross erected beside the rough rocky path. It was a crumbling pink and grey shrine. 'This is to remind the pilgrims of the journey of Christ to the Cross. Each station is symbolic of a certain part of the journey. We will see several of these little statues on the way up.'

'I can't wait.' He joined her on the step by the shrine and together they looked back the way they had come – down to the village and harbour of Vernazza, its colours sharpening in the light of the early sun, the silvery threads of dawn now dissipated into the deep blue sea.

'This was your idea, remember,' she said.

'It was about the only way I could think of to get any time

with you.' He turned to face her, close enough to touch. He didn't touch though. And she wasn't sure whether to be disappointed – or not.

She smiled. 'We are always busy at The Lemon Tree Hotel.'

'I've noticed.' He put his head to one side. 'You're Catholic, I suppose, aren't you, Isabella?'

'Lapsed.'

'Already?' he joked. 'How old are you? Nineteen? Twenty?'

'Old enough to know my own mind,' she flashed back at him. He was not in a position to try to get one over on her, as the English might say. Isabella certainly hadn't forgiven him yet.

He grinned. 'I can see that.'

'But I respect this place.' She shrugged. 'It's important to the locals. It means something.'

He nodded, paused for a moment, as if taking this in. He lifted his camera and took a few shots, but she guessed that he knew the pictures wouldn't capture it.

'Come on then. On to the next Station of the Cross.'

He groaned – but followed her lead.

The path was studded with olive trees, prickly pear, and cacti, and they were rewarded for the climb by the view of the ocean, which flooded their vision with every twist and turn of the Via Dolorosa. They stood together looking down in awe. The first church bells rang out with their usual loud, low, sonorous clang. Then came the next, and then another from a more distant village. Ferdinand laughed.

Isabella laughed with him. 'You should hear it at the weekend,' she said. 'It's a mad cacophony of bell-ringing, a sort of dance between bass and treble.'

'I hope I'll still be here.' He turned to face her. 'You love this place, don't you, Isabella?'

'It's home,' she said simply. And he gave her a look as if he understood.

'Is this it?' he asked when they reached a small and derelict stone building housing another shrine. 'Is this the sanctuary?' He lifted his arm to mop his brow. The building was surrounded by olive trees and it stood under the shelter of a pine; the ground was scattered with pine needles, and the blanket of the sea rolled and shimmered below and beyond.

Isabella threw back her head and laughed.

'What?'

'No,' she told him. 'This is the chapel of San Bernardo. I do not wish to worry you, Signor Bauer – but we are not yet even halfway.'

'Did I say I was tired?' Ferdinand grumbled as they paused for a swig of water.

Isabella watched the rise and fall of his Adam's apple as he drank. She could smell the fragrance of pine resin mixed with ozone and the herby vegetation that surrounded them. 'Are you?'

He shook his head, fixed her with a look from those cool eyes. 'We haven't even got started yet.'

Hmm.

The path was still steep, but Ferdinand seemed to have got into the pace of the climb and he began telling her how much he had enjoyed his visit to Lucca. She listened to the rhythm of his low voice, hearing the buzz of the insects around them in the background, conscious of the increasing warmth of the sun on her hair and face, the scents of the fragrant herbs that grew on the hillside – lavender and wild thyme. And she realised how much she was enjoying this morning hike with him, this rather strange and definitely secretive visitor to her land. He didn't belong here – of course he did not belong here – but he seemed to understand the place, he seemed to appreciate its serenity.

'Did you go to the amphitheatre?' she asked him. That was her favourite part of Lucca. It had been created in the first century AD for the usual gladiatorial shows and games, and, having been re-built since being abandoned all those centuries ago, it was still quite something.

'Oh, yes. A fascinating project. I was reading all about it.' She caught the enthusiasm in his voice.

'Project?'

'Mid-nineteenth century. The architect Lorenzo Nottolini had the old buildings of the ancient arena pulled down, and the inner area, with a slightly adjusted profile, became the present day piazza. It's ingenious – and stunningly effective.'

Isabella was impressed. 'You found out a lot in one day, Ferdinand.'

He gave a modest shrug. 'Just naturally interested in the architectural aspect.'

'Being in that line of work yourself,' she added.

'Exactly.' He gave her a rather strange look, and Isabella had the distinct feeling that he was about to say more. But yet again he held back.

She sighed. 'And what did you make of the amphitheatre from a professional point of view?'

'An excellent job.' He paused to catch his breath. 'There was music playing and the acoustics were amazing . . .' He broke off as if words were not sufficient to describe the experience.

She smiled and nodded. She understood perfectly. She could

hear in his voice how much he loved her country – despite his holding back. And that gave her a feeling of contentment. She didn't question the reasons why – not now. She just held on to it.

'Tell me some more about this trail,' Ferdinand asked her as they passed another pink shrine. Although the light was now so much sharper, he was still speaking softly, as if he didn't care to rupture the delicate atmosphere of the morning.

'It was originally used by the Vernazzan fishermen,' she told him. 'It was a link with the hinterland. And then the mule track became Via Crucis with all these colourful chapels – I have no idea when.'

'Did your family ever come here for sanctuary?'

'During the war years, yes.' Though here they were entering dangerous territory. 'The whole village came here. It was a refuge from the bombing, you know.'

Abruptly, he stopped walking. 'I love this place, Isabella,' he told her.

She knew it. She had recognised it in his voice and now she could see it in his eyes. 'Yes.'

'But I know my country was responsible for much of the destruction and hard times your people experienced during the war.'

Isabella hesitated. Was it really so simple? She thought of Giovanna – she would say that no, it wasn't. 'In part,' she agreed.

Ferdinand kicked at a stone on the pathway. He looked so miserable that Isabella reached out and put her hand lightly on his arm. His skin was warm and golden from the sun. 'But hasn't it always been that way throughout history?' she continued. 'Men of all nationalities' – and hardly ever women, she silently added – 'obsessed with power, greedy for control, trying to take over another man's land?' She spread both hands now, the gesture encompassing the stony path, the gnarled olive trees, the sapphire blue sea below. 'We can hardly blame an entire nation.'

'I suppose not.' Though he looked doubtful.

'We're all European now.'

'Yes, we are.' But he still sounded very serious.

Isabella wanted to take his frowning expression and fling it into the ocean. They had survived the war, had they not? People had died, but people always died. It was the cycle of life. 'And in Italy, we try to forgive and forget.' She nudged him. 'Life is for living, *no*? It is for enjoying the sun and the warmth, the food and the laughter.'

'Yes, you're right.' And at last he smiled.

'And it is for walking up to the sanctuary,' she reminded him. 'Come.' They might not be religious pilgrims, but she and Ferdinand were pilgrims of a sort; everyone was.

He shot her another of those appraising looks that she was getting rather used to. 'Isabella,' he said, 'how on earth did you get to be so wise?'

She gave a little smile. 'From the women in my family,' she told him. 'They are wise without even having to try.'

Finally, they reached the avenue of trees that led to the Madonna di Reggio. The sanctuary was situated in a large piazza of stately elms and ancient spread-eagled oaks, with benches placed for weary travellers in the dappled shade beneath. It was quite a spectacle, and Isabella was once again gratified by Ferdinand's audible gasp. 'We are now 310 metres above sea-level,' she informed him. 'Well done!'

He glanced at her rather sharply from the corner of his eye, but he was still smiling. 'It is a fabulous place.'

'And wait till you see the view.'

They passed the marble sarcophagus that collected water from a gargoyle set in a grotto of seashells, and Ferdinand took still more photos. Isabella suspected that she would be within the frame of many of them, but she didn't mind, it wasn't hard to keep smiling. 'How old is this?' he asked.

Isabella shrugged. 'They found it by accident,' she said, 'when a tree came down in a storm. The church was built in the eleventh century, but it seems likely that this was an old site of worship.'

He nodded. 'It certainly looks that way.'

She led them further through the wooded piazza where the sharp shadows of the trees cut through the morning sunlight and not another human figure was to be seen. They came to the church and peeked inside to admire the pretty painted ceiling and the marble pillars. The church possessed an air of sweet simplicity that Isabella had always loved. She remembered the first time she had hiked here with her grandmother – she was only about seven, she supposed, but even then, the shrines on the pathway, the old chapel, this sanctuary . . . The atmosphere, the sense of history, the strength of her people's beliefs – these had all fascinated her.

'Most of the locals are still very attached to the sanctuary,' she told him. 'We have a festival in August when a procession leaves from Vernazza for the Holy Mass.' She rolled her eyes. 'Plus a massive village picnic, of course.'

He laughed. 'Any excuse for a party?'

'You can bet your life.'

'Though it also shows what a strong community you still

have here,' he added. 'Despite people moving away to the cities, despite tourism.'

'We do. In summer people let out rooms, in winter they shut their doors, and in spring they open their arms out once more to the world.'

They strolled over to an ancient oak with a seat underneath at the top of the piazza to sit in the shade and admire the view. Isabella looked out over the coastline she loved: the green-cloaked mountainside, the terraced olives and vines and dazzles of yellow that were the lemon trees, the vast teal-green ocean. She could see the boats in the sea down far below, drifting in and out of sight like ghostly apparitions. Both of them were silent for a minute or two, just taking in the beauty of the scene.

'Most of the locals are still staunch Catholics, I suppose?' Ferdinand asked her. He sat down on the bench and she followed suit. Next to him – but not too close this time.

'Especially the older generations.' Isabella had been brought up Catholic, of course, but she had never let its rules dominate her life even while she appreciated the values that most religions were built on. Family values, being a good neighbour, trying your best to be fair and honest . . . She sneaked a sideways glance at Ferdinand. Definitely not stealing other people's paintings – these were the values that had always bonded her family and the community in which they lived, and these were the values by which she tried to live her life, just as her parents and her grandmother had before her.

'It's so peaceful up here,' he said. 'There's that sense of being on top of the world. I can see why they wanted to build a sanctuary on this spot.'

Isabella nodded. Peaceful it might be, but there was one

thing that she could not put from her mind any longer. She still needed some answers. 'But, tell me about the painting, please,' she began.

'Painting?' Those blue eyes were all innocence.

'Last night?' She poked him in the ribs. 'Luca Bordoni's Gabriel.'

'Ah yes.' He looked rather shamefaced. He leaned back against the broad trunk of the oak tree and let out a small sigh.

Isabella had no sympathy. 'Why were you so interested in it?' She held up a hand before he could speak. 'And please don't give me any more of that rubbish about how a painter catches the light or how you wanted to examine the frame.'

'Well—'

She stopped him again. 'And don't try to tell me that you don't want to talk about it either, like you did in Sestri Levante.' An image flashed into her head: Ferdinand Bauer stooping to kiss her. She blinked fiercely and it was almost gone.

'It's not easy, Isabella,' he said softly.

Outside the shade of the oak tree, the morning sun had strengthened, creating a haze of warmth that seemed to surround them. The occasional insect buzzed lazily by, a leaf stirred in the faintest of breezes, a bird let out a snatch of song. 'Life isn't easy,' she reminded him – a frequent riposte of her mother's when Isabella was young.

'Very true.' He gazed past her and down towards the sea, which was smooth and shiny, ruffled only by the occasional fringe of foamy water. His expression was thoughtful – and sad. 'What must it have been like, Isabella?'

So – was this a rhetorical question now? 'What must what have been like, Ferdinand?'

'Living in an occupied town during such a war? So much horror amongst so much beauty.'

So that was it. The subject was still on his mind – even amidst this serenity. And she supposed that it was natural – given the reason for his coming to Vernazza in the first place – for Ferdinand to brood. Up here, there was a sense of distance from the town, but also a feeling of protection; the sanctuary seemed to cradle Vernazza in its very palm. 'It was very hard,' she said. No point in lying about it, not now. And she herself had been quizzing Giovanna about it only the other day. It seemed that period of the past was currently on everyone's mind. 'There was no food and also no freedom. Men were being forced to fight or flee. I can't imagine the horror of it. Can you?' She turned to him.

He shook his head. Now, he was looking even more serious than before. 'My father spoke about it – not often, but certainly before I came here. I know it was different for him than it was for your people, he must have had food and a modicum of comfort.' He sighed. 'But I also know how much he hated it. How he longed for the war to be over. For things to go back to normal, I suppose.'

Isabella could see that too. Men were men, whichever army they were fighting for. There were good men and bad men. They all had their hopes and dreams. 'What happened to him when the war ended?' she asked.

Ferdinand shrugged. 'He did what he had to do to survive. He left Italy when he was told to leave Italy. He went back to Germany. He lived an ordinary life. One day, he met my mother – she thought it was too late for her to have children, but no, it turns out that it was not.' His eyes met hers. 'And here I am.'

And here he was indeed. Isabella was the first to look away. She looked down at the pale flagstones on the ground where puddles of sunlight were framed by the deep shade from the boughs and leaves of the oak tree. It was an emotionally understated story, but it moved her. She looked back at Ferdinand – he had closed his eyes for a moment and so it was safe. The way he spoke moved her. She loved watching the mobility of his face, the changing expression in his eyes, and listening to the fluent formality of his English. Most of all, she liked watching his mouth. His lips were full and sensual, the bottom lip narrower than the top. His teeth were even and white, but one of the eyeteeth was a little crooked and she quite liked this imperfection.

He opened his eyes and Isabella gave a little start of surprise. She forced herself back to the subject in hand. Best stay on course, she reminded herself. 'But your father asked you to come back here to Vernazza,' she pressed. 'Why did he do that?'

'Guilt?' He reached out to brush a tendril of hair from her face and she half-closed her eyes, shocked at the desire that shot through her from just this one small intimate gesture.

'For what exactly?' she whispered. Because – what had he done?

'He felt bad about his part in it all – even though he had no choice at times.'

'Mmm.' She could see the logic in that. It was a bit like survivor's guilt, she supposed. It wasn't Karl's fault that he was there – he hadn't asked to be part of any war.

He leaned forwards, his arms resting on his knees. 'And I told you about how he wanted to make amends.'

'Yes.' She frowned. 'But how can he do that?' Was there some local family perhaps who had been affected by something

257

that had happened? Did he want to give them money? The villagers of Vernazza would be far too proud to accept that.

'Isabella.' He took off his straw hat and put it down on the bench on the other side of him. He pulled the rucksack off too and put it on the ground by his feet. A dart of sunlight illuminated his fair hair and she could see the sweat glistening on his forehead.

'Yes?'

'You ask so many questions.'

'Yes.' And she was still waiting for some answers.

He leaned back again and looked through the leaves of the oak tree up to the sky. Then back to Isabella again. 'May I ask why you want to know? About my father? About what he did or did not do? About how he feels and why I am here?'

'And about your interest in the painting,' she added to the list.

'Yes – and about my interest in the painting.' He gave an exasperated laugh.

'Because I want to know . . .'

'Yes?'

'Who you are.' She hadn't meant to say this. She'd intended to say something glib and half jokey. *Keep it light, Isabella . . .* But it was the truth, and so why not say it? She wanted to know who Ferdinand Bauer really was. Was he a bad guy or was he a good guy? That was what it came down to in the end.

'Why?' He wasn't going to let her get away with that so easily. And his eyes hadn't left her face.

Because I like you, she thought. Because you've charged into my life, a life I was in total control of thank you very much, and you've made me wonder. About who I am, about what I want out of life, about *who* I want. But to say all that, would be going much too far. So, she said nothing and merely gave the tiniest shrug of the shoulders. Because if he didn't at least sense some of what she was feeling . . . And it was time for him to take the lead surely?

The silence between them was suddenly so intense that Isabella was sharply aware of her breath, his breath, and even the breath of the almost imperceptible breeze. It was magical. Who could break this spell?

He reached out and drew her closer. He held her chin and he kissed her. It wasn't just a brush of the lips this time. It was an exploratory kiss, a sort of *Am I allowed to do this?* kind of a kiss; at first tentative and then more confident, more sure. He smelt of the landscape they'd just walked through – dry-stone walling and the bitterness of olives – as if the land had almost become a part of him. And he tasted good: slightly minty and slightly salty at the same time. Definitely good.

They drew apart and stared at one another. Isabella was shocked at herself. She hadn't intended *that* to happen. She glanced sideways at the sanctuary. Wasn't this sacred land? Should she really be here, kissing a stranger? It was very nice though.

'I'd like to tell you more, Isabella,' he said earnestly. 'You don't know how much I want to tell you everything.'

Then do it, she thought. 'So?'

'But I can't.'

Right at this second, Isabella wasn't sure that she cared. Right at this second – sacred place or not – she rather wanted him to kiss her again.

He bent closer. 'Do you trust me?'

'No,' she said. But she guessed the desire was still burning in her eyes.

'Oh, Isabella.' He pulled her closer.

She wound her arms around his neck. She loved the feel of him – the taut leanness of his shoulders, the jut of his shoulder blades through the T-shirt, the touch of his lips, stronger and more passionate now. So, he was leaving soon. So, he was a thief. So, his father had committed war crimes – maybe.

She couldn't help herself. There were lots of things she should be doing, probably lots of things she should be saying too. But she'd rather stay here kissing him – all day long.

CHAPTER 27

Elene

Elene was baking – for breakfast and lunch. In the hotel, break-fast continued until ten-thirty and so was rather a conveyor belt affair, in order for everything to be fresh from the oven. But, ah . . . Their guests were on holiday – why shouldn't they relax and take their day at a slower pace? Elene was in an unusually tolerant frame of mind.

She added the remaining flour, salt, olive oil and rosemary to the yeast mixture that had already been warming for half an hour – making a start on the *focaccia* for lunch. Baking bread was a slow process, and this was one of Elene's specialities – a crispy, olive-oil crusted kind of *focaccia* with a soft puffy interior and a fragrance of rosemary to die for. She loved the process of making it – the kneading, the stretching of the dough to fit the pan, roughing it up with finger holes, adding a few simple ingredients – perhaps tomatoes and olives, or just rosemary, the final sexy drizzle of the olive oil, and a splash of salty water. Hot out of the oven, there was nothing quite like it.

Febe was making the *crema* for the next batch of *cornetti* – to

Elene's exclusive recipe; the brioche pastry laminated with butter to be shaped into perfect crescents – and so Elene had to keep an eye on this too. But she could tell from the sweet vanilla scent rising from the pan that Febe had got things right. A good cook should trust her instincts.

Elene inserted the dough hook and began to knead the *focaccia* dough. Ten minutes would do it; it should be soft, supple and sticky. This morning she had started off by making a *farinata* – this was comfort food at its best in Elene's opinion, a dish saturated with memories, tradition, and nostalgia. The *farinata* was already baking and she could smell its delicious toasty fragrance. Crisp and golden on the top, soft and moist on the inside, this thin savoury chickpea pancake should be eaten straight from the oven, plain or with either onion or *stracchino* cheese, and when Silvio was around, it generally was.

Marco popped his head around the swing door just as Elene was wondering where everybody had got to this morning. By now her mother and daughter were usually both sitting at the table, heads together, drinking espresso and comparing notes in that way they had that seemed to exclude anyone else who might be around. Elene kneaded the dough with a touch more ferocity. 'Hi,' she called. '*Va bene*, Marco?'

'Have you seen Isabella?' Marco peered around the kitchen. He was a sweet young man, and Elene suspected he had his eye on her daughter. But she doubted that Isabella was interested in the poor lad, he wouldn't have enough about him to challenge her.

'Not yet.' Elene continued working the dough. 'But she must be around somewhere.' Isabella was always up and around early. 'Is there a problem?' She sniffed. 'Febe?' she called. 'Have you checked the last batch of pastries?'

'*Sì, sì*.' Febe left her pan of *crema* and grabbed an oven glove.

'Not really. I only wanted to ask her about this order for cleaning materials.'

Elene clicked her tongue. Cleaning materials? Couldn't he see that she was busy? Surely breakfast was a lot more important than cleaning materials? 'Is she in the office?' She glanced around to see Febe whisking the *cornetti* out of the oven. The crescents were the same size and shape and perfectly golden. She nodded approval.

With a predictability Elene had now got used to, Silvio chose that precise moment to come in through the back door. 'Mmm.' He rubbed his stomach. 'Are those fresh pastries I can smell?'

'And going straight out to the dining area for the early birds,' Elene told him. 'Rosalie! Service *per favore*.'

'No, she's not in the office.' Marco frowned. 'I can't find her anywhere.'

'Isabella?' Silvio pulled off his boots and grabbed a pastry from the tray as Febe carried it to the hatch. 'She said something yesterday about going for an early morning hike.'

'Coffee?' Elene nodded to Febe. 'Could you make Silvio a quick espresso, please, Febe?' An early morning hike? She turned to Silvio. 'Who did she say she was going with?'

He shrugged. 'She didn't.'

Elene returned to her dough. 'And you didn't ask?' She shook her head in despair. Why did men never ask the right questions? 'Better see my mother about the cleaning materials then,' she told Marco, 'or wait till Isabella gets back.' What was she supposed to do? She had a kitchen to run.

Febe took the coffee to Silvio and he sat down at the table. 'Anything else to eat?' he asked, as if he was half-starved, poor man.

'The next lot of *cornetti* will be out in five minutes, *farinata* in ten,' Elene informed him. 'Febe, you can roll out the next lot now.' After the dough had rested for the fourth time, it must be rolled out into a circle. The circle must then be made into four sections and each section into five isosceles triangles. It was a delicate operation. Febe should end up with twenty triangles. Each triangle must then be rolled and stretched on to itself with the thinner tip tucked under each crescent so it didn't come apart during baking.

'What about the *focaccia*?' asked Silvio.

Mamma mia! 'It's for lunch.' She sprinkled some flour on to the marble counter and turned out the dough.

Elene's mother came into the kitchen looking as she did when she was going on an outing. She was wearing a tailored jacket and a different shade of lipstick. 'Good morning.' She smiled brightly at everyone, but the smile seemed forced; there was something brittle about her manner that worried Elene – it was as if at any moment she might snap.

'Do you know where Bella has got to, Mamma?' she asked her. She kneaded the dough just a little more. 'Silvio says she's gone on a morning walk. That's not like her, is it? Do you know who she might have gone with?'

Her mother frowned. 'One of her friends from the village perhaps?'

Hmm. Elene began to form the dough into a ball. The accustomed, repetitive movements were soothing. She glanced around to see how Febe was getting on with the next batch of *cornetti*. Traditionally breakfast wasn't a huge meal here in Liguria; most Italians grabbed a pastry while drinking espresso at the counter of a busy bar, devouring it with gusto rather than savouring it. But she was catering for all nationalities here at The Lemon Tree Hotel, and Elene liked to make it special. 'Where are you off to, Mamma?' The *cornetti* were under control and looking good. 'Coffee for my mother please, Febe?'

'Oh, I can get it myself.' But she looked exhausted, and had huge bags under her eyes.

Elene didn't like it. She cleaned the mixing bowl under the tap and dried it with a tea towel. 'Mamma?'

'Pisa.'

'Oh.' That was unusual. 'You didn't say.' Elene greased the bowl with a drizzle of olive oil and then replaced the ball of dough, turning it so that it was coated with the oil. She must refill this bottle from the demijohn, it was getting low. Usually if her mother was going out anywhere, she gave everyone plenty of notice, spent forever organising the roster, couldn't believe that the place could possibly still be standing when she returned.

'I told Isabella.'

Febe took over a plate of *cornetti*, and her mother and Silvio both helped themselves.

'Yes, I suppose that you did.' Elene covered the bowl loosely with greased plastic film and opened the warming oven. In an hour the dough should double in size.

'Come and sit down, Elene.' Silvio patted the seat next to his. He gave her a warning look. She knew what he was saying. *Don't mind so much. Why do you always mind so much?*

'Why are you going to Pisa?' Elene asked instead. She could feel the tolerant mood of early morning beginning to dissipate into the stress of the day.

'Oh, you know . . .' Her mother looked evasive. She took a bite of her pastry. 'Mmm, delicious, Febe, well done.'

Febe beamed.

265

'No, I don't.' That was why she had asked.

'Shopping . . . A new dress perhaps?' Her mother wiped her mouth delicately with a napkin.

'Ah.' She didn't believe that for a second. Elene turned away, busied herself taking the *farinata* out of the oven. It was crisp in all the right places and it smelt delicious. 'Will you see Papà?'

'Oh, yes, maybe.' She caught Elene's eye. 'Yes, I'm sure that I will.'

Elene felt again that protective instinct that she had felt before. Her mother had always seemed so invincible. And yet now . . . There was something different about her, something that concerned Elene and at the same time made her feel that she needed to help her mother in some way. To put a stop to this unaccustomed sensation, she went over to the machine to make herself a coffee. A strong bitter espresso should do the trick. Because she had done the right thing – hadn't she? When she had begged her mother to stay with her father? She had done the right thing surely, when she made her mother promise? Even if Silvio was right and she had wanted her mother to choose – it had been the right choice, had it not, for her to stay with Papà?

She packed the coffee in firmly and tapped the top of it for good measure. She inserted it into the machine and gave a sharp twist. Looking up, she noticed that Silvio was watching her. Ah Silvio . . . Lately, he seemed to have developed the skill of seeing into her mind, and it was most disconcerting. If it had indeed been the right choice – had it been right for whom? Herself, yes, and probably Isabella too. But had it been the right choice for her mother? After all, she might indeed have walked into a door. And if not? Had she ever considered

266

that her mother and her father might have been unhappy all these years?

As she turned, her mother got to her feet. 'I'll be leaving in about an hour,' she said. 'I just need to see to a few things in the office before I go.'

Elene nodded, watched her leave the room, not quite as confidently or elegantly as usual.

'So,' said Silvio.

'So, what?' Elene put her hands on her hips.

'We are left to our own devices.' Silvio sat back in his chair. He had demolished at least four *cornetti* and a large slice of *farinata*.

'Hmm.' It was, she thought, too good an opportunity to miss. 'I wonder if Signor Bauer has come down for breakfast yet?'

'Huh?'

She leaned closer. 'Perhaps you should go and find him, Silvio.'

'Find him?' He reached out for another pastry and she slapped his hand.

'With Bella and my mother out of the way it would be a good time for him to look around, take stock of the place, maybe take a few measurements . . .'

He stared at her. 'You said it would only be a few rough sketches.'

'Yes, yes, but he may want to do more than that. Who knows?' She remembered what she'd said to him – *who knows where it might lead?*

'I don't know, Elene.' Silvio was always on her side, only now he seemed reluctant.

'What's the matter?'

267

'They won't like it.'

'They won't know.'

'It feels wrong.'

'You're scared.'

'No.' He grabbed her wrist. 'I hope you know what you're doing, that's all, Elene.'

She felt a stab of guilt. Was she betraying her family? Was that what he was saying? Of course not. She was helping the hotel, doing something that would benefit them all in the long run. 'I know exactly what I'm doing.' She whipped off her apron. Lunch preparations could wait. The question now was – where was the Signor Ferdinand Bauer?

CHAPTER 28

Chiara

Chiara alighted the platform at Pisa Centrale. The station was light, modern and airy; a world apart from Vernazza. She made her way with determination towards the exit. She didn't want to be here. It wasn't anything to do with the city itself. Pisa did not have the charm of Florence, it was true – but then again, the culture of this city had not been as protected during the Second World War as that of Florence, despite the glories of the Camposanto frescoes and the many other art treasures it held. Her father had told her that after the war, Pisa was a skeleton of its former self; she had never fully recovered from the mines, the bombings, the destruction of her bridges. For a time, he told Chiara, the streets and piazzas were empty and Pisa was a dead town; even after the Liberation in September 1944, long-range artillery had continued to pound the city for three weeks or more.

It was all so hard to imagine. She walked through the terminal past the departure and arrival boards, the familiar paintings by Daniel Schinasi and the *biglietteria*, as the loudspeaker system blared its announcement of the next train arriving at Platform 1. There was an air of smooth efficiency about the terminal – trains were something else the Italians were good at, she reflected.

For Chiara, away from the obvious tourist attractions of the Leaning Tower and the rest of the Square of Miracles, Pisa was a charming city. And she knew it well. She came here when she wanted to go clothes shopping or to browse the galleries when she was feeling a bit stir-crazy. It happened – though Elene and the others would not believe it. She loved The Lemon Tree Hotel and Vernazza, but still, she needed to get away some-times. She loved wandering through the monumental cemetery that was the Camposanto, and never tired of looking at those fourteenth-century frescoes her father had talked of – the Camposanto's cool interior and pitted marble slabs seemed to tell such a complex story. Chiara also had an old schoolfriend here, Delfina, who had moved from Vernazza some years ago.

'I don't know how you can stay in that sleepy little place,' Delfina would say to Chiara from time to time. 'There's nothing there.'

Nothing but tourism, she meant – even then. But the land-scape that drew the tourists in was what Chiara also adored: the wild mountains, the terraced olive groves and vineyards, the romantic coves that were stamped into her heart.

She stepped outside. But no, this morning it wasn't the thought of visiting Pisa that was making her bite her lip with anxiety – it was what she might find here. It was another warm early autumn morning; good for the grape-picking, she found herself thinking. Isabella had been up in the mountains this morning when everyone had been looking for her – it turned out, she had walked to the sanctuary with Ferdinand Bauer.

270

Chiara frowned. And from the look on her flushed face when she got back it hadn't been a religious pilgrimage taking place. Chiara had to admit there was something charming about the young man, but still she worried. Who exactly was he, and why was he here? He didn't appear to be merely a tourist. Isabella was so young, so innocent despite the air of confidence she wore. Chiara would do everything she could to protect her.

She made her way over the decorative paved cobbles towards the fountain. A few people sat on the stone benches drinking take-out coffee. Occasionally too, Chiara had arranged to meet Alonzo here in Pisa, but over the past ten years, it had become more and more his haunt, and consequently it no longer attracted her in quite the same way. Pisa had become part of their separateness; acknowledged as his territory. Enough . . .

She paused by the cool fountain. She had the address written on a scrap of paper in her purse, but she knew the way; she'd looked it up before she came. It was only five minutes' walk from the station – the most insalubrious places often were. And so, she ignored the tree-lined road ahead, which she would usually take on her way to Via Roma, and instead turned right and down a side street where everything looked rather uncared for. Tired cars were parked in the road, litter strewn in gutters. The shutters of the apartment buildings were rusty, balconies were crammed with rubbish, and there was a general air of poverty hanging over the place. Alonzo's apartments couldn't be here, surely? Chiara fumbled in her bag for her purse to find the scrap of paper. Until Signora Conti's visit, she had imagined them to be smart and clean, attracting the professionals who worked in the city.

She could have waited at the hotel to see Alonzo, who had sent her a message saying he was returning to Vernazza tomorrow. She hadn't told him that actually she was coming here today. When it came to it, she might not even see him. But if she did, she wanted surprise to be on her side. She could have told him about their visitor, the rather brash Signora Conti. She could have listened to his explanations, his excuses. But she had chosen not to. Chiara found the address and checked the numbers in the street. It was further on. Some of the blocks had been modernised after all – presumably, Alonzo's was one of these.

In fact, as she walked, she could hear Alonzo already; recognise the tone of his voice – defiant, bordering on angry. She might easily have believed what he told her, accepted what he said, agreed that yes, this was his business not hers, put it out of her mind and continued running The Lemon Tree Hotel just as she always had. Signora Conti wouldn't come back – so, why not?

But instead, here she was. She passed a dimly lit café, gloomy in spite of the bright morning outside. A woman brushed past her, carrying a huge plastic laundry bag. And now, here was a shop window entirely covered in faded newspaper. Chiara had come here, because there had been something about that woman that had got to her. She must have been desperate to make the journey to Vernazza, to come to the hotel, to plead her mother's case. And so, the least Chiara could do was keep her own promise, to come here to see for herself.

She found the apartment block, though she had to check twice because it was as grimy and tatty as any other in the street. The balconies were crumbling, the wrought iron had rusted or was missing altogether, and there were no flowers, only a few broken terracotta pots to be seen. There was graffiti on the walls, and what looked like a snapped and fraying electric cable hanging down by the front door. *Mamma mia* – this was so much worse than she had feared. She rang the bell for Apartment 5 and waited. Minutes passed. She rang again.

She was about to walk away when at last the door creaked open. An old woman stood there – rather bent and certainly frail, since she was leaning on a stick. So, yes, this must be the mother of Signora Conti – Chiara could spot the resemblance, although this woman had a look of gentle warmth about her while the daughter had been brittle as a ginger snap. Chiara understood about brittle though – didn't she see it in her own daughter every day? – she knew what could lie underneath.

'*Buon giorno.*' Chiara spoke softly. 'Signora Gavino?'

'*Sì.*'

'Your daughter came to see me. My husband is your landlord. My name is Chiara. Chiara Mazzone.'

'Oh.' Her eyes widened in surprise. '*Buon giorno, Signora.*' The woman was immediately deferential. 'Come in, please. My apologies. I was not expecting visitors. So, you see . . . you catch me unawares.'

'It is quite all right, *Signora.*' Chiara stepped inside. 'Is the intercom not working?' she asked.

'I'm afraid not.'

'Hmm.' The communal hallway was not the cleanest and it could certainly do with a slap of paint. The floor tiles were dirty, thick cobwebs were tangled in the far corners of the ceiling, and there was a general air of neglect. But it was nothing too awful. She supposed most city apartment blocks of this calibre would be much the same.

She stood expectantly by the lift, but Beatrice Gavino tottered past. Chiara raised an eyebrow as she followed her up the communal stairs. The old woman clung to the banister, moving painfully slowly. 'Is the lift not working either, *Signora*?'

'No, not for a year or so.'

'A year!' Chiara clicked her tongue. That wasn't good enough. The old lady should not have to walk up and down from the third floor, for goodness' sake, especially not at her age.

It seemed to take forever for them to get to the third floor. From here, Signora Gavino led the way into the narrow hall of a small apartment. It was dark and dingy, and Chiara noticed the unmistakeable smell of damp. They entered the living room, which was furnished with an armchair and a sofa covered with a throw and a few scatter cushions – probably covering up something stained or threadbare, Chiara thought. Beatrice Gavino had tried to make the room cosy, but Chiara immediately spotted the worn rug, the light fitting hanging from the ceiling like a dismembered limb, the tears of condensation, and the paint flaking from the walls. The old lady had done her best, but the place was definitely in need of some urgent maintenance.

'I wondered. Could you show me the letter asking you to leave the apartment?' Chiara asked her. 'And perhaps your contract, if you have it to hand, *Signora*? Do you mind?' It was rather an intrusion, but she had to get some idea of how things stood before she stepped in.

'Of course, *Signora*, one moment please and I will find them for you.' The old woman hovered in the doorway. 'And in the meantime, can I make you some coffee?'

'Please. That would be most appreciated.' Chiara followed her into the kitchen so that she could check it out. On top of the stove was a two-ring unit attached to a bottle of gas.

Signora Gavino filled the ancient and battered coffee percolator and put it on the gas to brew.

'The stove doesn't work?' Chiara frowned. How many more things weren't functioning as they should? Many of the tiles were chipped or broken, and the grout was crumbling to dust.

'No.'

'You've told my husband about all these things, *Signora*?'

'*Sì.*'

And he had done nothing. Chiara looked around. There were a few dirty dishes lying in the cracked sink, but generally it looked as if Beatrice Gavino was keeping the place clean enough. But it hadn't been maintained. Some of the floor tiles were cracked too, which was unhygienic and probably a health hazard because the old lady could easily trip over them. Even the plinth below the units had fallen down and not been mended or replaced. There were grease stains on the ceilings and walls, and the creepings of black mould visible under the window.

'How long is it since anyone came to look at the apartment, *Signora*?' Chiara asked. 'There must be a regular maintenance check, surely?'

The old woman looked blank. '*Allora, Signora*, I'm afraid I can't remember the last time.'

Chiara frowned. No maintenance check then.

Back in the living room, Chiara sat on the sofa, added broken springs to the list of what was wrong with the apartment and sipped the bitter espresso. The old lady passed her some paperwork with a trembling hand and Chiara read the letter Alonzo had sent to his tenant. It was short and to the point. The apartment needed to be renovated (he was right about that, at least). Signora Gavino had been given two months' notice – and the letter was dated a month ago. No word of apology, no further explanation. She could hardly believe it. She scanned the contract. And it seemed that the period of notice was legal and above board.

'If I could keep most of my things here, then I could live with my daughter for a few weeks,' she told Chiara. 'We have told your husband that. It wouldn't be easy, but not impossible. And when the apartment is fixed up . . .' Her voice trailed. Her expression alone told Chiara that she knew she wouldn't be moving back in. 'Though the rent might be too high.' She sighed.

'How did my husband respond to your request?' It sounded reasonable enough to Chiara.

'At first, he didn't respond at all, *Signora*. Then he said it was too late. Since then we haven't managed to speak to him at all.'

Chiara nodded. Hence the visit from her daughter.

'Can you help?' The woman was gazing at her with pleading eyes. 'This is my home, *Signora*. I have lived here for twenty years. I don't know where else I can go. Or how.' She gazed around the simple room. The situation was obviously affecting her badly.

Chiara understood. But . . . 'Forgive me. But there are other apartments, *Signora*.' She had to say this. She guessed it was what Alonzo would say.

'Yes, you are right. I must accept it. I must move from here.' Her faded brown eyes were sad but brave.

But you shouldn't have to, thought Chiara. Alonzo had some moral responsibility here did he not? She found herself thinking of Giovanna. Their families were not even blood-related and yet they had always protected her, and the idea that Giovanna too could ever be treated this way by someone, that

276

she could ever lose her home and her security like this . . . This thought cut Chiara to the quick. And it was her own husband Alonzo who was responsible for this old lady's distress. She'd always known he wasn't perfect, but this showed a callousness that shocked her.

'My daughter and son-in-law will help me.' But the *signora* looked perfectly desolate at the prospect. 'Although . . .'

'And my husband?' Because there was more that Chiara needed to know. 'Can you tell me what sort of a landlord you have found him to be over the years?'

'What sort of a landlord?' The old lady looked away. 'Oh, not so bad, *Signora*, not so bad.'

Chiara suspected she was simply being polite. And after all, the evidence spoke for itself. 'But your daughter said—'

'*Pah!*' She swished this away with a gesture of her bony hand. 'People talk. She is angry. Always angry about something that one. And her husband . . .' She shook her head.

'I see.' Chiara finished her coffee. 'I will talk to my husband,' she said. 'And I will telephone you and your daughter. Do you have a phone here?' She doubted the old lady would have a mobile.

'Yes, there is one in the hall.' She wrote the number in a spidery and trembling hand on a piece of notepaper on the side table.

Chiara got to her feet and took it from her. 'I will be in touch in the next few days to let you know,' she said. 'Please don't get up. I can see myself out.'

'Thank you very much, *Signora*, *grazie mille.*'

Chiara shook her head. 'Let's wait and see.' She hadn't done anything yet. And she wasn't sure how much she could do.

Outside the building she bumped into Signora Conti

herself, who was talking to a younger woman. The *signora* looked just as she had when she'd visited The Lemon Tree Hotel, though it struck Chiara that here she did not look out of place. The other woman had jet black hair and was wearing a short denim skirt and high heels and an abundance of cheap jewellery.

'You came.' Signora Conti was clearly surprised to see her.

'I said I would.' Chiara held out her hand, and, after a moment's hesitation, Signora Conti took it. 'I've been talking to your mother.'

'And?'

'If the worst came to the worst, could your mother stay with you for a while – until she finds something else, I mean?'

She sighed. 'It's not me,' she said.

'Your husband?'

She shrugged. 'He's got a point. We're over-crowded as it is.'

Chiara nodded. 'I'll talk to Alonzo. I don't know what else I can do.' She noticed the two women exchange a sheepish look.

'Do you live here too?' she asked the second woman. Perhaps she could find out more from her.

'*Sì.*' The woman sounded defensive. She shifted her gum from one side of her mouth to the other and stared back at Chiara.

Chiara stood her ground. 'And do you have any complaints?'

'Complaints?' She groped in her bag for a pack of cigarettes and lit one.

'About the condition of the place, the maintenance, the rent?'

The woman let out a short laugh. 'Oh, don't you worry. It works just fine for me.' She looked Chiara up and down.

Insolent, was the word Chiara would use to describe this look, though she continued to hold herself upright and refused to feel intimidated.

'See you later,' the other woman said to Signora Conti. She pulled a key from her bag and let herself into the apartment block, slamming the door behind her.

Chiara shot a questioning look at her companion 'So what's going on with her?'

Signora Conti moved her shoulder bag from one shoulder to the other and winced. 'You don't want to know, *Signora*.'

'But Signora Conti,' Chiara steeled herself, this was why she was here, 'I do want to know.'

She let out a loud sigh and gave Chiara a long and appraising look. 'She has visitors,' she replied at last. 'Male visitors. Your husband, he turns a blind eye.'

Chiara gasped. 'You mean she's a prostitute?'

'*Ssh.*' She flapped her hands at her. 'No need to spell it out, is there? These things happen. We all have to live.'

'But is she?' Of course, Chiara knew that these things happened – but surely not in Alonzo's apartment block? He couldn't know. With his pride, he would be mortified.

'I suppose so, yes, if you want to call it that.' She seemed uncomfortable. 'But look, it's easy to think in black and white when you have money, *no*?'

Chiara took this on the chin. She was right. Chiara and her family lived in a privileged world. Even so . . . 'Is she the only one?' she asked.

'Probably not.'

'And what else should I know?'

The woman shot her a dark look.

'Come on now, think of your mother.' Alonzo had behaved

279

badly, no doubt of it. And she must know that Chiara might be able to help.

'A couple of tenants are dealers.'

Chiara flinched. 'Drugs?'

'*Ssh*. I told you. Keep your voice down.' She looked warily from left to right.

Madonna santa! Chiara was feeling dizzy now. She put a hand to her head. Surely Alonzo was not aware of all these things going on under his nose? 'My husband . . .'

'I wouldn't mention it to him.'

'But why not?' Chiara was struggling to understand. Naturally, she must mention it to him. The whole matter must be dealt with – it could not be allowed to continue. *Certo* this woman did not know Alonzo – not like Chiara did. He was a businessman, and he could be ruthless. He was greedy too. He wanted to get the best rent for his properties and he lacked compassion and any sense of moral obligation, as she had just discovered. But he wouldn't countenance drug-dealing and prostitution on his property – absolutely not. Of that she was certain.

'You seem like a decent woman,' said Signora Conti. 'You've got a fancy hotel. You're not like me and my family, not at all. But I like you.'

'Thank you.' Chiara wasn't sure what to say to that. 'I like you too. But—'

'And I don't understand what someone like you is doing with someone like him, to be honest.'

Chiara was conscious of a sudden chill in the air. 'Someone like him?'

'There's all sorts of ways of paying rent, that's all I'm saying. And it's only fair that you're aware of that, *Signora*. A nice woman like you. It's not right.'

'All sorts of ways?' Chiara frowned. What was she saying? What should Chiara be aware of?

'It's been going on for years as far as I know. And as for the drugs,' she added, 'the way I heard it, if he gets his money, he doesn't care.'

Chiara stared at her. She was in shock. Her mind was reeling. What sort of place was Alonzo running here? A brothel? A drug den? She was desperately trying to assimilate all this new information about her husband, and she was coming to an awful conclusion. *If he gets his money, he doesn't care.* Was this the kind of man she was married to? And what else? What did she mean about other ways of paying rent? For years? Surely, she wasn't suggesting . . . Chiara felt the chill of fear. How could she take all this in? *Mamma mia.* Until recently, that man had been in her bed.

'What will you do?' Signora Conti's expression was mildly curious. And there was something else. Chiara imagined that although she had wanted Chiara to know the truth for her own good, she was also rather pleased at being in a position to give it. Chiara was the one in the fancy hotel, and this woman lived a very different sort of life. But her husband was a problem to her too, so perhaps their lives weren't so very different after all.

'I'm going to pay my husband a visit,' Chiara told her. 'And after that . . .' She shrugged. After that, who knew? At this moment in time, Chiara could look no further ahead.

CHAPTER 29

Chiara

Chiara's mind was still buzzing with unanswered questions as she made her way towards the square. There was so much traffic it was making her head hurt. Scooters, trucks, cars, queued up at the traffic lights revving their engines impatiently; a bus careered around the corner as if it were going to plough right into the stately *loggia* of the Palazzo. She stepped out into the road without looking, the driver of a black Fiat blasted his horn, and Chiara jumped back again. She was shaking. 'Crazy country woman,' she muttered to herself. 'Pay attention. You're in the city now.'

But a walk might clear her head. She passed the bustling Palazzo, the row of orange trees, the marble benches, and the statue of Vittorio Emanuele II in the square. She could stop at one of the cafés with the burgundy parasols, but she didn't want to stop − not yet. She went straight on down the busy Corso Italia instead, which was lined with shops and tall narrow buildings. Funny, she'd never noticed how claustrophobic it was here. And how strange − that everyone was going about their business, continuing with their lives, not guessing how she felt right now, not caring.

Not keeping up the maintenance of his apartments was one thing. Chiara was surprised but not shocked at that. She'd always known Alonzo lacked the integrity of his parents, she'd always known he was lazy, greedy even.

So why in the name of Madonna, had she married him? That was easy. Just as she'd told Dante only days ago – oh, Dante . . . For a moment she felt a thrust of regret that was so startling, so strong that it took her breath away. She had married him because her parents had wanted her to. And when she came to think about it, what kind of crazy reason was that? Dante had been right in that respect. Her parents would be happy they were now related by marriage to Papà's oldest friend, they'd be proud they had an obliging daughter (*pah!*) but they didn't have to live with him, did they? They didn't have to experience the emptiness of a loveless marriage; a relationship based on little more than a business arrangement? Chiara had hoped that mutual respect and parental friendship could lead to love. But they hadn't. They had led to separation, to irritation, to chilly politeness. And now, even the mutual respect had gone.

Her breath was coming so fast as she hurried on that she thought she might faint. *Steady, Chiara.* She paused when she reached the Carmelite church. She stood in the doorway for a moment, looked up at the high vaulted ceiling, then took a step inside, her heels tapping on the cool black-and-white marble tiles. The simple wooden pews were empty, but at the altar a tray of candles burned and incense hung in the air. It was so peaceful, quite at odds with the busy and commercial street outside, and Chiara felt herself slowly grow calmer. She would give Alonzo a chance to explain, an opportunity to make good what he had done; she owed him that much at least.

On emerging from the church, Chiara walked more unhurriedly. She passed the fabulous stained-glass windows that she always admired when she came this way, and the *loggia* at the end of the road where the colourful antiques market was held on Saturdays. How many times had she browsed through the black-and-white photographs of the old film stars, examined the pieces of ornate jewellery, flicked through the records and thought of the old days? But today the *loggia* was just another empty space that seemed to echo her own state of mind.

At last she came to the River Arno. The reflections of the buildings fidgeted in the broad and rippling ribbon of water; earthy colours of ochre, rust and green. She walked over the bridge towards the building of peaches and cream. Alonzo's place was here on Lungarno Antonio Pacinotti – a charming part of Pisa that most tourists didn't see since it was a good twenty minutes' walk from Piazza dei Miracoli. The grand villas of the streets around the River Arno lacked the wow factor of the Piazza dei Miracoli and they couldn't match the charm of Florence. Nevertheless, they were quite something.

Chiara turned left and made her way along the busy pavement towards Alonzo's apartment. She glanced across the silky river to the chalky-blue villa with grey shutters. Beyond this stood pretty buildings in cream, mint and yellow, leading to the tiny Gothic church of Santa Maria della Spina and the Solferino Bridge just beyond. It was a lovely view, but it was Alonzo's view, and she had never stayed the night here, not once. She could say she always had The Lemon Tree Hotel to return to, she could talk about duty and how busy she had always been. True enough. But the deeper truth was that she had never stayed here because she had never wanted to. And she didn't want to be here now.

Because evicting a frail old lady from the apartment she'd lived in for twenty years, was another thing entirely. The ruthlessness of it made her shiver inside. And what else was there? Prostitution? Drugs? It was hard to believe. Chiara arrived at the terracotta building at the top of which was Alonzo's penthouse apartment. It was very grand, and a far cry from the apartments she'd just visited. She looked up. She had to find out if it was true. Her finger hovered over the brass bell. And there was only one meaning to be inferred by Signora Conti's comment about 'ways of paying rent . . .' Chiara swallowed. She pressed the bell, quickly, before she could change her mind. Signora Conti must mean that Alonzo was taking advantage of those women too. And this was too much, too awful to contemplate.

Alonzo answered the buzzer in a weary voice. '*Sì?*' No problem with the intercom here then.

'It's me.'

'Chiara?' His voice changed. 'What are you doing here? Has something happened? Is it Elene?'

'No.' She put his mind at rest immediately. She had married him for her parents, and she had stayed with him for Elene. But she didn't hate him that much – at least, not yet.

'Then . . .'

'Can I come in?'

'Of course.' The buzzer went and she pushed open the door. Chiara went up in the lift – taking a deep breath for courage, as it swept her noiselessly up to the top floor. That too was working. Things were certainly very different here.

The penthouse apartment door was open and she stepped

inside. It was light and airy with floor-to-ceiling bi-folding doors leading out on to a balcony.

'Chiara.' Alonzo was dressed in his usual dark trousers and shirt. He moved forwards to kiss her on both cheeks. She submitted graciously, though the touch of his lips seemed to sting her inside.

'Hello, Alonzo.'

'Is everything all right?'

She didn't answer. How could she, when nothing was all right and probably never would be again?

He cocked his head to one side, clearly curious. 'You are here to do some shopping, is that it? Why didn't you tell me you were coming?'

Chiara glanced around the apartment. It demonstrated Alonzo's taste. It was minimal, almost austere. There was a glass coffee table next to a black leather couch and on the other side of the room, a deep reclining armchair. In the corner stood Alonzo's desk – on this was his laptop, open, and the neatest pile of paperwork she had ever seen. Chiara almost smiled. Very different from the desk in the office she shared with Isabella. A newspaper lay on the arm of the chair; *Il Giornale*, the tabloid paper he preferred, was the only item of character in the room, the only object that could tell her anything about her husband. Which actually told her a lot.

'No, I'm not here to shop.' Chiara slipped off her jacket and put it on the back of the chair. She sat down. At once the room looked more lived in. 'I came to visit someone.'

'Ah – Delfina?' Alonzo was affable. He took her jacket and hung it carefully on a peg by the front door. 'And, how is she? Have you seen her yet? Lunch, is it?' He glanced at his watch.

How could it be only lunchtime after everything that had

happened today? 'Not Delfina, no.' Chiara wasn't sure how to begin. At any rate she would have to be ready to dodge the explosion. She pushed back the fear, the uncertainty. She must do this. 'I went to see Signora Beatrice Gavino.'

He frowned. Chiara could see him trying to place the name – which was appalling in itself. 'Signora Gavino? Who is she? Do I know her?'

'She lives in Apartment 5 – in your block in Via Giacomo Puccini.' She waited for his reaction.

Disbelief was followed by comprehension slowly spreading over her husband's face. Chiara watched, fascinated. And then came a flash of anger. 'Why the fuck did you go there?' He still spoke quietly. And he didn't come closer, not yet.

Chiara remained seated on the chair, though she was tense and ready to make her escape. 'Because her daughter, Signora Conti came to The Lemon Tree Hotel yesterday.'

'Her daughter?' He thrust a hand through his greying hair and shot Chiara a look of incredulity. He paced over to the window. 'That witch? I wouldn't believe a word she said.'

Chiara steadied her breath. 'I believed her. She was worried about her mother.'

'She had no right to go to you.' His fists clenched.

'But she had every right to try to get in touch with you,' she pointed out mildly. 'You are her mother's landlord, after all.'

He turned to face her. 'Yes, I am.' His eyes were hooded and she couldn't tell what he was thinking. He had never been a violent man, until the night he had found her having dinner with Dante. But at that moment she had seen it in him, felt his hatred, known how she had hurt him. And she knew that Dante was right – Alonzo was certainly capable of being violent again.

'She tried to contact you here,' she pointed out. 'She found out your other address. She came to The Lemon Tree Hotel to see you, not me.'

Alonzo's eyes narrowed. 'But you spoke with her.'

'I did.' Chiara recalled her initial annoyance with her husband when Signora Conti had arrived – that he had permitted such an intrusion into her peaceful hotel. How naïve she had been. How arrogant. Who did she think she was, really? Did she imagine herself to be some superior being who led some other-worldly existence, lived in a special and privileged place, one that should not be sullied by real life? Well, more fool her. No wonder that poor woman had looked as she had when she walked into The Lemon Tree Hotel. Chiara really couldn't blame her.

'And then, instead of contacting me and telling me what had happened so that I could deal with it, you took it on yourself to come here to Pisa.' He paced to the other side of the room, still looking out towards the river. 'That's interesting, Chiara.'

He was now between her and the front door. 'I was shocked at what she told me,' she said. 'I thought there must be some mistake. I wanted to see for myself.'

'See for yourself?' He still had his back to her. But she could see from the set of his shoulders that the anger was building.

'If it was true. If you would evict an old lady like that. If you were capable of doing such a thing.'

He spun around. His mouth was a thin line of fury and his expression was one of contempt. 'And so, Chiara, if a guest of your hotel should come to me with a complaint, I should not tell you? Is that it? I should simply investigate the matter myself? Behind your back, eh?'

Chiara bent her head. It was a fair point. 'I felt sorry for

288

her,' she said. 'I wanted to see if I could help her mother. I promised her I would come.'

He let out a sharp bark of laughter that made her flinch. 'So, you promised some low-life that you would poke your nose into your husband's business affairs? After we have agreed – have we not? – that the hotel is your concern and that the apartments are mine?'

'Signora Conti has had a hard life, Alonzo.' Chiara decided to appeal to his better nature. 'But that doesn't make her low-life.' Although she realised that she too was guilty of having made certain assumptions when the woman first walked into the hotel.

He took a step towards her, and Chiara flinched. But instead of grabbing hold of her, or – heaven forbid – slapping her, as he had done before, he strode once again to the door. He plucked her jacket from the hook and threw it towards her. It fell in a bright red puddle on the floor. 'The little you know,' he snapped.

Chiara did not pick up the jacket. She'd come here to say her piece and she'd leave when she was ready. 'Beatrice Gavino is elderly, frail, and vulnerable,' she said. 'She can't face moving. That tiny and grotty apartment of hers may be falling apart, but it's all she has.'

'You went there? You went inside?' His voice was a low growl.

'I told you I did.'

'To hell with that, Chiara.' Once again, he tore his fingers through his hair. 'What were you thinking?'

'Please reconsider, Alonzo.' If it would make any difference, she would get down on her hands and knees. 'I'm begging you. Let that poor woman stay in her apartment. Don't throw her out of her home.'

289

'No.'

'Is that your final word on the subject?' She wrung her hands together.

'It is.'

'Very well.' Chiara got to her feet – albeit rather shakily – picked up her jacket from the floor and slipped it on. She walked to the door, opened it, and turned back to him. She had an escape route now. 'What sort of place is it you run there, Alonzo?'

'What are you talking about now, woman?' But she could see he was flustered.

'Drugs? Prostitutes? Is it true what they tell me?' She paused. Did she dare to say it? 'And what about women of a certain profession paying you rent in kind?'

His jaw dropped and she saw it in his eyes – a flicker of fear, a hint of shame. Hesitation. Panic. This told her all she wanted to know. 'Please don't come back to the hotel tomorrow, Alonzo,' she said. 'I don't want to see you there.'

'Chiara . . .'

She shut the door behind her. It was true then. It was all true. She knew for certain now – she had heard it in his hesitation and seen it in his eyes. She didn't wait to call the lift. She half ran down the stairs and from the building, swinging the door shut behind her. She just wanted to be out of there.

She rushed back past the deli, the bike shop, the pharmacy, and the Royal Victoria Hotel to Piazza Garibaldi, and only then did she stop to catch her breath. A brandy. She staggered to a café table and sat down. A brandy would help restore some sense of calm. The statue stood in the centre of the piazza, hand on hip, sending her a pitying glance. A musician was playing on the far side of the square and people strolled past, eating *gelato*, chatting, laughing, discussing where to stop for a late lunch. The brandy came, and she took rapid restorative sips, the potent liquid catching at her throat.

When she felt marginally better she paid the bill, left the café, and hailed a cab to take her to the station. She wanted to get home as quickly as possible now. She wanted to be in her own bed, and she wanted to sleep. She wanted to see her family. What she didn't want to do – was think.

CHAPTER 30

Elene

Elene was in the kitchen after dinner. The clearing up had all been done and the others had gone home, but she lingered, unwilling to go back to the rooms she shared with Silvio empty-handed. She couldn't believe that she had lost them before she'd even had a chance to study the sketches Ferdinand Bauer had prepared for her. And she could hardly ask him to do them again . . .

She took out all her recipe books one by one and laid them to one side on the marble counter. She took a cloth and cleaned the surface, though oddly it seemed clean already, as if someone had been here very recently. Which made her think . . .

She hadn't managed to locate the young architect until after Isabella had returned from her morning walk and her mother had disappeared off on her mystery visit to Pisa.

'I could do a few sketches for you today,' he had said warily. 'But look, I don't want to go behind anyone's back, *Signora*.'

Elene knew he was thinking of Isabella. 'Don't worry,' she'd told him. 'They will all be delighted.' And she almost began to believe it herself.

This evening he had asked to see her after dinner, handed her a large brown envelope. 'Just a few ideas along the lines we discussed.' And he had looked around them, seeming ill at ease, perhaps worrying that the walls of The Lemon Tree Hotel had ears.

'That was quick work.' Elene had beamed. '*Grazie mille.* Thank you so much. I'll take a look later.' She could hardly wait. 'And how much do I owe you, *Signore?*'

'Oh, no no.' Signor Bauer seemed most embarrassed. 'I couldn't possibly take anything from you.'

'But why ever not?' Elene held the envelope closer to her breast. 'I must pay you for your time.'

Ferdinand Bauer brushed this off with a shake of his fair head. 'Not at all,' he said. 'It was nothing. It was my pleasure.'

Elene regarded him quizzically. A strange way to run a business indeed. 'Very well,' she said. 'Thank you again, *Signore.*'

He made his excuses and disappeared. Elene returned to the kitchen. She took a quick peek inside – there were several sketches; this looked most promising – and then tucked the envelope next to her recipe books. There were things she must see to, and too many people around. She would take a proper look later.

But later, when she went to retrieve it, the envelope had simply disappeared.

Elene smoothed the surfaces of her grandmother's old recipe book with her fingers. Her grandmother had died when Elene was very young – she could barely remember her, only perhaps the faint fragrance of her lavender perfume. She looked inside. From this book she had taken her grandmother's recipe for Ligurian lemon cake – one of her favourites – and not changed a thing. The pages were brittle with age and the ink had faded,

293

but her grandmother's voice was still there in her neat upright handwriting and the organised nature of the columns of ingredients and clear instructions. *Take the zest of a fresh lemon . . .* The recipe was made with olive oil and was moist and fresh as the fruit of the lemon tree itself. Elene sighed.

Slowly, she replaced each book on the shelf. There were her own recipes here, and books from Marcello, the chef who had first introduced her to the kitchen. From time to time friends and family had given her presents of recipe books from famous Italian chefs, but truth to tell, she barely glanced at them. The traditions she had grown up with had always been good enough for Elene.

She surveyed the books now back in line on the marble counter. The envelope was still nowhere to be seen.

'But who would have taken it?' Silvio demanded later. They were in bed, and she was trying to pretend that she was not worried. It was, of course, simply that she wanted to tell the others in her own time, to prepare the ground as it were. If someone were to find the envelope, if someone were to show her mother or Isabella the sketches . . . things could be taken the wrong way, that was all. 'Your mother?'

'No, of course not.' Her mother didn't even know about the sketches – no one did. And besides, Elene couldn't even remember her mother coming into the kitchen that evening. She'd been very quiet since she got back from Pisa. When Elene had asked her if she wanted dinner she had said she'd eaten earlier, that she was tired, that she would just go on up to bed if Elene didn't mind. Elene had felt it again – that unexpected surge of protectiveness. 'Are you all right, Mamma?' she'd asked her. 'Yes, *cara*. I'm fine.' But Elene didn't believe it – not for one moment.

'Who then?'

'I don't know.' But Elene felt like crying at the injustice of it. She had gone to all this trouble – and for what? 'Perhaps someone was tidying up?' Emanuele, Febe, or Raphael? They had all been around. It was possible . . . 'I'll have to ask them tomorrow.'

'Yes, my love, you should.' And Silvio had given her a most serious look. He didn't have to tell her how important it was that she find it, he didn't have to remind her that they wouldn't understand her motives or why she had done this without telling anyone.

Elene knew. It was imperative. She must find the envelope before anyone else did.

CHAPTER 31

Isabella

It was the following morning. Isabella's favourite sandals had come apart at the heel strap and her grandmother had suggested she take them to the cobbler in Monterosso al Mare. Their family had always taken their shoes to Passano's. These days, not so often, she supposed – more likely they'd buy a new pair, that was the way of the world. But she loved these sandals.

'I'm supposed to be on reception in half an hour,' she reminded her grandmother, who was still very far from being her old self. Perhaps she was just tired. Perhaps a visit to the doctor was in order, for Nonna was not as young as she had once been and she worked very hard. Perhaps Isabella should suggest they bring in more staff, so that Nonna could take a bit more time off?

'You were working all day yesterday, Bella.' Nonna shot her a sharp look. Maybe not so tired then . . . 'I have some correspondence to deal with, emails to send – that's all. I'll do it at the desk. You go to Monterosso for an hour or two.'

'But—'

296

'Go.' Nonna shooed her away. 'We're quiet today. We can manage perfectly well.'

'OK.' Her grandmother was right. At last the season was slowing down. Even the Signoras Veroni had left yesterday in a flurry of kisses and promises that they would be back next year. It was a lovely morning; early autumn sunshine was flooding through the open front door – the day beckoned.

However, Isabella loitered around reception for another twenty minutes, hoping that Ferdinand might appear. She saw an American couple who had arrived yesterday, who were 'fitting in' the Cinque Terre between Venice and Florence (Isabella heard this more times than she could remember, and hated it more than she could say), come to the desk and ask her grandmother about restaurants nearby. And she witnessed the latest tantrum of an English teenager – who must go to private school since she wasn't yet back there – who wanted to go and lie on the beach rather than hike to Corniglia. She said good morning to the sweet-faced older woman from Verona who was here on a nostalgic visit since this was the place where her late husband had proposed; and she sorted all their travel leaflets into piles that were marginally neater than they had been before.

Should she call his room? No. She had kissed him, but a girl had some pride. After their hike to the sanctuary the previous morning she'd spent the day half on a cloud. But clouds were insubstantial, and she might fall right through. Would anything come of it? She supposed it was impossible – obviously it was just a holiday romance. Which was fine. She shook her dark hair and adjusted a picture on the wall that was already straight. There was nothing *wrong* with a holiday romance. Only . . .

Yesterday evening, she had seen him dining alone in the

courtyard. The lamp above his head was shining on his fair hair, lighting it into pale gold. Emanuele had put on some moody jazz music; the buzz of low conversation and light laughter among the guests punctured the night, and the fragrance of her mother's pesto sauce was almost heady in the citrus-scented air. She'd wanted to go over to his table, say something casual and amusing, perhaps even join him for a nightcap. But . . . She faltered. She'd told him that morning that with Nonna being in Pisa she'd be busy all day. She'd thought she wanted the space to reflect. Now, reflection done, she felt restless. Now, space was the last thing she wanted, and she was uncharacteristically nervous too.

She had watched him push his plate away, and from where she stood she could almost hear his sigh of satisfaction. He pulled a sketch pad out of the bag at his feet and glanced around – Isabella stepped back into the shadows, not wanting him to see her observing him – and then he began to make some adjustments to a drawing, working fast with a pencil. So, he wasn't only in Vernazza on behalf of his father, and he wasn't only taking a holiday in a beautiful place – he was also working on some other project while he was staying at The Lemon Tree Hotel. He glanced across at the cloisters as if for inspiration, and Isabella had slunk away unobserved.

Now, their maid Perla passed Isabella in the lobby as she hovered.

'Have you done rooms Five and Six, Perla?' Isabella ignored her grandmother's pointedly raised eyebrow.

'Six is still in there. I've done Five though. He was up bright and early this morning.' Perla bustled off.

'I saw the Signor Bauer leaving before eight o'clock,' Nonna's dry voice broke into her thoughts.

'Oh.' Isabella blushed. No point in staying here any longer then. No doubt he had gone out for the day – and why shouldn't he, why should he hang around waiting for her to have some free time to spend with him, when she kept telling him how busy she was?

'Take care, Bella.' Her grandmother's dark eyes were gentle. 'Don't get hurt.'

'I won't.' Isabella forced a bright expression. Soon, he would be gone. Soon, her life would return to normal. And no doubt that would be a good thing. The trouble was though, that every hour she didn't see him was an hour where something seemed to be missing from her life. *Mamma mia* – had she really got it so bad?

Isabella pushed this thought away as she walked to the station and caught the train to the next village of the Cinque Terre. She loved the way the train hurled itself through the long, dark tunnels with the sudden explosions of bright sunshine that characterised the journeys between the five villages, and she sat back to enjoy. The train line cutting through the mountainous coastline must have been an engineering marvel for its day back in the late nineteenth century when it was first built, linking the villages to each other and to the outside world – though a far cry from the crowded tourist train it had now become.

Monterosso was very different from Vernazza, although geographically so close; there was an openness about the place – the largest village of the five – that was sometimes a relief when one was feeling a little hemmed in. It wasn't as stunning perhaps as the jewel that was Vernazza . . . Isabella stepped down on to the platform, lined with bougainvillea, palms, and oleander framing the glassy-blue sea beyond. But she liked the long sandy beach, the old town dominated by the ruined castle, and the narrow medieval *caruggi* – streets lined with multi-coloured terraced houses, divided by ancient stone arches and decorated with friezes in shades that remained vivid, despite the years of weathering.

From the station she emerged on to the promenade. This was tourist Monterosso al Mare with shops and stalls on her left selling bags, sarongs and beach gear, a central avenue of benches under oleander and tamarisk trees and on the right, the shoreline dotted with bright blue and orange parasols. People strolled along the promenade, leaned on the railings looking out to sea, sat on the benches with their coffee or *gelato*. Isabella began to relax. A lazy place and a lazy day – this was exactly the tonic she needed.

She headed for the old town past the panoramic 'window' through which one could see Punta Mesco, the promontory of the mountain and the old sandstone mines – stone once used to pave the streets of old Monterosso. She turned the corner and took the steps down to the lower promenade of Salita dei Cappuccini. The village was busy – the entire Cinque Terre remained busy although they were now well into October – but Monterosso seemed to thrive on it. Music trailed from the open doorways of cafés, the bougainvillea remained in full bloom, and there was a fragrance of baking dough and roasted tomatoes in the air that was making her stomach growl.

She had a few other errands to run before going to the cobbler, so she crossed the main piazza and took a narrow street under the arches that led to the black-and-white striped church of San Giovanni Battista where artists' easels were lined up under the *loggia*, and there were a couple of specialist shops that would sell what she needed.

300

Her purchases made, Isabella headed up the hill past the bar on the corner to the cobble-stepped street where old lanterns hung from peeling pink walls and plants spilled from over-hanging balconies. This was where Passano's Cobblers was situated – very aptly in the heart of the old town, because the Signor Passano was not just a cobbler, but a *maestro calzolaio*, a master shoemaker, like his father and grandfather before him.

The stone walls of the little shop made it seem more like a cave, Isabella thought, as she ducked inside. They were lined with dusty shelves on which sat neat rows of leather shoes, boots, wooden forms and moulds. Some shoes were shiny and new, some crusty and old – just like their owners presumably. The work counter was pockmarked with the stamp of tools, the well-oiled machines were no doubt the same ones that had been in operation for decades, and the overpowering scent – of leather, rubber, and glue – filled the air.

'Can you do anything with these, *Signore*?' she asked the cobbler. She liked Signor Passano. He looked about ninety, and still ran his business in the traditions of his forefathers. He was someone who would never be affected by the tourists who visited his town. He would never change, and neither would the way he worked.

'Let me see now.' He wiped his hands on his hessian apron, took the sandals from Isabella, and examined them, head on one side. 'I can re-stitch here.' He clicked his tongue – at the poor quality of the original construction presumably. 'Glue here.' He frowned. 'Can you leave them?' He held the straps of the sandals hooked over his little finger as if they weren't quite worthy.

'*Sì, Signore*.' Isabella nodded. He'd make a good job of them, she knew.

'Collect them the day after tomorrow.' He placed the sandals unceremoniously on the lowest shelf next to a huge basket of nails.

'Yes, of course.' She could always ask one of the staff to pick them up. 'Thank you so much, *Signore*.'

Isabella left the shop and walked back down the hill, past the old *loggia*. She stood for a moment on the corner opposite a dark pink house with green shutters. She blinked. Stared. Did a double take. But no, she was right the first time. Giovanna – of all people – was making her way slowly up the main street. She had a stick in one hand. With the other hand, she clung to the arm of Ferdinand Bauer.

Isabella was so shocked that she just stood there staring and didn't even notice the Ape swinging down the hill towards her until it practically careered into her amidst a torrent of hand gesticulations and swearing on the part of the driver. She jumped back into the shadow of the stone doorway, waving the driver away. She didn't want them to spot her, but there was no chance of that; they were walking with their heads together, thick as thieves. She frowned. What was going on?

When they had safely passed by the Conad supermarket on the opposite corner and were temporarily out of sight, Isabella darted down to Piazza Agostino Poggi. And there they were. She hung back, watching their retreating figures. They were making slow progress up the narrow street that was little more than an alleyway, looking neither left nor right. They were clearly on a mission. Then they disappeared again around the next corner, and Isabella hurried through the throng of tourists, past the rails of dresses and sheaves of scarves hanging outside the little boutiques on the street, in order to catch sight of them again.

They hadn't gone far. This time, Isabella stood in a café doorway to watch them. Giovanna was old, but still active. Isabella wasn't exactly surprised that she still visited the other Cinque Terre villages – she had plenty of friends dotted around here and there – though Isabella had imagined that these days people mostly came to her. But why Ferdinand? Had Giovanna asked him to accompany her for some reason? She had to know.

The road stretched ahead, lined with cafés and shops, bicycles propped against walls, tourists strolling through the *caruggi* streets. Just as they were once more moving out of sight into the maze of the old town, Isabella made a decision. She felt a bit silly, and she was no amateur sleuth, but she would follow them. How else could she find out what they were up to?

It wasn't easy. If they'd been walking fast, she could have followed their lead, but because they were going so slowly, she had to keep stopping; feigning interest in a scarf here, a leather bag there, a lunch menu somewhere else, while at the same time checking they didn't disappear out of sight. And she had to ensure that if one of them were to suddenly turn around, she could easily duck into a doorway, swerve down a side street or even hide behind a tourist. Isabella had never done anything like this before. In different circumstances it might even have been fun.

She waited by another café as they went further up the street. The scent of coffee was tempting, but she couldn't stop now. They were a bizarre looking pair. In those different circumstances, Isabella would have smiled and enjoyed watching them – one so lean, tall and masculine, the other small, bent, elderly. But where were they going? Was Ferdinand simply taking Giovanna to lunch? It didn't seem so – they'd passed plenty of good restaurants already, and why make her walk so far? It was crazy to be jealous of an elderly lady who she loved to distraction, but nevertheless Isabella felt the chill of it shiver down her spine. Why were they excluding her from this strange friendship? What exactly were they doing? And why hadn't she been invited to be a part of it?

They turned right at the top of the street. Isabella knew that the other main street ran parallel to this one for a while, and that they eventually met in a V-shape at the end of the road. She could see the door on the far side of the nearest building, so she took a chance and nipped through the grey and white café. The industrial-style lights were bright. She felt a surge of adrenalin. She had to hurry. She mustn't lose them.

She emerged from the café, and whoops, here was a problem. They were standing by the plane trees, almost right in front of her, deep in conversation. Isabella dropped back. Nothing to do but wait. After a few moments, they walked on, through the archways to where the road widened slightly. Isabella stayed close to the shops on the left-hand side of the road.

They turned off, and Isabella hurried towards the side street. But there they were again, this time standing by the oratory. She hovered by the fountain. Giovanna said something, he nodded, and they went inside. Wonderful. She could hardly follow them inside a church. Isabella retreated. She would just have to wait. The oratory was a simple building with a colourful and pretty rose window. But surely this wasn't their final destination? She sighed. She'd have to wait inside a shop that gave her a view of the oratory entrance – she couldn't risk them coming out and heading straight for her as they walked back into town. But this was easier said than done.

She was in luck, however. They emerged from the oratory five minutes later, Giovanna still hanging on to Ferdinand's arm, blinking like a mole in the sunlight. Isabella dodged back out of sight behind a plane tree. And, instead of retracing their steps to the main street, they turned right. Where now?

Her question was answered almost immediately. Giovanna pointed to an orange wrought-iron gate on the left. Ferdinand opened it, and Giovanna walked through, Ferdinand right behind her.

Isabella approached the oratory and stared towards the orange gate, still keeping her distance so that she wouldn't be seen. Clearly they were visiting someone. The courtyard garden of the building was full of greenery, so she couldn't see them on the path or at the front door. But whose house could it be? There was only one way to find out – and she'd have to act quickly just in case they came out again and saw her. There was nowhere to hide.

Ahead, she could see some steps that might provide a clue . . . At least the lemon trees and vines trailing over the high stone walls gave her some cover as she scurried past, not daring to hesitate by the orange gate, in case they might see her. She ran under an ancient stone archway and past a building – the butternut yellow Cinema Moderno. She'd never been to this part of town before, but she knew she had to get around the corner and up the steps before she was spotted. Perhaps she should simply double back and return into town? But by now Isabella was consumed with curiosity.

At the top of the steps she had a clearer view of the house behind the lemon trees. They must have gone inside – there was no sign of them on the path or on the street below. The house was painted peach, and had a wide balcony. She held her breath. It was a warm day. With a bit of luck . . . She dipped behind the wall at the top. Peered back. Yes. She almost cheered. She could see the balcony of the house. And a door was opening . . .

A woman passed by, glancing at her rather strangely. Isabella smoothed her hair from her face and stayed crouched behind the wall as if it were the most natural thing in the world.

The woman reached the bottom of the steps and took a right turn away from the house. Slowly, slowly, Isabella peered around again. If any of them happened to look up . . . If any of them happened to see her – how on earth would she explain her behaviour? Ferdinand would think she was mad as a coot. She stifled a hysterical giggle.

Three people were sitting around the table on the balcony, and they appeared to be having a serious conversation. Giovanna, Ferdinand, and Siena Gianelli. Siena? The retired nurse? Isabella knew that she was a close friend of Giovanna's and a frequent visitor to her cottage. She also knew that Siena lived here in Monterosso – though she hadn't known where. But why had Giovanna and Ferdinand come to see a nurse? Was Giovanna ill? Isabella held on to the wall to maintain her balance. It made no sense. If Giovanna was ill, then why wouldn't Siena have come to her? Or why hadn't they simply called out a doctor? And what did Ferdinand have to do with it all? Or was he the one who was ill . . .?

Isabella frowned. What should she do? Her fingers closed around her mobile in her bag. She could call her grandmother. Nonna would know how to handle this. But Nonna seemed to have enough problems of her own right now. And she remembered her grandmother's words about Ferdinand earlier that morning. No, not Nonna then.

Isabella couldn't stand here hiding behind a wall all day. She had work to do, she must relieve Nonna from her post on reception, she must get back to the hotel. And really – was it any of her business, what was going on here between the three of them? Perhaps not. With one last curious glance towards the three figures on the balcony, she descended the steps in the other direction and headed for the station.

But it was her business, was it not? Giovanna was her business. And Ferdinand too, if his kisses were to be believed. So . . . Isabella increased her pace. She would find out what this was all about if it killed her. So far, instead of providing answers for Isabella, all Ferdinand was doing was posing more questions. She now had even less clue what was going on. He had asked her if she trusted him, and she had given him an honest answer. No. He had kissed her, and she had responded. Yes. But if he still wouldn't tell her what this was all about, then where could they go from here?

CHAPTER 32

Chiara

That same afternoon, Chiara took her cheque book out of the desk drawer and made out a cheque to Beatrice Gavino. She decided to add a short note:

> *Dear Signora Gavino,*
> *Forgive me, but I was unable to persuade my husband to change his mind. Perhaps it is for the best? You may, after all, be able to find a more conscientious landlord.*

Chiara waited to feel some sense of her own disloyalty for referring to her husband this way, but it didn't come. This was a sign, she knew.

> *And besides, even if you stay, who is to say that your position might not once again be in jeopardy in the future?*

In Chiara's opinion, there wasn't much doubt about that.

For this reason, please accept this cheque. It is not charity. As the wife of your landlord, I do feel partially responsible for the position you find yourself in.

Yes, maybe she should have kept a closer eye on Alonzo's business as well as her own. Perhaps they should have worked as a team, instead of being separate entities. Perhaps then, things might have been different – in all aspects of her life.

She frowned with concentration. She didn't want the woman's pride to prevent her accepting the money: this would no doubt seem a large amount to Signora Gavino.

Frankly, I can afford to help, and I want to. This small sum will enable you to put a deposit down on a new apartment and perhaps pay the first month's rent too. Hopefully it will also cover your moving expenses. Whatever you decide, it is yours to keep. I ask only one thing – please do not tell my husband that I have given it to you. Think of it as a goodwill payment. I wish you well.

That should do it. She signed it with a flourish, put the note and cheque in a white business envelope, sealed and addressed it. In her opinion, there was still room in the world for a handwritten letter and a cheque book.

Her mobile bleeped with a message. She picked it up and sighed. Alonzo again. He had sent her five texts and tried to call her several times since she had left his apartment the previous day. Each text had sounded more pleading than the last. Each text sounded less and less like the man she knew.

Just give me one more chance, Chiara, she read. *For Elene's sake – just one more chance.*

How many chances could there be? How many chances did any man – or woman – deserve?

There was a knock on the door and Elene came in as if Chiara had summoned her with her thoughts. 'Mamma? Are you all right?' Her daughter looked unusually bright-eyed.

Clearly, she knew nothing of what had happened in Pisa, which meant that Alonzo hadn't contacted her, thank goodness. Perhaps Chiara shouldn't have been surprised at what she'd discovered there, but she was. And what now? She had made a promise to Elene. Was she going to break it? Could she break it? Or was she willing for her sham of a marriage to go on, even after this? She had told Alonzo not to come back to the hotel – but he would have to come back sometime, and they would have to discuss this some more.

'Hello, darling,' she said. 'I'm fine. Are you looking for something?'

Elene was flipping through some papers on the shelf. But admin was hardly her department. Usually she had to be dragged out of the kitchen.

'Yes.' She hesitated. 'There was a large brown envelope. I left it in the kitchen last night. I think Isabella must have moved it.' She seemed a little nervous.

'Why don't you ask her?' Emanuele had taken over from Chiara in reception two hours ago – surely Isabella was back by now?

Elene shot her mother one of her disdainful looks. 'Of course, I would, Mamma – if she was around.'

So, she was not yet back? Chiara was surprised, but it would do her granddaughter good to take some time away from the hotel. 'What is in this envelope of yours?' Chiara glanced through her own paperwork on the desk – there was no large brown envelope to be seen.

'Oh, nothing important.' But Elene's fingers were twisting at the tie of her apron. 'It's mine though. My name is on the envelope. And I haven't had a chance to look at it properly yet. So, if you come across it . . .'

'Of course.' Chiara shrugged. She hoped that she would not pry into Elene's business however curious she might be. She waited for her daughter to ask when her father was coming home, but she said nothing. Perhaps Elene was so concerned with the contents of this mysterious brown envelope that she'd failed to notice Alonzo's prolonged absence for once – which was no bad thing, because Chiara needed time to think.

'OK, Mamma.' Elene was still looking around the room as she opened the door and left the office. 'And don't forget . . .'

Chiara raised an eyebrow. 'If I see it, I will bring it to you straight away.' It was probably nothing. But it was curious, nonetheless.

It was late afternoon by the time Chiara picked up her letter to Signora Gavino. She would take it out to reception to go with the late post. Isabella had finally returned, looking surprisingly pale after her morning in Monterosso, and was now working on her laptop on the other side of the room. 'Isabella . . .'

'Yes, Nonna?' She looked up.

'Did you go to the cobblers?'

'Yes, Nonna.'

'And . . . Did you have a pleasant morning in Monterosso?'

A look of such innocence crossed Isabella's face that Chiara knew she was hiding something. 'Yes, Nonna.'

'Hmm.' Another mystery. Chiara left the office and shut

311

the door behind her. She had a quick word with Marco who was on duty, and glanced at the hotel register. Everything was as it should be. Guests were drinking aperitifs in the Cloisters Bar, and the courtyard beyond; some soft background music was playing. The hall and reception area were spotlessly clean. Although she'd been absent yesterday, all was running smoothly. No one was indispensable, it seemed.

Ferdinand Bauer stood at the foot of the stairs near Luca Bordoni's painting, deep in conversation on his mobile. His tone was urgent, she could tell that much, though she spoke very little German. Chiara gave him a polite nod as she passed by. She didn't know why he had come here, but she worried for Isabella. How could you tell who was a decent person on first acquaintance alone? Every woman needed a lie detector, a charm-offensive test – men too perhaps? Not knowing who could be trusted . . . *Allora*, this made life and love so much harder, that was all.

She stood in the doorway in the late-afternoon sunshine and put a hand up to her eyes to protect them from the brightness. The leaves of the olive trees seemed almost translucent; the rays of the sun had tinged them amber. The gravel path wound through the grove. It was so enticing that for a second she longed to dart along the path, run to a shady place, and lie down, the twisted roots her pillow.

Chiara shook the thought from her mind. For goodness' sake – she had responsibilities; she had a hotel to look after. Besides, she could dart along that path whenever she damn well liked. She was free. Wasn't she? This was her hotel, and she had no one to answer to.

But today, Chiara was finding it difficult to live with herself. How could she be running this beautiful and tranquil hotel here in Vernazza when her husband was allowing such terrible conditions to exist in his apartment block, and when he was evicting old ladies and taking payment in kind from a prostitute, no less? *Madonna santa* . . . She crossed herself – and it had been a while since she'd done that . . . And she had slept with him. He was her husband – she had slept with him before, afterwards, during. It sickened her to the core. He might even have given her some awful disease for all she knew.

Chiara shuddered. She had known when she made love with Dante that her marriage was over – perhaps she had known when Alonzo first raised his hand to her. She touched her cheek, remembering how she had felt in that moment. And now she also believed that he might do it again. It was unacceptable, unforgiveable. Was there really any way they could come back from this – what seemed like the last straw?

She turned from the afternoon sunshine. Ferdinand Bauer was still on the phone. She glanced quickly away. She could have sworn he had tears in his eyes.

CHAPTER 33

Chiara

Chiara pushed open the swing doors. Elene was still in the kitchen, though everyone else had left and gone home. Chiara dipped her hand into her bag. 'The envelope you were looking for – it turned up.' She passed it over. 'It was on the reception desk. Emanuele found it tucked into the register, it must have got caught up there by mistake.'

As she was talking, Isabella entered the kitchen. '*Ciao*, Mamma, Nonna.' She sounded unhappy too. Chiara thought about Ferdinand Bauer. Was it something in the air perhaps? It had been a long season – they all must need a break from the hotel, from the guests, from the endless demands of the hospitality business.

'*Ciao*, Bella.' Elene's attention remained fixed on Chiara. 'Did you look inside, Mamma?' She practically snatched the envelope from her and sat down at the table, tucking it into her bag.

'No, of course not.'

Elene narrowed her eyes.

314

Chiara spread her hands in righteous innocence. 'No, I did not,' she repeated more firmly. True, she'd been tempted – though only because Elene had made such a fuss about the thing. But perhaps she had learned over the past few days not to meddle in other people's business – in case you found out something you didn't want to know.

'*Va bene.*' Elene seemed mollified. 'That's OK, then.'

'But I looked inside, Mamma.'

Elene glanced up at Isabella. 'What did you say?'

'I read it. Sorry. And I think I need a drink, if you don't mind?' Isabella was already getting herself a wine glass from the kitchen cabinet, but she had her back to them, so Chiara couldn't see her expression.

She turned around. 'I didn't mean to pry.' Her eyes were red. She had been crying.

'Bella . . .' Chiara was filled with concern. 'What is it? What's wrong?'

'It was addressed to me, Isabella.' Elene rose to her feet. She looked furious. 'And I really can't see why a few drawings should have upset you so much.'

'Drawings?' Chiara looked from one to the other of them in confusion.

'I didn't notice it was addressed to you, Mamma.' Isabella brought over a bottle of white wine from the *Cantina Cinque Terre* along with three glasses, and came to sit down at the table. She didn't seem to want to look at anyone. 'I didn't see your name. Emanuele told me it had been left in the kitchen, and I assumed it was something to do with the hotel, so I pulled out the papers to check what it was, and . . .' She poured the wine. Her nerves were apparent from the way she spilt some drops on the table.

'And?' Chiara was getting a bad feeling about this. She picked up her glass and looked from one to the other of them again. She was certainly ready for a drink – it had been a tough day. But what could be so awful to make Elene desperate that they didn't see it?

'And it's personal,' snapped Elene. Her chignon had become unpinned, and there were two spots of red high on her cheeks.

Isabella raised a delicate eyebrow. She took a deep glug of her wine.

'And private.' Elene did the same.

Isabella put down her glass. 'Did you ask him to come here, Mamma?' she asked.

'What?' Chiara frowned. She took another sip. The wine was crisp, floral, and citrussy – it was one of her favourites, but it was hard to take any enjoyment from it tonight. She had no idea what her daughter and granddaughter were talking about – but they weren't happy.

'Who?'

'Ferdinand Bauer.' Once his name was out of her lips, Isabella's shoulders slumped.

'Of course not.'

'I don't understand.' Chiara was more confused than ever. What did that young man have to do with all this?

'Then why would he do such a thing?' Isabella blurted.

Elene shrugged. 'Because I asked him to.'

'Asked him to?'

'*Va bene.*' Elene sighed. She grabbed her mobile with one hand and repinned her hair with the other. 'I will call Silvio.'

'Why are you calling Silvio?' Chiara took another sip of her wine. It might help her get to grips with this conversation.

'You may as well all know. Who can keep any secrets in this place, eh?'

Chiara thought of Dante. She had a point.

'Bella knows already, and no doubt she will tell you the second my back is turned.'

'Mamma!'

'*Allora*, you are thick as thieves, you two.'

'But why do you need to call Silvio?' Chiara persisted.

Elene shot her a sharp look of disbelief. 'Two against one is never fair, Mamma.' She broke off to speak to her husband. 'Can you come to the kitchen – now? We need to talk. It's about the drawings . . .'

'Drawings?' Chiara still didn't understand.

Elene took another deep slug of her wine. 'I asked him, Bella, because he is an architect.'

'But . . .'

'And why not? It seemed like the perfect opportunity.'

An hour later they were on their second bottle of wine and they were still talking. Elene had laid the drawings out on the table between them and confessed – she had found out that the Signor Bauer was an architect when she had got talking to him one day, she had persuaded him to make a few drawings; they were just ideas, that was all, only ideas.

Chiara knew that Elene would never have just 'got talking' to an architect who happened to be a guest of their hotel. Elene didn't just get talking to anyone. And she wondered how her daughter had persuaded him. No doubt Isabella would be angry with Ferdinand Bauer for doing it – given how she felt about her mother's ideas. Still, Isabella had calmed down, and so had Elene.

317

They all looked over the drawings. They were only rough sketches it was true, but they were done sympathetically – perhaps then the Signor Bauer knew what he was doing after all.

'And so, what is this?' Chiara asked.

'The new bar.'

'On the roof of the old convent?'

'Well, why not?' Elene's eyes gleamed. 'There would be more space, don't you think?'

'And this?'

'An annexe for a fitness suite.'

'A fitness suite?' *Madonna santa*! What would the old nuns have thought of that?

The debate had been heated, and suddenly Chiara felt so weary of it all. First, Alonzo, and what she had discovered in Pisa, and now this. The wine had gone straight to her head. 'You should have spoken to me first,' she told her daughter. 'You should not have gone behind our backs like this.' She thought of her own parents, who had worked so hard to save this building, and she couldn't deny the feeling of betrayal.

Elene looked close to tears.

Silvio put a protective arm around her and, perversely, Chiara was glad about this. They had all had a lot to cope with recently. They all needed some rest.

'We have tried to talk to you many times,' he said stiffly.

'*Pff.*' What nonsense. They were always discussing possible improvements. There were regular meetings between the four of them, and any of them could put forward an idea for discussion.

'We feel you don't listen to us. We feel we are not important.'

'Oh, really . . .?'

'I am not important, sure.'

He held himself more upright, and Chiara was conscious of a small stab of guilt. It was not true. As Elene's husband and someone who worked hard in The Lemon Tree Hotel, he certainly was important. He was family, and a vital part of their business. But had Chiara ever regarded him in this way? The answer was 'no'.

'But Elene . . .' He tailed off. 'She feels sometimes that she is treated more like a paid chef than an equal partner, that's all.'

'I can speak for myself, Silvio.' Elene's eyes blazed.

He sat back. 'Then do it.'

Elene seemed to hesitate. She gave one of her defensive little shrugs. 'What he says is true.'

Chiara frowned. It was the first time Silvio had ever spoken up like this. Usually he left the talking to the women. She leaned forwards. 'We do listen,' she said. But perhaps not enough. It saddened her that they should feel this way, that Elene should feel un-valued. She had always felt that everyone had a clearly defined role within the hotel, and that this very definition was what helped The Lemon Tree run smoothly. But had she ever given them enough choice about this? Should she have done things differently – actively encouraged everyone to have more of a say?

'It's just that me and Nonna don't always agree with you and Mamma, Papà,' Isabella chipped in. She poured them all more wine. The second bottle was finished. 'We don't want things at The Lemon Tree Hotel to change. Right, Nonna?'

Chiara nodded. She wouldn't like to be in Ferdinand Bauer's shoes when her granddaughter confronted him about these drawings. But it wasn't just that she didn't want anything at the hotel to change. 'Though we shouldn't be entirely resistant to change, Bella,' she said. 'The important thing is to make improvements that enhance what the hotel offers, whilst still retaining its integrity. Is that not so?'

'Oh, yes.' Isabella nodded. 'Exactly so.'

'Elene? Silvio?'

'We never wanted to lose the integrity,' Elene flashed back. 'Having a rooftop bar does not lose the integrity. An infinity pool does not lose the integrity. A spa—'

'Elene.' Chiara put up her hand. 'Let's take one thing at a time, yes? Let's fix up a meeting tomorrow when we are all feeling fresher, when we have slept on it and had time to consider, perhaps? We will take notes. We will discuss everything properly. We will be professional, yes?'

'Yes, Mamma.'

'And this time, we will listen.' Chiara exchanged a glance with Silvio. And she had the weirdest feeling. Suddenly it felt as if he and she were on the same side.

CHAPTER 34

Isabella

Isabella couldn't believe how much had happened today. First, Monterosso and seeing Giovanna and Ferdinand – that had put her in a spin. Then she had got back to the hotel and unthinkingly opened an envelope addressed to her mother – she blamed her distracted state of mind for that one. And when she looked at the drawings inside . . . Comprehension had slowly dawned. Sketches of the hotel – but not of the hotel as it was now, but of the hotel as it might be in the future – if Isabella's mother had her way. A rooftop bar . . . An annexe with a spa . . . Isabella shuddered. What was she thinking of? The sketches were tastefully done, but really? What exactly was her mother planning? And more to the point – what would Nonna say?

But who . . . Isabella turned the envelope upside down, and a business card fell out on to the desk. She recognised it – of course. And then she remembered seeing Ferdinand having dinner alone that night, watching him as he took a sketchpad out of his bag, seeing him look towards the cloisters for inspiration. Inspiration! Ferdinand . . . Isabella wanted to go and look for him right there and then – only she supposed he was still in Monterosso. She wanted to shake him and demand some answers. How could he have done such a thing? How far had this gone?

Already confused about Monterosso and Giovanna, Isabella simply didn't know what to think. Ferdinand didn't return all afternoon, Nonna seemed too deep in her own thoughts to be disturbed, and her mother was busy with dinner. So, she waited. She left the envelope of sketches in the hotel register where her grandmother was bound to see it – she couldn't bear to tell her herself – but Nonna hadn't even opened it, although it was unsealed. And then it had all come out . . .

Now, it was getting late, after eleven o'clock, and she gave a little jump when she saw Ferdinand loitering outside the Cloisters Bar. *Aha*! Time to find out a thing or two. Was he coming or going? She couldn't tell. His hands were in the pockets of his jeans, and he was wearing a light blue collarless shirt, the sleeves loosely rolled to the elbows.

'Good evening, Ferdinand,' she said crisply. As if.

'Isabella. I was wondering where you might be hiding.' He took a step closer. Those eyes – they looked even deeper blue in this dim light.

'I've been talking to my parents and my grandmother.' She folded her arms as if to keep him at bay.

'Hotel business?' He seemed mildly curious, but that was all.

She shrugged. 'It is an ongoing discussion.'

'Oh?'

'My mother – she has plans to renovate The Lemon Tree Hotel.' She narrowed her eyes, waiting for his reaction.

'Ah.'

'Yes. She wants to bring it into the twenty-first century, she says. She wants to make it a five-star luxury hotel, a place that might attract the most discerning, the wealthiest people.'

'Right.' He frowned. 'And I take it, you don't want that?' He seemed uncertain.

Isabella rose to her full height. 'Nonna and I think that the hotel is just fine the way it is,' she replied.

'I see.'

'In fact, we love the traditional building, the history of *L'Attico Convento*, the old convent. My grandmother and her parents before her did all they could to preserve the integrity of the place,' she informed him. 'And I have always been determined to do the same.' Just so that he was in no doubt where she stood on the matter.

'Hmm.' Ferdinand rocked back on his heels and surveyed the crumbling pillars of the cloisters. 'I have to say that I agree with you. It's been expertly renovated. It's perfectly charming and unspoilt.' He even smiled as he looked out into the tranquil courtyard where the golden lamps were glowing.

The cheek of him. Isabella could hardly believe it. 'Then why did you do those drawings for Mamma?' she hissed.

'Drawings? Ah.' He had the grace to look embarrassed. 'Your mother asked me to.'

Well, she had guessed that much. 'You could have refused.'

He hesitated. Perhaps he was afraid of seeming disloyal – to his client. 'She made it hard to say "no".'

'Because of the amount of money she paid you?' And that was another thing that had annoyed her. The Lemon Tree Hotel was doing well financially, but like her grandmother, Isabella hated throwing money away. Her mother had her own ideas, yes, fair enough. But Nonna was right – she should never

323

have commissioned an architect to make sketches without consulting the rest of them.

'No!' He looked indignant. 'Because, she made me think that you all wanted it.'

A likely story. Just how could her mother have done that? 'And why, after all, would you have wanted to say "no"?' she parried, beginning to quite enjoy this sparring match with him, where – for once – she had the upper hand. 'You are an architect, are you not? You work freelance, I suppose? You take commissions?' Though she didn't really know even this much about him.

'Well, yes, I am, and so of course I take on certain projects. But . . .'

'But?'

'But in this case, I didn't agree with her plans.' Those blue eyes looked so innocent – it was quite amazing.

'Oh, really?' She was believing this story less and less.

'And so, I did the sketches simply as a favour to her, that is all.'

What was he telling her? 'A favour? So, she didn't pay you anything?'

He scuffed his feet on the flagstones. 'In fact, no.'

Did that make it worse or better? For a moment, Isabella couldn't work it out.

Ferdinand took advantage of that moment to grab her hands. 'I thought you wanted it too,' he said.

'And you couldn't ask me?' After all, they'd seen enough of each other to make that more than a possibility.

'Your mother – she said that it would be a surprise.' He grimaced. 'I thought it was intended to be a nice surprise – not a bad one.'

Isabella shook her head and pulled away. 'It feels as if you are always against me, Ferdinand.' And so why was she wasting her time even talking to him? There were so many things she didn't understand, so many secrets.

'No.' He pulled her closer once more. 'The opposite is true.'

'Those sketches . . .'

'You didn't like them?'

Isabella considered. 'They are good sketches,' she conceded. She took a step away and looked up at the building she loved so much. She must try to be objective. In fact, as they had sat around the table in the kitchen discussing her mother's plans, she had even, if she were honest, felt a faint sense of pride, that Ferdinand had made his sketches so *simpatico*. 'But definitely not what we want for The Lemon Tree Hotel.'

'I told you. I agree with you.' He came closer once more, smoothed her hair from her face. It was too much. Isabella could feel herself being drawn in – again, almost despite herself.

'Then . . . why?'

'It was more a case of damage limitation.'

Damage limitation . . . She could imagine now how it had been. Her mother asking him to do the drawings, Ferdinand not liking to refuse. He hadn't accepted payment, he had done them because he thought that Isabella would want him to. Was that how it had been? 'Why did you become an architect, Ferdinand?' she asked him.

'That's easy.' He smiled. 'I always had a passion for buildings. I was fascinated by them, even as a boy. They're representative of a part of history, don't you think? A culture and context.'

'Exactly.' Which rather proved her point about the ancient convent that had become The Lemon Tree Hotel.

'But it can also be about making changes within communities,' he continued. 'Looking at the bigger picture, architecture can affect social interactions and infrastructure. It can affect people's lives in a powerful way.'

'It certainly can,' Isabella replied crisply. She admired his sentiments – up to a point – and it seemed that this man could explain anything away. But how could he explain the rest of today's events? She was looking forward to hearing him try . . .

CHAPTER 35

Isabella

'I should also tell you that I spoke to my father earlier today.' Ferdinand sighed. 'I'm afraid that he has taken a turn for the worse. He has had the results of some tests through – and it's not good news.'

'Oh, Ferdinand. I'm sorry.' Isabella was immediately contrite. She put out a hand and gently touched his arm. 'Does that mean you'll be going home soon?' She hated the thought, but even without his father's illness, it was inevitable.

'Yes, I will have to.' He gave her a long look. Isabella tried to interpret it, but didn't have a clue. 'Every day here has been more magical than the last.'

'And today?' She couldn't help it. She wanted to believe every word he said, but the image of the three of them sitting around the table in Monterosso looking so serious, seeming so intimate, would not go away. But if he was leaving soon, then now was his chance to come clean about everything.

'Today?'

'Where did you go today?' She probed deeper.

Ferdinand seemed to consider. Isabella waited. Was it such a difficult question?

He leaned on a nearby pillar in that casual way he had. She could smell what she thought of as the evening scent of him – something soapy, a few glasses of wine, some pasta with a creamy sauce, a hint of lemon. 'I visited Monterosso al Mare,' he said.

'Ah.' At least he hadn't lied to her. 'And what did you do there?' She kept her voice light. But just because his father was ill . . . didn't mean that he wasn't answerable for his actions.

He shot her a sharp glance this time. 'What does anyone do there?'

Allora, they rarely went to take coffee with a retired nurse. Isabella shrugged.

'I walked along the beach, saw old San Francesco d'Assisi, looked around the *Centro Storico*. Nothing special.'

Nothing special . . . Isabella suppressed a sigh. Once again, she was getting nowhere with this extremely annoying man of mystery.

'And how about you?' He leaned still closer.

Did he even know that his voice could be so soft that it almost felt like a caress? Probably not, she decided.

'Another busy day at The Lemon Tree Hotel?'

'I took some time off this morning, as a matter of fact.'

'Really?' His eyes widened. 'Damn. Why didn't you say? We could have spent it together.'

And how would that have panned out with Giovanna and Siena? 'You weren't around. And anyway, it was a spur of the moment thing. I had some errands to run.'

'And now?'

'Now?' She glanced at her watch. It was a quarter past eleven.

'Are you busy now?'

Isabella shifted her weight to the other foot. Obviously, she wasn't busy now. It was late. Half of their guests were probably in bed already. Soon, Emanuele would be closing the bar. 'I was thinking about going to bed.' So, she sounded sarcastic. And why not? She felt sorry for him that his father was ill, she felt sad that he would soon be leaving, but the fact remained – he didn't trust her enough to tell her the truth.

'Isabella.' His gaze travelled slowly over her face. She felt almost immobilised by it. 'Could we have a nightcap together? I need to talk to you.'

Was he going to open up to her after all? She considered. She didn't feel in the least tired. 'I suppose that is possible.' She tried to sound more reluctant than she felt.

'Good.' He rubbed his hands together and turned towards the Cloisters Bar. 'I'll order us some wine.'

'Only a small glass for me.' She'd already had several in the kitchen talking with her parents and Nonna. And now more than ever, she needed to keep a clear head. She glanced outside to where the golden lamps were glowing – lighting up the blue agapanthus flowers, the dusky flagstones, and the lemon tree. Perhaps it was her overactive imagination, but sometimes that tree seemed almost to possess some spiritual power. The lemon was symbolic of bitterness and disappointment, she knew that. But she also knew that Christians had always linked the fruit to fidelity – a symbolism she preferred. The lemon tree would always be faithful and true – but how faithful and true was Ferdinand Bauer?

'Shall we go out into the courtyard?' she asked him. It was

329

a warm night, but it was getting late, and only a few guests still lingered out there.

He looked around, leaned back towards her. 'I was thinking about going somewhere more private,' he whispered into her hair.

Isabella shivered. She drew back, gave him a second glance, and he actually winked at her. Clearly, he was planning to seduce her. And the thought filled her with anticipation rather than fear. 'Well . . .'

On the one hand . . . Isabella wasn't a virgin – there had been a boy from the village with whom she'd hung out for a while a couple of years ago; it could have become even more serious, but Sergio got tired of always waiting for her to be free. And there had been another man at the hotel – a guest, who had come on to her and she had foolishly allowed herself to be flattered and made love to, not realising the obvious – that he was only staying at the hotel for a week and that he had a wife and a life back at home in Bologna. He was the reason she now tried to keep her working life separate from her personal one. He was probably also the reason why Nonna kept trying to warn her against Ferdinand too (well, one of the reasons anyway). Was it wise then to get entangled with another transitory visitor?

Isabella rapidly mulled this over in her mind. And then there was the other hand. On the other hand . . . Isabella's personal life *was* her working life – she had no other. Where else would she ever meet someone? Yes. On the other hand, she felt a distinct thrill.

Ferdinand was regarding her with some amusement.

'I'm not sure,' she said. What about the fact that she didn't trust him? What about the sketches? What about his father and his past life here? What about the big mystery between him and Giovanna that she wasn't in on?

He smiled – and despite his sadness about his father, it reached his eyes. 'Don't look so worried, Isabella,' he said. 'I just want you to myself, that's all.'

And suddenly she felt foolish. She liked this man, didn't she? She was attracted to him and she wanted to find out a lot more about him. 'Let's go and sit in the olive grove,' she said. She'd nip upstairs to get a wrap while he was sorting out the wine.

He laughed. 'OK. Do we need something to sit on?'

'Only the ground.'

They made their way into the grove several minutes later, Ferdinand carrying the wine in a cooler and Isabella holding the glasses. Despite what she'd told him, she'd decided to bring a blanket too. They settled themselves on this under the broadest tree, right in the centre of the grove, where there was just room to sit side by side in the comfortable mossy pouches between the roots, leaning against the knotty trunk. The olive grove was quiet and still; dense with night-time. But between the leaves and the olive-laden branches above, Isabella could see the globe of a full moon sending its eerie blue glow through the trees, dappling the ground with blue-pale light and shadows.

Ferdinand poured the wine and handed her a glass. 'To you and the Cinque Terre – both beautiful.'

Isabella laughed uneasily. 'To the Cinque Terre,' she echoed.

'You know . . .' He leaned back against the tree trunk. 'My mother would have loved it here.'

'Would have?'

'She died when I was eleven years old.'

'That's awful.' Isabella put a hand on his arm. 'I'm so sorry. You were just a boy.'

'We were very close,' he added. 'She never visited Italy, but she told me lots of stories about her life in England when she was a girl.'

'She lived there?'

'She was British, yes.'

'Oh, I see.' And why not, of course? It was just that she had assumed Ferdinand was German through and through.

'You must miss her,' she murmured. She tried to imagine how it would feel for an eleven-year-old boy to be deprived of his mother. How hard it must have been.

'I do. We both still do. But now that my father . . .' His voice trailed.

Now, he was losing his father too. Isabella's heart went out to him. And she realised how lucky she was. Her family argued like crazy, and her grandfather spent much of his time in Pisa, but at least they were all still healthy and intact.

'And you were right.' He put his hand on hers. 'I'll have to go back home soon.'

'Of course.' Isabella was no longer that naïve girl who had been flattered by an older man from Bologna. 'But have you done what you came here to do?' She thought of Giovanna and this morning in Monterosso al Mare.

'Not yet.' He sipped his wine. 'At least not entirely.' His brow clouded. 'But there have been some unlikely developments.'

'Oh?'

'There are some things I must tell my father.'

Isabella picked up her own glass. This was the same wine she had been drinking earlier, but it tasted so different in the moonlight, almost like nectar on her tongue. 'So, you have not yet . . .' she hesitated '. . . made amends?'

He eyed her intently. 'If it was my secret, Isabella . . .'

'Yes?'

'Then I would tell you everything.'

Sitting here, so close to him in the moonlight, it was tempting to believe him. She leaned in closer. She could feel the warmth of his skin, his breath against her neck. 'Whose secret is it?' she asked. 'Your father's?'

'Yes.'

'And what about Giovanna?'

He put a finger to her lips. 'One day,' he said, 'I will tell you everything, I promise.'

One day. That sounded as if he were envisaging some future meeting. 'But . . .'

'Isabella.' He put both their glasses to one side and knelt in front of her. His fair hair looked dusty in the moonlight, and she reached out – an involuntary gesture – and ran her fingers through the softness of it.

'I have not brought you out here to talk about my father's secrets,' he said.

'Then why have you brought me here?' He had said he wanted to talk. She watched his mouth. She could see the sadness there, even in the faint curve of his smile.

'You were right the first time. I am a man, you are a beautiful girl.' He put his head to one side and regarded her intently.

Isabella wriggled under his scrutiny. 'I see.' She could move away of course – but she didn't.

'I didn't expect to find you here, Isabella.' He smoothed her hair from her face. 'I didn't expect there to be such . . .' he hesitated '. . . such a complication.'

'A complication?' She'd heard more flattering descriptions. But she was trying to understand.

He held her face in his hands and he kissed her – a long, deep kiss that seemed to travel far inside her, twist in her belly, and liquefy into desire. *Mamma mia* . . .

'In a day or two I will leave,' he murmured into her ear. 'But I will come back.'

Would he? Could she take that risk? Isabella slipped her hands under his shirt and around his waist, feeling the warmth of his flat belly, the ridges of his back, the knobs of his spine. Slowly, she brought her hands back, undid the buttons of his shirt, one by one, starting at the neck, not taking her eyes from his.

'Isabella,' he murmured. The sadness was in his eyes now too. She wanted to change that. She wanted to make it better.

She pushed the shirt from his shoulders, her palms on his warm skin.

He bent his head, let out a small groan, and she pulled him closer to her breast.

Her hands dipped lower to the waistband of his jeans. She fought with the buckle.

He raised his head to look at her. 'Are you sure you want this, Isabella?'

She nodded. Their breath was growing faster, more urgent. She pulled the buckle free and slipped her hands lower.

He paused, his hands under her blouse now, but stopping short of her breasts. His eyes as he looked at her were dark and hungry. 'Really sure?'

'Yes,' she breathed. She pushed the secrets to the back of her mind. 'Yes, Ferdinand, I'm sure.'

CHAPTER 36

Chiara

Alonzo turned up the following morning as Chiara had guessed he would. He wasn't the type of man to take no for an answer, certainly not the type of man to be told he couldn't come home.

He came into the office. Fortunately, she was alone. 'Chiara,' he said sternly, 'we need to talk.'

'Very well.' She mustered all the dignity she could. 'Let's go to our rooms.' This was not going to be a public occasion. She was going to remain calm – she only hoped that Alonzo would do the same.

Once inside, with the door closed, he turned to her. 'So – have you had enough time now to think things over?'

Chiara had had more than enough. 'Yes,' she said, 'and I can't see any way forward for us, Alonzo.' She had thought and thought. 'The distance between us has grown too wide.' Because it wasn't just the violence or the way he ran his business in Pisa. It wasn't just his lack of compassion and integrity, or the fact that she did not love him as a wife should. Neither was

335

it Dante and the way she felt about him. It was everything. She had thought she could keep her promise to Elene, but the only way she could do that would be to betray everything she believed in – and that was one step too far. Her recent discovery had tipped her over the edge. She could not stay married to this man and retain one small grain of self-respect.

You should be proud of what you have done here, Dante had told her. *You have achieved so much*. And she was. She had. But . . . It was one thing to stay with Alonzo after he had slapped her – one could say she had pushed him; she had been with Dante after all, and crucially, it was only Chiara who was being hurt. But it was quite another thing to stay with him now, knowing what she knew. She was deeply ashamed. And so. 'Our marriage is over,' she told him.

He laughed. 'What there was left of it, hmm?'

'What there was left of it,' she agreed. But it was no laughing matter. Somehow, she had to explain this to Elene. Somehow, she had to live with the knowledge that she had let her down – again.

He turned away, then back to her. Raised an eyebrow. 'And Elene?' He knew her so well. He knew which buttons to press, where her guilt would always lie.

Chiara tried not to let her shoulders slump. 'I'll talk to her.'

He frowned.

'Oh, don't worry.' She kept her voice level. 'I won't tell her about what goes on in Pisa – that's your affair, as you pointed out. And I won't tell her—' She put a hand to her face, touched her cheek. Not for his sake – but for Elene's. She didn't want to be the one who made Elene think badly of her father. Let her keep her love for him, her belief in him; Chiara didn't want her to be hurt any more.

336

'Elene will be devastated,' he said. And to his credit, Chiara could see that this affected him deeply. Elene was his one soft spot perhaps; his love for her a redeeming factor in all this.

She bowed her head. 'But we can't keep using our grown-up daughter as the only reason for staying together,' she said gently. She had done all she could for Elene. Now, she must let it go. They might never be close, but neither would they be close if Chiara chose to continue living such a whopping and unacceptable lie.

'Of course, I know the real reason for your sudden morality.' Alonzo walked over to the window and stared out at the olive grove.

Chiara tensed. She knew he wasn't the kind of man to accept this without a fight. 'The real reason?' she echoed.

'I'm not stupid,' he said. 'This has all happened since Dante Rossi tried to force his way back into our lives.'

Chiara remained silent. She watched him. Where was he going with this?

'Pisa is your excuse.' He turned around to face her once more, his eyes cold.

Chiara wondered how she could ever have thought they might grow to love one another. She was only just acknowledging quite how far they had grown apart.

'My business dealings, the way I lead my life, are your excuses. But I know better.'

'It's not just one thing, you're right.' She kept her bearing erect and still. 'It's many things. What point is there staying together when there's no love between us?' It was an appeal to his better judgement. *Forget your pride. Let it go.*

He took a step closer to her, then another. 'It's him,' he said. 'Isn't it?'

But even if he was right, even if her feelings for Dante, suppressed for forty years, had been the trigger . . . Alonzo was responsible for his own actions – as human beings they all were. 'It's everything,' she insisted.

'Everything, hmm.' He rocked back on his heels. 'Very well, have it your own way.'

Chiara blinked at him. Was he giving in so easily? It seemed unlikely.

'But if our marriage is over, then I shall expect some compensation, my dear.'

'Compensation?'

He clicked his tongue. 'Really, Chiara, you are supposed to be a business woman, are you not? Financial compensation for the funding my parents put into The Lemon Tree Hotel.'

'But that was before we married.' She stared at him.

'Oh, I think we both know the nature of their deal, do we not?' He was smiling now. 'You could even call it a dowry I suppose – though that seems a little old-fashioned. But then – our parents were old-fashioned, as we both know.'

Chiara's mind went into overdrive. Of course, he had a point. Their parents had shared a deep and strong friendship – which was why Alonzo's parents had invested in the hotel. And in a way their marriage had been part of it. She thought quickly. Just how much was he talking about? If she knew Alonzo, it would be a lot. 'And Elene?' she demanded. 'And Isabella?'

He shrugged. 'What do they have to do with it?'

'It's their inheritance.' What was he thinking of? If he destroyed The Lemon Tree – or even tried to – then he destroyed his own family. 'Would you take that away from them too?'

He seemed to be considering this. 'The hotel could afford some compensation,' he said smoothly. 'I have to live.'

'You have your own business interests, Alonzo,' she reminded him. 'Can you not make a living from them?' Though it was hard to keep the sarcasm from her voice. 'They are not at risk surely? Unless there is . . .' she hesitated as an idea occurred to her. Because she didn't want to let him have any part of The Lemon Tree Hotel. His parents had put in the money yes, but in all the years they'd been married, Alonzo had given the place almost no support . . . 'some chance of exposure.'

'Exposure?' He shot her a quick glance.

Now it was her turn to shrug. 'If you understand my meaning,' she said softly.

'Why you—'

'Alonzo.' She put up her hand. She had been ready for the moment in which he would lose his cool. And she wouldn't have threatened him – if he hadn't threatened her hotel, her family. 'I don't think it would be such a good idea to hit me again.'

He hesitated.

'You should leave,' she told him. 'You should talk to Elene, you should get some things together, and you should leave. You are a father and a grandfather as well as a businessman, you know.'

It was hard for Alonzo to lose face, she knew that. But she also knew that she had given him no choice. So, before he could argue further, Chiara swept from the room. She would talk to Elene. It was done, and now there was no going back. Her daughter would have to understand.

CHAPTER 37

Elene

Elene looked up when her mother came into the kitchen. She saw the look on her face. More trouble? She was relieved at the way her mother and Isabella had taken the discovery of Ferdinand Bauer's architectural sketches – it could have been a lot worse. She had always known in her heart that they wouldn't go down well – why would they, when her mother and Isabella preferred the hotel to be stuck in the last century? And, of course she had envisaged telling them in a very different way – a gradual way, a more gentle and persuasive way. But given the circumstances – and she was still cross with Isabella for opening that envelope – her mother's moderate reaction had been a welcome surprise. *We shouldn't be entirely resistant to change, Bella* . . . That was a new one. She supposed that her mother and Silvio had been right – she shouldn't have gone behind their backs. But it was done – and maybe after all, some good would come out of it.

'Mamma?' She slipped off her apron. It was time for a break. 'Is something wrong?'

Her mother hesitated. 'You look tired, darling,' she said.

'It's been quite a morning.' Elene decided not to tell her about Ghita going home sick and Febe confiding in her that she was pregnant. Her mother looked exhausted too – they all were. It was time for the season to start winding down at The Lemon Tree Hotel.

'Do you have a moment? Your father's just arrived and he wants to talk to you, but I wondered if I could have a quick word first.' And she looked around as if Papà was about to charge into the kitchen after her.

'That's fine. Shall we get a coffee?'

'Or perhaps some fresh air.' Her mother took her arm and steered her out of the back door. 'I want to talk to you in private,' she murmured into her ear.

Oh, dear. But Elene submitted with good grace.

They walked through the kitchen garden. 'I don't want to pile more pressure on to you, when I can see you're exhausted,' her mother began.

Oh, dear, Elene thought again.

'But I have to be honest – with myself and with you.'

Elene steeled herself. 'Is this about the drawings? We did say we'd discuss each one—'

'No.'

'No?'

Her mother hesitated. 'It's about your father and me.'

Elene felt a deep sense of foreboding. 'Go on, Mamma.'

The scent of flowering sage and thyme rose up to meet them as they came to the edge of the herb garden. Her mother trailed a hand through the purple flowers. A bee buzzed crossly. 'We have decided to separate, *cara*.' She held up a hand before Elene could say anything. 'I know you don't want it. I know you hate the thought of it. But we've made the decision – and now we have to see it through.'

Elene sighed. 'We?' But there was such a note of finality in her mother's voice – she knew it was hopeless.

'Your father and I. You see, darling, we've grown apart. We both love you – and that will never change, believe me. But we don't love each other – not any more.'

'What happened?' Elene knew something had happened in Pisa – she just knew it. Her mother had been acting strangely even before she left, and when she came back . . . Had they had some sort of showdown there?

'Nothing specific.'

Elene narrowed her eyes. She was lying.

'I can't tell you exactly,' she amended.

Elene shrugged. It was one of her defensive shrugs that made it look as if she didn't care – but what did Mamma expect of her? And what difference did it make, really? Her father spent such little time here – Silvio was right. But in her heart, she felt something sink still lower. Her family – breaking apart.

'I'm sorry,' her mother whispered.

'You promised not to leave him.' Elene supposed it was selfish to remind her mother of that. She supposed she should never have extracted that promise from her in the first place. But she had felt so frightened. She couldn't explain that childhood fear – not to Silvio, not to her mother, not even to herself.

'I know.' Chiara reached for her hand and clutched on to it as if she needed some reassurance from Elene. It was a strange feeling, because her mother had never really needed anything as far as she knew, and she wasn't quite sure how she felt about the role reversal that seemed to be taking place between them.

'And I tried,' her mother said. 'But things have changed. I'm so sorry to let you down.'

Elene nodded. The full impact of what her mother was saying seemed not to be sinking in. Did that mean that she had been expecting it? Or was she so cold, so heartless that she didn't care?

Her mother was still talking. 'I made that promise to you in good faith, I really did. But I cannot keep it.'

'Did Papà find out?' Elene pulled her hand away. She felt as if she should maintain a defensive stance. 'Because if he did – I didn't tell him, you know.'

'Find out?'

'About Dante Rossi.'

Her mother shook her head. 'No, he didn't find out.' For a moment she gazed towards the olive grove as if she were thinking of some other time. 'That wasn't the reason, Elene,' she said. 'This has nothing to do with Dante.'

Was that true? And did it even matter now? 'And Papà?' she asked. 'Will he live in Pisa?' Would he still visit them? Would Elene have time to visit him?

'You can ask him yourself.' Her mother hesitated. 'He's coming to talk to you too.'

Elene looked at her, really looked at her, and she suddenly felt ashamed. 'I shouldn't have made you choose,' she blurted. 'Silvio was right. I should never have made you choose.'

When Elene returned to *la cucina* fifteen minutes later, sure enough, her father was waiting to speak to her.

'Papà.' She walked into his arms.

He held her for a moment without speaking. 'Will you forgive me, Elene?' he said at last. 'I never meant for this to happen.'

'There's nothing to forgive. If the love has truly died between you . . .' Elene drew away. Why was it so easy to give affection to her father and so hard to respond to her mother? She'd almost given in to it a few minutes earlier outside in the olive grove, but something always stopped her. Was it because they were both strong women, both too determined to get their own way?

He tipped up her chin so that she was looking into his eyes. 'I haven't behaved well,' he said. 'I'm your father and I've had to be reminded of that fact. And . . .' His voice had a tremor to it that she'd never heard before. 'Well, never mind.'

Once again, Elene had the sensation of being thrust into a different role. 'I understand,' she said, though she didn't. 'I just want you and Mamma to be happy.' And slightly to her surprise she realised that this was what she wanted. 'And for everything to stay the same,' she added. Which she wanted even more.

'Nothing will change, Elene,' he told her. 'You'll see. You can take time off and come to Pisa. I'll buy you lunch.'

She laughed.

'I'll still come to Vernazza – and buy you lunch there as well.'

'You will?'

'I most certainly will. Just as I said: nothing will change.'

CHAPTER 38

Chiara

The following evening, Chiara took Giovanna over some supper. She hadn't seen her since her return from Pisa and she wanted to make sure that all was well. More than that, she realised, as she knocked lightly on the front door and let herself into the cottage, she needed Giovanna's touch of quiet sanity in her life. Half an hour or so with her old aunt would be soothing and just what she needed after the last few days. Alonzo had taken some things and left the hotel. None of it had been easy, and there would be many more difficulties ahead, but Chiara was relieved that it was done. As for Elene . . .

'Chiara.' Giovanna came into the kitchen. 'How lovely to see you, my dear.' She was looking well.

'Aunt Giovanna. Good evening to you.' They exchanged kisses, and Chiara gave her the bowl of pasta.

'*Grazie mille*, my dear.' Her old eyes were bright as she sniffed appreciatively.

'Prawns with courgettes and saffron,' Chiara told her. Elene had such a touch with the saffron – and whatever else was going on in her life, it never seemed to affect her abilities as a chef. The sauce would be creamy with a red warmth, just a hint of winter fires embedded within. Though Chiara did not want to look ahead to winter too soon . . . She was conscious of a feeling of dread, of loss, that she wasn't accustomed to.

'Do you have to rush back, my dear?' Giovanna leaned forwards in a conspiratorial manner. 'Can you stay for a small *aperitivo*?'

'I'd love to.' Chiara was still getting to grips with everything that had happened over the past few days. Pisa, Alonzo, and not to mention Elene and Silvio's ambitious plans for the hotel.

They'd had a further meeting to thrash out a few ideas – 'thrash' being about the right word for it. Isabella was reluctant for change – though truth to tell, she looked so starry-eyed that Chiara wasn't sure her granddaughter's mind was on the job at all – while Elene and Silvio seemed to want to change everything. How much of this was connected with the news of her parents' separation and impending divorce, Chiara had no idea. Nevertheless, she found herself in the role of mediator – soothing, questioning, compromising. Because yes, she did want Elene and Silvio to feel valued and to have more of a say in the running of things. But she also had to stay true to her parents' vision and the original nature of The Lemon Tree Hotel . . . And she was beginning to realise something else: the hotel was an important part of her life, but it wasn't everything. This was a shock.

Giovanna opened the fridge to reveal a blue glass bottle of wine chilling in the door. Heaven knows where it had come from – there was no label, and the cork was fixed and tied around with rough string. But Giovanna had so many visitors – no doubt it had been produced in a local family vineyard and given to her as a token of goodwill.

'Would you do the honours, my dear?' She handed the bottle to Chiara.

'Of course.' Chiara located the corkscrew in a drawer and opened the bottle with a flourish. It made a satisfactory 'pop'. Fizzy wine, no less.

She fetched two heavy crystal glasses from Giovanna's kitchen cabinet and poured the wine. They raised their glasses. 'To you and your continuing good health, Aunt Giovanna,' she said.

Giovanna's old face was wreathed in smiles. 'And to you, dear Chiara,' she said. 'And The Lemon Tree Hotel, of course.' They clinked glasses. For some reason that Chiara couldn't fathom, it felt like a celebration.

'Shall we sit outside and catch the last of the day's sunshine, my dear?'

'Why not?' Chiara followed her through to the terrace where a few hens were clucking around on the cobbles as usual, the olive trees glinting silver in the early evening sun.

When they were settled on the bench, amidst the terracotta pots of scarlet geraniums, with the wine bottle and a bowl of fresh almonds between them, Giovanna sat back and folded her wrinkled hands on her lap. 'You look tired, Chiara.' Her expression was concerned. 'I hope you're not working too hard, my dear?'

She was tired, she knew it. This business with Alonzo had taken it out of her, and the hotel was still busy although the main season would be coming to an end soon and several of their guests were leaving in the next day or two. 'I'll be fine, Aunt. We're beginning to wind down. Soon, I'll be able to relax a bit more.' She swirled the wine around the heavy crystal glass. Though how could she relax with all these potential

347

renovations to worry about? And if they went ahead? She imagined the disruption, the dust, the noise, and had to close her eyes for a moment to take the thought of it away.

'I certainly hope so.' Giovanna took delicate sips of her wine, like a bird. 'But is it just the hotel that is bothering you, my dear? The last few times you have come here . . . *Allora*, I don't wish to interfere, but—'

'You're right.' She might as well tell her. 'It's Alonzo.' Soon it would be common knowledge. Not that this bothered Chiara – in some ways, that too would be a burden lifted. She would no longer have to pretend.

'Alonzo?' Giovanna raised a questioning eyebrow.

'We are separating, Aunt Giovanna. Please don't be shocked. We haven't been happy for a while, and now . . .' She was tempted to unburden herself further, but held back. She would keep Alonzo's secret – and her own.

'I see.' She took another sip. She didn't seem shocked in the least.

'You're not surprised?'

'Not surprised, no.' Giovanna leaned forwards and patted her hand. 'Your parents only wanted the best for you, *cara*, but . . .' She shook her head sadly. 'Our parents cannot tell us whom to love.'

'Very true.' As always, Chiara was struck by her aunt's quiet wisdom. She might lack experience of affairs of the heart, being tucked away up here in the grounds of *L'Attico Convento*. But she seemed to know so much.

'But why now?' Giovanna seemed to be speaking her thoughts out loud – and it was a reasonable question.

Chiara took another sip of the wine. It was light, fizzy and delicious. 'I found out some things,' she admitted. 'And someone came back – someone from the past.' She let her gaze drift to the olive grove, where a few of Giovanna's hens were loitering, as if they were wondering just how adventurous to be. The olive grove would always remind her of Dante and how she had once hoped . . . But what had happened with Dante seemed so far away now.

'Ah. Someone from the past.' And for a moment, Giovanna too seemed preoccupied with her own thoughts. 'But what things do you mean, my dear?' Giovanna followed her gaze and clicked her tongue gently. Her girls waddled back towards their coop.

Chiara shook her head in mild disbelief. '*Non importa*. It doesn't matter what, Aunt.' She still couldn't help wondering though. When had it begun – that business in Pisa? Who had seduced who and how many times? She lifted her face to the early evening sunshine. It was as warm and comforting as the wine sliding so easily down her throat was chilled and delicious. Did these questions matter though? No doubt it was only her pride that needed to know the details.

Giovanna gave one of her wise nods. 'Have you told Elene and Bella?'

'Yes. They both know.' At least, there hadn't been quite the explosion she had feared from Elene. Perhaps Elene had finally realised how bad things had got between her parents, how they had hit an all-time low. Was that Silvio's influence? She guessed that it was. He grounded Elene.

Chiara realised that she should have been more supportive of her daughter's decision to marry Silvio back in the day. It was just that without love . . . There had been certain parallels in her own marriage and that of her daughter, and this had worried Chiara. But there were crucial differences too. Elene had chosen Silvio of her own free will for the qualities she perceived in him. And Silvio — a good man, undeniably — had always adored her. More than anything, Elene had not been in love with another man. So perhaps Elene was one of the lucky ones. Chiara hoped so. Perhaps for Elene, love had grown.

Chiara let out a small sigh. That moment when Elene seemed to understand at last how things really were for Chiara, had been one — like so many moments in the past — when they might have drawn closer, understood what the other was thinking and feeling, re-kindled that mother and daughter bond and found some common ground. Chiara had held her breath. She had reached for her daughter's hand and longed for that closeness. It was a hard-working hand and for some reason she felt bad about this — as if she had chosen Elene's career. Which in a way, she had, she supposed. How could she make it happen? What was the right thing to say, to do? But the moment had passed, just like all the others before. Once again, Elene's barriers were up and she had headed inside, back to the kitchen as she always did.

Isabella had also been upset of course, but she seemed more concerned about her grandmother than anything else. 'We will manage,' she kept saying. 'Don't worry, Nonna. Everything will be fine.' Then again, Isabella didn't know about Dante, about all the recent troubles with Alonzo. Neither of them knew that he had hit her though — and Chiara prayed that they never found out.

As for Ferdinand Bauer's sketches . . . Chiara didn't know what would happen about those either, but she realised that the important thing was to trust in her family — because together, they were strong. When there was no trust, no communication — that was when people went behind one another's backs; there

350

was no sense of loyalty any more. So, they would continue to discuss Elene and Silvio's proposals as if they had come to them first; they would give each one the time, thought, and practical consideration it deserved.

They had started with a discussion about the proposed rooftop bar. And it was undeniable that, disruption aside, it could be a potential asset.

'Just think of the views,' Silvio had said, and Chiara had nodded her agreement. 'It would free up the tables in the cloisters for the restaurant too,' he added.

Chiara saw Elene throw him a grateful glance.

She gritted her teeth. 'It's quite a good idea,' she said firmly. 'Bella?'

'We will have to get estimates before we even consider it.' Her practical granddaughter would keep hold of the numbers, and that was good too.

'Perhaps start with that then?' Chiara suggested. 'And then when the figures come back, we will discuss the proposal some more.'

'*Va bene*,' said Elene. And Chiara saw her squeeze Silvio's hand, tightly. So, it was worth it. It was all worth it. Because if necessary they could embrace change – it was the way of the world.

'These things happen.' Giovanna pushed the bowl of almonds towards her. 'You mustn't worry too much, my dear.'

Chiara took an almond and ate it absent-mindedly. The olive grove beyond the terrace always seemed closer to her heart at dusk, when the light was fading and the night was ahead.

'But I suppose you are thinking: what next?'

Chiara looked at her aunt sharply. That was exactly what she had been thinking. 'I don't know yet, Aunt.' She would tell

351

Giovanna about the hotel renovations, but not yet, not until they were more certain.

Giovanna put her head to one side. 'Who are you most concerned for, *cara*? Elene? Isabella?' She gave a throaty chuckle. 'Not me, I hope.'

'I am always concerned for you, Aunt.' Impulsively, she leaned across and gave Giovanna a little squeeze of the shoulders.

'You do not need to be,' her aunt told her sternly. 'I am feeling better than I ever did. And I have a strong constitution for change – better than yours perhaps.'

'You're probably right.' Chiara laughed. She considered her aunt's question. 'I'm not concerned for Elene. She will get used to the idea, and she has Silvio.'

Giovanna nodded. 'He is a good man.'

'And Isabella . . .'

'She will be fine too.' Giovanna sat back, a satisfied smile on her lips. 'She also will have the support she needs.'

Chiara stared at her. 'You can't be talking about Ferdinand Bauer?' For she was certainly meaning something of that nature.

'Perhaps. Perhaps not.' Giovanna shrugged. 'Ah, but they are certainly taken with one another those two. Who knows?'

'But . . .' Where to begin? 'He will be returning to Germany soon, you know, Aunt.'

'Oh, yes, I'm sure he will.'

'And he's just a guest, isn't he?'

'Is he? Ah well, yes, perhaps he is.'

Chiara frowned. How forgiving could she be? Over events she had witnessed with her own eyes? Events that had affected her old friends and compatriots so deeply?

'But we will see, oh yes, I'm sure we will see.' And those eyes twinkled as if there was much more she could say.

'Indeed.'

'So, you are free to do what you need to do, Chiara.' Giovanna poured more wine for them both with rather a shaky hand.

It struck Chiara that she had rarely seen Giovanna drink wine before. Had something else happened that she didn't know about?

'Well, you know there is still the hotel . . .' Leaving Alonzo hardly meant that she was free.

'A short holiday perhaps?' Giovanna clapped her hands. 'Yes. Why not? It would do you so much good, my dear.'

Chiara considered. A holiday was an attractive prospect. She might even be able to avoid some of the disruption when work started on the rooftop bar. If it started . . . But it would be nice to get away long before that. 'I haven't been on a holiday for a long time,' she agreed.

'*Ah, sì.*'

In fact, when had she gone away? Practically never. And how she longed to travel. She was weary of all these disputes over the future of the hotel. It would be so good not to worry, simply to let go. 'And now that Isabella is old enough to take charge – with Elene and Silvio's assistance, naturally.'

'Yes, naturally so.'

'I might actually do it,' she conceded. She took another sip of wine. It really had the most delicious floral bouquet.

'Think about it some more,' Giovanna advised. 'No need to go too far. But I would leave Italy, at least. Spread your wings. Some parts of Europe are very lovely in the late autumn, I have heard. And you can always take an umbrella, hmm?'

Giovanna seemed very taken with the idea. And perhaps her aunt was right – the family didn't need her so much any more, Alonzo certainly was no longer in a position to need her, and even her beloved hotel . . .

'You cannot please everyone,' Giovanna shook her head. 'It is impossible, my dear.'

'Oh, I know. You're right.' For her entire life, she realised, she had always done what other people wanted her to do. She had always tried to live up to the expectations of others. First her parents, then Alonzo, then Elene.

'Now, it is time to live for yourself.'

'Mmm.' It was a seductive idea. Chiara got to her feet. 'Thank you, Aunt. But for now, I must return to the hotel.'

'Of course, my dear.'

'Shall I put the wine back in the fridge on my way out?' She bent to kiss her.

'Oh, leave it here, if you will.' And she'd swear Giovanna's eyes actually sparkled with mischief. 'I may treat myself to one more glass with that delicious-looking pasta you brought.'

On the way back, as Chiara walked through the darkening olive grove, the idea of a holiday seemed to take root and begin to grow. She couldn't please everyone, no, and it was true that a change of scenery would be most pleasant. This break with Alonzo – perhaps it was a turning point. She could easily go for two weeks – even three weeks maybe – the hotel could manage without her. It was not so long. And yet, it was long enough, certainly, for what she had in mind.

Around her, the olive trees spread their protective branches. This place was a cocoon. She felt safe here. But what would happen if she took a step out of her comfort zone? Did she dare? One could not experience a sense of liberation unless one

354

had been tied down. So. It was her place of safety. But, maybe Dante had been right about the hotel also tying her down, stopping her from doing other things. Maybe he was right in all sorts of other ways . . .

She paused and listened to the faint rustle of the trees, a sound that was so familiar, so entwined with her memories, her past. And her future? Could she really be free to make such a choice? It was a concept almost alien to her. But yes, Giovanna was right. She needed this, and so she would go. She felt a new confidence in the future and perhaps that was what happened when you found the strength to break free. As for the rest – *allora*, it was ambitious she knew. But it was good nevertheless, to have a purpose in mind.

CHAPTER 39

Elene

Elene was serving the last of the desserts when her mother and Isabella came into the kitchen. They both helped themselves to pasta and salad, and no doubt they would be sampling some of her latest Ligurian lemon cake for dessert. She put a couple of slices aside.

They were chatting – hotel business – throwing the occasional comment her way. Elene was only half-listening. Last night she had told Silvio about her parents' separation.

'What point is there in them staying together, my love?' Silvio had said. 'If they no longer love one another? If they have grown apart? If they lead separate lives?'

'I suppose you're right,' she had conceded. Though it was easier for him to accept – they weren't his parents, after all.

He drew her closer and into his arms – something Elene had found herself resisting less and less lately. 'You don't want them both to be miserable, do you, my love?'

'No,' she whispered into his shoulder, so grateful that he was always there for her. 'I don't want that.'

Now, Elene clattered about the kitchen, putting the cake tin into the sink to soak, loading cutlery into the dishwasher. The scent of the lemon cake hung in the air – cleansing and fresh. She knew Silvio was right. And now her mother seemed to be making an effort to understand Elene's issues about the hotel. Maybe she felt guilty. Maybe she was trying to redress the balance. But at least they were talking about it.

Nevertheless, there was a time and a place for everything. Right at this moment most of her attention was focused – as it so often was – on her food and its presentation. The Ligurian lemon cake was delicate and golden brown as honey. Elene liked to serve it with only a dusting of icing sugar – it was moist already, and needed nothing more.

'So, I was thinking – a short holiday perhaps? The English family are leaving tomorrow morning, the Americans the day after that.'

Elene glanced sharply towards her mother. She was going away? But her mother never went away.

'You could manage, couldn't you? The three of you?' She glanced towards Elene now.

Elene raised an eyebrow in lieu of a reply and turned her attention back to the cake. A twist of olive leaves would make a pretty garnish and signify the fact that the lemon cake was made with olive oil, but no doubt people would try to eat them, so best not.

'A holiday? Yes, Nonna, of course you should go.' But Isabella sounded concerned. She too must have noticed how tired her grandmother was looking these days. But then again, it was hardly surprising – after everything. Elene sighed.

'But will you go alone?'

Elene plucked her little sieve from its hook and spooned in

the icing sugar. She tapped it on the side to achieve the light frosting she required. *Basta.* She moved on to the next plate.

'I think so, yes.'

'And where will you go, Nonna?'

There was a beat of silence. Once more, Elene's attention was caught. Her mother wouldn't go far. Florence perhaps? Siena? Or did she want something a little more relaxing? If so, this was hardly the best season for it. Everything in Italy was winding down. Soon it would be autumn, and Elene would be thinking of the next season's recipes: the nuts and the mush-rooms, warmer sauces and autumnal treats.

'I think I shall go to England.'

Elene dropped the sieve. Icing sugar clouded the tiled floor. She looked down. It was very unusual for her to be clumsy in the kitchen, and so her mother and her daughter were now looking at her too.

Isabella jumped up to fetch a floor cloth. Elene retrieved the sieve and rinsed it under the tap. But her mind was spinning. England. Her mother was going to England. So that was how it was.

'Why are you going to England, Mamma?' She turned to face her. As if she didn't know.

Her mother met her gaze, eyes steady. There were streaks of grey in her dark hair, which on Chiara, naturally, looked effortlessly chic. Whatever she wore, however old she grew, her mother was beautiful still. Elene could see it, and no doubt Dante Rossi could see it too.

'It's just a holiday, Elene.' She forked up a mouthful of pasta and then pushed her plate away. Unfinished. 'Two weeks off, that is all.'

Just a holiday? To England? Elene took the dessert plates

over to the hatch where Rosalie was waiting. They were the last ones.

She turned back to her mother. 'And will you see him?'

Isabella had sat back down again and was looking from one to the other of them in confusion. She knew nothing about all this, and it was not Elene's place to put her straight. But it had all happened so quickly. Her mother was certainly wasting no time.

'No. At least . . .' Chiara hesitated. 'I don't know where he lives.'

Elene narrowed her eyes. There were ways of finding out such things.

'Who, Nonna? Who might you be going to see?' Isabella chipped in. At least she was eating her pasta with some gusto, Elene was pleased to see. She wondered how her mother would explain.

'I have a friend, Bella,' she began.

'*Pff.*' A friend? Elene trusted that this would show her feelings on the matter.

'His name is Dante Rossi. You may remember, he came here recently . . .'

'Dante Rossi . . .' Isabella was wide-eyed. She stared at her grandmother. Elene guessed her mind was working overtime. She would be wondering now. Weren't they all?

'I have not made any plans to meet up with him,' Chiara said firmly.

Elene wiped the kitchen counter down with soapy water. But they would meet up – she knew it. And if they met up, they would be together again, sure as day. And if that happened . . . Would her mother consider leaving Italy to be with him? Was that why she had raised so few objections to Elene and Silvio's plans? She felt as if she couldn't stop moving and doing. If she stopped moving and doing . . . If her mother left Italy . . . Suddenly, she felt bereft. 'Really, Mamma?' Then why was she going there?

'But, yes, he spoke of his life in England, and yes, I would like to see something of the country. Why not?' Her mother's voice was calm, but there was something more. It was as if some decision had already been made.

'When are you leaving?' Elene asked quietly.

'The day after tomorrow.'

'So soon, Nonna?' Isabella frowned. 'But—'

'I have already been in touch with Emanuele about covering for me,' Chiara assured her. 'Lucia is going to come in to help in the bar. And things are quieter now.'

She had planned it already – and so quickly. Elene couldn't let it rest. 'Are you going to look for him, Mamma?'

Her mother sighed. 'Elene . . .'

'After he . . .' Hit you, she was going to say. But of course, she could not. She must show some discretion. If Isabella had not been in the room, then it would be different.

'You don't understand, Elene.'

But what was there to understand? Elene had seen the evidence with her own eyes. The mark of a slap on her mother's face. She didn't know what had gone on between them that night – she didn't want to know. This was enough. Somehow, this man had edged between her parents' less-than-stable partnership, and he had forced their parting. To Elene it was as plain as day.

'And when you find him?' Elene couldn't stop. 'What then? Will you ever come back to us?'

Isabella gasped. 'Nonna?'

'Of course, I will.' Her mother reached out to put her hand on Isabella's. At the same time, she looked across at Elene with dark eyes that were so sad, it was all Elene could do not to rush over to her, not to hold her, not to hug her and tell her that everything would be all right. She couldn't respond though, she just couldn't. Instead, she bustled around the kitchen putting her utensils away. Everything must be clean and organised. She must focus on *la cucina* – just as she always had.

'But what about the hotel, Nonna?' Isabella asked in a small voice. Her daughter too seemed out of her depth. Elene realised that they all were.

'The hotel will be fine, my darling. We'll go through the timetable of shifts in the morning and you will see. I told you. It is a holiday, nothing more.'

'And the other changes – the plans we discussed only yesterday?' Elene knew it had been too easy. Her mother was the embodiment of The Lemon Tree Hotel – this place meant everything to her. And the thought of her not being here . . . Elene wiped the same counter down three times before realising. Could they manage? She steadied her breathing. Yes, they would manage. They had to. If it came to it, she and Isabella could take over the helm.

Her mother was still speaking. 'Isabella, you should go ahead and get some costings just as we agreed. It is only a holiday, I keep telling you . . .'

Who was she trying so hard to convince? Elene frowned. Wait until Silvio heard about this – her mother, barely separated from her father and already heading for England to search for Dante Rossi. The rest of them left to look after things at the hotel for God knows how long until she found the man who had slapped her around. Was she mad?

For a moment Elene thought of Silvio with longing. He was the sensible voice in her head. What would she do without him? She hoped she never had to find out.

'The three of you can manage perfectly well without me.' Her mother's voice was brisk and businesslike as ever.

For a moment Elene couldn't help feeling pleased that she trusted them. But this was scarily unlike her mother. Chiara always wanted to be in control.

'Are you sure you're only going for two weeks, Nonna?' Isabella looked anxious.

'Two or three. Certainly not more than a month, my darling.'

'A month?' She gave an audible gulp. 'But you won't leave for ever?'

'Of course not, Bella.'

Elene saw her mother put her arms around Isabella to comfort her. There had always been such an easy affection between the two of them. She felt herself tense. She pulled her apron off so roughly that she heard the neck stitching go.

'This is my home,' her mother said. 'You are all my home.'

And when she looked over, she saw her mother's dark eyes fixed on her.

'I will come and get you if you don't return,' Isabella said staunchly. She pulled away from her grandmother's embrace.

Chiara laughed. Isabella looked very fierce. Even Elene wanted to smile.

'Elene?' Her mother was waiting.

'Yes, we will manage.' Elene had a lump in her throat. She swallowed it whole. 'Of course, we will manage.' If she said it enough times, naturally, it would be true.

'So, you don't mind if I go?'

Elene knew what her mother wanted. She required emotion – she always did. She wanted to comfort Elene just as she had comforted Isabella. She wanted tears, words, anything she could hold on to. That was her way. But Elene felt contrary. Her mother had left her father. She was on her own now.

So she just shrugged as she always did. 'Haven't you booked it already? And besides, it is only a holiday, as you say.' Because even her mother could make nothing of a shrug – although no doubt, she would try.

CHAPTER 40

Isabella

The night after her grandmother had left for her trip to England, Isabella couldn't sleep. She eventually drifted off at about 2 a.m. and then something woke her. But all was quiet in The Lemon Tree Hotel. It must then, have been a dream.

There was so much to think about – no wonder it was hard to relax. So much to dream about too. The renovations her parents were so keen on having done that they had gone behind Nonna's back to have drawings made – and by Ferdinand of all people. The fact that Nonna had gone away – and her mother's insinuation that there was some darker purpose to her trip and that she'd be gone for longer than she'd said.

Dante Rossi . . . Isabella had known, hadn't she, that something was up with that man; Nonna had been behaving so strangely. And she was sad, of course, about her grandfather, though truth to tell, he had never been a strong force in her life, he had never been around for long enough. Isabella wasn't afraid of managing the hotel while her grandmother was away – she knew she wasn't alone, and Nonna had already covered most eventualities with her usual smooth efficiency. Nevertheless, things were changing.

And then of course, there were the delicious feelings that had been creeping and sweeping all over her ever since she had made love with Ferdinand Bauer in the olive grove just a few nights before. She closed her eyes and let out a small sigh. She had been so cross with him about the drawings. She still was – though she understood why he had done it; her mother could be very persuasive, and Ferdinand must have thought he was doing them all a favour. Even so. How could it have turned so easily into passion?

In the darkness, she allowed herself to relive for a moment the touch of his hands on her shoulders, her breasts; the intensity of his eyes in the moonlight as he seemed to leave her for seconds and go to some other place. She'd gone there too, of course. And then he had held her in his arms and they had stayed there under the olive tree until her limbs had grown stiff and her skin shivery with goose-bumps. Their love-making had been better and bolder than anything she'd known before – more tender than the outright lust of the man from Bologna, more subtle than the youthful fumblings with Sergio. She sighed once more. It had almost been too good, too right.

She had seen Ferdinand since then of course. They had snatched a coffee the following morning – Isabella well aware that she was hollow-eyed from lack of sleep and that her face and lips were sore from his kisses. But she didn't care. They'd had a drink together too that evening in the courtyard after her grandmother's announcement about her forthcoming holiday.

'Everyone needs to get away sometimes,' Ferdinand had said.

'But Nonna . . .' Only she couldn't explain. It was just that her grandmother didn't need to go away – why would she? Her whole life was here at the hotel – or so it had seemed until now.

She waited for Ferdinand to suggest that they went to her room or his. After all – how long did they have? He would surely be leaving soon. His father was stable, he said, but when he returned to Germany he would stay with him until the end. Was he waiting for something? Did that something concern Isabella? She was expecting him to suggest another stroll in the olive grove perhaps. She wanted it, and yet at the same time she was scared of it, which was perhaps the most confusing feeling she'd experienced in her whole life.

When they left the courtyard, he kissed her goodnight – a long deep kiss that made her ache for more. 'Ferdinand . . .' She didn't want to waste time where this man was concerned.

But he had held back. Did he imagine he'd taken advantage of her? Did he regret those hours in the olive grove? She didn't think so. At any rate, they'd gone for a walk this morning, when she took a break, along the *Sentiero Azzurro* towards Corniglia. Not all the way, but far enough for her to show him the prickly pears and the olives high up on the mountainside, and the spectacular view of Vernazza below. 'I have to return to work,' she told him, 'otherwise we could walk further along the path.'

'We can do the walk another day.' He stroked her cheek with his forefinger.

'But you're leaving soon,' she reminded him. She didn't dare ask exactly when.

'I know.' He frowned.

What was it then? Was he not ready to go? Had he not done what he had intended to do? Or was it his attachment to Isabella that kept him here? She couldn't help hoping so. 'Ferdinand . . .'

'I'll come back to Vernazza,' he told her again.

'Don't make any promises,' she warned. It was what she wanted, but she hardly dared hope. She knew what it was like when someone returned to their own life after a romantic holiday abroad. The romance faded just like the sunshine. And the memories too. But she didn't regret what they'd done. How could she?

'I will come back,' he repeated. 'After my father—'

Now, another sound made her sit up like a shot. It was definitely coming from downstairs. She checked the clock. 4.45 a.m. Who would be creeping around at this time of the morning? Surely not a guest – it was too early even for the dawn risers. And it was far too early for any of the staff to be here. A burglar? She swung her legs out of bed, got up, and grabbed her robe from the hook by the door. Her room was nearest to the stairs; if anyone was to hear something it would be her.

Silently, she eased opened her door a crack and listened. Nothing. Could she have been mistaken? She frowned. Should she wake up her parents? Not at this hour. If there was nothing to see they'd be none too happy. And if there was anything to see?

She'd find out. But surreptitiously, so she could back off if there really was anything to worry about. She looked around the room. There was nothing she could use as a weapon, but she felt she ought to have something. She grabbed the vase from the windowsill. It was made of glass and heavy enough to make her feel a bit safer.

She crept out of her door and on to the landing. The lighting was kept at a low level at night-time, and it was still on, casting an eerie yellow glow along the corridor. What would she say if one of the guests were to appear? How would she explain the fact that she was wandering along the landing in her night clothes holding a glass vase? But she mustn't worry about that now – being spotted by a guest was the least of her problems. Isabella approached the top of the stairs. First, she must see if there was anyone down there.

She tiptoed down the first few steps and peered around the curve of the staircase. She couldn't see much from here, but the front door appeared to be closed. That was good. Probably not a burglar then – they'd leave it open for a quick getaway, surely? She froze. She could hear something though – a soft rustling. Perhaps someone was at the desk in reception. They didn't keep any money down there, but who was to know that?

She hovered, torn between going back upstairs to fetch someone – but if she did, that would give whoever it was a chance to escape – and going down a bit further to find out more. It could be legitimate after all. It might be her mother or father, going through some paperwork (until recently she would have found this idea ludicrous, but after the revelations of the other night and the contents of the envelope she'd found, she wasn't so sure). Or Emanuele – who, with Lucia, was living in while her grandmother was away – deciding to get some work done before breakfast. In fact, now she came to think about it, that was much more likely. So, she'd just try to see a bit more . . .

Isabella edged around the curve of the stairs knowing that when she'd done so she would have a full view of the black-and-white tiled entrance, and that whoever might be in the lobby would equally have a full view of her. Worst-case scenario:

she could run back upstairs and scream. She cursed inwardly. Why hadn't she thought to grab her mobile – then she could at least raise the alarm that way? But . . . Her hand stilled on the banister. What if they had a gun?

Oh, for goodness' sake! How likely was that? She would have said she'd been reading too many crime novels, only when did she have the time? She took another step. She had to know.

Someone – and in the next millisecond she knew who – was kneeling on the floor in front of the niche that always held Luca Bordoni's painting of the Archangel Gabriel. Only the painting wasn't there. It was on the floor, and the man kneeling on the floor beside it looked to be taking apart the gilt frame with a screwdriver.

Isabella didn't waste time considering what she should do. She thundered down the remainder of the stairs, the glass vase still in her hand. He heard her, of course, and twisted around. He looked guilty as hell.

'Ferdinand!' She stared at him. She had the glass vase held high, but she was hardly going to smash him over the head with it. Wasn't this the man who she had imagined herself in love with? 'What in God's name are you doing?'

CHAPTER 41

Isabella

'Isabella – put that down,' hissed Ferdinand. He didn't get to his feet.

She realised that she was still holding the glass vase above his head. 'What the hell is going on?' She sank to her knees beside him, lowering her voice too, though she had no clue why. He was obviously stealing their painting. He was a liar and a thief. Why shouldn't she shout out for someone to come? Why shouldn't she sound the alarm? Why shouldn't she smash this vase over his head for that matter? She put the vase down beside her.

'You must be quiet,' he warned.

'But—' How dare he! Isabella saw red. She began to get up, but he pulled her down again. He put his arm around her, and she pushed it away.

'Please,' he said. 'I can explain.'

But he didn't have to. Suddenly it was all very clear to her what was going on here. He was dressed in black jeans and a T-shirt, with a fleece tied around his waist – like a burglar.

He had planned the whole thing. That was the reason he was here at the hotel in the first place. 'Your father asked you to steal this painting.'

'No.' He gripped her by the arm. 'Yes. Look—'

'Let go of me.' She shook him off once more. 'This painting – it is worth a lot of money, yes?' Because surely that was the only conceivable reason for anyone wanting to steal it.

'No.' His shoulders sagged, and Isabella had to force herself not to feel sorry for him. 'Yes. Let me explain, Isabella.'

'You don't have to.' She pushed him, and he nearly lost his balance. He shot her a look of such hurt that she almost relented – but, how could she? 'You came to this hotel under false pretences.' She remembered how he had been when he first arrived, the way he had looked around – yes, and paid special attention to Giovanna's father's painting, even back then. 'You snaked your way into my affections.'

'No.' He looked outraged at this suggestion. 'I had no intention—'

She held up a hand. 'You deceived me. You refused to tell me why you were really here. You waited for an opportunity. And then you tried to steal our painting.' She looked down at the half-dismantled frame. 'You can hardly deny it.'

'Yes, Isabella, but you don't understand . . .' He glanced up the stairs, but there was no one there, just the shadows of the banisters.

'Then explain.'

'I don't want this painting,' he began.

Isabella had to acknowledge the possible truth of this statement. She looked at the picture in the dim light. It had a simple charm in the awkward formation of the angelic figure, the way the yellow-gold pigments of the archaangel's halo caught the light. But its charm was in its provenance – the fact that Giovanna's father had painted it and given it to the nuns at the convent, and that it had remained here at The Lemon Tree Hotel ever since, one of the silent reminders of the building's history. How could it be valuable to anyone else? 'Why would you?' she echoed. She was still trying to work it out.

'But it is not so simple.' Again, he looked up the staircase, clearly worried that although they were speaking in low voices, someone might have heard them talking and be about to appear at the top of the stairs just as she had done.

'It wouldn't be.' It seemed to Isabella that nothing at all was simple where Ferdinand Bauer was concerned. And how many times would she be expected to give him the benefit of the doubt?

He seemed to come to a decision. 'Come with me.' He began to bundle his tools into a black canvas bag she hadn't even noticed before. A burglar's toolkit, she found herself thinking. Who was this man, and why had he come into her life?

'Go with you where?' Isabella didn't move. She couldn't believe that after being caught in the act of stealing their property, he was now expecting her to go off with him somewhere.

'You can carry the bag and I'll carry the painting. It's heavier than I expected.'

'No way.' She almost shouted.

'*Ssh.*' He shot her a pained look. 'Someone will hear. Someone will come.'

'Good.' Isabella folded her arms. 'Because this painting is not going anywhere, Ferdinand. This painting is going right back on the wall where it belongs, and you are going to tell me exactly what this is all about before I phone the police.'

He reached out and touched her shoulder. Despite everything, she felt a treacherous shiver of desire. 'I will explain, Isabella,' he said. 'But for the moment, I'm asking you to trust me.'

'Trust you!' She couldn't believe he'd even used the word. And anyway, hadn't she already told him she didn't trust him? And that had been before she knew he was nothing but a common thief.

'Take the bag,' he pleaded. 'Quickly, before someone comes.'

'But where are we going?' Against her will, she seemed to catch his urgency. She sighed, picked up the bag.

'To Giovanna's.'

'Giovanna's?' She stared at him. He was full of surprises.

'This was painted by her father, was it not?'

She nodded.

'Then you can't object to us taking it there now, can you?'

Could she? Isabella considered this. He could be lying of course. It could be a trick. But his blue eyes looked so infuriatingly honest. 'What if someone sees that it's gone?' It wasn't too long before there would be people up and around. And the absence of the painting had left a gaping emptiness in the niche opposite the stairs. It was inconceivable that no one would notice.

'You can say you took it to Giovanna's.'

'But what would I have taken it there for?' Isabella was struggling. And how had it come about that now it was she instead of he who must come up with a cover story?

'Look. Never mind. We'll think of something.' He grabbed the painting. It was big and bulky, but he managed to hold it under one arm with some difficulty. 'We must go there now, quickly.'

Still, Isabella hung back. 'But why?'

'It's private there. It's the best place. And Giovanna . . .' He sighed. 'Maybe she can help me make you understand.'

So, Giovanna was in some way implicated in this? Isabella thought about the morning she'd seen them both in Monterosso. There was certainly a lot to explain. She glanced at her watch and shook her head. 'Ferdinand, it's only five in the morning. We can't go charging around to Giovanna's at this time. She'll have a heart attack.'

'She'll be awake. Come.' Already he was by the front door.

'But I'm not even dressed.' She looked down at her flimsy nightgown.

He gave her a long look. 'Wear this.' He pulled off the fleece that was tied around his waist.

Isabella put it on and followed him. She felt as if she had little choice if she was going to find out the truth. But – at five in the morning? She realised that even his damn fleece smelt of his body and now it was so close to her skin she was breathing the scent in. And how come Ferdinand Bauer, who had been here only a couple of weeks, seemed to know Giovanna Bordoni better than Isabella did – when she'd known her aunt her whole life?

They stumbled down the gravel path in the pre-dawn semi-darkness, and plunged into the gloom of the olive grove. Ferdinand flicked on a torch. 'Take this.' He handed it to her. He had certainly come prepared.

'Were you always planning to go to Giovanna's?' she asked him.

'At some point, yes.' He flung his spare arm around her shoulder. 'Don't worry, Isabella. It will be fine.'

Fine? How could it be fine? The man she had imagined herself in love with had just stolen a painting from her beloved Lemon Tree Hotel. Now, they were haring through the olive grove to take it to the old lady who had lived at the convent, and whose father had painted it anyway. It made no sense. It certainly was far from fine.

Ferdinand shifted the painting under his arm and led the way down the path towards the cottage. At least Isabella only had to carry the tool-bag. Which still made her an accomplice to the crime, she realised.

'Maybe we can get it back on the wall before anyone wakes up?' He almost seemed to be talking to himself.

'Back on the wall?' He wanted to get it back on the wall? 'But you're stealing it!'

He let out a bark of laughter that echoed around the grove. 'Oh, Isabella, I'm not stealing it.'

And she supposed that if they were taking it to Giovanna's, then in a way, he wasn't.

But even if he wasn't stealing it, something equally dodgy was going on here, and now it seemed that Isabella was implicated too. How, she wondered, was she ever going to explain this to her parents and to Nonna?

CHAPTER 42

Isabella

At the cottage, Ferdinand gave a cursory knock on the door and walked straight in. He propped the painting against the wall in the dim, narrow hallway. 'Giovanna?' he called softly. 'Are you up?'

Sure enough, Giovanna appeared at the kitchen door. She was still dressed in her nightclothes, but held a small cup of steaming espresso in her hand. 'Ferdinand!' Swiftly, she turned back to put her cup down on the table. '*Buon giorno.*' She reached to kiss his cheek.

Isabella registered the tenderness in the way he held her. But surely they hardly knew one another? She waited in the shadows.

Giovanna saw the painting he'd put down by the front door. 'You have it then?'

'Yes.'

Then she saw Isabella. 'Bella!' And she beamed.

Isabella moved towards her. She had known this woman all her life – but now she was starting to think she didn't know her at all. 'Aunt Giovanna?' She felt herself held by the surprisingly strong arms that had always represented safety to her.

'Isabella caught me in the act.' Ferdinand gave a wry smile.

'Oh, my!' Giovanna gasped and put her hand to her mouth, but Isabella could see that her faded brown eyes were twinkling. So, she found this amusing? How could that be?

She stood her ground. 'Will you tell me now?' She addressed this to Ferdinand. 'What you were doing, and why you wanted to come here?'

'Isabella . . .'

'I did as you asked. I even carried your bag.' She glared down at the black canvas tool-bag she had lugged through the olive grove. 'But now I think I deserve an explanation.'

'She certainly does.' Giovanna nodded. 'I will make coffee. While you tell Isabella what she needs to know.' She bustled back into the kitchen.

'In that case, I will.' Ferdinand took her hand and they followed Giovanna into the tiny kitchen. The aroma of freshly brewed coffee was still lingering in the room, and a tray of *cornetti* sat on the worn marble worktop ready for baking.

They sat down at the small wooden table. Isabella traced a pattern in the wood – a pattern she'd known since childhood, probably a pattern made by her own mother or grandmother as they had sat here with their pencils and crayons while Giovanna tended something simmering on the stove.

Ferdinand took a deep breath. She could feel him bracing himself for what he had to say, but this time she had no sympathy. This time she would find out the truth.

'You know that my father was here in Vernazza during the war?'

'Yes, of course.' He had told her that much already. Isabella

377

glanced at Giovanna, but she was busy loading coffee into her percolator and did not react to his words.

'And you probably also know that certain people were stealing valuable works of art from their rightful owners at that time.'

'Yes, I knew that.' Isabella had heard the stories from some of the more elderly villagers who had lived through the war years. There had been paintings in the Sanctuary of Madonna di Reggio that had apparently never been recovered, and some marble carvings too. She was sure her grandmother had told her there had once been some valuable artefacts and paintings in the old convent too . . . She glanced back out into the hallway where Luca Bordoni's painting was just visible propped against the wall. Though that picture was certainly not one of them.

'Not just German soldiers,' Giovanna said from her position by the stove. 'During wartime everything is at its most vulnerable. People and precious objects. And if there is a person of any nationality who is corrupt or greedy . . .' She let this thought hang in the air. '*Allora*. So much is going on, no one notices if things disappear.' She clicked her fingers.

Isabella blinked. But she could well imagine. 'What disappeared?' She looked at Ferdinand.

But it was Giovanna who replied. 'There was a certain painting in the convent.' Her tone changed; she sounded lost in her memories, almost spellbound. 'Ah, *sì*, it was very beautiful. It was of the Last Supper. The artist had used gold leaf to get a special effect, an almost ethereal glow.'

Isabella couldn't help smiling at the dreamy look on her face. She rather wished she could see that painting – and all the other splendours that Vernazza used to own. 'Who was the artist?' she asked her aunt.

She spread her hands. 'I don't know. I was young, of course. All I knew at the time was that it was a painting of great value. The nuns revered it; it was a masterpiece.'

'And it was stolen?'

'Someone had their eye on it apparently,' Ferdinand told her. 'My father overheard a conversation in the castle one night. He knew that the painting was at risk.'

Isabella raised an eyebrow. Call her cynical, but how could Ferdinand be sure that it wasn't his father who had had his eye on the painting? After all, wasn't he the one who had wanted his son to come here to 'make amends' for what he had done?

Giovanna put the pot of coffee down on the table. She fetched her delicate and worn porcelain cups from the dresser. 'Karl was one of the good men,' she told Isabella, as if she knew what she was thinking. 'He had to follow orders, of course, they all did. But he didn't want to be here, Bella. You must understand that he didn't want to fight, and he certainly didn't want to hurt anyone or steal their property.'

She sounded very sure about that. Isabella decided to let it go – for now.

Ferdinand glanced at Giovanna. 'My father decided to save the painting,' he said simply.

'How?' Isabella leaned forwards. This was getting interesting.

'There was another painting. A much larger picture.' Ferdinand got up, went into the hall and came back with the Bordoni under his arm. He held it up for them to see.

'My father's painting.' Giovanna smiled. 'Oh, he was no expert. It was a hobby, that was all. But he loved his artwork, and after my mother died it was all he had left . . .' Her voice trailed.

'Oh, Giovanna.' Isabella put her hand on her old aunt's arm. She knew that both Giovanna's parents had died young – her mother in childbirth, and her father at the start of the war. How lonely she must have been. She must have been so grateful to have been taken in by the nuns at the convent.

'But tell Bella what Karl did,' Giovanna urged Ferdinand. She poured the coffee, a small espresso for each of them.

'According to my father, it was a risk. He couldn't be sure that it was possible. But he had an idea. One night, he broke into the convent and took the Last Supper painting from the wall.'

Like father, like son, thought Isabella.

'Or to be more accurate, he was let into the convent,' Giovanna corrected with a wry smile.

'By you?'

'By me.'

But her aunt hadn't even been living there at that point – had she?

'He removed the canvas from the frame, then he took down this picture and he removed the hardboard backing.' Ferdinand paused to add milk to his tiny espresso. 'Thank you, Giovanna.'

'And?' Isabella was impatient.

'He inserted the canvas of the Last Supper into the cavity of the Bordoni canvas and frame. He re-tacked the hardboard backing on to the Bordoni, broke up the other frame, and left it under a pile of firewood. And so . . .'

All three of them stared at the picture of the Archangel Gabriel.

'Did you know?' Isabella asked Giovanna. Had she known all these years?

'I let him in, but I didn't know what Karl was going to do.

He didn't want me to know – in those days the less you knew the better, my dear.'

Isabella could imagine.

'And the truth is – we don't even know if it is still there.'

Well, what were they waiting for?

Giovanna sipped her coffee. She seemed content to wait, and Isabella realised that there was more to come.

'My father naturally assumed the painting would have been lost, found or destroyed many years ago,' Ferdinand went on. 'It was during the war. These things happened as Giovanna has explained.'

Isabella frowned. 'But why didn't he come back here after the war had ended, to find out for sure?' It seemed the obvious and most natural thing to do.

'I asked him the same question.' Ferdinand gulped down the rest of his coffee. 'He said that he was ashamed.'

'He would have wanted to put it all behind him,' Giovanna said softly. 'The war, the atrocities, the hardships, things that he was forced to do. He would have been ashamed of his country, ashamed of himself. He must have felt guilty. There were so many bad memories he would have wanted to let go.'

'I think you're right.' Ferdinand nodded. 'He buried himself in his work to all accounts – especially until he met my mother.'

Giovanna patted his shoulder. 'And until he had you, my dear,' she added.

Isabella raised an eyebrow once again. This story was fascinating, and everything rang true. Her dear aunt Giovanna would recognise the truth if anyone did, and, after all, she had been there at the time . . . But something didn't quite fit. Something seemed to be missing. Isabella was sure that there was still more to come.

'It was difficult for your country after the war.' Giovanna poured more coffee for Ferdinand.

'That's true.' He smiled his thanks. 'For many years people of other nationalities did not care so much for my father's.'

'Bella?' Giovanna offered the coffee pot.

'*Grazie*, Aunt.' She drank her coffee down in one, and accepted the refill. 'And the painting? What did he do about that?'

'He decided to leave it to fate.' Ferdinand shrugged.

'He wasn't tempted then – to come back and try to reclaim it for himself?' Isabella had to ask. These two had both accepted one version of the story, but they could be mistaken. Everyone was open to temptation.

He shook his head. 'At the time, he only wanted to help the convent and the village. He only wanted to minimise the theft, the destruction.'

Which was very magnanimous of him – considering he had no connection to their village whatsoever.

'And then, as I told you, he imagined the paintings must both have been lost. Or destroyed.' He glanced at Giovanna, shot her a sad smile. 'I suppose, truth be told, it was easier not to come back.'

'So, what changed?' Isabella couldn't take her eyes off Luca Bordoni's painting. Could that other more valuable painting still be hidden under this canvas? Was it even possible after all this time? She was desperate to know. She couldn't believe that Ferdinand had been able to walk past it every day not knowing, not doing anything about it. No wonder he had kept staring at it. 'Did your father change his mind when he became ill? Was that it?'

'No.' Ferdinand sipped his coffee. 'It was more of a random thing.'

'Go on.' This was getting more intriguing by the second.

'My father was reading an article about old monasteries and convents in Italy, and how many of them had been converted into hotels.'

'Like ours.'

'Like yours. Exactly.' He paused. 'The old convent in Vernazza was mentioned in the article. It piqued his interest, naturally. The memories must have come flooding back. He mentioned it to me and I suggested we look it up online.'

Isabella already knew what he was going to say next. She had been responsible for a large part of The Lemon Tree Hotel's website design. She knew there was a photograph of the staircase, the black-and-white tiled lobby, the very niche where Luca Bordoni's painting had always hung. 'You saw an image of this painting,' she said.

'Yes.'

'And Karl remembered it,' Giovanna added. 'Of course.' Her eyes softened.

'And he told you – about what he'd done?' Isabella sipped her coffee more slowly this time.

'Not then, no.' Ferdinand glanced away. It was approaching sunrise. The pale dawn was creeping through the small windows in the kitchen, pooling the smooth flagstones with lighter tones. 'He must have spent some time mulling it over, trying to decide what to do. But by then he was too poorly to travel. So, that's when he told me the story.'

'He asked you to go and recover the painting.' Isabella sat back in her chair. 'To get it back for him.'

'No, no, my darling.' Giovanna waved an arthritic finger. 'He asked Ferdinand to recover the painting, sì, but he also told him that if by some miracle it was still there, he should

383

give it to any of the nuns who might still be living near Vernazza.' She nodded with satisfaction. 'Or otherwise to give it to our town, our community, to someone who could be trusted to do the right thing. To have it authenticated and valued before the community decided what to do with it. He was very clear, was he not, Ferdinand? That was what he wanted to do.' She clicked her tongue. 'He did not want it for himself, Bella, not at all.'

Isabella was beginning to see. 'He wanted to make amends.' She exchanged a glance with Ferdinand. That was what he had said, and now it was making sense. If the painting was there, if it could be recovered, if it was indeed as valuable as they all thought it was, then the community of Vernazza could in some way benefit from the money it might raise. It wouldn't make everything right. But it would be something.

'Exactly.' Ferdinand once again added more milk to his coffee and drank it down in one. Like Isabella, he must be feeling pretty hyper by now. And Giovanna seemed to realise this too as she got up to put her tray of pastries in the oven.

'My first task was to discover if any of the nuns were still here, or someone else who had been around at the time, and you helped me with that as soon as I arrived.' He beamed at Giovanna. 'You told me about Giovanna, and I learned a lot more about what had happened from her.' He sent her aunt a knowing look.

Giovanna smiled back at him. 'Ferdinand told me the full story,' she said. 'It was quite a surprise, I can tell you.'

'And not the only one,' Ferdinand added.

Isabella remembered the day Ferdinand had arrived at the hotel, how he had sought her out and asked her to introduce him to Giovanna. She remembered her old aunt's reaction too – how forgiving she had been, how she had welcomed Ferdinand into her home. Since then . . . they had really bonded.

'He told me about his plan to look inside the frame of my father's painting. If there was nothing there, well then, we would know that someone else had found the Last Supper and that it was lost for ever. But if it was still there . . .'

'Then I could hand it over to Giovanna for safekeeping.'

'And I could take it to our community and tell them the whole story.' Giovanna retrieved her *cornetti* from the oven. They were golden and smelt divine. She brought them over, still on the baking tray. 'Or at least part of the story.' She chuckled.

Isabella took one of the neat spirals. She'd had no idea that her aunt was so secretive. Cautiously, she bit into it, crisp flaky pastry giving away to a hot, sweet custard centre. She blew on the pastry and took another bite. She hadn't realised how hungry she was.

'So why was it such a big secret?' she complained when she'd finished the next mouthful. Ferdinand could have told her all this days ago, and they could have examined the painting together. 'Didn't you trust us?' It was ironic that all this time Isabella had been unsure whether to trust Ferdinand because he wouldn't tell her exactly what he was doing here, and now it turned out the positions had been reversed without her even being aware of it. He didn't trust her family. That was hardly a decent foundation for any kind of relationship.

Giovanna held up a hand. 'That was my fault.'

'Your fault, Aunt?' That was impossible. Their family had always looked after Giovanna – she would have no reason not to trust them.

'Ferdinand's father knew that it was a delicate situation,' she explained. 'He didn't know who had bought the convent, of course. He didn't know that it was in fact one of the very rebels who had been running away that night and whose compatriots had been shot.' She shook her head sadly.

Isabella thought of the great-grandfather she had never known. 'Ah, yes.' That made sense. If he had known this, he would have been even more wary of the family's reaction.

'But what he did know was that the painting had originally belonged to the covent, and that therefore it would have been sold to the new owners along with the other contents of the building.'

'So, any part of it would automatically belong to my family,' Isabella said, her mouth still full with her next bite of *cornetto*. 'But couldn't you trust us to do the right thing?'

'I promised my father to keep it a secret,' Ferdinand said. 'And Giovanna told me I should respect that wish – for now.' He swallowed his pastry in one. 'You made that very hard, Isabella.'

She supposed that she had. Not that she was about to apologise. But if she and Ferdinand hadn't become so . . . er, close, then the problem would never have arisen. 'Hmm,' she said.

'I didn't know you, Isabella,' Ferdinand said. 'Not then.' He reached out his hand and took hers. She liked that feeling a lot.

'And I was concerned too, my dear,' Giovanna admitted. 'Elene and Silvio had so many plans for The Lemon Tree Hotel . . . How might they react if the money to do everything were to land in their laps?'

Isabella gaped at her. 'You know about all that?'

Ferdinand squeezed her hand. 'It's my impression that Giovanna knows everything that goes on around here,' he said.

He had a point. But: 'I'm certain my parents would also want to do the right thing,' Isabella said staunchly.

Giovanna nodded. 'And I think you are right, Bella.'

'But don't offer them the temptation, is that it?'

Giovanna seemed evasive. 'Some things are best kept quiet,' she murmured, 'even from those you love.'

Ferdinand was fidgeting. 'Enough talking,' he said. 'We have to get this painting back on the wall before anyone notices it's gone. Don't you think it's time to find out if the Last Supper is even there?'

'Most definitely,' said Giovanna.

Isabella jumped up to get the tool-bag from where she'd dumped it in the hall. 'Come on then, Master Criminal,' she said, putting it down next to the Archangel Gabriel. 'Let's do it.'

CHAPTER 43

Isabella

'Shall we open it up outside?' Giovanna's faded old eyes were twinkling with excitement.

'There is more room outside, yes, why not?' Ferdinand agreed.

The two of them, Isabella thought again, were thick as thieves. Literally. She looked down at her flimsy nightdress and shrugged. She wasn't cold. She was still wearing Ferdinand's fleece on top of it, and besides, there was far too much going on to be cold.

He carried the Bordoni painting under one arm out on to the terrace. A pink misty dawn made the morning sky look like a watercolour. Isabella let out a small sigh. It seemed paintings were very much on her mind . . .

The hens were clucking inside their coop, eager to get out into the fresh air, and Giovanna clicked her tongue. 'I must let out my girls.'

Ferdinand and Isabella exchanged a glance. The situation would be funny – if it weren't so serious. Ferdinand placed the painting carefully on the wooden table and assembled his tools beside it. They waited in silence for Giovanna to return.

She fussed around, unlatching the low door that was strong enough to deter any wild animals that might want to try their luck. Then she fetched some grain to toss on to the cobbles. Ferdinand glanced at his watch. Isabella knew what he was thinking. They had to get the painting back where it belonged before anyone from the hotel was up and about. If they didn't . . . At this moment in time she was unable to think of any plausible reason why she and Ferdinand might have taken the Bordoni down from the wall, let alone why they might have spirited it away through the olive grove and to Giovanna's cottage . . .

At last, Giovanna returned, and Ferdinand set to. He turned the painting face down and picked up the screwdriver. 'We must take off the back.' He eased the screwdriver under the lip of the worn gilt frame. It was stiff and, of course, it resisted.

'It has been many years,' said Giovanna. 'It is a bit like taking off the lid of an old paint pot, no?'

'A bit.' Ferdinand gave a grim smile. He was being rather gentler than he would have been with a paint pot, easing the screwdriver in a bit all the way around, and gently prising the hardboard apart from the wooden frame.

It creaked.

Giovanna nodded. 'A good sign,' she said.

Isabella supposed it showed the picture hadn't been tampered with – at least not lately. She realised she was holding her breath, and she exhaled slowly.

Ferdinand went around the frame a second time with his screwdriver. This time the gap between the hardboard and the frame was wider, and he could insert it more easily. The tacks that held it in place had come out a few millimetres, and he took his pincers and meticulously removed each one, placing them in a pile on the far side of the table. 'And now . . .' He prised the hardboard further apart from the gilt frame. Dust motes flew out into the morning air. He eased the hardboard backing away.

Giovanna and Isabella peered over. Now that the backing had been removed, it was possible to see the back of the frame that held the Bordoni canvas in place. All was intact, but in the centre of the frame's cavity was a smaller canvas, face down, kept in place all around its perimeter with balls of scrunched-up newspaper. There was indeed another painting here – that was immediately obvious. But was it *the* painting?

'*Madonna santa,*' whispered Giovanna. She crossed herself.

Ferdinand took out the balls of newspaper. 'It must have been all he could find,' he muttered.

His father would have had no time to think about long-term protection. He would have had to think and act fast. And if he hadn't used the newspaper, the second canvas – which was smaller – would have moved around within the Bordoni's larger frame cavity, Isabella realised. People would have guessed that the frame housed something else other than the painting on show. The smaller canvas would have made a noise and been discovered almost straightaway. This way though . . . The smaller canvas was protected and could remain undetected. Until now.

Ferdinand had taken out all the newspaper. He reached into the cavity of the frame and he took hold of the smaller canvas with both hands.

Isabella held her breath again.

He lifted it up and turned it around for them all to see. 'It is here,' he said – rather unnecessarily.

Because here it was indeed. It was nothing short of a miracle that this painting could have been hidden under the Bordoni for so long. It was quite dazzling. Isabella blinked. She'd seen other depictions of the Last Supper – it was a popular subject of course, inspirational, she imagined, for many artists, especially those painting in the Renaissance. But she'd never seen one quite so bright. There was a luminosity in the yellow, ochre, and saffron of the disciples' robes and hair, a soft light in the sky through the pillars beyond. In the light of the morning here on Giovanna's terrace, the hidden painting glowed.

'Ah, *sì, sì.*' Giovanna's voice was soft and tender. 'I remember this painting from when I was a girl. It hung in the convent, in the vestibule. It was the first thing one saw on coming into the building.'

'It's beautiful. Is it very old, do you think?'

'Fifteenth century perhaps?' Giovanna sounded uncertain. 'And it has great character.'

That was undeniable. Isabella couldn't take her eyes off it.

'But who is the artist?' Ferdinand was peering at the signature. 'Did he donate it to the convent do you think?'

Isabella came to her senses. The signature was illegible, but could easily be authenticated by an art expert, she imagined, when the time came. 'Never mind that now,' she said. 'Now you must get the other back, Ferdinand. *Pronto.*'

'Of course.' Ferdinand laid the Last Supper reverently on the table. He took the original hardboard backing and, jiggling it about a bit, he fixed it into place on the original frame. He glanced at the tacks he'd just removed, discarded them with a shake of his head and pulled a packet of new tacks from the canvas bag. Deftly, he tapped them in with a small hammer, and the gilt frame was back together again, looking much as before, the gilt just a little more cracked perhaps. He was becoming quite the expert.

'See you later.' He kissed Giovanna on both cheeks.

Isabella stepped forward, and he took her hands. 'Forgive me?'

Isabella met his gaze. 'There is nothing to forgive,' she said. He had loyalty to his father – that was good and right. But ultimately, he had indeed come here to make amends to their community, and Isabella respected that. She would have preferred that he had trusted her enough to tell her the truth before now. But . . .

He gave one last look at the painting, and at Isabella. And then he was gone.

Isabella and Giovanna gazed down at the painting. 'It is a good picture,' Giovanna remarked.

'Yes, it is.' Isabella could tell it was valuable – although she still had no idea who had painted it or how it had been acquired by the convent in the first place. There had been so many wonderful Italian artists. She turned to Giovanna. 'What now?' What would she do with it?

'We must wrap it carefully . . .' She frowned. 'Wait here.'

Which wasn't quite what Isabella had meant.

Giovanna returned with a wad of tissue paper.

'You're going to wrap it in that?'

She shrugged. 'It's better than clingfilm.'

'And then what?'

'And then, after someone has looked at it, the painting will go to our community,' she replied, 'just as Ferdinand's father wants it to.'

'Will our community want to sell it?' It seemed a shame, after all that effort.

Giovanna smiled. 'It rather depends on what it is worth, my dear. It could be valuable. It might be painted by some artist whose paintings are rare and highly valued. Only an art historian will know, I suppose.'

Isabella scrutinised the painting. She thought of the story of the Last Supper. On the evening before his death, Jesus called his disciples together for supper, knowing that it would be his last. Before the meal, he washed the feet of everyone attending. During the meal he disclosed the fact that he would be betrayed by one of his twelve followers. He shared the bread and wine, eternal symbols of his body and blood, as depicted in this painting. In this picture, Jesus was the only figure dressed in a dark robe – the disciples wore robes of many colours. They had been drawn with various expressions of worry, disbelief, animation on their faces; only Jesus looked serene and set apart. One of the disciples – maybe Peter? – was whispering in another's ear. Which one was Judas? The one who looked the most worried, she supposed.

'It's quite something,' she said.

Giovanna nodded. 'Ah, sì, it is special. It is a reminder of what we have lost. But also, my dear Bella, it is a reminder of what can be saved.'

CHAPTER 44

Chiara

Chiara had flown from Pisa to Gatwick and caught the train from there to Weymouth. It had been a long journey and she hadn't found it easy travelling alone. It was all so different, so strange. Before leaving home, she'd planned her itinerary – at least in the early stages; after that she would have to wait and see – but making the journey was another thing entirely. A hard knot of anxiety sat in her belly. The unfamiliar surroundings, having to depend on a transport system in an unknown place, the not knowing what she would find . . . It was definitely a step outside her comfort zone. Was she mad to have come here at all? She hoped not, but only time would tell.

She wasn't sure what had come first – the idea to get away or the urge to find Dante. It had begun with that conversation with Giovanna, and had taken root in the olive grove that meant so much to them both. Could she be brave enough? She'd made her travel arrangements quickly, so there'd be no time to worry about it or change her mind. Even so, she'd lost count of the times she'd felt unsure, been tempted to turn right around and go back home. But she hadn't. She didn't have the luxury of certainty, but she had to at least try.

The train journey to Weymouth was lengthy enough to make her relax, and it was fascinating to watch the scenery of England sweep past. It was just as she'd read and imagined, just as Dante had told her. Grey skies with shimmerings of silver mist, crowded platforms in built-up suburbs giving way to quieter and older towns and villages. As the train got closer to its final destination, there were harbour towns of Bournemouth and Poole – both in East Dorset, she knew from looking at the map she had bought – and the views became more rural. Fields of a vibrant green, with woolly sheep grazing, old yellow-stone farmhouses, winding streams, and trees with leaves of red, russet, amber, and yellow. Autumn was cooler here, yes. But it certainly wasn't all grey.

According to her map, Weymouth was the most easterly part of West Dorset, so this was where Chiara was starting her Dorset journey. She'd booked into a small hotel on the sea front, and spent the next day finding her bearings, walking around the town and trying to get used to the fact that she, Chiara Mazzone, was here in England at last. It all felt so strange – not just the language, but the people, the place. There was a bleak chilliness to Weymouth that was at first unsettling and then rather soothing. The beach was sandy, the Georgian architecture rather grand. But she could see straightaway that this was not the right part of West Dorset. She must move on.

Back at the hotel, Chiara emailed Isabella. She couldn't simply stop thinking about them. Had she left them in the lurch? She hoped not. She had been looking after The Lemon Tree Hotel for so long that even here, as unsettled as she felt, as unfamiliar as everything was, the hotel in Vernazza remained close to her thoughts.

Is everything all right, Bella? she asked her granddaughter. *Are there any problems? Is your mother OK? And you? How are you?* She considered asking about Ferdinand Bauer, but managed to stop herself. It was not her business. Look at how everyone had interfered in her love life when she was a girl, and look at the results.

The reply pinged back in minutes, while Chiara was still sitting staring out towards the sea, lost in a dream – showing her that Isabella was working on her laptop, probably while sitting in reception. She imagined this in her mind's eye and gave a satisfied nod.

Everything's fine, Nonna. Mamma's fine too. How is England? Are you managing all right on your own? Anyway, don't worry about us – just enjoy your break!

No mention of Signor Bauer, she noted. Was that good or bad?

Chiara thought of Elene. She wasn't one for emails, so maybe she'd send her a text message later. She had no idea how Elene had felt about her going away. She hadn't liked the thought that her mother might try to find Dante – that was natural. But any other concerns she had hidden well. Chiara suppressed the age-old twinge of guilt. *Basta.* Enough. She remembered what Giovanna had said. She was doing this, not for her daughter, but for herself.

The next day, Chiara consulted her map, and the girl in the hotel reception and, according to her instructions, caught a bus from the king's statue (George III apparently) to Abbotsbury, where she spent the rest of the day exploring the pebbly beach and the swannery. She even walked up to the atmospheric

St Catherine's Chapel on the hill, which reminded her of their hilltop sanctuaries in Italy. Some things then, were the same the world over. She looked out over the impossibly green fields towards the sea. Abbotsbury was a pretty village – though rather manicured for her taste, but again, it wasn't the right place. It most definitely wasn't Dante's place.

Chiara tried not to panic. This wasn't a long stretch of coastline – it ran from Weymouth to Lyme Regis, and she already knew from pictures she'd seen that Lyme wasn't the place Dante had described – so she must be getting close. The helpful girl in reception at her hotel in Weymouth had booked her into a small place in the village, so she would stay the night and then move on. Thank goodness she had only brought a small suitcase. She didn't want to rush through all these parts of England that she had longed to see, but on the other hand, the true purpose of her visit continued to burn steadfastly inside her. She had to see him – just one last time.

From Abbotsbury she booked into a small B & B in Burton Bradstock further up the coast. She went there by taxi this time – the buses were not frequent in this part of the world, and Chiara resented the waste of her time spent in waiting for them. But by the time she got to Burton, travelling along an open, scenic and hilly road that boasted spectacular sea views over Chesil Beach, Chiara was beginning to see the attraction of West Dorset for Dante. This road alone almost rivalled the beauty of her own Cinque Terre, though the sea was vaster and arguably less picturesque. But she could sense what held him here.

At first, it seemed that Burton might be the place. Chiara left her bags at the B & B – my goodness, she was beginning to feel like such a nomad – and walked along the beach road to Hive. Her confidence was growing with every day that passed; her life in Italy – her old life – almost seemed to belong to a different Chiara. This new woman was still finding her bearings, it was true; she was a stranger in a foreign land. But she was becoming braver. Perhaps she was even settling into a new version of herself – a more adventurous woman who was ready and willing to explore new places, find new horizons.

Chiara almost gasped when she reached Hive Beach. Because surely here were the golden cliffs? She walked over the beach towards the sea, almost blinded by the brightness of them in the afternoon sunlight, half expecting someone to shout out her name. The water was grey, green, olive, and about every shade in between. Chiara was fascinated by it. If there wasn't such a chilly breeze she would have wanted to swim – and there were a few people and a dog braving the elements and splashing around in the waves.

She found a sandstone path that led up to a rather run-down hotel (Chiara was relieved she wasn't staying there) and a house that apparently belonged to some famous British musician, according to a dog-walker who seemed to want to make conversation. Beyond this, it was possible to walk along the cliff to a place called Freshwater Beach, and then back along the river. But there was no Italian *gelato* – just a rather nice seafood café on Hive Beach, and a very English ice-cream parlour. Chiara tried not to feel too disappointed.

'Is there somewhere nearby that sells Italian *gelato*?' she asked the girl behind the counter. She had auburn hair and green eyes – a striking combination.

The girl looked a touch annoyed. 'Have you even tried our ice cream?'

'No. Yes. Oh, I'm sorry, yes of course I'll have the vanilla please.' It was probably the safest. Chiara took the proffered cone. 'I'm looking for someone, you see,' she explained to the girl. 'He's Italian. He makes ice cream.'

'Ah.' The girl's voice softened at the hint of romance. 'You should have said.'

Chiara paid her with the unfamiliar coins. 'I know he lives somewhere in West Dorset,' she confided. 'And I know there are cliffs like these.' Which sounded a bit mad. What kind of person in this day and age searched for a compatriot on the basis of a description of some sandstone cliffs? But from Dante's description, she thought she'd recognise the place, and in her heart, Chiara knew Burton Bradstock — beautiful though it was — wasn't it.

The girl frowned as she handed back her change. 'You could try West Bay,' she said. 'It's not far. Outside Bridport, just along the coast road.'

Chiara headed back to her B & B to investigate this further. Rather to her surprise, she was beginning to enjoy her adventure, but she hoped she'd find Dante soon. Was she being foolish? Was she on a pointless mission? Was she far too old to be thinking this way? Chiara steeled herself. She was only fifty-nine. Who knew? Perhaps it wasn't too late. At the very least they could talk. At the very least she could tell him how sorry she was that it hadn't worked out between them. And meanwhile, she could experience a taste of his beloved Dorset for herself. Because if she didn't even try . . . How would that make her feel for the rest of her life without him?

Back in her room, Chiara looked up B & Bs in West Bay. There was one just up the hill called West Cliff that had a sea view, she read. It sounded perfect. She called the number.

The woman sounded very pleasant. Yes, there was plenty

of room, she said, as long as Chiara was staying two nights or more. It was the end of the season, and not yet half term.

'I could come this afternoon,' Chiara told her.

Her current landlady offered to take her to West Bay for a small charge to cover petrol. 'There's still a railway station down there in the bay,' she told her. 'Though much good it does anybody.'

'There are no trains?' Chiara was curious.

'There were trains to Bridport and West Bay once upon a time,' she said. 'Until the branch lines were closed in the 1960s. Come to think of it, I believe they closed the station at West Bay even earlier. It never quite took off as a holiday resort, I reckon.'

Chiara wondered why they would have stopped the trains like this. It seemed short-sighted to say the least, and if they could have a train station in a place like Vernazza . . . But it was a pleasant drive, and she sat back in her seat to enjoy it. Even if she didn't find Dante – and at this thought her new-found courage almost failed – then at least she would have travelled to another country alone, she would have gone somewhere different, done something that didn't involve The Lemon Tree Hotel or her family. That would be an achievement in itself.

They turned left off the main road and soon came to a village with a large car park, a hotel, and a distinctive mound of small ginger pebbles piled so high on the beach that it was impossible to view the sea. Chiara felt a pull of excitement deep in her chest. There was a disused railway station just as her landlady had said, and a harbour lined by kiosks selling fish and chips, burgers, seafood, and . . . ice cream. Chiara hardly dared look at these kiosks as they passed by in her landlady's car. Had he mentioned a kiosk? She couldn't recall. Boats gently nudged each other in the harbour. There was a hotch-potch of build-ings in the village – some old, some newer; some pretty, some entirely defeated by the elements they must have fought for so many years. It was, she decided, exactly the kind of place Dante Rossi would feel at home in. Not too neat, not too rundown. A real place, with sea air and a slightly weary soul.

They drove up a hill, and Chiara glanced back to see a path snaking up a grass-covered golden cliff. The sea was visible now too. Broad waves were crashing on to a ginger and gravelly beach, and the sea rocked and gleamed in the autumn sunlight beyond. Chiara's heart did a double flip. She had the strongest feeling that this was indeed the place.

CHAPTER 45

Isabella

It had been a strange few days for Isabella.

Aware that she was still only wearing Ferdinand's fleece and her flimsy nightdress, she had hot-footed it back to the hotel and sneaked in the rear entrance through the kitchen. Her mother was already up doing the breakfasts though, and naturally, she spotted her.

'Bella! What on earth are you doing?'

'Oh, I just went outside for a walk, Mamma.' Isabella edged towards the door. The sooner that she made it up to her room, the better.

'In your nightclothes?' Her mother's eyebrows rose.

'It was such a lovely morning.' Isabella gestured towards the window. 'For October.' Fortunately, the sun was indeed shining. 'I didn't want to hang around and er . . . get dressed.' She laughed. Did that sound convincing?

'Really?' Her mother frowned. 'If your grandmother were here I'm sure she wouldn't be happy about that, Bella. I mean, what about our guests? What sort of impression are you giving them of The Lemon Tree Hotel? We have our professional credibility to consider, you know.'

At least, Isabella thought, she hadn't said anything about a missing painting. Ferdinand must have got it back in time. 'There was no one around, Mamma.' She moved closer towards the door. She had to make sure this was the case, that the Bordoni Gabriel was once again hanging in its rightful place and had not been missed. She crossed her fingers behind her back. 'It was so early when I went out. Only just dawn.'

'So where did you go?' Mamma wasn't letting her off that easily.

'To Aunt Giovanna's.' That much at least was true. 'Then we had coffee and *cornetti*, and got talking, and I just didn't notice how late it was.'

'Hmm.' Her mother nodded.

She could always rely on Mamma to understand delays where food was concerned.

'And how is Aunt Giovanna?'

Isabella thought of her aunt's expression when she had seen the painting of the Last Supper. It had been worth being there just for that. 'She's well.'

'Good. I'll take her down something to eat at lunch-time. I'm making a squid-ink risotto.' She frowned at her daughter. 'Better get dressed quickly then, Bella.'

'I will.'

In the lobby, the Bordoni hung just as it always had. Only . . . Isabella put her head to one side. It might be a little off-centre. But there was no time to do anything about that now. Fortunately, it was still too early for guests to be around, and she was able to slip up the stairs and into her own room without being seen. She shut the door behind her, leaned against it, and exhaled. What a morning it had been so far . . . So, was that it? Was that the full mystery of the missing painting and the reason for Ferdinand's presence at The Lemon Tree Hotel? She couldn't rid herself of the feeling that there was something more.

Over the next two days she was too busy to think about it too much however. Her grandmother had been right – they were getting quieter now that it was late October, but there was a lot to show Emanuele, who had taken over her grandmother's shifts on reception, and there were other problems with deliveries and bookings that she had to manage alone. Her mother had told her about Febe's pregnancy and that she wouldn't be working next season. With Nonna away there was plenty to do.

Ferdinand had not yet left the hotel to return to Germany – he'd been here now for almost three weeks – and yet she'd swear he was keeping out of her way. They'd had drinks and coffee, snatched a quick walk, and even had dinner one evening, but there was none of the intimacy of the night in the olive grove. He was still here – which had to mean something. And she'd been so sure of how he'd felt . . . But if that was the case, why was he now creating a distance between them?

Isabella was due some time off for sure. Ferdinand was nowhere to be found, and many of their guests were leaving because the weather was certainly on the change. She looked outside. It had been a fine early autumn and it had hardly rained for months, but now the sky was dark and heavy with clouds. Even so, she needed to get out, she really did. With Nonna away and their planned renovations on hold; with Ferdinand playing some sort of waiting game . . . She felt unsettled. She'd go down to the village, she decided, buy a few supplies, spend some time by the harbour at the water's edge, and try to shake herself out of this mood.

She took a bag and a light jacket and scarf and set off through the olive grove. The wind was whipping the branches of the trees – perhaps there would be a storm? When she got to the cliff edge she stood looking out over the prickly pears and juniper. The ocean was not smooth and glassy as it had been for most of the summer, but thick and green, blurred by mist, the waves smashing on to the rocks that surrounded Vernazza in rolls of fizzing and foaming water, spraying on to the cliff side. The clouds were darker towards Monterosso, and it was so hazy that it was even hard to make out the contours of the village from here. There was a grey bleakness to the landscape today that made her shiver, a kind of eerie calm. Even the houses didn't look as colourful as usual. The low cloud was certainly putting a dampener on the scene.

She thought of her grandmother, in Dorset. No doubt it would be even bleaker there. Was she looking for Dante Rossi – this man who'd had such an effect on her when he visited The Lemon Tree Hotel earlier this month? Isabella still felt sad that her grandparents' marriage had come to an end – you didn't expect it somehow of your grandparents . . . Weren't they, after all, too old for that sort of thing? But she'd always had so much respect for her grandmother, and so she instinctively trusted Nonna's decision. There were reasons, there must be. Although surely she wasn't about to fling herself into another relationship at her age? And if she found Dante Rossi in Dorset, if she did embark on a relationship with him . . . What then? What about The Lemon Tree Hotel and her life here with her family?

The sky was growing still darker as Isabella made her way

down the steeper steps into the village. There were still plenty of people around, even though the wind was beginning to whistle down the narrow alleyways. Tourists came to Vernazza all year round – though not as many now in the last week of October as invaded the tiny town in the summer. And although tourism was their business, Isabella thanked God for that. Everyone needed some respite. This village – her village – had never been meant to house so many people, it had never been intended for so many feet to walk the cobbles, for so many strangers to use the little shops and cafés. It was a strain on Vernazza – not to mention on those locals who didn't make their living from tourism and had nothing to thank it for.

The first drops of rain fell as Isabella was approaching the small harbour down the narrow walkway by the pink, yellow, and terracotta houses. The green wooden shutters in most of them had been drawn closed. The boats had already been brought on to the piazza as they usually were when there was a forecast of bad weather. And it was raining harder now, fat drops splattering on to the pavement. Some people were already dodging into shops, cafés, and bars to avoid the down-pour that was now looking to be a certainty.

'*Ciao*. It's looking bad.' A restaurateur she knew greeted her as he started stacking together the chairs outside his place. He looked up at the sky. 'There goes the lunch trade, huh? It's the *scirocco*. You should get home.'

'In a while.' Isabella walked on past the piazza – usually it was full of orange and blue parasols on the tables outside its restaurants and bars, but today the boats were crammed in side by side under their blue and white striped covers, and the tamarisk trees were waving in the wind. Some tourists were still around – but they were all tucked safely inside the bars and the cafés, sheltering from the rain. She passed the strangely deserted beach and harbour and walked on up to the far promontory where the water was glistening on the jetty and rocks and where the sea was choppy and wild.

Some brave souls were sitting high up on the striated layers of rocks watching the sea – whooping as the waves crashed ever closer, as the water spluttered and washed on to the jetty, as the white spray flew up towards them. A couple of young guys she knew were even swimming off the harbour arm where the tourist boats usually came in, diving into the foaming water and allowing the next wave to bring them right up on to *terra firma* again. She couldn't help laughing. It was a long-established tradition in Vernazza – and it unquestionably entertained the tourists. As for the two boys – it made them look macho, and they clearly loved the attention. But even they were looking around, assessing the weather and the tide. With a laugh and a joke between them, they grabbed their towels and retreated to the steps that wound towards the castle, *Castello Doria*, where people were lined up hanging on to the railings, watching the heaving ocean.

Isabella climbed up the slippery rocks to escape the water beginning now to swirl around the paved concrete of the jetty. She loved the freshness of the rain and the way it changed the water in the harbour to a glossy, milky green. Vernazza had its share of winds and storms – this sort of weather was pretty much the norm for this time of year, and she knew it wouldn't be dangerous. Even so . . . She looked up. The dark clouds were thick and fast-moving in the sky, and the wind was increasing. It looked ominous. Yes, it could be a bad one. It was probably crazy to sit on the rocks and watch the waves, but at the very least it would clear her head.

She stayed as long as she could, even though she was beginning to get wet through. It was cleansing somehow. But as time went by, the rain was becoming heavier and the wind stronger. She realised she'd skipped lunch entirely. The last of the wave-watchers headed for the nearest café, and Isabella followed them. She should get back to the hotel. The tide was rising into a wall of water, and she didn't want to be swept out to sea by a freak wave – anything was possible on a stormy day like this. It was hard though, even walking down the street. The water level was rising and now she was soaked to the skin. Her teeth started chattering and she realised belatedly that she had stayed out much too long. The storm was going full pelt – she could hardly see in front of her.

Suddenly, everything went crazy. Chairs left outside the cafés began to tumble downhill. People were shouting, screaming, crying with fear. People were panicking, rushing around, diving into doorways and fighting to keep the doors closed and the water out. What had happened? What was going on? Someone grabbed her and, just as they did, she peered through the driving rain and thought she could see . . . No. What looked like a torrent of mud sliding towards her. Getting deeper. Getting thicker. Sliding down the road so fast. It was impossible – wasn't it impossible? She blinked. There were rocks and debris too – thundering down from the mountainside carrying everything that stood in their path along with them. The noise was deafening. There was the shriek of a whistle. And water. So much water . . . the rush of it filled her head.

Isabella screamed. The lights went out. She could smell gas – sickly sweet. She slipped on the pavement, only it wasn't the pavement any longer, it was something dark and slippery and alive. There was a whirlpool of water in the entrance to the café, and beyond it a snapshot of the frightened faces trapped inside. And then she was gone and she was down and the smell was in her head – the smell of mud and water and gas – and everything went even blacker than before.

CHAPTER 46

Chiara

Chiara met the owner of the B & B – a cheerful, middle-aged woman with a mop of fair curls and kind blue eyes who introduced herself as 'Jacqueline Bennet but please call me Jackie' – and was shown to her room. It was pleasant, light and airy, and had a view down the hill towards the orange sandstone cliffs and pebbles of Chesil Beach.

Chiara thanked her and stood for a few moments alone at the window. From her vantage point, she couldn't actually see the harbour or the kiosks. But something was still telling her that this was the place. And that same something was tugging at her to take action. This was why she was here. She must walk down there and see. Be brave at last.

She checked her appearance in the mirror, combed her hair – though no doubt the sea breeze would have something to say about that – and carefully re-applied her lipstick. She changed into a pair of well-fitting trousers and flat ankle boots more suitable for this terrain, and tied a silk scarf loosely around her neck. Her jacket was light, but designed to protect her from the cool autumns and winters of the Cinque Terre, and it buttoned up suitably high.

Dante, she thought. She examined her face in the mirror. What would he think when he saw her? How would he react? Did she look any different from how she had looked in Italy? Were there already a few more frown lines after what she had discovered in Pisa, her subsequent separation from Alonzo, the revelations concerning Elene and Silvio's plans for the renovation of the hotel? She wasn't sure. It had been a harrowing time. They said that older people became invisible, but Chiara was determined to stave that off for as long as possible. She wasn't old, not at all, not by any stretch of the imagination. And she hoped she would never be invisible to Dante. He may not have forgiven her for letting him down again – but she believed that he would always see her.

As satisfied with her appearance as she would ever be, Chiara picked up her bag and went downstairs. Jackie had given her a key so she could come and go as she pleased. And now, Chiara couldn't wait to get out there.

Instead of walking down the road, she turned towards the cliff path, just visible down a narrow, grassy alley. The wind immediately caught at her hair and stung her skin with its autumn chill. Chiara dug her leather gloves from her pockets and pulled them on. The cliff wasn't high at this point; it was green, and the path dry and stony. The sky was a silvery grey, and the cliff-side opened up into something more like a sloping meadow, with wooden benches planted every few metres, to make the most of the view down to the sea. The water was grey-green and lively, the waves rolling to the shore, their rivulets of white foam seeping into the gravelly sand. The air was fresh and salty. Chiara drew great lungfuls into her chest – it felt as if it had been a long time since she had breathed so fully. It was, she thought, her kind of air.

This path ran on and up to a grassy cliff-top, but Chiara took the downhill slope that led to a concrete promenade above the shoreline of grey rocks and ginger pebbles crumbling into coarse sand. Beyond the next pile of rocks, she could see another beach; concrete steps led down to ground level, and a few people were wandering along by the water's edge. They were kicking at the sand, throwing balls for their dogs (and what a lot of dogs there were, here in Dorset!) a father and his toddler playing tag with the oncoming waves, the little girl shrieking with delight.

Chiara watched them for a moment, thought of Elene, and smiled. In the days when Elene was young, she and Alonzo had mostly been too busy to play with their daughter down at the shore. And perhaps that was why Elene had become the way she was now – fiercely independent, emotionally distant, seemingly always quick to take offence. But it was so easy to look back and think that one should have done things differently. At the time . . . She sighed.

There were no definitive rules to parenthood, and one was thrown into it within the context of life at that moment. Fighting to keep The Lemon Tree Hotel afloat had taken all her energy; at times it had seemed that it must surely go under. By the time Elene was born, more people had started visiting Cinque Terre, this was true. But they were coming on day trips from Pisa, Portovenere, La Spezia; they were not staying in Cinque Terre hotels. And when her parents died . . . It had seemed imperative to keep The Lemon Tree going.

Chiara felt a surge of regret. But . . . The Lemon Tree Hotel had seemed the most important thing in her world. She had to make it work. And yet, it was just a hotel, as Dante had always said. Whereas Elene was her daughter. And Dante . . .

She strolled to the edge of the harbour as if she had all the time in the world, as if that man might not be within reaching distance once again. The square harbour was full of boats – fishing vessels, rowing boats, the odd pleasure craft – and lined with these rather quaint old-fashioned kiosks, like beach huts she supposed, that she had glimpsed from the car earlier. *The Snack Shack*, she read. *Rachel's* . . . It was the last week of October, and decidedly chilly, but they still had tables and chairs set up outside, people drinking tea and coffee, and eating ice cream. Ice cream . . .

Chiara looked around her, suddenly sure that Dante might leap out from behind the harbour wall. But no, he would not. It was far too low, and besides, he did not know that she was here. If she wanted to, she could still change her mind, move on, forget this crazy adventure and go home. He would never know that she had even been here. Because she had worked to save The Lemon Tree Hotel for Elene, for her family, for Isabella, and the generations to come; she had worked for her parents' legacy to live on. She still did.

Dante had threatened all that. He still did.

Gulls were screeching, circling over a fishing boat unloading its catch. Crabs and lobsters in frayed pots were being pulled up on to the harbourside. Ice boxes of shiny grey fish with surprised eyes were being dumped unceremoniously on the ground. The gulls swooped closer, almost grazing the harbour wall, their cries insistent, demanding. Children were crabbing along the jetty, dropping nets into the clear water, filling buckets with shrimps and tiny crabs. More and more, Chiara liked the feel of West Bay. It was down to earth, real

413

and uncompromising. Windy and raw. Not beautiful perhaps, but her sort of place.

She walked along the harbourside. There were more kiosks on the far edge, over the road. Selling fish and chips, seafood, burgers and . . . She stopped so suddenly that a young man wearing headphones and a leather jacket cannoned into her and she had to turn and apologise. 'Sorry. So sorry. I just—'

'No problem.' He raised a hand. His voice was gentle and had that West Country lilt that Chiara had already heard around these parts. 'Are you all right?'

'Yes. Fine. Thank you.' She smiled and let him go past. Because she had seen the sign outside the blue and white kiosk. *Italian Gelato.* She took a few tentative steps forwards. A young couple were just leaving with cones of what looked like chocolate and pistachio. Well of course, you could enjoy *gelato* at any time of year.

Chiara took a deep breath. She stepped closer. The man behind the counter had his back to her. But he was unmistakeable. Silver and grey hair. Lean and muscular neck and shoulders, though slightly more bent these days than before. A blue shirt, a white apron, blue jeans. He turned. Dark eyes.

'Hi. What can I—' He stopped as his eyes met hers. 'Get you?' he murmured.

'Hello, Dante.' Chiara smiled. He looked so wonderfully familiar, so dear.

'Chiara,' he said. 'What in God's name are you doing here?'

414

CHAPTER 47

Elene

Elene was in the kitchen that day as usual, making her *Buridda* – a Genoese *secondi* of fish stew which was one of her staple autumn recipes.

She chopped the onions, sniffing and turning her head away every so often as she did so. Over the years, she had found ways to lessen the tears – would that it was so easy in life . . . But onions were onions, and there was little you could do about tears. *Buridda* was worth it – the name was Arabic in origin and it was one of the oldest recipes she knew, originating from medieval times when Arabic merchants had visited the port of Genoa to trade. Back then, it was mainly a meal for the poor of course, since leftovers could be used, and Elene was not too proud to still make the dish in this way.

It was a strange day – there was a peculiar atmosphere in the air – she could feel it, even tucked away in *la cucina* on her own as she was this afternoon. The day seemed unusually dark, and she had switched on all the lights – maybe it was because it had been raining steadily and there had been so much dry weather of late that they weren't used to it. But when she'd gone outside with her espresso earlier for a break, the atmosphere had seemed heavy too, with a sense not so much of calm but of premonition. It had been heavily misty. Stormy weather, she concluded, was on its way.

Elene gave a little shiver and moved over to the other counter to chop the celery. This was another technique for avoiding the onions, and it was easy to do on this, one of the increasingly rare occasions that she was on her own in the kitchen. Her mother had been right. The Lemon Tree Hotel was quiet at last. The seemingly endless flow of visitors that had continued from March through to mid-October had thinned now to more manageable levels. Which was a good thing as far as Elene was concerned. Normally she liked to keep busy, but she also relished some relaxation too. And she enjoyed being alone in her kitchen trying out new recipes, revelling in the old – it gave her precious time to think.

She moved back to the onions. They might make her tearful, but they were such perfect globes of glistening white, and they lent such flavour to any dish. Onions were so simple and yet so versatile – they were perhaps one of her favourite ingredients of all time. She closed her eyes for a moment and blinked away the sting of an onion-tear. What then was her mother doing now, all those miles away across the sea in England? Elene sniffed. Had she seen him? She'd said she didn't know where he lived, but *certo* she would have found out by now. Elene knew her mother. She would not go all that way on a whim or a whisper. She would have found him for sure.

Elene moved now to the carrots, already peeled and topped and tailed. She preferred them sliced thinly in rounds for this dish, and she had a special knife she used for this. She selected

416

it, took a breath, and moved into action, the repetitive rhythm of the slicing soothing her in some strange way as it always did. *Just a holiday*, her mother had said. But then she said a lot of things. Elene paused in her slicing. She could see how it was. It was just the three of them now – Elene, Silvio, and Isabella. And that was just fine.

She opened the back door to cut some parsley from the kitchen garden. Goodness, but it was gloomy out here even though for the moment it had stopped raining. The trees in the olive grove seemed to shiver in the shadows and it was hard to believe it wasn't yet four in the afternoon. Elene looked up towards the terraces and the scarred hillside. The dry-stone walls so important to their agricultural history were not maintained as well as they had once been and so they were more vulnerable at times of heavy rain – without the support of their walls, those terraces could create an avalanche. The Cinque Terre was no longer a land of agriculture – and tourism was responsible for that in part. She bent to cut a handful of parsley and lifted it to her nose to sniff the fragrance, brought out more fully by the rain.

Silvio was sure that Chiara would come back. 'This place is her life,' he had said to Elene more than once over the past few days. 'Your mother would never leave here.'

'Hmm.' But Elene couldn't help but notice that he said 'this place' not 'you', nor even 'Isabella'. Her mother might love her family, Elene knew that she did, but Elene still felt unwanted, discarded even. Because what came first – that was the question? That had always been the question.

Just as she was about to go back in, Elene paused. She thought she could hear a sound in the distance – a kind of rumble. Thunder perhaps? She returned to the kitchen and shut the door with some relief as the rain started up again, more persistent now. She was glad that she was not out in it, that was for certain.

She heated some olive oil in a large pan and began to fry the vegetables and herbs. It was comforting. The aroma from the onion, celery and parsley rose enticingly from the pan and, as if he'd been summoned by the intoxication of it, Silvio charged into the kitchen from outside.

'Don't forget to wipe your feet on the mat,' Elene said quickly. Silvio had a habit of not noticing the mud. Probably because he wasn't the one who cleared it up afterwards.

'It's whipping up rough out there,' Silvio said.

'I know. Maybe Mamma is having better weather even in England, eh?' Elene added the sliced anchovies to the pan. The smell of anchovies was unique, and she'd always loved the variety of shiny silvery greys that were available in the market. Sometimes she liked to fry them and serve them in cones *da asporto*, as a nod to Vernazza street food at its best.

'Maybe.' Silvio tugged off his boots. 'That's me done for today. Unless there's anything to see to inside?'

'I don't think so.' Elene stirred the juices.

Silvio came up behind her and clasped her waist. He buried his face in the back of her neck and planted a kiss there.

It tickled. Elene laughed. 'I'm cooking.'

'I can tell.' He didn't move away. 'I'm quick like that, you know. Perhaps that's why you married me.'

'Perhaps it was.' Elene could smell the earthiness of him combining with the fragrances emanating from her pan. Normally, she would have pushed him off without further ado. She had pushed him away so often when she came to think about it – because she was too busy or too tense, too angry

418

or too anxious. Now, though . . . She allowed herself a small tilt backwards so that she was resting against him. It had been a long time since she'd been able to relax fully. She closed her eyes – just for a second. Mmm. They wouldn't be able to do this if they hadn't been alone in the kitchen.

'When will it be ready?' Silvio sniffed appreciatively. But his voice was low, as if he had appreciated the change in her.

'It depends on whether or not you leave me to get on.' But Elene managed to add the fish without moving away from him.

'Can I pass you something?' he murmured into her ear. 'Anything at all you need?'

She smiled. 'The mushrooms.'

'*Va bene.*' He shifted only slightly to pass them over.

'The pine nuts.'

'Hmm.' He shifted again.

'And the white wine.'

'Ah, don't tempt me.' This time he had to step away, and she felt the sudden draught of air between them and wanted to pull him back.

'Remember the days?' he asked her.

'What days?' She paused in the adding of the ingredients, the slow layering of the dish, the putting together – which was the part she always liked the best.

'The old days, my love.' He passed over the bottle of white wine. 'You and me. A bottle of wine. A dish of your special *trofie al pesto.*'

The days when her parents had been her parents and she hadn't given a thought to the fact that they might separate. The days when she and Silvio had been young, and so much had seemed possible. She added the wine, blinked back a tear that wasn't an onion-tear at all.

'Hey . . .' Silvio turned her around to face him. He tilted her chin. 'No regrets, Elene?'

'No regrets.' She flung her arms around his neck and for the first time in years she realised that this was true.

'What were you thinking about then?' He stroked her hair. There had been such a tenderness in Silvio lately. She supposed that she had stretched him to his limits over the years. But the closeness that had lately grown up between them was special. And with it was a gentleness born of a love that was no longer young, but which had become so strong with the years, almost without her noticing.

'I was just thinking about that man . . .'

'What man?' he frowned.

'You know.' She couldn't bear to say his name. She turned back to stir the *buridda*. When the wine had evaporated she would add the passata and the spices. 'The man who came here, the man in England, the man Mamma has no doubt gone to see.'

'Ah.' He sighed. 'So, you are thinking of that again.'

'And why shouldn't I?' Elene pursed her lips, stirring the *buridda* more moderately now.

'Because it makes you worry.' He turned her back to face him again. It was like some strange dance they were having here in *la cucina*, Elene thought. 'It makes you anxious, my love.'

'I can't help but worry.' She looked up at him, into his eyes. He had helped her with so many things, her Silvio. But this, this was beyond even him. 'He is a violent man. A disruptive man. A destructive man. I have seen the evidence, you know.'

'Your mother is a sensible woman.' Silvio held her in his arms. 'Trust me. She knows what she is doing. It may be that this man, this Dante Rossi, is not so bad as we imagine.'

420

'Then . . .' But Elene couldn't say it. *Who had hit her?* Her mind had thought it, but her voice couldn't speak it. If she said it, it would become real.

'Let it go, Elene.' He ran his thumb along her cheek and she leaned against him once more. After a few moments he kissed her head and smoothed her hair from her face. She looked up and he kissed her lips. It was a long kiss, a strong kiss, a kiss she didn't want to end.

'Silvio,' she whispered. How long since they had kissed that way?

'But what about the food?'

She punched him playfully in the stomach. She couldn't remember the last time she had felt like this, acted this way with him, her husband. He'd talked about the old days, but had they ever really enjoyed each other without her fears, her worries, her insecurities sitting on their shoulders throughout?

'It will take at least an hour to simmer.' Modestly, she looked down at the floor. 'And so, if, as you said, you have finished for the day . . .' She could hardly believe she was saying this. She wasn't sure she had ever said anything like it before.

Silvio looked as if he could hardly believe it either.

But as they stood there staring at one another, there was a noise, as if the heavens had opened. There was something that scared Elene about the noise and Silvio must have felt the same because he rushed over to open the back door. The rain was lashing down. He swore softly. 'I can't see a bloody thing. But something's happening out there. Let's go out the front.'

In the lobby, a few people were milling around talking excitedly. 'What's going on?' Elene addressed this to Emanuele, who was on reception.

'There is a storm,' he said. 'Rain and . . .'

'A mudslide,' someone shouted. 'I saw it – down in Vernazza. I was on the upper path heading back here. I saw it racing down the mountain, a river of mud. Tables and chairs, rubbish bins, cars even were being swept up in the torrent. *Madonna santa*! People were rushing into shops and bars to escape. But they couldn't keep out the water. It was wild. Crazy, I tell you. And the noise . . . I've never seen or heard anything like—'

A landslide. Elene felt the panic deep in her belly. 'Isabella.' She grabbed Silvio. 'Where is Isabella?'

She saw the fear flare suddenly in his eyes. 'Jesus . . .'

'Emanuele? Where is Isabella?' Elene was conscious of the hysteria in her voice. But he must know. Someone must know. 'Where is our girl?'

CHAPTER 48

Chiara

The following morning, Dante picked Chiara up from her B & B. 'Wear your hiking boots,' he'd told her.

'I don't have any with me.'

He laughed. 'No worries. You'll be fine. This walk will be nothing – not after the mountains of the Cinque Terre.'

Chiara hoped he was right. These cliffs of West Dorset weren't so steep admittedly, but they were very muddy.

The previous afternoon, it had taken Dante a full hour to accept the fact that she was even here. Chiara knew how that felt.

'I'm on holiday,' she had replied to his question. 'That's what I'm doing here.'

'On holiday?' His eyebrows had shot up to his hairline and she'd had to laugh.

'Why not?' She shrugged. 'You told me about the place and I have to admit, it sounded pleasant enough.'

'Pleasant enough?'

Chiara wondered when he was going to stop repeating everything she said. 'What would you recommend?'

'Recommend?'

She clicked her tongue. 'Which flavour?'

'Oh, liquorice, if you are a fan.' At the mention of ice cream, he seemed to come to his senses.

'I'm a fan,' she confirmed.

'Definitely liquorice then.'

'It was a shock, that is all,' he told her over dinner that night in the West Bay Inn. He had recommended the lobster, and she was happy to follow his directive once again. This was his town now after all.

'How do you imagine I felt when you turned up unannounced at The Lemon Tree Hotel not so long ago?' she retorted.

'My God,' he said. 'It already feels like very long ago to me.'

'Is that so?' But Chiara had to agree. When she thought about everything that had happened since . . .

'But you came here alone?' Dante looked around the cosy bar as if some holiday companion might suddenly vaporise and join them at their table. *Allora*. That too had happened before.

The waitress brought over their wine. Dante poured them both a glass, and Chiara took a tentative sip. It wasn't the wine of the Cinque Terre, but it was good nonetheless.

'Completely alone,' she confirmed. '*Salute*.'

'*Salute*.' Again, he raised an eyebrow.

And he deserved an explanation. 'I needed a break,' she began. 'It has been a very busy and eventful end to the summer.'

Dante picked up his glass. 'I wonder what your husband might say to that.' He held the red wine up to the light as if he might see some answers there.

'Alonzo and I have decided to separate.' She said this quickly, could hardly look at him. 'I don't want to go into the details.'

424

He shrugged. But if she had been expecting his eyes to light up with hope – they didn't. And why should they? She had rejected him twice already. If nothing else, his pride must have taken quite a battering.

'So?'

'So, as I already said, I thought I'd take a holiday,' she said. Keep it simple – that was probably the best way. After everything that had happened between them she felt strangely insecure. She didn't know what Dante felt now. She couldn't tell. She'd never seen him so in control of his emotions.

And they had kept it simple – so far. Over dinner she had told him about Isabella and Ferdinand Bauer.

'She should give love a chance,' Dante had said.

'Ever the romantic,' Chiara had been able to tease.

And she had told him about Elene and Silvio, and their plans for renovation, the sketches made by the Signor Bauer himself.

'A bit cheeky of them,' he observed, cracking a claw and extracting the meat with the lobster fork.

'You are not joking.'

'But, Chiara, my dear . . .'

'Yes?' She raised her eyes and found herself staring into the dark brown depths of his.

'Why was your daughter unable to express to you how much she wanted things to change?'

'That's a question I have been asking myself,' she admitted. She mixed a little mayonnaise dressing with her salad. It was an Italian-style salad, a nice mixture of leaves, and really very good. Elene's feelings on the matter were something she had already tried to address, but she felt there was a lot more to be said. What would it take, she wondered, for Elene to tell her what she really thought – about everything?

'And Alonzo?' He asked this at the end of the evening, even though Chiara had told him she didn't want to discuss it.

'He will live in Pisa full time.'

Dante nodded. 'And so, you thought you could come and find me, and . . .'

Give our love a chance at last, thought Chiara. But he looked so despondent. Did he imagine that she thought she could just click her fingers and he would come running? *Was* that what she had thought?

'Didn't I mention, Dante?' Chiara finished the last of her wine. It was time to return to the B & B – alone. 'I felt I needed to take a holiday, that is all.'

Of course, both of them knew that wasn't all. How could it be?

Today, Dante took Chiara up the cliff in the other direction. He pointed out the places where the sandstone had eroded. 'The cliff, it is vulnerable,' he said. 'To the wind and the rain.'

She nodded. They were all vulnerable.

They walked down on to another beach where a few small wooden boats had been discarded on the pebbles and left to rot, the peeling paintwork just a snapshot memory of what they had once been.

'This is Eype,' he told her. 'It's my favourite beach around here. I come here quite often.'

Chiara gazed over the pebbles to the earthy green waves rolling in to shore, leaving arcs of white sea-foam on the beach behind them. 'It's lovely.' Even on this blustery October day. It was not like the beaches of the Riviera Ligure di Levante naturally – nothing could compare to Sestri Levante and the Bay of Silence . . . But it was wild, and it had a sense of vastness and clarity. She could certainly see the appeal.

Dante took her up the lane and across Eype Down to a small café attached to a farm.

'Dante!' A silver-haired woman sitting at an outside table jumped to her feet. 'I was coming to see you later.'

'Hello, Maddy.' He spread his hands and grinned.

That grin, thought Chiara. It was good to see that grin. But who was Maddy, so able to inspire it?

'Well, as you see, here I am.'

'But not with your *gelato*,' she teased. Her blue eyes sparked with humour. She was around their age, Chiara guessed, with a slim figure and a ready smile. She felt a small stab of pain in her chest. Was it jealousy? They seemed to know one another rather well.

'I took a day off from the *gelato*,' he admitted. 'Don't hate me.'

'How could I?' She beamed.

Chiara stood there feeling totally excluded. She had been an idiot to come here. She should have known. Of course, Dante was going to meet someone else eventually – an attractive man like him. Clearly, he already had – which was why he had been so reserved the night before. And how could she blame him? It was a miracle he had waited so long – if he had in fact waited at all . . .

'Hello there.' The woman – Maddy – smiled at her, and Chiara attempted a graceful smile back. She must make the best of it and then leave as soon as she could in order to preserve what little dignity she had left. 'Hello.'

'This is Chiara.' Dante seemed to realise that he had been remiss with the introductions. 'A friend from Italy.'

A friend . . . The casual words stung. 'I'm pleased to meet you.' Chiara extended a hand.

427

'And you.' Maddy's eyes were frank and curious as she shook it. 'Are you here on holiday?'

Chiara avoided Dante's amused glance. 'Yes,' she said. 'Just for a day or two.'

'A day or two?' Dante turned to face her. 'That is all?'

'Well, I can't have you skiving off work in order to show me around,' she threw back at him. 'There are the fans of your famous *gelato* to consider.' Because she had now tried it, and it was very good.

'You have a point, my dear.' Maddy laughed and waved them away. 'Go ahead, have your lunch and your catch-up. I'll be in touch later, Dante, OK?'

'OK,' he said.

They were quiet as they walked back along the cliff-top.

'She seemed very nice,' Chiara said at last, 'your friend.'

'Oh, she is.' Dante paused and gazed out towards the grey-green ocean. The clouds were building. It looked as if they were in for some rain.

'I'm glad,' Chiara blurted.

'Glad?'

'That you've met someone.'

There was a pause. It grew longer and longer, and still she couldn't look at him.

'Chiara.'

At last, she turned. 'Yes, Dante?'

'Why have you come here – really?'

She shook her head. The sea breeze was catching the words from her throat and she felt she couldn't say a thing.

He took a step closer. He put his hands on her shoulders. 'Maddy is just a friend,' he said. 'She happens to have a husband – I have supper with them sometimes. They live only three doors away from me.'

'I see.' Now she felt even more of a fool. But he hadn't made a move towards her the night before. Here she was, on her own, on his territory, and he had given her nothing but a chaste kiss on the cheek. 'But I'd expected . . .' Her voice trailed. What had she expected? Dante wasn't one given to fleeting liaisons – he had told her as much. He wanted a long-term relationship. He always had. When they had spent the night together back at The Lemon Tree Hotel after her argument with Alonzo, that is what he'd thought they were embarking on.

'You have turned me away not once but twice,' he reminded her now.

'Third time lucky?' she whispered.

He chuckled and pulled her closer, into a proper hug. 'I've always liked a woman with a sense of humour,' he growled into her ear. 'But . . .'

'But what?'

He drew away from her once more. He still hadn't kissed her, and she was beginning to doubt he ever would. 'What is the real purpose of your visit?' he asked again. 'The truth now.'

A gull shrieked in the darkening sky. Chiara took a deep breath. 'I wanted to see you.'

He nodded. 'I'm not an arrogant man, Chiara, but I had gathered that much.'

Chiara stood up straighter. 'I'm not making assumptions, Dante,' she said. 'I know I've let you down – more than once.'

'This is true.'

'And I don't even know if anything could ever happen between us now.'

He gave her the eyebrow.

'But I wanted to try.' There, she'd said it. But of course, he must have known.

'Did you indeed?' He stroked her hair from her face and tucked a stray tendril behind her ear. The gesture was almost unbearably tender.

'I wanted to let you know that I care.'

He stared at her for what seemed like minutes. Would he kiss her now? Apparently not. Instead he tucked her arm in his. 'It's too cold to be discussing this on the cliff-top,' he said. 'We will go to my house. We will talk. We will drink wine, and I will cook you dinner.'

Chiara caught her breath. This was what she had wanted, but . . . 'I could leave,' she said.

'So soon?'

'Maybe tomorrow. If I'm in the way, I mean.'

They negotiated the path downhill. 'You're not in the way,' he said. 'But I don't know if I have the strength to let you hurt me again.'

'What do you mean?' Chiara felt the tears sting her cheeks. But she knew.

'Can you give up The Lemon Tree Hotel?' he asked her. 'That is the bottom line, *no*? Would you be ready to leave your life in Italy and come here to be a part of mine?'

Chiara knew that at this point she had to be totally honest. 'I don't know.' She sniffed.

'Exactly.' He quickened his pace. 'So, are you asking me to leave this place, this place that I have made my home, this place that I love?'

She shook her head.

'Are you asking me to give up my business?'

'No, of course not.'

'Because it may only be *gelato*.' He sounded very defensive now. 'And it may only be a kiosk by the harbour . . .'

'But it tastes good,' she finished for him.

'Yes.' He shook his head in mock despair. 'It tastes good, and it is my life.'

'I understand that, Dante.' And she did. What had she been thinking when she came over here? She hadn't really thought, had she? She hadn't grasped the implications – that she and Dante lived so far apart from one another, one of them would have to leave.

She couldn't ask him to leave Dorset. It wouldn't be right. Which meant that if she wanted to be with him she would have to move over here – there was no other way. Even Elene had recognised that fact. Chiara would have to leave the hotel she loved, Elene, Isabella, Giovanna – everything and everyone she cared for. Could she do that? Did she have the courage? Was she ready to give up so much?

'*Bene*.' He patted her hand. 'I needed you to understand. But it is good to see you, Chiara.'

'And you.'

'And perhaps after I have cooked you dinner,' he suggested, 'we can talk about this some more.'

Chiara sighed. 'All right, yes.' So, she had to come to a decision, Dante had made that plain. He would not allow her to throw herself into his arms. He would be making no grand gestures and it would have to be her this time who made all the sacrifices. Otherwise . . .

It would not happen. Chiara hung on a little tighter to his arm. She had come all this way – but for what? She could have

431

Dante, but not her life in the Cinque Terre – she would lose her precious Lemon Tree Hotel. Or she could have a life there – but without the man she loved. That was her decision – and she had to make it tonight.

CHAPTER 49

Chiara

Dante's house was exactly as she might have imagined it if she had ever allowed herself to think about it in any detail. He lived in West Bay in an old fisherman's cottage just off the sea front. It was small and white with tiny square windows and was perhaps in need of a lick of paint, but it was perfectly formed and had views of the snaking river and the impossibly green hills beyond.

It was funny to see Dante working in the kitchen, shirt-sleeves rolled up, wearing an over-sized navy and white striped apron, while she sat on his antique brown leather sofa, legs crossed, sipping a delicious gin and tonic he'd made for her earlier. They'd talked so much today about so many different things – she felt that she was getting to understand how he lived his life here in England for the very first time.

He was pan-frying two whole plaice that had been caught in the bay only hours before, and serving them with sautéed potatoes and a crisp green salad. He'd allowed her to peel the potatoes, but nothing else. 'Relax, Chiara,' he'd said. 'You are on holiday, is that not so?'

'As you like.' She was happy to accept the tease. And so, she had done just that – it was so pleasant to relax, here in his territory, after all. She chuckled as he whisked the potatoes into another pan, doing the cooking in the same way he seemed to do everything – with gusto.

'Something amusing you?'

'It's just that . . .' How could she explain? It wasn't only the gusto. It was the pure domesticity of it – a situation that she would never have envisaged. She and Dante had spent such a short time together over the years when you counted it up. There had been those first two encounters – one in Corniglia when he had sent off those boys who were bothering her, and one in Vernazza when he was looking after the old lady. Followed by Chiara's dreams about destiny . . . There had been their passionate and whispered meetings in the olive grove not long afterwards, there had been plans and promises – most of which had never come to fruition. Then he had left, and when he returned all those years later, there had been walking and more talking, drinks and dinner and then . . . At last, a night of love.

Chiara took a sip of her drink, hoping it would cool the heat that had risen to her cheeks on remembering that night. And what a night it had been for two people far from the first flush of youth. 'We don't even know each other very well,' she said. 'And yet here we are.'

'*Allora*. Here we are indeed.' He turned and brandished a spatula at her. 'Talking about whether we might spend the rest of our lives together.'

'Exactly.' She put her drink back on the glass-topped coffee table beside her. 'I thought of you though, Dante,' she said. 'I thought about you a lot, you know.'

'Ah — at least in the beginning.' He turned back to his pan, but she knew he was teasing again. This Dante was not as uncompromising as the young Dante had been. He was gentler, more mellow — and his sense of humour had improved since coming to England, for sure. She relaxed back further into the sofa. The enticing fragrance of the plaice and the dill and lemon with caramelised garlic wafted in the air.

Chiara breathed in deeply. 'And beyond,' she assured him. 'I imagined you making your living here in England, finding your way in your new life, chatting up all the single women in West Dorset . . .'

'And there are quite a few,' he pointed out — rather unnecessarily in Chiara's opinion.

'I even imagined you coming back to Vernazza.'

He grinned at that. At last. How she loved that grin. Dante seemed to put all of himself into his grin. 'But by the time I actually did come back — you'd stopped expecting it, I think?'

'I certainly had.' She regarded him over the rim of her glass as she picked it up to take another sip. There was something about gin and tonic — something deliciously anticipatory and crisp. She re-crossed her legs. 'And did you ever think of me, may I ask?'

'Every day.' Expertly, he turned the fish in the pan.

'Dante . . .'

'The woman I wanted the most. The woman I could never have.' He tossed the sautéed potatoes in the other pan. 'Ready, I think.'

He brought the food over and dished it up on to their plates. Chiara took a sniff. 'Mmm. It smells divine.'

Dante opened a bottle of Sauvignon Blanc and they sat down at the table squashed between the kitchen and living area of the open-plan ground floor. Even the stairs rose up from this space – every square centimetre had been used. It was definitely, Chiara thought, a house for one. Would she want to live in this tiny cottage? Would it give her the space she needed? She looked around. Pictures of the sandstone cliffs at West Bay on the white walls, a Turkish rug on the bleached floorboards, wooden blinds at the windows.

'What?' He poured the wine. '*Salute*.'

'*Salute*.' They clinked glasses, and she picked up her knife and fork. 'Just that there's nothing Italian here at all.'

'And why should there be?' He sliced into his fish and breathed in the aroma.

'Because you are still Italian,' she reminded him sternly. 'I thought there might be something from our homeland here in your house.'

'There might be.' He raised an eyebrow. 'You haven't seen the bedroom yet.'

'Dante . . .' She took her first bite of the fish. It was so full of flavour, and melted in her mouth. Even Elene would have approved. 'This is delicious.'

'Thank you, *Signora*.' He bent his head.

'You are very welcome.' But where did they go from here? Chiara took another mouthful. Who would have thought that Dante would be such a good cook? Today they had discussed every subject under the sun. She knew how he lived his life here in West Dorset – how many hours he worked, how he got on with the people, what he did in his spare time. She knew where he liked walking, what films and plays he'd seen, what music he listened to these days. They'd got on to politics – of both Britain and Italy, and had even touched on football. As for her life, she had told him what had led to her eventual break with Alonzo, and many other things besides.

'Are you lonely, Chiara?' he had asked her.

'Not at all,' she'd replied. 'How could I be lonely with my family so close by? With The Lemon Tree Hotel, and all our guests to look after?'

'So, let me guess,' he said now. 'Were you wondering – how can I even think about giving up my very fulfilling life in Vernazza for a man I've hardly spent any time with?'

She shrugged. 'For a man who is barely more than a fantasy,' she teased. Because two could play at that game.

He leaned forwards. 'And yet,' he said.

'And yet.' His eyes were still dark and still smouldered just as they always had. His hair was grey and silver now, but gave him a dignified look that was just as attractive as the piratical charm he'd had in his youth.

'I came all the way here to see you,' she reminded him.

'You did.'

'You still move me.'

'And you me, Chiara,' he said. 'And you me.' The look in his eyes told her he wanted to take her into that bedroom of his, and she had to admit that she ached for it too.

'And although we haven't spent so very much time together . . .' she paused '. . . still, I know you.'

'Sì.' She saw the understanding in his dark eyes. She had known him from the first moment they met – and he her. It had indeed seemed to be destiny.

'So . . .' She forced her attention back to the food. It was far too good to waste.

'We fell in love.' He took another mouthful and washed it down with some wine.

'Yes.' Now, that she couldn't deny.

'And whereas some people fall out of love, divorce, die, or simply forget one another . . .' He let the words hang.

'The feelings between us remained the same.' Her voice wasn't much more than a whisper now. She put down her cutlery. 'We didn't forget. But it's crazy isn't it, Dante? I mean, before tonight I've never even seen you cook a meal.'

He speared a potato. 'And I hate to point this out to you, my dear Chiara, but I haven't seen you cook at all.'

'What?'

'Perhaps you can't.' His eyes shone with humour now. 'Perhaps I am considering taking on a woman who doesn't know one end of *la cucina* from the other, hmm?'

'Why you . . . You!' Chiara picked up her knife and fork again and returned to her meal. The fish was so delicate; the potatoes crisp on the outside and fluffy inside.

He took pity on her. 'But you're right. I understand what you're saying.'

'Do you?'

'Yes. You're saying that we are contemplating a huge life change with someone we hardly know. We may not have forgotten one another. But is this feeling between us real? Or is it some romantic dream?'

'Exactly.' She sipped her wine.

'Have we been thinking of each other all these years because we haven't met someone else we could be happy with – or were we unable to be happy with that someone else because the right person was someone else?'

'Hmm.' Put like that, it sounded even more complicated than she had thought. Chiara helped herself to more salad. The

438

dressing he had prepared was also very delicious, with just the right hint of balsamic.

He put his head to one side, considering. 'Perhaps it depends on what we think about love?'

'Perhaps.' Or perhaps they shouldn't even have started this conversation.

'Perhaps we shouldn't try to analyse what it is we have between us? Perhaps we should simply give in to it, don't you think?'

Now, he was reminding her of how he had been when he came to The Lemon Tree Hotel. Intense, persuasive, seductive, charming, irresistible . . . She dared to glance up at him. He had finished eating, and had folded his arms, a small smile playing around his mouth. She looked away. Really, anyone would think that this was just a game to him. 'But it pays to be cautious,' she remarked.

'Does it?'

'Well, yes. Just as you were saying earlier. We don't want to hurt each other all over again. We need to be sure.'

'And are you sure, Chiara?'

'Yes.' She answered almost without thinking. Perhaps she shouldn't be mixing gin and wine after all.

'Sure enough to leave The Lemon Tree Hotel and come to live here in West Bay with me?'

Chiara couldn't escape the feeling that Dante had somehow manipulated the conversation so that it would arrive at this point. Was she that sure?

She thought of Elene and the coolness she often saw in her eyes. If Chiara wasn't there, Elene might flourish. She had Silvio and Isabella – this independence could be just what her daughter needed. She thought of Isabella, who seemed

439

to understand her grandmother and The Lemon Tree Hotel so well. Isabella was young. She would miss Chiara, but she would find a nice young man, and she would throw herself into the business just as her grandmother had done before her. She thought of Giovanna, who sadly must be getting to the end of her days. The others would look after Giovanna, Chiara had no worries about that. And she thought of The Lemon Tree Hotel and all the love and work she had put into it.

Could she ever leave? It was her legacy from her parents – but it was a legacy that she could now hand over to Elene and Isabella. She had done her job, and they could be trusted. Giovanna had been right – it was Chiara's time now. And finally, she thought of her beloved Cinque Terre – the blue skies and seas, the colourful houses, the prickly pears and the olive groves, the scent of lemons in the courtyard. Dante was right though. It was just a place. It was just a hotel – however much she cared for it. It wasn't – it should not be – everything. Because Chiara only had one life, and this was the man she loved.

'Yes,' she said. 'I'm that sure.'

Dante's eyes widened. 'Really, Chiara? You would give it all up and come and live here with me?'

'Really, Dante. I would, yes.' She took a deep breath and pushed her plate away. She couldn't eat another thing.

He took her hands over the table. 'I never thought I would hear you say that,' he marvelled.

Chiara had never thought she would say it either. She got to her feet. 'Will you hold me?' she asked.

Almost before the words were out of her mouth, Dante had taken a step around the table and she was in his arms, feeling the strength of him, the softness of his touch, the scent that was Dante's alone.

They drew apart. 'My love,' he whispered. He cupped her head in the palm of his hand. They stared at one another, and this time Chiara didn't look away. He kissed her, slowly at first and then with a gathering urgency, and she could feel herself responding to every touch of his lips, every breath that he took.

'Dante,' she said. 'I think I would like to see the bedroom after all.'

He chuckled. 'Sounds like a plan, *cara*.' And then he was suddenly serious. 'We have so much to plan, you and I.'

He was right. You couldn't analyse love or how it worked, how a spark could take you and hold you. It was more than enough that it was there.

Chiara's mobile began to ring. She turned. 'I should . . .'

'Of course.' He stepped back. 'And then I have something more to confess to you, my love.'

'Really?' Distracted, she picked up the call. It was Elene. 'Elene? How are you, darling?'

'Mamma.'

'What is it?' There was something in her voice. Some need that Chiara hadn't heard for so long – if at all.

'Mamma – it's Isabella.'

'What?' A surge of panic made her legs buckle. She dropped back into the leather sofa, her senses on high alert. 'What's happened to her? Tell me.'

'She's hurt. There's been a terrible landslide. She's in hospital.'

'In hospital?' A landslide? 'How bad is she?'

'Bad enough.' There was a pause, and Chiara could hear the emotion in her daughter's voice, she could feel her tears. 'Mamma, we need you. Please – will you come home?'

CHAPTER 50

Isabella

Isabella was conscious of her mother sitting by her bed. 'Where am I?' she managed to whisper. Not in her own bed in The Lemon Tree Hotel, that much seemed certain.

'In hospital, my darling.' Her mother gently squeezed her hand. 'You're in hospital in La Spezia.'

Hospital. That made sense. Isabella closed her eyes. She couldn't think about it now. She was too tired.

Later, or the next day perhaps, she was aware of nurses drifting past. Sometimes one would come up to the bed and talk to her, their face close and kind. Sometimes, Isabella thought she spoke to them, sometimes, she did not. She was conscious of her father too, she instinctively sensed his worry. The hospital was warm and yet clinical, the sheets and blankets felt heavy on her legs. From time to time someone helped her sit up and she drank water through a straw. Or there was a doctor asking her questions she couldn't seem to focus on. People swam in and out of her vision. Once, her grandfather was there by her bedside, and she felt faintly surprised to see him. Her head hurt.

442

Some time on, and gradually things became clearer. Her mother was still there. Often, she read to her in her cool, clear voice. 'Do you remember anything, Isabella?' she asked her.

'I don't know.' But then Isabella tasted the fear that she had felt that afternoon and she began to remember. She remembered that morning in Vernazza, the dark ominous grey of the sky, the fast-moving clouds, the sense of premonition that she had blithely ignored. She remembered the fat raindrops and sitting on the rocks by the far promontory watching the wild waves send spray high on to the harbour arm. She remembered a whisker of fear as she scurried down to take shelter, aware of the rain getting harder, the wind howling, the water around her feet suddenly becoming a brown river. And the noise; the rush and the dark noise, before she slipped and fell.

'What happened?' she whispered at last.

'There was a landslide, my darling.' Her mother was holding her hand again. She seemed different here in the hospital, quieter and more tender. And she seemed to be here all the time. But if she was here . . . What was happening with the hotel? Was Nonna looking after things? But no, Nonna had gone away, she remembered that too . . .

'Nonna?'

'She's on her way here.'

'What happened to me, Mamma?' Isabella turned and looked into her mother's eyes. 'I fell, didn't I?'

'Yes, you slipped on the pavement, we think.' Her mother winced. 'It was chaotic, by all accounts. Someone grabbed you and pulled you into the bar. I haven't had time to find out who. People were sheltering there.'

'Sheltering?'

'From the mudslide. It was taking away everything in its path, you see. Bins, chairs, tables, cars even.'

Isabella stared at her. She remembered it now – the brackish-brown torrent of mud and water roaring like a monster, moving like a living creature, sucking up the town. What would have happened if no one had pulled her into the bar? Would she simply have been swept away and drowned in a sea of mud? She shuddered.

'Hush, darling.' Her mother stroked her hair. 'You're safe now.'

'Was there . . .' Isabella frowned '. . . much damage?'

Someone swore softly and Isabella realised her father was at her bedside too. 'Papà?'

He came around to take her other hand. 'Vernazza is all but destroyed,' he said. 'The mud, the rocks, the water, the debris . . . It all swept down from the mountains and raged through the town, burying it four metres deep. It wasn't just one mudslide my love, there were a lot more.'

Isabella struggled to take this in. 'But . . .'

'You mustn't worry.' That was her mother now. 'You had a bad knock to the head and a few cracked ribs, otherwise just cuts and bruises. You're getting better, everything will be fine.'

'But Vernazza?' Isabella could hardly believe it. There had been landslides before, but nothing like what her father had just described.

'Yes, it is a terrible thing,' her mother acknowledged. 'But people are coming together and working to make good. Volunteers have been helping those who were trapped in their houses on the top floors. Foreign visitors have been evacuated in boats already.' She squeezed Isabella's hand again. 'We will rebuild the town. We still have our spirit, and we can recover.

It can be done.' She looked over at Isabella's father and let out a small sigh. 'But you mustn't think of it now. You must only think about resting and getting better, my darling.'

'Was anyone hurt – badly hurt?'

'I'm not sure. Perhaps. It's all been a bit muddled and confused. A few people are missing. No one really knows yet.'

'The gas . . .' She could remember the overpowering sickly-sweet smell of it. It was almost the last thing she did remember.

'The town's five-hundred-gallon propane tank was ripped off the hillside,' her father told her. 'The whistling noise it made was unbelievable – it went down into the town while it was still spewing gas.'

'I remember that whistling noise,' she whispered.

'There, my darling, don't think of it now. Silvio . . .' her mother broke in.

But Isabella wanted to know everything. 'And the hotel?' She could feel a sense of panic flying through her now.

'The hotel survived.' Her mother reached over to put a cool palm on her forehead. 'You're hot. I should call a nurse . . .'

'I'm fine.' Isabella felt a flicker of irritation. But the town . . .

'We weren't in the direct pathway of the mudslide,' her father explained. 'There was some power loss and telephone lines have been down. The railway station is out of action too of course, for the moment at least. But no damage to The Lemon Tree to speak of.'

'Thank goodness.' Isabella closed her eyes and then opened them again. 'Ferdinand,' she said.

'Ferdinand?' Once again, her mother looked at her father. That wasn't a good sign. Isabella would have expected him to be here too.

'He hasn't been here to see me?'

'He checked out, my darling, don't you remember?' Her mother patted her hand.

'After the landslide?' Isabella was confused. She didn't remember. And she would remember that, surely?

'Before.'

'Ah.' Which was why he hadn't been to see her. Like Nonna, he probably couldn't get through. He would be in Germany by now. Did he even know about the landslide? Had it been bad enough for the news to have reached other countries? Isabella shifted in the narrow hospital bed. She felt clamped down by the sheets, imprisoned by them. But something was bothering her about this. That was it. She certainly did remember. And he hadn't said goodbye. 'But did he leave a note for me? A message?'

'I don't believe so, darling.' Her mother frowned. 'Are you certain you didn't know he was leaving?'

'No.' And he hadn't said goodbye. How could he have left without saying goodbye?

'What does it matter?' her father growled. 'We have other things to think of now, you know.'

Isabella felt a tear crawl from her eye.

'I'm sorry, my darling.'

She couldn't bear to see the pity in her mother's eyes. Her mother knew that it mattered. She understood. Isabella sighed. Nonna had been right then. Ferdinand had come here for his own reasons – or for his father's reasons, she should say. He had got what he came for, and now he had left – without a word to her. He had used her and then discarded her. He hadn't ever trusted her – that was the truth. This explained why he had created a distance between them after they had uncovered the

446

painting of the Last Supper – he had detached his emotions; she had not been mistaken about that. And now Vernazza . . . Another tear crept out from under her closed eyelids. And now her beloved Vernazza was destroyed, and nothing would ever be the same again.

CHAPTER 51

Elene

Elene stood to one side so that her mother could sit next to Isabella. Chiara looked exhausted. She had hugged Elene the second she entered the room, a proper big hug that had taken Elene by surprise. It had also felt wonderful though. There was nothing quite like the hug from your mother, the woman who had nurtured you, given birth to you, unconditionally loved you. She wiped away a tear. She was so emotional these days – it looked as if Isabella was going to make a complete recovery, but even so, since the landslide, Elene had felt as if she were riding on an emotional roller coaster, dissolving into tears at the slightest provocation. It really wasn't like her at all.

'I came as quickly as I could,' her mother whispered into her hair. 'Are you all right?'

'Yes, Mamma.'

'And Silvio? And Aunt Giovanna? The staff?'

'All fine.'

'*Va bene.*' She drew away. 'How is she?' And now her

attention was fully focused on her beloved granddaughter, propped up in the hospital bed, a wan smile on her face.

'Better. She will be fine.' Elene followed her mother over to Isabella's bedside.

'Bella.' She took her hand. 'Darling, Bella. I leave you for five minutes and what do you do?'

'Nonna . . .'

Elene smiled as she watched them, her mother and daughter. Why had she ever resented this closeness between the two women she loved best in all the world? She really couldn't remember. What did it matter? They were all safe, and it didn't seem important now.

After half an hour, her mother got to her feet. Isabella was tiring. Clearly, she was ready for some sleep. But she was frowning and she hadn't let go of her grandmother's hand.

'You mustn't worry about anything, Bella,' Chiara was telling her.

Isabella half opened her eyes. 'That's what Mamma keeps saying.'

'And she is right.'

Elene caught her mother's eye as she looked across at her. She gave her a small nod. Isabella hadn't stopped asking about Ferdinand Bauer, and Elene knew her mother's views on that subject. She wanted to ease her daughter's unhappiness, but she didn't know what to tell her – Elene didn't know what to make of his sudden departure either. It was a little odd that he had simply left without saying goodbye, and rather a coincidence that it had been on one of the last trains that had departed from Vernazza before the terrible mudslide occurred. But some men could not be trusted, that was the truth.

Elene was lucky that she had Silvio. He had been her absolute rock since this awful disaster – she didn't know how she would have managed without him. When they'd realised that Isabella might be down there . . . Silvio had wasted no time. He was a man who would support his family no matter what, and she felt that she was fully appreciating this for the first time. As for love . . . She sniffed, and her mother looked up sharply. *Allora*, it seemed that love had crept up on Elene, softly, softly. Unless, that is, it had been there all along.

'But so much is destroyed . . .' Isabella too was crying again. All their emotions were so close to the surface, and it was the same with everyone Elene had spoken to since it had happened. No one could quite believe it. They had survived – at least most of them had survived – but what was left of their town? Silvio and Elene had seen it from their vantage point above. It was a shell of its previous self, barely a muddy whisper of its former beauty.

Elene took a tissue from the box on the bedside table and gently dabbed her daughter's eyes. 'It can be rebuilt,' she said staunchly. Though already she knew that the task of rebuilding Vernazza would be long, hard, and complicated. Even so, she had seen her people working together to unload emergency supplies on that first day after it had happened, some of them trying to dig out the mud burying Piazza Marconi with their bare hands, and she had witnessed such generosity of spirit that she had felt quite humbled. Because of these things she was sure that Vernazza would survive and rebuild – thanks to the strength of its people, its community.

'Yes.' Her mother caught her arm and gave it a little squeeze. 'Vernazza and those who love her will start again. You can start again too, my Bella. Together, we can all come back from this, my love.'

Elene listened to her words and wondered what they meant. Was she coming back to them, back to The Lemon Tree Hotel? Had her mother found Dante Rossi in England? And if so, what had happened between them?

The two women had coffee in the hospital café while Isabella was sleeping.

'Perhaps I shouldn't have asked you to come back,' Elene said. 'I suppose I overreacted. I could have waited, at least. I shouldn't have made you cut short your holiday when you haven't been away for so long.' At the time though it was all she had wanted: for her mother to be here, to help her, to support her. Isabella was hurt and it was an instinctive reaction. Elene had been terrified. She hadn't known how bad it was. Her father had come to the hospital too, of course. He had visited his granddaughter and asked if there was anything he could do. 'No, Papà.' She was glad that he had come – but what could any of them do except wait for Isabella to recover?

'Absolutely not.' Her mother sat up straighter in her chair. 'Of course you had to let me know what had happened. I would have been furious if you had not.'

Elene smiled. Her mother furious was not something anyone would want to experience.

'And I would not hesitate for a moment. Naturally I would have come home as soon as I possibly could – even if you had not asked me to.' She nodded to emphasise her point.

'Thank you, Mamma.' And she had called it 'home'. Elene took her hand and squeezed it gently. It was quite something to know that you only had to ask, and that someone – that special someone – would drop everything to be by your side.

'But tell me what happened in Vernazza?' Her mother's eyes were sad. 'How bad is it?'

Elene began to tell her what she knew and what she had found out since. They were getting more information every day. 'It began as a severe rainstorm.' She remembered that morning in the kitchen. She'd been making her *buridda*. Silvio had come in and . . . She smiled at the memory – though it seemed so long ago. 'I noticed a strange atmosphere outside. But I thought it was a storm brewing – nothing more.'

Chiara nodded.

'And then it increased. Within hours the storm was raging. The rain and the wind were so strong – they lifted soil, vines, rocks, all the plants that were growing. Everything gathered together into a massive mudslide that came down in a torrent from the mountain.'

Chiara shuddered.

'People realised what was happening – but not at first. They ran for shelter, roads were closed, the electricity went down—'

'And Isabella?'

'Isabella happened to be down in Vernazza at the time.' Elene paused. 'She hadn't been quite herself . . .'

Her mother grimaced. 'Ferdinand Bauer?'

'I think so.' But Elene hadn't really talked to Isabella about it, had she? In many ways she'd been as guilty as her mother before her – of getting on with her own life, of imagining that Isabella was fine, that she'd get over it, that it was just a mild flirtation, a crush, something that would easily pass . . . she hadn't tried to find out what was wrong.

'And?'

'And she was running for shelter when she slipped in the mud pouring down the street in Via Roma.'

'And hit her head?'

'We think so.' Although everything had been so noisy and chaotic that they would probably never know for certain.

'And then someone pulled her to safety?'

'Apparently so. The water level was rising inside as well as out. In the cafés, shops, and bars it got to more than half a metre. People had to go up to the next floor to escape it – if they were able to.'

'So the townspeople were trapped inside their own houses?' Her mother was aghast.

Elene nodded. 'Everyone was trapped. It was a complete nightmare. A continuous wave of mud thundering down from the hilltops, carrying everything that stood in its path along with it in a river of mud and rainwater.' She sipped her coffee. It was more bitter than she preferred, but it still hit the spot. 'Someone at the hospital took a video from above Via Roma – she showed me. And I saw some of it for myself when we went down to look for Isabella. It was horrendous, Mamma. Cars and trucks being sucked into this muddy brown whirlpool. Rubbish bins, car bumpers, tables, patio umbrellas. And the noise of it! It was like the worst kind of thunder. Entrances and exits were blocked, the water level was still rising, entire buildings were beginning to collapse.' There had been plenty of time in the last few days to hear the stories – each one more horrific than the last.

'My God, no . . .'

'But, yes. At the Blue Marlin they broke down the back wall of Massimo's restaurant just to escape the flood up an abandoned set of stairs. Good for Massi, eh – he helped an awful lot of people.'

'It sounds as if he did, oh, Elene . . .' Chiara shook her head. There were tears in her eyes.

'Some people gathered for safety in the gift shop at the station, others were taken to Al Castello. Everyone who can do, has helped out, giving water, food and shelter.'

'Al Castello . . .' They shared a glance. They both knew that centuries before, villagers from Vernazza had defended themselves from pirate raids in this very building. The irony was not lost on them.

'Many citizens and tourists gathered at the City Hall – apparently they knew already that things were going to get worse. They got food and shelter there. By then it was a case of damage limitation, I suppose.' She sighed. 'And then there was more.'

'Another landslide?'

'A worse one.'

'What happened after that?' her mother whispered. Her face was pale.

'More buildings buried deeper, more buildings collapsing. People must have thought their end had come. It was pitch black by then, of course. Around midnight the rain began to let up and the rescue process began.'

'When did you find Isabella?' Her mother seemed distraught. She had entirely lost her usual air of calm; her eyes were wide and her hair was in disarray from the number of times she had torn her fingers through it.

Elene realised that her mother did not need to know everything. And so. She would not tell her of the woman who had clung to a tree stump wedged in the wall for hours before she was rescued, or of the man who had died in order for his family to be saved. She would not speak of how she and Silvio had left the hotel and gone down as close as they could get to the town. She would not tell her of the hysteria, the

454

panic, nor that they too had brought people up to The Lemon Tree for shelter and safety on higher ground – all the time still searching for their Isabella – searching, hoping, praying that by some miracle she had survived. She would not tell her that Silvio had risked his own life to find his daughter. Her mother could read between the lines – but she did not need to know the worst of it. Elene would protect her from that, at least.

She told her how, when daylight broke the following day, helicopters were able to fly in to help the search and rescue effort. Trains and boats had stopped operating, and the hiking trails leading to and from Vernazza were blocked. For now, there was no other way in or out. By the next day, boats were able to come in close enough to take people to La Spezia. On that day they found out that Isabella was alive. But that first day after it had happened . . . Elene would not be able to live through those emotions again.

'Thank God you and Silvio were safe.' Chiara grasped Elene by the shoulders. Her voice trembled. 'And Aunt Giovanna.'

'And the hotel of course,' Elene heard herself saying.

Her mother threw her a reproving glance. 'The Lemon Tree is just a hotel,' she said. 'We must remember that, Elene. We are talking about people here. Our family. Our community.'

'Yes.' She was right – though Elene had never expected to hear her say it.

'Our community . . .' Her mother seemed lost in thought for a moment.

'And us,' Elene said. 'I've been thinking about us.' Because that was part of it. And she wanted to shake off the resentment. She wanted them all to make a new start, not just Vernazza.

Her mother pulled back. 'Us?'

'You and me,' Elene confirmed.

455

'Oh, Elene . . .' Her mother looked as if she wanted to hug her again.

Elene found herself blinking back another of those damned tears. 'When something happens to someone you love . . .'

Her mother was nodding. 'Life's so short,' she agreed.

'Exactly.' They clasped hands.

'I've always loved you so very much, Elene.' Her mother bit her lip. 'I didn't give you enough of my time, I see that now. I didn't value you enough or give you enough of a say. But I've always loved you so much.'

'You had other things to do. Hotels to save.' Elene smiled back at her. 'I understand. Truly I do. And you know, I didn't have a bad childhood, all things considered.'

Chiara laughed as she embraced her. 'I'm glad to hear that at least,' she said.

Later they walked arm in arm back to the ward.

'So, did you find him?' Elene asked at last. She was curious to know.

'Yes, I found him.'

'And?' Elene wondered how much she would mind what her mother might be about to say.

'And he insisted on coming back here with me.'

'He's here?' Elene stopped walking. She hadn't expected that.

'Oh, don't worry.' Her mother seemed quite blasé. 'He's back at the hotel. I don't think he's quite ready for my family yet.' She chuckled.

'I'm surprised.' Elene wasn't sure what she had expected – but it wasn't that.

'He's a good man,' her mother told her. 'I was in such a state

456

that he insisted on coming with me. And I'm sorry to tell you this, my darling, but that man is the love of my life.'

Elene turned to her, registered that glow in her mother's eyes once more. 'He wasn't the one who hit you, was he?' Though they were very hard words to say.

She shook her head. 'He didn't hit me. Dante would never hit me, Elene.'

Hadn't she known it? 'I see.' And what this meant was a truth that she must learn to accept.

'I walked into a door, as I always said.'

'Mamma.' She wouldn't let her mother lie to her – not any more.

Chiara sighed. 'Very well. But don't blame him too much, my darling. I too must shoulder some of the responsibility.'

'Why, Mamma?' Elene thought of her father and the love she had always felt for him. He had asked her to forgive him, because he would never ask her mother to do the same. Could she? He was her father, whatever he had done.

'I loved Dante Rossi long before I met Alonzo,' Chiara told her. 'I wasn't fair to your father. I married him to please my parents, but I could never quite stop loving Dante. Which was a disaster for all of us, I'm afraid.'

Elene absorbed the words. Her mother had never spoken so frankly to her before, and it explained a lot that she had never understood. *Allora*. She had a feeling that she and her mother would be able to speak a lot more honestly to one another after this.

'But you tried?'

'Oh, yes, my darling, for many years I tried.'

Elene sneaked a look at the woman by her side. So, there was one more thing she needed to know. Was her mother going to

457

leave Italy for good – was that what was going to happen? Was she going to go and live in England with her Dante? Would she leave her family, her community, The Lemon Tree Hotel? Could she really do such a thing – after this?

CHAPTER 52

Chiara

Chiara and Dante were in Vernazza. The train station was not yet open – even for residents – and many roads remained impassable. But Dante was a man who made it his business to organise things, and he had borrowed a boat to take them there by sea. He held out a hand to her, and Chiara climbed out on to the jetty. She was grateful for the contact, grateful that he was here. He seemed instinctively to understand so many things – how Chiara felt about this town, how she needed to see it, right now in its raw and battered state, to see for herself how bad things really were.

And they were bad. She couldn't speak at first, she just looked around her, appalled. The harbour itself was barely recognisable. The beach had been replaced by a massive pile of mud on which she could see the splintered remains of a few battered blue and white boats that had washed up to shore. Via Roma was still covered in mud – in fact the mud rose so high that it entirely obscured doors and windows.

As they walked slowly down the street, taking in this strange and unfamiliar landscape, Chiara recognised a first-floor balcony that now appeared to be on ground level, the sign for the pharmacy once hanging above its door also now level with the ground. Opposite this, the top of the awning of *Vineria Santa Marta* was the only part of the shop still visible. She was walking on top of people's businesses and homes – all buried under the mud and rubble. It was surreal and deeply disturbing.

Luckily, they had been sensible enough to wear waterproof boots. Around them, men in yellow and orange vests were already working with cranes and diggers to remove the mud, other people were wandering through the streets still looking lost and disorientated. Chiara recognised a few people she knew and she spoke with them in shocked whispers.

'It is barely believable.' She clung on to Dante's arm as they walked further up the street. The oleander trees in terracotta pots had been swept from the centre of Via Roma, even the colour had been leached from the fascias of the houses; everything seemed to be brown. The thick mud had splattered the walls and roofs. Fragments of buildings and other wreckage was strewn everywhere – pieces of wood, bits of plaster and stone, broken car parts, bins, sections of balconies, rocks of all sizes and endless tangles of vines. Telephone and electricity wires were down, thrown haphazardly into the road. The little chapel had all but disappeared. In the centre of Via Roma was a pile of debris running the whole length of the street, which had already been cleared away from the houses. But how could they get rid of so many tons of mud? Chiara couldn't imagine.

'Oh, Dante,' she said. 'Vernazza is destroyed.'

'It's still there,' he said. 'It's hidden, but it's still there.'

'Dante—'

'Don't say another word.' He held her close as they walked back down towards the harbour again.

'If there is anything we can do,' Chiara kept saying to the people they passed, who had lost their possessions and possibly their houses too. 'If you can get up to The Lemon Tree Hotel, there is someone there who can help. There's shelter at least, and we must have some provisions. We will take it from there.'

Back at the harbour, Chiara lifted her face towards the sea. It was no good. 'I have to say it, Dante,' she told him. She had been sure, she really had. But this – this had changed everything. It wasn't just a question of helping her family or looking after the hotel. It wasn't even the fact that for the first time she had seen the vulnerability and fear in Elene's eyes, or how much this had moved her and made her long for that new start with her daughter. It was so much more than that now – there was a whole community needing her help. They needed to stick together, they needed to work as a team. There were years of work ahead to salvage the beauty of Vernazza and return their village to its former glory. She could not walk away.

'You don't need to,' Dante said softly. 'I know you need to stay here in Vernazza. I know you need to be with your family.'

'Yes,' she said. 'I'm so sorry, my darling, but I do.'

He put his hands on her shoulders and faced her. 'You want to help with the rebuilding, I know.'

'Yes.' She was glad he understood. But even so, to lose him again . . . Her heart was almost breaking.

'You wouldn't be you if you didn't want to do that.' He drew her closer.

Chiara folded her body against him. He felt so good. She remembered how he had reacted when that phone call had come through from Elene. He hadn't questioned her decision to leave immediately – not for a second. He had given her brandy, made her sit down, gone online and booked them the very first available flights to Pisa. 'I am coming with you,' he had said. 'There is absolutely no way you are going through this on your own.'

He had taken her back to the B & B to collect her bags, and he had held her all night, not wanting or expecting anything other than that Chiara would allow him to stay close and comfort her. He had driven her to Bristol the following day and he had been beside her ever since. While she visited Isabella in hospital he had been finding out what they could do, who needed help, how he could get her over to Vernazza to see the damage for herself. And now . . . He was the sacrifice. 'But, Dante . . .'

'Hush.' He held her more tightly still. 'It will be OK. I will be here too.'

'No.' She looked up. She would not allow him to do this again. Why should he give up everything to come here – for her? Why should his entire life be put aside?

'You don't want me here?' But there was a small smile on his lips.

'It's not that.' He must know it wasn't that.

'These are my villages too, cara.' He looked out towards Monterosso, which had also been damaged, though not as badly as Vernazza. Dante's home village of Corniglia had suffered too of course, but not so severely, since it was built on higher ground. Nevertheless, they would go there on the way back to see if any of his old friends needed help. Any past hostilities would have been long-forgotten – they would all support one another now.

'I know, but—'

'I was always going to come back here with you,' he said softly.

'What do you mean?' She frowned, recalled what he had said about Dorset and his life in West Bay. 'What about your business? Your home? The life you have made there?'

He shrugged. 'I have made some money out of my *gelato*, Chiara. It may be only ice cream, but it has served me well. I have had no family, no commitments.'

'I'm sorry.'

'Not your fault, *cara*,' he said sternly. 'It was my choice. But I have made enough to support myself. If I can't find casual work in some local hotel . . .' He shot her a conspiratorial glance '. . . I will be happy to take early retirement, believe me.' He sighed. 'Once we have sorted out this mess, at least.' And he nodded back to the sad little town.

'Early retirement?' Chiara echoed. What a lovely thought. She and Dante living in some little cottage on the hillside. With a view of lemon trees, olive groves, and the Mediterranean Sea.

'Forgive me.' He took her hand. 'I only wanted to be sure of your feelings, before I told you all this. I was about to come clean – do you remember?'

Chiara thought back. Yes, there had been something he was about to say – just before that phone call from Elene. She realised what he was telling her. 'You were testing me,' she breathed.

'Can you blame me?'

After everything that had happened? 'I can't, no.' The image of that fantasy cottage swept into her mind. Could that be possible? 'But you love Dorset,' she reminded him again.

He smiled. 'This is true. It was the right place for me – at the time.'

463

'And now?' Despite everything that had happened, despite the destruction all around them, Chiara felt a spark of hope.

'Oh, Chiara, don't you know? I love you and the Cinque Terre even more.'

CHAPTER 53

Isabella

Isabella was feeling much better now, and it was good to be back in her beloved Lemon Tree Hotel, even though she was still supposed to be resting. She'd had all the tests, and everyone kept telling her that apart from her cracked ribs and a few bruises, she was fine. The trouble was that she didn't feel fine.

It wasn't just the trauma of what had happened – thankfully most of it was a blur, though she still sometimes woke from a nightmare where all she could hear was the sound of rushing water, all she could smell was gas. And it wasn't just the destruction of Vernazza – she still had to see that for herself; her mother and Nonna had tried to protect her from knowing the scale of the disaster, but thankfully plenty of other people talked, and there were lots of other stories she'd heard that hadn't been censored in the least.

Besides, she believed that Vernazza could come back from this. There were so many people who loved the town. Already, the mud was being cleared, the railway station would soon be re-opened – at least for residents – the phone lines were once again operational. It would take months before the debris was fully cleared, years probably before Vernazza shone as brightly as it had shone before, but it would happen. Vernazza would come back from this disaster.

Ferdinand though . . . That had been a big blow to her self-esteem. There had been moments in their short relationship when she had doubted him – quite a lot of moments, truth to tell. He had been evasive, dishonest even. He had come here to uncover a painting, and she had, by his own admission, got in the way of his plan. She wasn't sure she fully believed him, even now. He had become distant in those last few days. And yet . . . She had to admit – and she'd had plenty of time to mull this over during her convalescence – that despite all this, she had thought he might be the one for her. There was something about him that had touched her so deeply, something about him that made her keep coming back for more. She had hoped . . . Oh, how she had hoped. And this bitter disappointment just wouldn't go away.

There was a light knock on her bedroom door, and Giovanna slipped inside. 'Bella.' She approached the bed, a wide smile lighting up her wrinkled face. 'I am so glad you are safe. So glad that you have come back to us.'

'Oh, Aunt Giovanna.' Isabella held out her hands. Her ribs didn't really allow her to hug anyone yet, but she squeezed her old aunt's hands as hard as she dared. 'It's wonderful to see you. You were unharmed, I hope?'

'We were lucky.' Giovanna drew up a chair. 'I heard the rain and wind, but I had no idea how bad things were.' She sat in the chair and smoothed her black skirt. 'Your mother came and brought me back here to the hotel, just in case. But the cottage

466

is still standing. I am back at home. And now everything is as calm as ever.'

'And the painting?' Isabella whispered. Surely everything hadn't been entirely in vain?

'The painting survived too,' Giovanna told her. 'And it will be a gift that Vernazza needs – it will help a small amount towards the rebuilding you know, it will be a good start.'

She was right. 'It was a terrible day,' Isabella said.

'Oh, yes. First in the morning, young Ferdinand called back to Germany like that, rushing around, not knowing what to do for the best, then—'

'What did you say?' Isabella frowned.

'He must have caught one of the last trains before the line was out of action,' Giovanna mused. She didn't seem to have any idea of the effect her words were having.

'But why was he called back so suddenly?' Isabella sat up straighter in the bed. Her head was beginning to hurt again, and she struggled to concentrate.

'But don't you know?' Giovanna seemed confused. 'He told you what had happened, did he not?'

Isabella shook her head.

'It was his father. Karl.'

Was she imagining things, or did Giovanna have tears in her eyes? Really, the emotion flying around here at the moment was affecting everyone in so many strange ways . . . 'What about him?' She knew that he'd had some test results back, she knew that he didn't have long left, and she knew that Ferdinand had promised to go back and look after him until the end. But what was true and what was pure fabrication? Where Ferdinand Bauer was concerned, she simply had no clue.

'He deteriorated very suddenly. Ferdinand was told he had only hours to live.' Giovanna bent her head. 'And so, he had no time to lose if he was to see his father before he died.'

'That's so sad.' Though Isabella was surprised that her aunt was so affected by the news. 'Were you fond of Karl Bauer, Aunt?' she asked.

The old lady nodded. 'Very fond.'

'I see.' Though really, she didn't. 'Was that why Ferdinand left without saying goodbye?' It certainly explained why he had left so suddenly – and she could hardly blame him. For a moment she thought she could see a chink of light in their story, though she hardly dared. It was easier not to expect anything, not to be disappointed once again.

'Oh, but of course, my dear.' Giovanna lifted her head. 'Though before he left, he was desperate to find you.'

'Desperate?' echoed Isabella. She remembered the distance between them. Could that really be true?

'Quite frantic.' Giovanna seemed very certain. 'He'd looked for you in the hotel, he told me. Then he rushed down to the cottage to tell me about Karl, asked if I'd seen you, there were things he regretted, he said. Then he told me he had to get back to Germany straightaway . . .'

Things that he regretted? Did that include making love with Isabella in the olive grove perhaps? 'I was in Vernazza,' she said softly.

'Of course you were, my dear.' Giovanna reached across and patted her hand. '*Allora*, he said he would write you a note, he said he would call you, he said that you would understand.' She scrutinised Isabella, her head on one side like a bird in that way she had. 'You do understand, don't you, Bella?'

'I never got a note,' Isabella said. She fidgeted with the

468

bedcovers, aware that she sounded rather like a petulant child. And she didn't understand.

'The landslide, the chaos, the panic . . .' Giovanna shrugged. 'Maybe the note got lost?'

'Maybe.' Very likely in fact, she had to concede. 'But he didn't call me either.'

'Did you have your phone with you?'

'Yes. No. I think I put it on silent.' She struggled to recall. She remembered wanting to be alone, to think. She remembered the noise of the waves, the rain, the wind. And then she lost her bag and her mobile with it at some point – when she fell or was dragged to safety perhaps. And the phone lines here were still down.

'So, he still doesn't know?' Giovanna's faded brown eyes were wide. 'He doesn't know what happened to you?'

Or doesn't care, she thought. 'Aunt Giovanna – you always want to see the good in people.'

'That, Bella, is because I am an old woman. And I have learned that most people are intrinsically good.'

How could she say that after the war she had lived through? In Isabella's opinion it was Giovanna who was so good that she was almost deluded. 'But you know there are many people, darling Aunt, who act selfishly, who act with cruelty, who are greedy and only think of their own self-interests.'

'Yes, I do know that, Bella.' Calmly, she folded her hands in her lap. 'Although there may be good reason for their behaviour if you look far enough back into the past.'

Isabella sighed. 'Has it never occurred to you that Ferdinand Bauer might have wanted to retrieve that painting for his own reasons, reasons that were very different from the ones he told us?'

Giovanna shook her head. Her eyes were sad. 'Oh, Bella,' she said. Clearly not.

Her disappointment was obvious. Not in Ferdinand Bauer, but in Isabella herself to think such a thing. But perhaps she just needed to be convinced? She took a breath and charged on. 'I mean, why would he or his father want to help our community? What link do they have with us?'

'During the war—' Giovanna began.

'Oh, the war!' Isabella brushed this away. 'Karl Bauer might have felt guilty at how he behaved, but you said yourself he wasn't so bad as the rest of them. And he was in the middle of a war where men had to obey orders or be punished for it – you said that too.'

'It's true.'

'Yes, but it's not enough, is it, to go to all this trouble? Not only to hide a painting, but then send your son to recover it, to risk being arrested as a thief, just to help some community you had some dealings with years ago during the war.' Isabella wasn't sure where all this was coming from. Some of it she hardly believed herself. Perhaps then it was coming from this bitter disappointment she was feeling.

'It wasn't just because of that, my dear.' Giovanna was still watching her closely.

Isabella couldn't help smiling. She was so good that still she couldn't see it. 'What was it then, Aunt?'

'I first met Karl Bauer when I was helping the runaways who were hiding in the convent,' Giovanna said. 'He was after them, so of course I assumed he was like the rest of the soldiers.'

Isabella thought of Ferdinand. 'But he wasn't?'

'No. He caught us out, you see. We weren't expecting him, and our runaways were there for the taking.'

470

'Oh, my goodness!' Isabella realised that the runaways had included her great-grandfather. 'What did he do?'

'He let them go. He shot me a look, took in the situation at a glance, gave them enough time to run.' She smiled grimly. 'He told me later he planned only to sound the alarm once they'd had the chance to escape. But his colleagues were close behind him. Which was why not all of them managed to get away.' She sighed.

'It was a risky thing to do.' Isabella thought of her great-grandfather. He might have not lived then, if it hadn't been for Karl Bauer. He certainly would never have bought the old convent. And The Lemon Tree Hotel – not to mention Isabella herself – would never have been born.

'I was very grateful to him,' Giovanna admitted. 'But it was more than that right from the start.' Her voice grew softer. 'From the moment I met him, I saw something in his eyes and I sensed there was good in him. He was kind. He didn't want to be there. He didn't want to hurt anyone. He was a pacifist, he told me.'

'Then he shouldn't have been fighting in any war.'

'No, Bella, he certainly should not.'

'So, you befriended him, is that it?'

'Yes.'

Was that a blush rising her to her aunt's withered cheek? Isabella stared at her. Suddenly she understood. 'You fell in love with him?'

'I met him in the olive grove of the convent that night. I was not living there then, remember. I was just a young girl of eighteen who went up to the convent for bread and soap.'

Isabella saw where this was going. 'And..?'

'I was attracted to him. Very attracted. We began meeting

whenever we could. It was difficult – it was wartime of course, and there was great shame attached to sleeping with the enemy. But . . .' She smiled. 'By then, I had already fallen in love.'

'What happened, Aunt?' Isabella could feel the intensity of her aunt's emotions. It was written in the lines of her face, the expression in her eyes, the wistfulness of her smile.

'He had to leave. The German forces were withdrawing. We barely had time to say goodbye.'

Which chimed rather a chord.

'But the war went on. And . . .'

'And?'

'I never heard from him again.'

Isabella didn't know what to say. It was such a sad ending to her aunt's story. 'Did you try to contact him?'

'In those days we didn't do that kind of thing,' Giovanna admitted. 'It was harder to keep in contact then. And anyway, we were on different sides.'

'But if you loved one another . . .'

'We did. But I think we both accepted that it wouldn't last.' Such a sad look crept on to her face that Isabella wanted to reach out to her. 'I suppose there was a part of me that hoped that one day he would return.' She shook her head. 'But he never did.'

Isabella thought about this. It would be easy to blame Karl Bauer for letting down the young girl who was in love with him. But she supposed Giovanna was right, and wartime made it harder. It must have been years before he would have been able to come back. Life went on. And how did he know whether or not she might still be waiting for him? 'His son came back though,' she said. Which had to mean something.

'Yes.' A light seemed to shine from Giovanna's face. Isabella could almost see the young girl in love that she once had been.

'I recognised him the second I saw him – he has exactly the same eyes.'

Those eyes, thought Isabella.

'He is a good man – like his father. I saw that too.'

And he also likes to disappear without saying goodbye, thought Isabella. 'Did you tell him about you and his father?' Though she knew the answer already. That was why they'd had an immediate bond, why Ferdinand had spent so much time with Giovanna, why he took her the painting. It explained everything really. Only – she thought of that day in Monterosso – not quite everything.

'Yes, I told him. And he told me something rather special too.'

'Really?' Isabella leaned forwards. She didn't want to miss a word.

'That his father always regretted not getting in touch after the war ended. That Karl had been ill when he first returned to Germany and unable to travel for some years – which was why he never came back. That he had eventually been very happily married. But that he still thought of me sometimes . . .'

Isabella heard raised voices coming from downstairs. She put her hand over Giovanna's and gave it another squeeze. Her words were very moving and she could see how much Ferdinand's visit had meant to her aunt. But who was this making so much racket in the normally tranquil surroundings of The Lemon Tree Hotel? Two women – was that her mother and Nonna? – and a man. She looked at her aunt. Surely it wasn't . . . Giovanna nodded.

'Ferdinand?' she whispered.

She heard them coming up the stairs. 'I'm not sure that she's well enough to see anyone,' her grandmother was saying.

'My mother's right. She's been through so much and—' her mother was adding.

'She'll see me,' said Ferdinand.

Isabella and Giovanna shared a complicit glance. 'You need to tell Nonna the full story, Aunt,' she whispered.

And then Ferdinand charged into the room, followed by Isabella's mother and grandmother hot on his heels.

'Isabella!' He strode over to the bed. 'Are you all right, my love?'

My love . . . She wasn't sure whether to yell at him or kiss him. Although looking at him now, she couldn't quite remember why she wanted to yell at him at all.

'Bella, I tried to stop him coming in,' her grandmother said. She looked concerned.

'It's OK, Nonna, Mamma.' Isabella found that she was grinning at Ferdinand – grinning like a fool. 'I'm fine,' she said. 'Honestly.'

He reached over to kiss her – oh, so gently – on the lips. He was so warm, so close . . . 'I didn't know,' he murmured. 'I came back – as soon as I heard.'

'And your father?' She put a hand on his arm. The warmth of his skin even seemed to come through the light sweater he was wearing. *Mamma mia* . . . Suddenly she felt like crying all over again.

'He passed on the evening I got back.' He glanced at Giovanna, and Isabella saw the compassion in his eyes – even at a time like this he was thinking of others. Her aunt had been right – he was a good man.

'I'm sorry for your loss, Signor Bauer.' Nonna and her mother were still hovering in the doorway like two over-protective hens. 'But . . .'

474

'Thank you.' Ferdinand smiled so sadly at them, that after a rapid glance across at Isabella and Giovanna, as one they withdrew from the room. Her mother whispered something in her grandmother's ear. Nonna nodded and closed the door. Those two were a lot friendlier these days, Isabella found herself thinking. And her mother seemed to have altered her opinion about Dante Rossi too. So perhaps some good had come out of this after all.

Giovanna rose to her feet. 'But before I go . . .' She leaned over and managed to put a shaky arm around them both. 'I must tell you the end of the story, my dear.'

Ferdinand sat down on the bed, holding tightly on to Isabella's hand.

'Yes, Aunt?' She regretted all those silly things she'd said and thought about him. She hoped he would never let go.

'A few months after Karl left Vernazza, I discovered I was pregnant.'

Isabella's hand flew to her mouth. She hadn't expected that.

'What could I do? I was shocked and I was ashamed. I couldn't get in touch with him – and even if I could – what would he have been able to do about it in the middle of the war years?' She sighed, and her thin shoulders slumped a little. 'I knew my mother was going to go crazy with the shame of it. I didn't know where to turn.'

'Oh, Aunt Giovanna . . .' Isabella could imagine how alone she must have felt.

'So, I went to the nuns at the convent.'

Of course. Isabella should have guessed.

'I told them everything. They took me in and arranged for the baby to be adopted when it was born.' She sighed. 'I promised not to try to contact my child, and that was easy

475

since I had no idea where my baby might have been taken.' She sneaked a look at Ferdinand.

'How awful for you though.' Isabella's heart went out to her.

'But the dear woman who gave my daughter such a good home and such a good life told her the truth just before she died, and so, my daughter – she came looking for me.' Giovanna beamed.

'So, you were reunited?' Isabella was surprised that none of her family had known any of this. Her aunt Giovanna was very good at keeping secrets.

Giovanna chuckled. 'She didn't have far to go to tell you the truth, my dear. She only lived in Monterosso al Mare.'

Isabella's mind went into overdrive. She remembered that day in Monterosso. The three of them on the balcony. 'Siena,' she breathed. 'Siena Gianelli is your daughter?'

'A good guess, my dear.' Giovanna nodded. 'She certainly is. And I have been so proud of her – she has been a wonderful nurse in the Cinque Terre, and she is a lovely woman – thanks to her adoptive family, you know. She and I have become very close friends.'

'But why did you never tell us?' Isabella knew that her grandmother and mother would have loved to welcome Siena into their family. They would never have made Giovanna feel ashamed of what had happened, they would never have judged her.

'I didn't tell anyone the truth – I am old, but in some ways, I am still ashamed of being an unmarried mother, I suppose. If Siena had wanted it – *allora*, I would have happily and openly declared our relationship. But she had her family to think of too, so we decided to keep it to ourselves.'

And it was quite a secret. 'You told Ferdinand though?'

Giovanna put her head to one side. 'However did you know that, Bella?'

'Let me guess . . .' Ferdinand had narrowed his eyes and was scrutinising her closely. 'You saw us that day in Monterosso. Correct, my love?'

'Correct.' Isabella decided not to admit she had followed them – it made her look rather suspicious after all. 'I just happened to be passing that day.'

Ferdinand threw her a look that showed he might be unconvinced, but that it didn't matter anyway.

'Siena is Ferdinand's half-sister.' Giovanna patted his hand. 'I had to introduce the two of them.'

'A sister.' He grinned. 'I can't tell you how happy I was to hear that – I always thought I was an only child. And as for my father . . .' He took hold of Giovanna's hand. 'He was devastated not to have known, for you to have coped alone, and so sad never to have met her. But he was also so thrilled to see that picture I took of his daughter before he died.'

Later, after Giovanna had left the room and they were alone, Ferdinand lay down on the bed next to her, and she snuggled up close. 'I'm so sorry about your father,' she told him.

'Thank you.' He tucked a tendril of hair away from her face. 'But I'm glad that he got to know about Siena. And he was glad too – that I'd met them both, and that I'd met you, of course.'

'You told him about me?' This made Isabella feel very warm inside.

'I told him that just like him I'd fallen in love with a place and a woman.'

'You did?'

'And that unlike him, I was going to go back there the second I could to get to know both of them a whole lot better.'

'But . . .' All sorts of thoughts were careering through her head. 'What about your job?' was what she actually said.

He laughed. 'I work freelance.'

'Ah, yes.' How could she forget?

'And something tells me there might be plenty of work for an architect like me around here.' He put on a modest look.

Isabella narrowed her eyes. 'An architect like you?'

He shrugged. 'Someone *simpatico* to the origins and culture of a place, someone aware of the complex history?'

'Hmm.' Isabella suspected that he was teasing her – again. But he was right. She didn't think that finding work would be a problem, at least not if her mother had anything to do with it. 'But you seemed so distant,' she murmured, 'in those days before . . .' She couldn't bring herself to say it. Before the tragedy. Before the landslide. Before Ferdinand had left The Lemon Tree Hotel.

'I was worried,' he said. His blue eyes were earnest. 'I hadn't meant to draw you into the whole thing. I knew that I cared for you. But had I taken unfair advantage of you? Was I ready to take that next step? Were you?'

'And what did you decide?' She had to forgive him for his caution. It was a huge decision – to move to another country, to consider starting a new life with someone you had only known for such a short time.

'I think you know the answer to that.' He sighed. 'I realised it the morning I left. I knew I had to go back to Germany, but I didn't want to leave. What was I doing? Why the hell hadn't I just taken you in my arms and told you that I loved you and made love with you every opportunity I had?'

'It's never too late,' Isabella murmured.

'But I nearly lost you . . .' Once again he stroked her hair from her face. 'I would never have forgiven myself—'

'Hush.' She caught his hand. 'It wasn't your fault.' She took it to her lips and kissed the palm gently. 'And your father?' she whispered. 'Did he approve of you coming back here?'

'You bet he approved.' And then he kissed her once more on the lips. With tenderness, with love, and with a lot more passion now that Giovanna, her mother, and her grandmother were – thankfully – no longer in the room.

ABOUT VERNAZZA (SOME SPOILERS HERE . . .)

The town of Vernazza gave me this story in many ways. I first visited in 2001 and loved it on sight. When I next visited the town in 2008, it had already become much more of a tourist destination – unsurprisingly, its beauty and that of the surrounding landscape were hardly going to go unnoticed. On my next visit in 2017 I saw the heart-breaking evidence of the storm of 25 October 2011, mostly from photographs, as – incredibly – the town had since been rebuilt.

This storm wreaked havoc on the entire Cinque Terre region of the Levante on the Italian Riviera. The severe flooding and landslides almost totally destroyed Vernazza – burying the small town in more than thirteen feet of mud and debris. More than twenty inches of rain fell in under four hours – about one third of the average total annual rainfall for the area. Six people died.

After the storm, an organisation named 'Save Vernazza' was formed by three women: Ruth Manfredi, Michele Lilley, and Michele Sherman. Their aim was to raise money and awareness of the problems facing this unique environment, to restore Vernazza and protect it for the future.

On the Save Vernazza website (www.savevernazza.com) it is possible to read some harrowing individual stories. The people of Vernazza showed great resilience after the storm, and in days they had commenced the necessary rebuilding. Geologists and engineers were brought in to assess the damage and to give advice for future protection and stabilisation. Save Vernazza have since expanded their aims to promote sustainable tourism through educational programmes that will help preserve the culture of Vernazza for future generations.

Vernazza has now been restored to its former glory. But it is a busy tourist town and the organisation urges visitors to respect the hiking trails and to support the local community by eating their food and drinking their wine. Maintaining the olive groves and vineyards will help to prevent such a disaster from occurring again.

ACKNOWLEDGEMENTS

Thanks to Vernazza. I have tried my best to be faithful to its spirit. The outside locations in this book are all real enough, but the people came entirely from my head and do not exist outside of this story. I would like to think that The Lemon Tree Hotel could exist on the hillside outside Vernazza, but of course it does not – which is a shame because if it did, I for one would like to go there . . .

If I have made any mistakes, or caused any offence to its residents in the way I have made use of this location that I love, I apologise unreservedly.

Thanks to the talented and hard-working team at Quercus, who make it happen. First and foremost the amazing Stefanie Bierwerth, who is always supportive and encouraging, and whose wonderful enthusiasm is legendary. Even better, she is an excellent editor and a joy to work with. I'd also like to thank Jon Butler and other members of the brilliant team: Olivia Mead, Olivia Allen, Katie Sadler, Rachel Neely, Laura McKerrell, and anyone else who has worked on this book. Quercus have shown their faith in me, and I am hugely grateful.

I'd like to thank my agent, the talented and perceptive

Laura Longrigg of MBA, for her continuing support. She is always there for me, and always on my side, and I appreciate her more than I can say. Louisa Pritchard of Louisa Pritchard Associates also deserves my thanks – she works so hard with MBA and markets and publishers overseas, for which I am hugely grateful.

In Vernazza I met the artist Antonio Greco who shared with me his personal story of 25 October 2011, and showed me some incredible photographs of the devastation caused by the mudslides. He created the plaque in the village: *alle sue donne*, which pays homage to the women who supported Vernazza after the storm. I'd like to thank Antonio for his generosity and time, and also Gianni Franzi, who runs a restaurant by the harbour and who has written a charming and nostalgic memoir: *Vernazza – Snow Always Comes from the Sea*.

Other books that I used in my research and that I found invaluable were: *Beautiful Ruins* by Jess Walter, *The Rape of Europa* by Lynn H Nicholas, and *Saving Italy* by Robert M Edsel.

Thanks to all my family for everything that they do and everything that they mean to me. That's my son Luke, Agata and Tristan in Copenhagen; my daughters Alexa and Ana, and my husband Grey. Grey takes all the photographs on my research trips, is always full of ideas, and has to listen to me droning on about the story before, during, and after I've written it. I'm sure it isn't easy being married to someone who spends so much of her time in another world. Family – I love you all, you are amazing.

Thanks to friends who go beyond the call of duty in their support for my writing – particularly Wendy Tomlins, June Tate, Laura James, and Anita Count. Thanks to writers in the groups I meet with – in the RNA, in Andalucia, in Dorset, especially my newbie writers' group of Maria Donovan and Gail Aldwin – I hope we are an established group by the time you read this. Thanks to all the writers who I love reading (too many to mention!) and all those writers who give support both in person and on social media – you know who you are . . . Thanks to the Bloggers who are honest, supportive, and very quick readers (!) – may I say that your reviews are perceptive, insightful, and highly appreciated.

And thanks to you utterly gorgeous readers – without you, where would we all be?